BREAKING
THROUGH THE
DARKNESS
Love Always Wins

DAWN SINGLETON, PhD, DNM

Breaking Through the Darkness: Love Always Wins

Copyright © 2021 Dawn Singleton, PhD, DNM

ISBN

Paperback	978-1-68547-018-0
Hardcover	978-1-68547-019-7
eBook	978-1-68547-020-3

Library of Congress Control Number: 2021921433
Printed in the United States of America

101 Foundry Dr,
West Lafayette, IN, 47906, USA

www.wordhousebp.com
+1-800-646-8124

Table of Contents

Chapter One
Earth School

Thoughts drifted through my mind as a young child that there was some deep reason as to why I was brought to this Earth School. That being on Earth was a test or initiation in my faith and strength as a spirit in a human body. Now believing this to be true, I am convinced this is meant to be shared.

"Have not I commanded thee? Be strong and of a good courage; be not afraid, neither be thou dismayed: for the LORD thy God is with thee whithersoever thou goest (Joshua 1:9 KJV).

Suffer or Act

It is a cosmic principle that we either suffer in imbalance or act to create balance. Though we may be habituated to the discomforts of imbalance, and even perceive it as balance, we cannot grow in such a state. Growth is progress and progress is the soul's purpose. By shining the light of yoga on the imbalances that we keep veiled in darkness, we illuminate the road to the inner realms as well, and as balanced beings, we progress on the path to our soul (By Aadil Palkhivala).

Every drop is inconsequential, nothing in the grandness of the ocean, but when they all move together, as one body—therein lies the power. From the surface it may remain tranquil for many days, months even, but its strength is not gone, merely dormant. Below the surface, no matter how still, are unstoppable currents moving unimaginable volumes of briny water many thousands of kilometers. From above it seems no more alive than a bucket of water, yet below is more life than the skies above or the land it kisses. Truly it is another world, an alien landscape. It is one we should visit with reverence.

Swimming underwater, descending further down, deep into the moving currents of the blue ocean waters, she comes across an ancient building. Exploring, her bright green eyes come across concrete steps which appear to be made out of some type of white stone or was it marble, part of an

1

ancient building from long ago? Travelling further, her hands reach out, touching the steps as if she remembers something which has been long lost from memory at least for some time and with great determination plunges deeper down into the depths of the now darker cool ocean waters. While at this ancient building people materialize, some are familiar and other faces she does not recognize. A few of these people are very old friends of hers from long ago. Suddenly a woman's eyes catch her attention, someone she has known, possibly having a very close relationship to as a young girl or was it a past life? This woman mournfully repeats numerous times, "So many long years, Ember, so many long years." As she shakes her head, this message is repeated over and over very slowly with great deliberation. These words are voiced from the depths of the soul, in a gut-wrenching deep agonizing groan as their eyes lock in a knowing that is deeper than words could ever be expressed, by the wisdom behind their communication. As hard as it is, she averts her gaze and begins to search deeper into the ocean depths. Her piercing eyes of green emit rays of light flickering within them, as if they are turning on memories long lost. Continuing, deeper to the bottom of the stone steps she circles around the building, proceeding in her exploration of these ancient ruins at a steady leisurely pace. The building is very old and medieval in its structure with huge gray massive stone pillars. Taking time, she touches lovingly the granite pillars, exploring their exquisite detail. Slowly ascending upwards through the sometimes strong currents, she peers once again into the all-familiar piercing eyes which touch the depths of her soul but this time becomes aware of many eyes in the background watching her. Slowly, she rises up. Finally arriving at the surface of the water, her eyes open wide and her throat gasps powerfully as her lungs take in a deep breath of air. Feeling as if she is drowning, her tears begin to gush like a dam has just been released, relieving the aching pressure on her chest. So much deep-seated sorrow inside her causes her to convulse from the deepest part of her being, forcing her lungs to release unexpressed heartache. She mourns. Not understanding exactly what she is experiencing, she knows something is happening beyond her comprehension and continues to weep relentlessly. It feels good to be alive. She is on her journey to freedom.

Is life one big puzzle in which someone above is trying to shape all the pieces in order to put them together with the goal of intending to create a masterpiece that brings forth warmth, peace and beauty, or is it just a bunch of random occurrences that are not interrelated? All the people in this book play out a very important role. None are to be judged from afar; they are all heroes in creating a beautiful revelation about life and what is important to mankind. Without them, this could not have occurred, because each one of them was necessary for the role they played to create the quantum happening. This occurrence broke the bonds of the physical death which came through in a magnificent way in love, communicating joy, bliss, and happiness beyond comprehension because of love. And here goes the story of darkness to light. Without darkness, there would be no light. This book is dedicated to my beautiful parents, Thelma Jane and Lester Paul. In part, this book was written to work out the events that played in the magnificent revelation in my life and meant to bring provocative thought, not judgment on anyone. You will find it very different than most people's lives but I hope, with it being written, to bring some understanding of what it is to deal with what society calls mental illness. Maybe this horrible disease can be prevented. I believe it can be.

Freedom

Being a child represented freedom—frolicking in the fields unimpeded from the outside world and not becoming involved with the troubles of others, but living in a world of sheer bliss. Listening to the music of birds in the early morning just before rising from a restful sleep, waking up to the sweet aroma of freshly baked cinnamon bread just made that morning, heading outside to discover what new flowers had bloomed overnight. I remained outside just to climb a tree at my own whim. This was my life. Life was truly glorious, and I was absolutely in love with life! Life is all about the events in our lives that have a strong emotional component and I latched on to those experiences with fervor and due diligence—the events that were created through caring and love. At my young age, I didn't remember anything that caused pain or distrust—anything which really made any kind of impression on my three-year-old psyche. Life represented to me trust and the feeling that all was well.

Our Friend

There was one particular event in my young mind, that made a great impression on me, and its memory is instilled in my brain as if it happened yesterday. The setting is a very windy, snowy time of the year and on this particular winter day we were snowed in, making travel totally impossible on our country road. Snow was piled several feet high on Donegal Springs Road. Silvery flakes drifted down, glittering in the bright first light of morning, and the red bird swooped down to nestle in its pine tree. The weather was frosty and the snow was glittering, like white sequins lying all over the floor. The horizon was a candy red as the sun shone a dandelion yellow along with strokes of carrot orange. It was a crisp white, pristine covering that had transformed the landscape for weeks, making it a magical land full of wonder and undiscovered mysteries.

Early in the morning my Dad worked tediously removing the snow from our front door which made it very difficult to open. He did this every morning because the wind blew fiercely, threatening to imprison us in our home, piling high against our doors. In fact, it had been like this for fourteen days, so our friend, Don Jaldeman, came with a horse-drawn sled and picked my mom, dad, sisters and me up to take us into town to get groceries. Don was a very good friend of my parents who attended the same church: Shady Pine church. He was a good, fine man. My sister and I were three years old at the time of this event and our older sister, Kay, was thirteen. There was so much excitement and adventure attached to this particular occasion it was easy to remember. The aroma of his massive horse permeated around us as he pulled us along on our sled. Air spiraled toward the horse's nostrils as he took the cold winter air in them and then exhaled; creating billowing swirls in the air as he proudly pulled the carriage to our destination. Going merrily along, my parents sang Christmas songs as we headed into town. We lived far out of town on a country road which would be attended much later by the snow plow and Don knew we needed groceries, "What are friends for?" he exclaimed. So off to town we went on our winter wonderland adventure all snuggled and warm with coats, hats and mittens.

Before we showed up into the World, our mother planted a beautiful garden of flowers at their modest home in Florin. This is the home my older sister lived in until she was ten years old. Unfortunately, on this particular day the squirrels decided to dig many of Thelma's flowers out of the ground and when she looked at her garden, she began to cry. Lester could not take hearing her wails and went outside and yanked every flower out of the ground and said, "Now you don't have anything to cry about!" This story was told many times to me by my mother. My father definitely exhibited a very hot temper and a low resistance to stress in his younger days but as he matured, he slowly evolved in grace and developed the character trait of patience, thank heavens!

Living in a small home in Florin, close to Brubaker Store, my mom acquired a job working for the owner of this small convenience store located within walking distance of their home. Marilyn, the owner of this small store, became one of Thelma's good friends.

New Arrivals

Knowing their small home was not going to accommodate another baby, when Thelma received the news that she was three months pregnant, they decided it was about time they started thinking of a bigger place. Kay, their only child, was nine years old by now, and played a big part in the household. It was a very smart idea, because little did they know they were going to have twin girls! Deciding it was time to enter the world, we were born at Lancaster General Hospital. As my mom finished giving birth to me, she was in for a huge surprise, having no idea that there was another little person waiting her turn to take that plunge through the birth canal and out into the world. This exciting event happened minutes later, in fact exactly two minutes. Wow, two baby girls! Oops, double the trouble!

Our home on Donegal Springs Road was built by Lester, using his own bare hands with the help of a very good friend of his, Big Red. Big Red was a high school teacher and assisted him whenever possible in this project. Red and Lester worked hard; they focused on the vision of the finished product. Constructed around the constraints of the weather elements, they labored sometimes late into the evening as well as on weekends. Lester also worked his full time job at the shoe factory during this time, so he was definitely putting all of his extra energy to good use before we were born.

Back at the ranch home, during nap time, we took up the sport of taking off our diapers and seeing how far we could throw them. We stood up in our cribs and gave them a toss across the room, and if they were messy, better yet—that got painted on the wall, yuck! Our mother felt like pulling her hair out because it seemed as if our naps were short lived, and we took it to our favor, with every opportunity we had, to get ourselves into trouble just like puppies do. One usually played the part of the instigator while the other played out the act, egging each other on. Puppies can absolutely make you crazy, and we were like puppies. Eventually, we became strong enough to climb out of our crib, and took the liberty of playing in our room together; using whatever was in the room for our inventions.

We both wore rings on our pinky fingers. It was my mishap that while happily playing in our playpen outside in the back yard; I decided to take my ring off. I put it into my mouth and then decided to swallow it. But instead of the ring going down into my stomach, it got caught in my throat and by the time my mom found me my face was a bright blue. Frantically, she hung me upside down and luckily the ring did eventually pop out as I gasped for the fresh country air.

My sister and I had thick curly light brown hair which was cut short and we both had dimples, which made it very difficult to tell us apart. In fact, most people could not. My parents eventually figured it out, although they admitted when we were babies they became a bit confused as to which little body belonged to which name. With all the energy that comes with being a toddler, we definitely were a handful. As babies, we cried a lot with colic—at least that's what my mom told me. My dad and mom took us to the shore and our cries could be heard the whole way there and back as well at the hotel. Eventually we did grow out of it, giving some room for Mother's stress level to ease up a bit.

Playing hairdresser outside, we experimented using our scissors to do new hairdos, creating short bangs or whatever came whimsically into our minds or we thought might be fun to try. Without much thought of any due consequences, we practiced trimming each other's eyelashes and eyebrows. When Mother scolded us, we looked at each other and shrugged our shoulders, thinking it was not a big deal. Inside the home my parents gave us a special wall just to use for our art activity. It is where we drew pictures using our crayons. This entertained us for hours, keeping us occupied for awhile in our toddler years.

Chapter Two

Nature's Art and Stories of Love

It was wintertime. Snowflakes piled upon each other, forming hills and canyons which were created by the frigid winter wind. Nature fashioned a masterpiece using the barren trees as its canvas, making them come alive with twinkling sparkles. Unusually shaped, luxurious crystals formed by winter air could be seen hanging from the branches with the remaining bright red berries from the fall season. Peeking pristinely out from the white freshly fallen snow, icicles hung like Old Man Frost's beard and sparkled in the winter sunlight like jeweled daggers. This memory is one of the many memories etched into my being as a young child.

Today was one of those truly magical winter wonderlands which I had the opportunity to notice and appreciate. I was drawn to look out the window and watch the red birds frolic in the snow-laden pine trees. Some still had impressions of the pine cones that hung from them, many protruding out boldly, looking like an ornament for a Christmas tree. The snow formed drifts which traveled up to our windows and meticulously painted designs, a masterpiece which only nature could create, free for anyone to enjoy. Immediately, my attention was drawn to my dad. As he shoveled, his breath could be seen circling in the cold, crisp air, enticing me to adventure outside. So dressing up with boots, mittens, scarf and hat, I was swept away in ecstasy in this gorgeous winter wonderland. Sledding and building igloos all day in the fields kept me occupied for much of the time. Hiking great lengths along the winding country road created so much adventure for me, filling and refreshing my soul. Worries were not even a word in my vocabulary. As snowflakes shimmered softly falling gloriously from the sky, my spirit was fed and refreshed, and I felt one with the world and my dance with life.

Years later, my parents purchased snowmobiles and off we went together through the drifts, enjoying the wind on our cheeks. Snowmobiling gave us the opportunity to snuggle close, wrapping our arms around each other's waist as we went along. Finally, after hours of snowmobiling, we peeled off our wet cold clothing from our bodies, carefully spreading them out to dry close to the cozy fire Dad had started. Together, we enjoyed hot chocolate at the kitchen table in that warm, simple ranch home. These days blessed us and we gazed contentedly out our picture window watching the red birds that danced delightfully amongst the snow-decorated trees, providing us plenty of entertainment. This was the home which I knew without a doubt was mine. This was where many wonderful childhood memories were made. In the backyard a huge oak tree stood tall, and it was here where frequent visits were made.

The Gnarly Root

Underneath me the ground was lumpy with roots that protruded through the soil and my clothing. They twisted like snakes that turned to stone, writhing upward one final time before descending deep into the earth to take cool refreshment from the water table below. It is here where I quietly listened to the sounds of nature about me while sitting on a large gnarly root that peeked through the Earth. Knowing that I was supported by the nature fairies that frolicked around me, the magic of life was real and supported me with unconditional love.

One day, I was dared by my neighborhood clan, at the spunky age of three, to cross our country road to fetch our kitten, contently lounging under some brush. Deciding to take the dare, and engrossed in the challenge, I dashed across the road without much thought. But unfortunately, on my way back, I clumsily tripped on my own two feet and landed in the middle of the road, clutching as tight as possible my favorite kitten to keep her safe. Little did I know, a huge truck was traveling toward me on that winding road and my physical life was very close to being snuffed out. My neighborhood friends covered their eyes as the truck approached but in the nick of time it came to a halt, its tires squealing just inches away from my tiny body. My friends hid their faces in angst seeing my horrible predicament, and afraid to look at the result. They just screamed.

The truck driver's face turned a bright shade of red and then appeared as if it changed to blue. In shock, his teeth chattered and his body quivered as he tumbled out of his truck a total wreck. My mom heard the commotion of the horn blaring and the screeching of the wheels as the truck skidded to a stop and came running outside as fast as was humanly possible. In humiliation and dismay, when I finally got up I darted to my home, tore off my clothes and jumped into the bathtub, taking refuge while the frustrated trucker talked to my mom.

Little did I know, this was only the beginning of the many dangerous episodes these neighboring children and I would be sharing. But at the time I felt shame-faced, having caused so much distress and angst in the bus driver and Mother. As I grew in stature, we learned to deeply love the family that lived to the right of our home. Love connected us, bonding our friendship.

Two little girls with curly light brown hair which curls softly around their ears, play late into the evening, frolicking outside from morning to dusk. They spend their time with the children living next door, who comprise of a motley group of various ages. Even with the diversity in their ages and personalities, everyone is included that desires to play.

Today, the one twin watches with green eyes of longing because she can only imagine how it feels to be touched in such a loving way. Fascinated, she watches as a young mother tenderly and lovingly rubs the feet and body of her baby, who will eventually become one of her younger playmates. This young mother explains that it is important to touch your baby because it is essential to create an environment where a baby can relax. Also, touch puts invigorating boundaries on a baby's body. Her new playmate thrusts his legs out over and over, cooing happily as his mother rubs his skin gently. Not completely familiar with this in her own home, at least not with her mother, she does remember times when her dad used to snuggle with her and look lovingly into her wide open eyes. But that all mostly has ceased, and longingly she yearns at the memory.

Independence

At five years of age, I proudly exhibited my independence. I strolled with my neighbor friends a far distance on Donegal Springs Road. One of our destinations was the Summer Park and Recreation program which was in close proximity to the Crossroads Mennonite Church, where we later attended Bible School together. Very excited to be on our journey to this new exploit, we chattered amongst ourselves. Since we were in good company this long walk did not bother us at all, and we were excited about this new experience.

But nothing compared to the feeling of running free in the country fields, where my most valuable lessons in life were taught to me. Spooky Nook Road and all of the stories behind its name fascinated us. Spooky Nook Road is an offset narrow windy country road from Donegal Springs Road and along it are found many mature trees with thick gargantuan branches. Colossal arms seemed to stretch out toward us as we walked on this narrow country road and sometimes a weird sensation formed in the pit of our stomachs because of this road's tall tales involving ghosts and goblins. These stories often fueled our imaginations, making them run rampant. But on the other hand, these massive trees also created a safe haven for squirrels to take shelter for the winter as well as for birds to create their nests in the springtime. But most of the time, stories of ghosts and goblins entertained our imaginations as we frolicked carefree with our neighbor friends along Spooky Nook road.

Mairzy's bed was located to the left and my bed to the right. Without a doubt some kind of special bond existed between us, which I felt no one could ever break or tear apart. When living at the ranch house my bedtime routine was to jump into bed, slap my bubble gum onto the bedpost and read verses from my tiny Bible. When finished, I carefully placed it on my head rest to review in the morning.

Looking at that innocent child, I now realize that a strong force guided me, preparing me to be strong, supporting my knowledge that there is so much more to life than what the eye sees, and that love shines above all pain, hardship, depression, oppression or evil. Love always wins. One of my favorite verses is Matthew 13:31, 32, "The kingdom of heaven is like a mustard seed, which a man took and planted in his field. Though it is the smallest of all our seeds, yet when it grows, it is the largest of garden plants and becomes a tree, so that the birds of the air come and perch in its branches." And Matthew 17:20, " I tell you the truth; if you have faith as small as a mustard seed, you can say to this mountain, 'Move from here to there' nothing will be impossible for you." I love these verses which let us know how powerful we can be. Later this verse proved to be true.

During the hot summer months our bedroom converted to a hot furnace, creating an oppressive blanket of unbearably high temperatures. This heat forced us to get out of bed and bound into a tub full of cold water. If the weather was muggy and hot enough, the same routine was done a few times a night into the wee hours of the morning, giving us some relief from the oppressive heat. All throughout the blackness of the night, giggles and soft voices were heard coming from the bathroom as stories were exchanged between us in the bathtub, while Pinky, our little spotted dog, looked on.

Trips to the grocery store were special outings in which Mairzy and I waited in the car patiently, while our parents shopped for groceries.

Being of preschool age we were promised a pint of ice cream, one for my sister and one for me to enjoy, which was straightaway brought out by our father upon arrival to the store. This cool delight entertained us until they finished shopping in peace. I guess you can say our family had a strong belief in the value of ice cream! Since air conditioning was not an option for the car or home, we appreciated the ice cream, enjoying the coolness of its touch which helped our bodies to cool down until our parents were finished shopping. It always worked out, and by the time we were finished with our pint, bags full of groceries were loaded into the trunk to accompany us home. In the evening, we felt really lucky when my dad got the privilege of putting us to bed. After our wheelbarrow routine which ended at the foot of our beds, he tickled us until tears came. Not much later the sleep fairy came to visit us, leaving a trace of a smile on our faces, as we dreamt of enchanting places.

The tooth fairy, another visitor who frequented our room quite often, left coins which were found under our pillows in return for being able to carry off our teeth. Picturing the tooth fairy, huffing and puffing carrying a tooth, amused and amazed me. This supported my belief in another world out there with all kinds of magical creatures. My face lightened and my eyes danced as my imagination ran wild with animation at these thoughts of magic.

Many Saturday afternoons my sister and I proudly sat in the back seat of Dad's new black model T. Lester cranked down his window and puffed leisurely on his cigar, making clouds of smoke that billowed out his left front side window. Usually adorned with a new cap, his elbow propped out the window, Lester drove leisurely on the back country roads while we sat in the back seat, looking out at the beautiful rolling hills. Later, Lester's cigar-smoking days were short-lived by choice or just maybe Thelma had some influence on him. Was this a leisurely drive especially for us, or was it to give my mother some peace and quiet? Whatever the reason for this outing, I sure did feel special.

Two sisters run happily over to the neighbor's property to play on the swing set, beckoning their friends to come out and swing. The next door neighbor's family home has many siblings, making great playmates for these two little girls who are by now swinging with enthusiasm, laughing as their green eyes twinkle with excitement. They enjoy each other's company as well as their neighbor friends.

Later, to their surprise as they sway and oscillate high into the sky, the old rusty metal swing set begins to slowly topple back and forth. Feeling as if they are falling in slow motion, this makes them howl with laughter all the harder. Then the old swing set tumbles over with all the children aboard.

Oblivious to the mishap, the twin's mother is heard calling their names to come home for an excursion to the grocery store. Enjoying the soft breeze upon her skin, her bubble is burst this carefree morning as her mother announces, "Ember, you will soon have to wear a shirt because kindergarten is coming soon. You cannot go without a shirt to school, it is not acceptable." Her inquisitive jade green eyes mist with wetness because she does not understand. School does not sound like fun anymore and she dreads the thought.

Sharing my life story is not to condemn or bestow negative, depressing judgments upon experiences or people, but written to express that I have witnessed a higher power, and that the events that we create on our specific journey to experience are for our soul and for spiritual growth. Grateful and honored to have experienced a small part of this higher power while living on Earth, I found love is the strength we search for and is all that really matters. It is the power within and is found in such depths in the spiritual dimension that we have a hard time grasping the importance of it on this earthly plane. However it is more real than the homes we sit in or the cars we drive. It is the kind of love we feel when we look at our spouse and our children or even our pets. In its purest and most powerful form, this love is not jealous or selfish, but unconditional. Even the villains that play a part in our lives are doing us a favor, though it is difficult at times to grasp that idea, particularly those that torture or mutilate any living creature. But there is a greater depth of knowledge than what we can comprehend in this physical plane. Many people can get caught in the human condition and become covered by so much foreign energy that the brightness of their soul spirit connection is covered with darkness.

My parents had sent me confusing and conflicting messages on an emotional level as I grew up, but I came to understand it on a higher level and became terribly saddened with the turn of events. Ultimately sorrow and the destruction of our family unity were not too far away.

After finally going out the door leading from the shoe factory, he begins his long walk. Now finally on his last stretch home, he reaches Donegal Springs Road.

A little blonde green-eyed girl stands at the end of the driveway in the late afternoon sun, waiting patiently to see her dad's silhouette on the distant horizon. She knows that he will be bringing a piece or two of special candy home in his shirt pocket. As she sees him in the distance with the golden globe of the sun above him, a feeling of joy comes over her and it is difficult for her to contain the glee that bubbles inside her. She so loves and respects her father, and with longing, desires to look into his caring eyes. As he draws near and gets to the end of the hot macadam driveway, he lifts her up in the strength of his arms. Looking into her radiant face, he reaches into his pocket. With great wide eyes, her heart bursts with great anticipation as to what treasure is brought home today. She loves her dad.

With a twinkle in his eye and the happiest face mankind could ever have, my dad came home with a cute puppy or two in his arms. Lester's face always beamed with radiant happiness as he showed us his findings. These free puppies were found on the farms nearby and landed in our home quite often. One of the last farm puppies that jumped from his arms into mine was black and white, having the cutest pink belly, justifying her name: Pinky. I mourned and cried for days when Pinky was accidently kicked by my horse, King. Death was difficult for me to understand. One day you are around and the next second you are gone, but where? Knowing I would never be able to touch her cute little belly again, or give her the daily baths, made it all the more frustrating. Eventually I became so angered, I demanded God to show me, "Where did my Pinky go?" I received my answer a lot later in life. With her accidental death, many tears came as if they would never end, but as time went on the suffering became more bearable.

Mother Earth

Life was full of many mysteries. The cool soft touch of the grass under our feet, the myriad sounds created by nature, the different tastes of fruits and fresh vegetables from the garden, seeing the miracle of new flowers bloom throughout the warmer months, the feeling of the soft snow falling upon our heads, observing the leaves turn to beautiful bright reds, oranges and yellows and being pleasantly surprised by the new growth peeking from the blanket of Mother Earth in the Spring--all these vitalized our senses. Experiencing these changes the seasons brought forth filled our cups to overflowing and our hearts sang with joy. Lying on the soft luscious grass on my back, I peered up at the clouds as they drifted by and I daydreamed for hours.

The sky, is a perfect bare canvas, offers clouds nonetheless which shift and drift begging interpretation... such is the nature of art. –Jeb Dickerson

A bee sting or two was a normal summer occurrence and we did not give any thought to wearing footwear. We took our chances. If we did so happen to step on a bee, we ran inside to tell Thelma, who immediately focused on helping us with our dilemma. She retrieved a large pail of water, putting plenty of baking soda in it. A wooden chair in the kitchen was designated for the injured victim to sit, where the bruised foot was soaked in Thelma's concoction to help reduce the swelling. One of the onlookers was asked to retrieve the tweezers for pulling out the tiny little stinger. This procedure was done with extreme care under the scrutiny of all our playmates, which most likely by now were standing in a circle around the patient.

My foot always became swollen about twice the size of my normal foot and the option of wearing shoes for attending church was physically impossible. Therefore, I gained the privilege of wearing my Dad's sock until my foot returned to its normal size. Also, poison ivy plants were very prevalent in the woods where we played. The signs of this mishap were extremely uncomfortable and itchy, making your face become like a swollen melon, leaving only slits for your eyes. These incidents never deterred us from the luxury of being able to feel the ground under our feet and to explore the woods. Spending hours in the Spooky Nook Creek gave us the opportunity to experience the surprises it elicited. As we explored its nooks and crannies its secrets were slowly unfolded, though hidden from the common observer. Sometimes swimming in the deeper parts of this creek, we watched inquisitively as different species of fish passed by us and discovered different homes of muskrats and many other animals. A wealth of natural beauty to explore was right at our fingertips, entertaining us for hours, and we lost all track of time in its magnificence as the hot steaming sun looked down upon us in the magical world we'd tapped into. Eventually, as we climbed out from the banks of the creek all kinds of little creatures were found between our toes which might make someone cringe, but we simply were not affected by their presence and picked them off one by one as we talked cheerfully amongst each other.

Winter

There is a freezing chill in the winter's air that brings crispness to the leaves that crunch beneath feet and makes cheeks turn rosy red with every sting of winter's breeze.

Looking through the barren winter trees we spy a family ice skating on a very crooked frozen creek. Two little girls each with dimples are seen slipping and skidding along on their skates, laughing as they go. Their father is holding one of the little girl's hands. Gazing lovingly down upon her, Mother walks happily along on the ice holding hands with her twin sister. Swinging and swaying on the ice, they sing what a wonderful world it is.

We etched architectural designs for tree houses which needed materials such as sticks, old scraps of plywood and anything else that was available at the time. These designs were put on big sheets of paper which were spread out on the ground. This is when we took the time to discuss our plans, making any changes if needed. Later as we evolved, a leader was chosen who designated a certain task to each child, which was their responsibility to complete, playing an important role in the construction of the tree house. In the beginning we took a vote on who we wanted to take charge, but eventually our own unique formula evolved. Later, it became automatic as to who did what in the construction of the tree house. Discovering this type of joint effort made it so much easier to create a unique masterpiece each time.

When we were mere toddlers, our first tree house was made from cow dung and small bits of twigs. It was a structure that we could not possibly fit inside. Our older sister witnessed us amidst one of our projects and immediately ran home, ratting on us. This created a huge spectacle. We had to sit and listen to many lectures as to why the use of this particular choice of painting media was not acceptable, but instead gross and disgusting.

Later upgrading our tree houses, they were built big enough to enter and a secret code was used for access, which was found hidden in the tall branches of the many trees that we climbed.

Climbing every tree that was possible brought tranquility, quieting and comforting my soul. As I nestled myself high in the branches, a feeling of great awe came over me as the beauty that surrounded me yielded peace, and gave me a respect for its unlimited knowledge. The bark under my hands acknowledged me with all its nooks and crannies, encouraging my senses to come alive. As I listened to the rustle of the leaves, a sense of great stillness was brought into my soul, bringing forth awareness that I was an intricate part of this very special place called Earth which is somehow connected to the many galaxies unknown to man in one huge matrix. In the spring, I carefully peeked into the nest of birds and then sat patiently on a branch nearby, watching for hours as robins built their nest from twigs and leaves. Sometimes nature gave me the opportunity to observe baby birds peck from inside their shell, ready to make their entrance into the world, and I quietly giggled with anticipation. Nature and its life rhythms utterly captivated me.

Our neighbor's family cat was found lying in a window well, getting ready to go into hard labor. She was discovered by Mairzy, as she lay with her belly swollen with kittens preparing to become part of the wonderful creatures on planet Earth. Coming upon her by accident, Mairzy ran excitedly and summoned the crew as she put her finger to her mouth signaling us to be quiet. Each and every one of us gathered around in reverence, stilling our small bodies so as not to disturb her, while she labored hard in the middle of the hot summer afternoon. We watched in total reverence as she gave birth to eight tiny kittens. Each kitten displayed a different color and design and was given special attention by this devoted mother. We had the opportunity to witness many more births in the neighborhood, but this birth always held a special spot in my heart because it was my first experience watching a mother give birth to her babies. A very considerate mother cat with her little onlookers, she seemed to smile after her labor was finished and purred loudly, gazing out at our very earnest somber faces. We were in awe of life rhythms.

Computers, video games, or cell phones were not available and playing outside was so much more fun than watching television. One of our activities used for entertainment was a hard metal barrel used for rolling down a steep hill. The main goal of this game was to remain in the barrel while plummeting down a steep bumpy hill. Huddling together, we discussed different techniques that we thought might be beneficial to help keep our bodies in the barrel. Various strategies involved safety precautions in what to do if you did so happen to fall out of the barrel. Of course, the only way to discover if anything worked was to give it a try! The barrel entertained us for hours and eventually we graduated to steeper and more challenging hills. Exhilaration filled our bodies, as we learned to let go of our fears and trepidations. Bravely, one person climbed into the barrel and then when the passenger was ready, the playmates gave the barrel a push and ran alongside until it began its descent down the hill. Stopping at the top of the hill, they watched as the barrel gained speed, rolling and plummeting down a very bumpy hill.

Our summers came alive with the exploration of new frontiers and, by trial and error; we seemed to always discover another activity which got our attention before boredom totally encompassed us. Donegal Springs Road had so much to offer with all its off roads and farms, providing endless fields in sight just waiting to be explored for adventure! Our walks on the country roads, which sometimes were quite far from our home, gave us the opportunity to visit the many different farms.

On one of these particular hot afternoons, after searching and exploring various barns at whim, we came across a sow giving birth to her babies. As the piglets were being birthed, we became very concerned about the size difference to the sow, the piglets were so tiny and fragile compared to their huge mother. Later, we were informed by the Wise Wizard that the mother pig had some kind of innate intelligence as to the position of each piglet. Not knowing about this innate intelligence, a large amount of our time was spent positioning each piglet so that the sow did not accidentally crush them by lying on them. Each piglet was introduced to their mother by putting them up to her snout. With unfaltering focus, we proceeded to show each piglet the way to a teat of their very own. With our mission complete, we sped home on our bicycles as the sun's glow began to lower toward the horizon, etching pink streaks throughout the sky.

The Kind Wizard and Life Rhythms

One early summer eve, just as dusk started to fall, Grandpa Kentin came across baby opossums clinging to their mother's dead body lying in the middle of Donegal Springs Road. The sky was beginning to create a masterpiece of colors, as it prepared for the moon to make its entrance and Grandpa Kentin knew that the babies' lives were in jeopardy from other travelers on the road. Hence, being a kind man, he collected them up and, using his shirt as a knapsack, he carried them home. That evening he gave us a bit of advice on how to take care of the baby opossums, showing us how to prepare a special formula to feed these precious babies. So every day it was our responsibility to feed each baby. Using a makeshift bottle from a syringe, we nursed the babies until they were healthy and strong and eventually they were given their freedom at the crooked creek.

Once in awhile, Grandpa Kentin took the motley crew on special trips, and today is one of those very special days. An interesting-looking character, wearing black pants with black suspenders and a wide brim hat, he embellishes his look further by sporting a long grey beard. He is a kind man of sorts and is in his seventies, which seems ancient to these small children who look up to him, calling him the Kind Wizard.

This afternoon, piling excitedly into his big white station wagon, some of the lucky children find their seats in the far back. Sitting down on the tailgate, they let their feet dangle freely from the open end of the station wagon and enjoy the warm summer breeze with all the magnificent scents of summer. Now sitting side by side, they giggle as they watch the hot macadam road pass by them. The Kind Wizard is happy to be taking his load full of passengers to a place way out into the country where they have never been before and his eyes sparkle with anticipation. Nearing their destination, their excitement mounts as their eyes detect a long wooden diving board seen in the distance. Their elation increases as he comes to a stop and the children take a deep breath with wide eyes full of wonder. They take one look at this lake and know immediately it is a kid's paradise. It's a swimming hole, complete with swans and a wooden diving board!

This particular neighborhood had other playmates but the Kentin family was our second home, where most of my time was spent as a young child and we are friends to this day.

The Kentin garden was very well pruned, having many different kinds of vegetables growing from it which thrived heartily because of its well tilled fertile soil. But as with any garden it came with weeds. Every year it became a ritual to till the earth and plant seeds with our neighboring family. After this annual ritual it seemed like in no time just like magic, green shoots appeared in the warm spring air. As this garden matured, we had the chore of helping the Kentin family weed their garden and it was on one of these particular summer mornings, I discovered a bunch of fur. This ball of hair was hidden, embedded under the green beans which showed much promise of a hearty harvest. Snuggled safely in this nest of fur was found the tiniest baby mice. They were found at one of their most vulnerable times of life, not in the world long enough to have the opportunity to develop fur to cover their naked bodies, and safely hidden from view by the heavy foliage. After I showed Dottie, the oldest child in the Kentin family, the nest, she seemed to have all the answers on how to take care of them. She informed us it was most imperative to keep them warm. So, I decided it best for her to take care of them. Regrettably, I was so disappointed when the news got out later regarding what happened to these precious beings. Mice do not survive in an oven set at warm.

Guilt set in when I realized I was the person ultimately responsible for their early demise, due to my hastiness and lack of respect. I held myself accountable for removing them from the comfort of their nest, inconsiderate of nature's flow and the rhythm of life.

Every Easter, we always had the opportunity to go into town and choose our very own peep from a window full of cute fluffy peeps of every color imaginable. Each peep came with its unique color because of being dipped in a grade food dye. The process of how these peeps bodies changed into adult chickens fascinated me and stirred my curiosity to find out more about this innate intelligence which guided their bodies to change, rapidly at times. They rested while this intelligence worked quietly in the background and then pizzazz, just like magic, a small minute change is seen in their bodies or a quite noticeable transformation, leading them to eventually evolve into adult chickens. At first sporting their different colors, our peeps entertained us for endless hours but as the days went by, they magically changed from their colored fuzzy down into a few adult feathers. Later we were delightfully surprised by their changing voices, which matured into a deeper tone instead of the tiny soft peeping sounds. We watched in amazement as their bodies developed into adult chickens. When fully grown, they were given the freedom to run around in the field with our pony or horse, and later became our meals. Lester showed no hesitation to using a hatchet and a piece of wood to accomplish the execution. Somehow, our mother found it amusing and said, "Ember and Mairzy, come look out back at the stable and see the chicken running around without a head!" At the time, I didn't give it much reflection but did think, "That is horrible! Why revel in someone's mishap. Grownups!"

Yes, life was grand. Warm weather events such as nursing school, cooking classes, and many other activities were meticulously organized by the oldest Kentin sibling, *Dottie, who was four years our senior.*

One of these events was a mock wedding which was planned to the greatest detail. *Invitations are handed out amongst the neighborhood. It is a week before a very special event is going to take place, a wedding celebration.*

On this special occasion, all the participants are beautifully and elaborately adorned. The bride's gown and the flower girl's dress were all carefully sewn by their oldest playmate and her mother. Also, responsible for the other outfits of the members of the wedding party, this mother, and daughter team has been working hard together. Bubbles of excitement are in the air as a multitude of fresh flowers are being skillfully arranged into fresh bouquets from an array of just freshly picked flowers that has been spread out on a card table. Morning and night seem to stand suspended in time, as beams of glimmering rays of light begin to show on the horizon. Finally finished, the twins' mother is placing her fresh arrangements of colorful tulips, fragrant lilac flowers and bright yellow daffodils on the tables for the guests, while Dottie and her mother are putting the finishing touches on the wedding cake which was made from scratch diligently in the kitchen early morning. Much later, Dottie is placing a bride and groom figurine in the center of the wedding cake. She sighs in satisfaction and, standing back, she smiles in admiration at their masterpiece.

Quietly, everyone now watches—

It is Rex's turn, the youngest girl of the Kentin family. Slowly, she begins to walk the path leading to the altar, carefully dropping a multitude of colorful rose petals along the way from her basket. Next in line is the ring bearer, cameras are quickly retrieved as the adults smile at how adorable everyone looks. Now the big moment arrives which everyone is waiting for, here comes the bride! Standing in a line, the wedding party looks on with wide eyes as the bride is led to the altar. After the pair's I do's, a multitude of helium balloons are released into the sky and the groom shyly lifts her lace veil. Looking into her soft green eyes, he kisses her. These children are eager willing participants, and love to play in the world of make believe. Life as a child is glorious with cake and most of all love. Life is meant to be celebrated. Next week, another wedding is held but with Mairzy as the bride and, of course, a fresh homemade cake but a different flavor.

A strong firm hand held onto my little hand as I braved the huge ocean waves. The excitement was overwhelming being amidst the swells of water that came toward me. My father made me feel safe and secure as my small body was swiftly lifted above the swelling waves. Consoling me, he said, "You have no need to be afraid; I have you." I fondly hold onto these memories of life and what I believe life should represent at such a young age.

In the big vast ocean a proud dad holds the tiny hands of two little girls close by his side. As a wave approaches them, these two toddlers feel sheltered. The sky is a violet-blue as the sea gulls swirl in the fluffy, shimmering white clouds overhead. They dive for their next meal as the magnificent ocean swells and splashes. The sun rays shine through the seawater, creating diamonds of sparkling lights dancing on top of the ocean waters. To an onlooker, they appear fragile and tiny in comparison to the magic of its vibration.

On the boardwalk, the seagulls overhead perform acrobatics swooping, zooming from the sky as they detect their dinner which two twin sisters hold way up into the sky for them to see. Later, a multitude of seagulls can be seen hovering and swooping down upon these two little toddlers, covering them with their many white, gray flapping wings. The girls giggle and squeal in delight as their small bodies shake with laughter. Their parents look on holding hands, smiling with grateful hearts.

The beach grass and sand dunes created a great magical playground for my sister and me. There was always something to explore found along that old rickety beach fence with the seagulls nearby. Thelma and Lester's hearts sang and this is how they would have wanted life to be forever. Later, Mairzy did an oil painting of this picture, capturing the moment in time. How horrified they would have been if they knew that their life was to turn so sour.

Being older we remained on the beach all day long, sunning and swimming for hours in the vast ocean while our parents stayed tucked carefully under a huge umbrella. In the evening, we walked the boardwalk until we were totally exhausted; visiting every store possible, while Thelma did what she was good at: shopping. She loved to look at the diamond rings that seemed to be priced just right, and she managed to bring at least one home from our travels. Looking forward to a sausage sandwich with green peppers, Lester headed for the same stand every year. By the time we returned to our hotel, our bellies were very full and our skin was a little sore to the touch, but morning brought a new beginning with refreshed and renewed bodies.

Games

One of our all time favorite pastimes was taunting the cows. Our clan puffed out our chests and ran boldly up to these huge beasts grazing in the middle of the pasture. We waved our arms, wiggled our hips, daring them to chase us and with very little encouragement, they stampeded toward us. Some of us were barely three years of age, which made the cattle appear even more massive. This inspired us to run like the wind. Screaming and hollering, we scattered across the pasture with our sight only on the barbed wired fence. Very much aware of the importance in not getting caught in the barbs of this rather high fence, we barely had enough time to scoot out of the way as they charged us. This game could go on for hours at a time. Being very young we were too naïve to know better. And when we did know better, the excitement outweighed any common sense. But whatever the reason, we chose to overlook how dangerous this sport was as a childhood game. We were very happy no one ever found out about this particular game which lasted into the later elementary school years.

The normal games were also a part of our play time—games such as: king of the mountain, hopscotch, dress up, jump rope, freeze tag, steal the flag, hide and seek, foursquare, baseball, sledding, skating, doctor, nurse and a game called find my tail. At the time, my sister and I thought it odd that a boy would have a tail and frequently had serious discussions which took place in the evening just before bedtime, trying to figure out how it was possible for this to be. Very naïve as children and with lots of amusement and a chuckle, we understood what it meant as we became older, that is, at least my sister inferred what it meant. She said, "Now think about it, Ember, you have to know what they mean!" When at last an association was made, the light bulb went on, and I exclaimed, "Really, gee whiz, yuck!" So when the boys played that game again, our only retort was laughing and saying, "Oh, please, save your breath, we are over your taunting! Stop it; we know what you really mean!" The boys' faces turned a crimson red.

We played hard into the early evening and during our baseball season my fingers became all black and blue, swollen from not catching the baseball correctly. The pain of my jammed fingers coerced me to learn to play as well as the boys—In fact, better.

The pussy willow tree was rescued from intruders, the Japanese beetles. Perceiving that somehow mankind was benefited by removing these nasty beetles from the delicate leaves of the pussy willow bush, gave us great satisfaction. Different fates were picked out for these pesky critters, drowning by quicksand, or being sautéed in a frying pan with our little stove. Ants also received the same fate. This took a bit of time because our stove had to be turned on and heated up, while a designated child retrieved the oil to put on the grill. This activity went on for much of the day because the pussy willow tree was the home of many Japanese beetles, and we were determined to save the beautiful leaves of this tree. We believed we were on a special mission of saving the pussy willow tree which definitely deserved our help, because in the spring time it gave us beautiful bright yellow flowers and in the fall brought soft fluffy silver flowers which looked just like the fur of a cat.

A pussy willow is a tree, I called it both but early in the life of a pussy willow tree, it looks just like a bush or a shrub. If you keep it trimmed back it resembles a bush but the pussy willow is a tree and can grow twenty to thirty feet high or more and, like other willows, it is soft-wooded.

It is popular for its soft, grayish, fur-like buds on long, straight stems. The buds begin to open very early in the spring, making great indoor arrangements that are long-lasting. Thelma brought them indoors to brighten the room. Pussy willows bring with them the expectations of spring and a new gardening season ahead! We loved our pussy willow tree, which Lester was found trimming every autumn!

Our neighbors purchased a rubber swimming pool and shortly afterwards, my dad found a metal tin drum used for animal feed, making a sturdier swimming pool. Using his ingenuity and creativity, Lester found this particular feed bin from one of his farmer friends and instantly became our hero. Already playing in the neighbor's rubber shallower pool, we usually began with the neighbor's pool and when bored with that particular pool, ran and jumped together into the feed bin filled with colder water. These two pools cooled and entertained us during the hot sweltering days in Pennsylvania as we gleefully galloped and jumped. Sprinting from pool to pool, our laughter was heard throughout the neighborhood as we kicked in the cool water. What a wonderful way to spend time on a hot summer day, and the sensation of the fresh cool water upon my skin on those hot humid days made my senses explode with ecstasy.

Halloween

It was not unusual for us to go out trick or treating for a week or two, our celebration lasted a rather long stretch of time. Materials were gathered together by Dottie and her mother and were piled high on the dining room table. During the season, this table was used to design and create costumes, which could be very elaborate or as simple as a sheet.

In the farmer's field, whispering is heard as the children discuss their next set of plans. Very careful not to be noticed, they slowly emerge from the tall grass and proceed to cross the field to their next home. As they come near, they reach into their paper bags and fling field corn with all their might on to the wooden porch of an old fashioned farm house. Using this field corn is an upgrade to their Halloween fun which adds fuel to their excitement. Immediately, sprinting as if their lives depend upon it, they scatter into the fields of tall grass where they will meet later.

Their imaginations grow rampant and wild. Pretending to be hunted down for this mischievous antic, they quietly cover themselves with the tall grass in the farmer's field. Remaining still and low for what seems a coon's age, only soft whispers can be heard from the tall grass during the pitch blackness of night. Eventually emerging, they brush off their costumes, covered with grass, straw and gnarly burrs, and they are ready for their next adventure.

In due course, adding another exciting fun activity to Halloween, different colored soaps were gathered together to use for decorating the windows of cars. Vehicles could be seen driving throughout the neighborhood on Donegal Springs Road, and also in our small town of Shady Pine, showcasing our artwork. Some of these designs became very elaborate and the children of Shady Pine knew that we were most likely responsible for these intricate designs made from soap, which evolved into our trademark during Halloween. Children smiled with their secret, as cars drove by with designs not yet scrubbed clean.

When growing up as a child being sick wasn't too bad, although there were times it felt like I was in the pit of hell. But the times when sickness only meant a sniffle or two, sickness was bearable. I lounged in bed, pampered by my mom, who prepared me poached eggs and dry toast. It was really nice. Also, a shot of whiskey was retrieved from the neighboring family, a very important part of the ingredient in helping to bring my health back. I found this to be a very interesting concept, and a peculiar fact that Thelma resorted to liquor to heal the sick. She never touched the stuff and was not at all in favor of having it in the home, but gave me a shot of whiskey to help me recuperate!

So when school could not be tolerated another day, my body was held close to the hot register for a while until it felt nice and warm. Next, tiptoeing to the kitchen as quiet as humanly possible, I found catsup and mustard in the refrigerator and squirted both into my mouth and waited for that perfect time to scurry to the bathroom. Running to the bathroom, I held my stomach as if in gut wrenching pain. Mother looked at me very worriedly. She was a bit gullible or maybe I was just very smart, but regardless, with a concerned look on her face she hastily went to retrieve the thermometer. After taking my temperature, my goal was met with a day off from school. Spending time with Mother even if it meant feigning sickness was really nice for a change!

The Rapture and Scary Things in the Dark

The rapture was talked about a lot in Church, how one day you are on Earth and in a split second you disappear, with the possibility of family and friends being separated forever. This thought was incomprehensible to me and horrified my whole being, literally tearing me to pieces to think of such a dreadful, heinous experience. One afternoon after a long day of school and finally arriving at my bus stop, I was very glad to jump off. Thrilled to be finally home, I ran up our driveway and opened up our screen door leading to the kitchen, looking for my mother. Announcing my arrival, I expected to see my mother's face but instead found nobody in sight. This was very unusual at our home. Going through our home I called, "Hello! Is anyone home?" Immediately, I thought back to the sermon on Sunday at church. "Oh my, the rapture has finally come like the preacher said and I have been left behind, separated from my family forever!" Convinced this event had taken place brought the most shocking feeling in the pit of my stomach, making it churn and reel.

Ultimately, my mom finally did appear and calmed my unrelenting sorrow. She smiled softly, looking into my eyes, and I realized soon my fears were not authentic, but only my fragile psyche acting out a church sermon which was constantly being preached at us. Everything was the same as before. In fact nothing had changed at all! Is fear love? I thought God is Love? Death totally freaked me out, and I could only imagine the terror people felt as they stood at the edge, looking into the bottomless pit of hell getting ready to make that plunge. It was important to do the right thing or else it was curtains for the unbelieving and misbehaved because they got to burn for eternity. It was not a very pretty sight to imagine such gruesome continuous torture!

The Closet

How could I not be fearful of the night that was shrouding the world in front of me in pitch-black darkness?

My twin sister and I shared a bedroom, each having our own twin bed. The clothing closet in our room entertained my thoughts about the bogeyman. This closet was made from knotty pine, displaying all kinds of intricate designs from the natural decoration of the wood. My bed was the furthest from the closet on the left hand side of the room, giving me a bit of security. At least I felt a tad safer than my sister who was adjacent to the apparition's home. Of course, if the ghastly apparition in the closet did not get you, almost anything could be lurking under the bed. Sometimes in the wee hours of the morning, my eyes decided to pop open as if they had a mind of their own and I swore there was someone or something standing right next to my bed. As this apparition stared at me quietly in the pitch blackness, I periodically got the courage to call my sister to help me, thinking Mairzy could save me. But she was usually sound asleep. Realizing that my position was revealed in the room made me feel more vulnerable and all the more queasy. I froze into position after my arms, hands and eyes were very quietly tucked under the sheets. Fear curled up inside me and clung to my ribs, settling uncomfortably in my chest. I didn't doubt the feeling was there to stay, reminding me of its existence every time I opened my mouth to breathe.

Amazingly the deep release from my horror came with sleep. It is where I escaped from my own agonizing and fretting about something that probably was a figment of my own imagination, or was it? If for some reason it did exist, fear took over my being and the perseverance to find out and face it was not going to happen—at least not then. However, as time went on, this kind of hiding was not even an option.

King

As the morning sun is just starting to arise with glimmers of it peeking over the horizon, children can be seen sitting on a wooden fence, patiently waiting to take their turn to ride a horse named King. While they wait, they are happily making bets on who will stay on King's back.

This horse has his own game and a couple tactics of playing it. One way is to rub his weight against the side of his shed to scrape the passenger off from his back or maybe surprise them by quickly changing his direction, darting into his barn. It was usually in the barn where he won, and King bucked hard with the intention of sending the young equestrian catapulting from his back into the scratchy hay of his stall. Once in awhile, the equestrian's face glowed with excitement as he or she came out of the pony shed, still clutching onto King's thick mane.

Today, the onlookers cheer as bets are being made on the outcome of each individual rider's fate or victory. The father of the twin girls sits for awhile with this group of children, pleased with his accomplishment of building this sturdy wooden fence made by hand just for King. There could be as many as twelve children seen lined up on the fence participating in this special event. The word boredom was not even in their vocabulary; it just did not exist. Today, the cherry tree's massive limbs create an upper balcony seat for a few children who wish to view the game from above. It is where the aroma of blooms of whitish pink flowers drift throughout the air, splashing a kaleidoscope of red hues in the sky as the sun rays stream, making sprinkles of diamonds through the air for all to enjoy.

Later that day all the children are seen climbing this massive tree to find a seat on the thick branches, enjoying a beautiful view of the endless fields and the fragrance of the luxurious cherry blooms. The scent of the perfume spiraling up from the blooming peony garden down below adds an extra dimension to the smells which spring ushers in. This is heaven on Earth.

Stroking his soft mane and gently putting on King's bridle, I hopped onto his bare back and off we went, galloping through the fields. Not our only horse, but having a pony before, King gave me plenty of practice time to horseback ride. It was a liberating experience to be on such a massive creature, generating a whole new meaning of being, and a mutual respect was developed between us over time.

Mairzy enjoyed riding King too, but her riding days were later cut short after being thrown from his back into the wooden fence. Forcefully striking her head on the fence, she blacked out and when she finally gained consciousness, she crawled back to the house and headed to the couch. Becoming very sick, she vomited throughout the night into the wee hours of the morning. We kept her accident a secret, but our parents were informed about the accident a few weeks after her mishap.

A horse named King carries a young passenger bareback. The child is clutching onto his soft mane as he propels his massive body forward. Snuggling her nose into his mane, she enjoys his scent, as she's done many times before. Today, King is guided to trot through the maze made yesterday, paths made by the children in the tall grass of the pasture. At the end of this maze, King comes out galloping with his little passenger, releasing her from any cares of the day. She loves the feeling of the air which blows through her light brown hair and takes in the smell of the autumn air as her green eyes glisten brightly in the sun rays. As this powerful animal moves forward, he fills his nostrils with breath, and releases from his throat a soft neighing sound. Happy to be free, he shakes his shimmering blonde mane passionately.

Most people do not get to experience what I did in a lifetime. Those beautiful lazy hazy summer days and freedom to run barefoot as a child gave me memories to hold onto, sustaining me and strengthening me for a journey that was before me. My Bible was a book frequented often as a child, as I memorized many verses that spoke to my soul. Maybe I had a deep inner knowing that evil existed, and somehow knew its power could be the source of havoc and destruction in a family. The love of the heart, uncontaminated, represents power and strength which is insurmountable. It cannot be prevailed over and to me a great example of this love was the life of Jesus. Reciting the Lord's Prayer repeatedly in my head prepared me for what was to come, and the spiritual battle later on in my life. I was blessed to witness this power of love, which brought me to my knees in awe.

The Crossroads Mennonite Bible School was a summer haven for kids. It is where I was encouraged to memorize many Bible verses which were later used as an anchor in life. In my later teenage years, I walked to this church and sat in the window sill at night to ease my troubled spirit.

On a country road a motley group of children stroll with the brightest eyes, full of anticipation for their first day of Bible School at Crossroads Mennonite

Church. They giggle and talk amongst themselves as they walk along, relishing each other's company on this rather long walk to the church. Not giving it much thought, they like the idea of walking. The anticipation of learning Bible verses and becoming a part of all the fun activities of Bible School, fuel their souls forward on the hot country road.

From the open windows of Shady Pine Church, the children can be heard singing robustly. 'This Little Light of Mine' and 'I got the Joy of Jesus Down in My Heart' are songs that feed their spirits and set them free to soar, preparing them for the tumultuous storm clouds that come to rock the deep seas.

The Shady Pine Church Vacation Bible School had a fun-packed program which my sister and I faithfully attended every year. It was a grand experience involving many different art projects, water games, puppet plays and it was made complete with badges, snacks, stickers galore and most important, love. My parents attended this church since they were young teenagers and had many friends here.

Summer days, lying upon the cool grass, I gazed dreamily up to the sky and filled my world with fantasy as the clouds took different shapes and forms, floating lazily in the sky. I thought how heaven must be unique because, to me, heaven was on Earth.

Every summer, Mairzy and Ember attend a church camp affiliated with the Shady Pine Church. On this particular summer day, Thelma and Lester have arrived early to pick Mairzy up because homesickness encompasses her whole being. Since this camp is weeklong, her sister is very torn on what to do. But after a bit of agonizing, she decides to stay for the week alone without her. Bunking with their roommates alone without her sister in the cabin is a very new and different experience for her and not too much later she realizes just how much her sister is missed and how very important her presence is to her. At a very early age she comes to an understanding exactly how important it is to show appreciation to the ones we love.

Thelma had signed us up for the week that was designated for our grade level in school and with just a bit of money, we attended this camp complete with turtles, frogs, salamanders, creepy insects of all sorts, ping pong tables, arcade activities, art projects, outside fountains, great meals, singing, Bible lessons and many different board games. Also, this camp had a myriad of games and activities outside for us to explore. There were sports, organized hikes, treasure hunts, a swimming pool, canoeing and many intricate obstacle courses that challenged the spirit, making a child's dreams come true.

Sacred Area

The sacred area is a very wide open area of grass where a simple large wooden cross stands strong, brilliant in the energy it elicits. Long wooden benches are arranged in many rows to sit in silence and worship. Children gathered and meditated together here in silence, generating a portal of powerful omnipresent love energy. Later their voices of praise are magnified throughout the forest.

On a beautiful sunny bright Sunday, a dream comes true for a very excited child, who has been praying with fervor that her parents' excursion to the lake is going to manifest. Mount Gretna is a beautiful manmade lake and after church, they would visit this lake with only one stipulation: that the day is without clouds. Food prepared the day before is loaded into the trunk of their car; potato rolls made from scratch, fruit salad, fresh vegetables, homemade potato salad, baked beans, pies and cakes are only a few of the items taken with them. Steaks placed in a cooler packed with ice are the responsibility of their father who is very proud to be in charge of the steaks. He is a master steak griller.

Immediately upon arrival, Thelma searches for a special spot to lay out the feast, as Lester prepares the grill for the steaks. Lester and Thelma work together as a team, each being responsible for a specific task, while their sandy blond twins wander off to explore the terrain nearby in search of small critters and cute bugs. They do not take the chance in exploring too far because their stomachs growl in great anticipation for the picnic which is being prepared. Later, sitting with their father, mother and older sister, their heads are bowed in prayer, as their father offers a prayer of appreciation for the food prepared. Lester believes in the importance of the family, calling himself a family man.

We allowed all our inhibitions down, playing relentlessly. We played until the sun started to set on the hills and the sky displayed a multitude of colors, always painting a different masterpiece each time. Mount Gretna was the location of our first swimming lesson. It is here where Lester and Thelma took turns demonstrating the skill of doggy paddling on land. Advising us exactly what was needed to accomplish this skill, which sounded quite easy because all you had to do was keep your head above the water, move your hands like a puppy and kick your legs as hard as possible. Quickly moving to the next part of the lesson, my father picked up my small body and gave me a gentle throw off the pier into the shallower part of the lake, deep enough that standing was not an option for a small girl like me. Therefore, imitating a puppy and kicking as hard as possible, I floundered through the water not knowing exactly what to expect. But as my body began to relax to the water's caresses, swimming began to make some sense and instead of panicking, I chose to let go, trusting the outcome. Promptly, my parents got into the water and encouraged me to swim to them, and the most absolutely extraordinary feeling of freedom came over me. "This must be heaven!" I thought. Next, my sister had a turn and surely must have done just fine because of all the smiles on everyone's faces.

Later swimming became a passion of mine and the fantasy of being a mermaid entertained me for hours. Mount Gretna was an enchanted haven, complete with diving boards, canoes to rent, a very long swing over the water and many wooden rafts which enticed us to swim out to the middle of the lake. It was fun to discover an unoccupied raft, claiming it as our own, at least for awhile. Once in awhile, I discovered Mairzy sunbathing happily on a raft. Climbing up the slippery ladder I joined her and we relaxed together watching the various shapes and sizes of water creatures swim enchantingly by us as we basked in the rays of the mid-afternoon sun. Water spiders hopped as if they walked on the water across the diamonds of color created by the sun's rays. Dragonflies flitted here and there with rainbow-colored wings.

A dragonfly is a beautiful sight on a summer day or early evening. The dragonfly has the ability to reflect and refract light and colors. It is often linked with magic and mysticism. With their shimmering wings and delicate form, they appear to come directly from the land of Faerie. Their spectacular colors shine with iridescence in the sunlight. These colors take a time to develop, giving the idea that with maturity our own true colors will come forth. Just as light can bend and shift and be adapted in different ways, so can the archetypal forces associated with the dragonfly. Dragonflies yield the message that life is never what it appears to be. The dragonfly is one of nature's shape shifters. It inhabits two realms, air and water. The first two years of their lives dragonflies live in the water, on the bottom of ponds and streams, and are called nymphs. As they age they go through metamorphosis and take to the air. As water represents the emotional body and air represents the mental, those with this animal power will frequently find themselves trying to maintain a balance between their thoughts and emotions.

A swing located in the middle of the lake has a big launching pad and is still a very popular destination for swimmers. Using the long metal ladder, people climb up onto its platform and wait patiently to take their turn. This is not the normal swing seen at parks but has extra long ropes attached to a metal bar to sit upon, giving swinging a whole different perspective. Today, people are seen traveling way out over the lake on this long swing resembling a special ride seen at many amusement parks. They perform many tricks from it such as: flipping, standing, diving, hanging or just sitting upon the metal support it offers. My curiosity was evoked further by the huge turtles that swam and hung out around the massive platform of this swing. Later I discovered from a very knowledgeable adult that they were snapping turtles. A real sense of respect for their space was developed over time. Later a sliding board was erected, which was the longest sliding board ever invented, complete with curves and hills. It was the grandest sliding board ever seen by mankind. The area where the sliding board was erected had a multitude of different water creatures, unlike the habitat of the location of the swing. Being very different in environment, we discovered a fresh new wealth of creatures, one of them being tadpoles. Tadpoles fascinated us and were caught in a net to be brought home to be attentively watched as they transformed into frogs. Amazing how one day they looked like fish, eventually developed legs, and magically changed into frogs which were able to live on land. They too, just as the beautiful dragonfly, begin their life only living in water.

As this lake changed, I also changed and matured into a young lady, but the spark of enthusiasm felt for this place always flickered inside me, waiting for me to remember.

Our dad was so much fun to be around and, boy, did he make Mairzy and I laugh. If caught in a good mood, our dad took turns with us and played wheelbarrow, holding our ankles as we walked on our hands throughout the hallway to our bedroom. Giggling until we got to our beds, we fell down totally dog-tired. In the basement, a challenge was made to wheelbarrow up the many steep steps. Usually taking the challenge, we made it to the top with our arms aching and a lot of grunting. At the top of the steps, our dad tickled us until we cried for mercy. Later, finding our way to our bedroom, we clambered into our beds. It is here where a deep contentment came over us while my sister and I shared stories with our little dog named Pinky, snuggled close by our sides. A sense of peacefulness floated in, our eyes slowly closed and we were fast asleep with Pinky, who was already in another world dreaming. I loved my dad and knew without a doubt his love for us.

Pinky

The twin sisters love night time; it is time to play with their dog, Pinky, and share tales made up at whim. Relaxing, they prop their legs up on the headrest of their beds stretching their thin bodies. They cradle their heads with their arms, getting ready for their nighttime activity which includes Pinky. The placement of their twin beds, only a couple feet apart, makes this game very convenient for Pinky to be an eager participant. So, let the game begin! Pinky stands up immediately at their playful calls, jumping from one twin's bed and then turning and bounding to the other one's bed. Excited by their summons, Pinky wags her tail, madly enjoying the sport of it all. Ember has fallen in love with Pinky and what this spotted puppy represents to her about life. Life is good to these two little girls who are innocent, bubbling with joy.

Encouraged to take weekly baths, their dad's responsibility is to make sure that this happens for these two little girls. He is currently preparing their bath water, making sure the temperature is just right. Now, his voice can be heard calling them from the bathroom, summoning them to please come. Immediately upon hearing his voice, they stop their playing, hop up from their beds and skip playfully to the bathroom. Dad is waiting for them with a full tub of warm water and bubbles. Later, the happiest and most innocent voices bubbling with enthusiasm can be heard from the bathroom, as these sisters talk amongst themselves. Life is vivid and vibrant, and their hearts and eyes glow with light.

Biking was another activity which enabled me to explore the endless miles of country roads. While riding my bike to Brubaker's grocery store, I practiced holding an intention to manifest a piece of candy which was easy to obtain because my mom always made sure it came true. She so happened to work at this small grocery store in Florin.

A tomboyish mishap with a mini-cycle was responsible for the permanent tattoo created on my knee. A boy who lived across the street was filled with immense pride because of the recent purchase of his new mini-cycle and invited me to hop on to take a ride down our country road. Experiencing the air as it billowed through our hair enlivened our senses and we felt free and one with the bike, but this feeling left as quickly as it came. The cycle had the mishap of becoming caught in the shoulder of the road. The force of the bike hitting the macadam propelled us through the air like a rocket as our legs and arms flailed out of control. My knee was badly bruised and was deeply embedded with gravel. Taking one look, my mother immediately transported me to the town doctor who was conveniently the father of a boy I had befriended in school. Upon arrival, he took me into his office and proceeded to ask me questions as he meticulously and torturously scrubbed my wound with what appeared to be a Brillo pad. Having no compassion or empathy for my moans, he examined my wound with intense scrutiny to make sure every piece of the gravel was excavated from it. This procedure seemed to take forever to do, and unfortunately, stitches were not even an option because most of my flesh was lost on the road. The boy steering the cycle had the misfortune of breaking his leg in multiple places, and the bone protruded through the skin, making the sight of it really disturbing. Therefore, his riding days were cut short and his mini-cycle was stored away for what seemed a coon's age. My bruise eventually evolved into a special permanent design, with a great story behind it.

Later that summer, a cement bridge leeringly came into my sight as my out-of-control bicycle headed toward it. My bike kept on accelerating as it descended down the steep country road, and I knew without a doubt trouble was closing in fast. Traveling at such a high speed made it impossible to steer or stop my bike. Luckily, my body came out of this mishap just fine with only a few scrapes, bruises and scratches; but the long two hour's walk back home with my bike in hand was very grueling. My bike had taken on a different form by now, looking like a broken accordion. Slowly limping home, to me this voyage seemed long and hot, but I was very careful not to panic which would have made everything even worse. Finally arriving home, Mother saw my predicament and immediately took my bike from me. She helped me to get cleaned up and bandaged my scrapes and bruises. The next day the broken bike was sent off on a one-way ticket to never return, but not much later a brand new red bike was found parked in our driveway.

While heading to visit our sister, Mairzy and I invented different games to help pass the time and ease the excruciating boredom. Being prisoners in the backseat of our parent's Cadillac made us feel extremely fidgety, but we hoped the torture of the trip would be well worth it. Finally, after arriving at our destination and exchanging long hugs, Mairzy and I ventured outside and preoccupied ourselves in exploring the new landscape, while the adults engaged in deep conversation.

Later that day, Kay suggested a unique place to go swimming. She described the location as a beautiful majestic lake having ice cold water, surrounded by huge pine trees. This idea sounded so good to us after having been confined in the car for such a long time. Off we went to find the lake. Arriving at our destination, our eyes became wide with excitement and anticipation exploded in our beings.

And before even testing the waters, we run to the lake and jump right into the freezing water. Splashing and laughing after our bodies enter the frigid waters, we nimbly climb out to the top of the high rocks that jut out precariously from the embankment. Without hesitation, we catapult our bodies from these overhanging boulders that look as if they will tumble down to the lake below and make a giant splash. Holding our bodies into tight balls, we propel down deep into the green frigid waters below. Resembling cannonballs, we make funny faces at each other as bubbles of air come out of our noses. It is so beautiful at this lake and the very frigid air makes the water feel warm to our skin, enlivening our already heightened senses. Nothing is going to keep us from the luxurious sport of swimming.

While driving back to my sister's home after swimming, a sore spot was detected on top of my head, which definitely got my attention. This spot did not go away and appeared as if it was slowly increasing in size. We made an appointment with one of Thelma's favorite doctors, and promptly as we returned from our family vacation, my worried mom straightaway took me to his office. After a couple of deeply concerned doctors took a look at the inflammation on top of my head, they all came to the conclusion that part of my skull needed to be removed because the bone on my head was disintegrating. Concerned that this inflammation was going to spread further and therefore generate more difficulty later, my head was shaved and the hospital became my home for many weeks—weeks which seemed like forever.

The evening before my arrival at the hospital, going downstairs to do my regular dancing, I came across Mother fretting and crying. Being the evening before my admission to the hospital, she was so worried and concerned about me. I said, "Please stop worrying; everything will be just fine because God will take care of me." She looked up at me, and with those words, her face released the pain of worry and love radiated around her. That was one of my first lessons on the power of the spoken word and how energy can change with intention.

After some time, when feeling more up to it, a beautiful scrapbook was created from the many cards given to me from all of my friends at school as well as my friends from the Shady Pine Church. This occupied some of my time at the hospital, but a great deal of time was spent sleeping because the procedure wore and tore at my already thin body. My worried mother accompanied me most of the time, sometimes spending the night.

Just as I had said, within a few months time, with a white turban wrapped around my head to protect the raw wound, I was eager to romp and play once more in the corn fields. Joining my neighbor friends and sister, we made endless trails throughout the autumn wheat. This is where most of our time was spent those fall days. Playing and planning in these fields of dreams, we created magic. The best memories were made during this time, setting me up to remember and win the battle over what was to be encountered later in my life.

Bread Soup

The Kentin family taught those around them so much about life by showing respect for each other and demonstrating the power of this energy called love in people's lives. It is more important than the material things we acquire—our jobs or accomplishments. It overrides all and is the essence of life, giving beauty in an array of multidimensional levels. With money scarce at times for this family, they tore white bread apart into a deep bowl and poured milk over it. This made a type of soup for their dinner, and they had this quite often. Hard working in order to be able to pay bills, their mother acquired a waitress position at one of the all time favorite local restaurants of the townspeople. This is where she spent long hours to earn money for their household. Working hard together, the children did family chores, while their mother was away bringing in an income which in turn strengthened their unity as a family. The oldest sibling, Dottie, was given the responsibility for assigning the household chores to each of her siblings and to make sure they stayed on task. I watched in admiration as our neighbor friends showed me with enthusiasm how they prepared bread soup for their evening dinner with such an attitude of pride and painstaking deliberation, as if the feast was being prepared for a king. This mind-set fascinated me, because I never had to experience any kind of lack in my life, and they showed me that lack was a word that does not have to be experienced. The poorest people might not even think about their situation as being one of lack; whereas someone who has it all, might perceive an experience as being unbearable. It all depends on how you look at it. Rexie, the youngest girl in the family, thought it was really nice how a meal could be made out of two items, milk and bread. "Simple," she said, "but tasty!" Her eyes brightened at the thought.

During this time of my life, Thelma decided that wearing a hairpiece to hide my bald shaved head was very important. This humiliated and drew attention to me even further, which enhanced my feelings of shame and embarrassment about my lack of hair. If not for that stupid revolting hairpiece, I would never have given a thought to my shaved head and would have gone on with life as if nothing happened. But having no choice except to wear this hideous piece, the unnecessary attention heightened my feelings of shame and responsibility. I blamed myself for my twin sister's plight. Because she had to wear a stinky hairpiece, it made the whole ordeal seem bizarre. Mother was insistent when we were young, well into elementary and junior high, that we dress alike. Not crazy about our mother's idea, we absolutely hated it, so depending on who chose what we were both going to wear that morning, the other brought a change of clothing to school in their backpack. We worked as a team until finally our battle was won in high school, and we were able to pick out and buy our own clothes that fit our own unique preferences.

My twin sister acquired the biggest lump on the top of her head which became very soft to the touch, and within days her hair fell out there. We were playing softball at the playground. She was the catcher and missed the ball and *bull's-eye,* it landed smack on top of her head because, instead of paying attention to the game, she was involved in looking down at some interesting bugs that appeared in front of her. The force knocked her backward, flat onto her back into the dirt and immediately her head swelled up, making her look like a cone head.

Our concerned mom sat Mairzy in the small bathroom in our ranch home and periodically checked her head, rubbing calendula on it to encourage the process of healing. It appeared odd that both of us had some kind of head issue, hair falling out or shaved. Mairzy's head exploded out and my head sunk in. My injury, a sunken crater, became permanent, and Mairzy's injury healed completely.

We were encouraged to take piano lessons when attending third grade in elementary school and later organ lessons were incorporated into our practice time. Developing a real appreciation for music, every morning before leaving for school we each took turns practicing a half hour. First, our practice time only encompassed the piano and later the organ was added for another fifteen minutes, and eventually, our practice time evolved to an hour allotted for both instruments. Mairzy ate breakfast, while I practiced or vice versa, switching place after our timer went off and by then it was time to say goodbye to our mother. We hurried out the kitchen door, crossed

Donegal Springs Road and climbed aboard the yellow school bus. It is here where I reflected upon my life, and enjoyed the scenery of the many rolling hills and open countryside, eventually passing forests and smaller wooded areas with streams as other passengers were picked up along the way.

In the beginning, our piano lessons were held at the school during school hours. But in junior high school, I had permission to walk into Shady Pine for lessons at our teacher's studio and later walked back to school to finish my remaining classes. This was not a big deal because walking was what one did to get to a destination. In high school, we needed a more advanced teacher. So our mother transported us once a week into Lancaster, about a good forty minute drive, to Loretta Burchell's studio to take lessons. We were dropped off together, while Thelma went shopping. Never shown where the bathroom was located, I roamed aimlessly and desperately around the home searching for one, but unable to find it decided the best thing to do was to water her flowers. Feeling a little lost for any other options and way too embarrassed to ask, I was extremely backward around adults.

Eventually, our dedication to keeping on schedule with our piano and organ lessons gave us the confidence to perform in front of the congregation of the Shady Pine Church. It is here where we were invited to sing duets. Intermittently we took turns playing the accompaniment on the piano and sang from our hearts. One of my favorite songs was, 'You Can Smile' which is about the importance of your attitude in life. If sour grapes come your way, your attitude and, of course, a smile will change the way you feel, which is easier at times said than done.

Acquiring the honor of being chosen to play the part of Mother Mary in the elementary musical for Christmas, I felt very special. Absolutely loving all the practice time that came with it, I gave it my undivided attention. I didn't comprehend at the time that the music teacher was Lester and Thelma's best friend, which may have factored into my receiving that part. Oh well, regardless, being picked definitely boosted my self-esteem and confidence in my voice because out of everyone who tried out for the part of the fifth-grade classes, I was chosen.

Thelma and Lester's good friend, Joyce Rosskee, reliably played the organ at Shady Pine Church every Sunday. She was also responsible for directing the church choir, and in charge of the choir's rehearsal time every Wednesday evening. When Joyce thought that the choir was ready, they performed the new arrangements the following Sunday in front of the whole congregation. Lester was dedicated to the choir and rarely missed the opportunity to join choir practice held once a week. He sometimes sang duets with Kay, who sang like a lark and had a unique melodious voice that gave me goose bumps. It was difficult or maybe just plain impossible for me to ever measure up to her bright caring personality and love for music because playing outside was so much more important than music could ever have been in my life at that time.

The Hole

My parents supported me in my desire to become baptized at the Shady Pine Church. Shady Pine is a quaint town where everyone knows each other, sometimes learning too much information about each other's lives. Gossip ran rampant in this small town with a few town criers holding megaphones at the city border, making sure they shared the gossip with all town dwellers as well as any newcomers. Somehow, they acquired the knack of how to obtain these juicy morsels of information about people's lives and made it their business to make it well known throughout the town. There must have been some undisclosed place where they went secretly to major in gossip.

This Church had a hole cut into the floor with a board over it which was removed for baptisms. They filled this hole with water and when it was my turn to be baptized; my body was guided backward under the cool water. One of the biggest concerns of mine with this procedure of being baptized was the dread of experiencing the cold heavy wet clothing and getting water up my nose. I went through the motion but recall very little of it, only remembering the sense of being scared, cold, and soaked to the bone—anxious for it to be finished!

Daydreaming, —she arrives at a small clearing in the forest, a glass-clear lake. The sun is like a celestial fireball in the sky with brilliant beams that shine onto the land and make the lake a-glitter with golden sparkles. In the afternoon, the sun becomes a muted, wax melt-yellow but shafts of light still pour through patches of white fluffy clouds onto the lake while speckled trout arch into the air and plop onto the water's surface, seeking to grab a fly close by.

Her soft green eyes dream of a magical place where the sun shines as her friends: birds, trees, flowers, animals, fairies, and many loving spirits begin to surround her. On this occasion, they have gathered together to witness her special commitment and special moment in time... There is a buzz in the air; they just love celebrations. Now is the time, it finally is here and they are very excited because they have just finished creating a beautiful robe from flowers and moss, with the help of the flower fairies. The flower fairies have just finished using a huge pine needle to sew the remaining few flowers together, putting the finishing touches on this beautiful emerald green robe.

—Gently, her godmother touches her back and the young girl allows her body to descend slowly into the warm pool of water, hidden deep in the jade- green forest. This body of water contains many colorful crystals emitting rays of love and water lilies with hues of pink and fuchsia. A multitude of fish can sense the celebration, as they jump to join in on this joyous occasion. Before emerging, she swims and enjoys the energy this pool of water emits, and then floating quietly on her back, streams of sunshine glimmer throughout the forest's canopy, making the rainbow wings of the dragonfly shine with iridescence. She giggles with delight as the dragonflies twist and turn, always changing direction. Then they hover in front of her before quickly flying backward, putting on a show for her.

Much later, after she emerges, her copper brown silk slip falls gracefully to her feet onto the bright velvety green moss. Waiting for her are swarms of fluttering robins with deep red bellies, which carefully place her emerald green robe around her shoulders. Delicately led to recline in a pile of heavenly scented daisies, she smiles as a fresh breeze welcomes her to enjoy the streams of sunlight now cascading through the tall blue evergreens. Later, her many friends join her with a glass of fragrant water, prepared by using the nectar of blue honeysuckle flowers. It is a baptism in Love, a memory never forgotten.

Death

The most unusual and embarrassing behavior occurred at a funeral where we accompanied our mother. Sitting next to Mairzy during this sober event, I felt the whole pew come alive and begin to shake. Curious as to what was causing the vibration, my eyes glanced over to Mairzy to see if she noticed anything peculiar, but she definitely was not in any shape to talk. Covering her mouth with a tissue so no one noticed, she was busily working on stifling her giggles which were bubbling up and out of her shaking body. She tried to conceal her laughter the best she knew how, which for no good reason decided to erupt from her being at this very inconvenient time. Pondering why this was happening, I thought, "Odd, this event is supposed to be sad!" and as soon as the thought came, out of nowhere a giggle came from within me. Immediately my eyes looked down to quiet my mind, pretending my head was bowed in grief. But that didn't deter them; there they came again—bubbles of laughter! As I sat on the hard wooden bench, it became progressively more like torture to stifle the waves of laughter that followed as my face turned strawberry red, making my body feel as if it had hot coals inside it. This behavior created much embarrassment for each of us, but mostly for our mother, who was furious. Anxious for the funeral to be over, we left as quickly as we could in hopes that no one noticed us.

Unprocessed grief was released in laughter—another of life's lessons. Emotions have to flow.

Sewing was an art taught to me by my mom, which required much patience and time on her part. We designed all kinds of clothing together, such as; kilts, skirts, dresses, shirts and anything else imaginable made from a piece of fabric which gave us a special connection. Sewing empowered Thelma. Definitely very talented with her hands, she could easily sew a dress together or a kilt full of pleats in a day without giving it much thought. Decorating and planning parties also played a very important part in her life. The Sunday school church group came over once a year around Christmas time for a social. These ladies taught me how to really party.

The excitement was hard to contain as it got closer to the time to open the gift which was received during the gift exchange. I waited with such anticipation allowing my imagination to run rampant. Funny, a gift was always received that rocked my soul. I had no idea that secretly, Thelma took the time to buy a special gift just for us on this festive occasion! Afterward, the ladies shared stories while leisurely munching on all kinds of delicacies brought by each of them, which included Thelma's myriad of amazing entrees. Fun games, silly in nature, created much gaiety amongst these women and were always part of these festive parties, one including the white elephant gift exchange. I never quite understood why a "white elephant" gift exchange; there was never a white elephant or even a normal elephant at the party!

Watching her mother put on her makeup, she lies on her back on her mother's bed, stretching her thin body out. Patiently, she is waiting for their excursion to a country farm market called Roots, which displays all kinds of food items and goodies. It is a warm summer day and all the vendors will be there busily selling their fresh produce. After finishing her make-up,

Mother asks if she would be so kind as to give her a foot massage before they leave for their excursion and straightaway, she jumps up from the bed and sits on the footstool to massage her mother's aching feet. Although it sounds rather corny, she loves when her mother calls her Emby. This nickname gives her a sense of deep warmth and a feeling of being loved. Life is so peaceful and perfect with Love.

Rescue operations for baby birds that toppled from nests occupied much of our time during the spring and the summer months. These little creatures were nurtured until old enough to spread their wings to fly. During this season of transformation and birth, we questioned exactly how much we were really helping these baby robins, who had the horrible plight of falling out of their nest before they were old enough to fly. Sometimes we even knew exactly which nest the little creature fell from. The bird was placed in a homemade nest using twigs and leaves and fed worms and water from a dropper. Pondering if the robin should have been put in its nest, we were advised that after we touched it, the mom would ignore it, picking up our scent. The nestling would be shunned. So we took it under our wings, taking care of the youngster the best we knew how.

One afternoon, while my sister attended a youth meeting at the Shady Pine Church, I decided to look at her robin which was so carefully placed on the headrest of her bed. Without receiving permission from Mairzy, I fed it a piece of bread. Oh, how I wanted to take back my actions and turn back the clock of time. I agonized over my stupidity and hastiness. As much as I wanted to, I could not figure out how to save the robin's life. Hanging my head in shame, my conscience forced me to tell the truth to my sister. It took her a long time to forgive me for the demise of her robin, but it took me much longer to forgive myself for feeding it such a large piece of bread.

Huge billowing winds had the strength to upturn trees, ripping a nest from the sturdy oak tree. Even with its mother's meticulous work of making the nest as sturdy as possible, she could not keep the winds from plucking it from the crook of a tree where it was comfortably snuggled. A tiny baby robin from this nest is found in the tall grass next to the swing set. It never had the opportunity to learn to fly because its wings were underdeveloped and weak. She is well aware that if certain boys discover this young bird, it surely will come to harm. She has watched these boys throwing small birds with all their might, aiming them at a particular tree. It is a sport enjoyed tremendously by these boys. Sprinting to the tree to see if they succeeded, their screams of victory can be heard from afar. "Yes! Bull's-eye, we got it." They're delighted with their successful attempt in finding the crumpled fragile body in a lifeless heap after striking the old oak tree.

So carefully picking it up, not wanting to bring attention to herself, she quickly wraps it in her dress and waits for the school bell to ring. After the recess bell rings, without delay, she enters the now empty classroom and hastily goes to her desk. Lifting the top of her wooden desk open, she uses tissues to fashion a soft nest inside her desk. Gently she places this little creature in its new temporary home and as soon as she is satisfied, she quickly closes the top of her desk. She is very happy her desk is next to the open window which makes the task of keeping this bird's arrival a secret a bit easier because the sounds from the outside birds blend in with the chirps coming from her desk. Although she wants to quiet her prized possession so it is not discovered by the teacher, all day long happy chirping could be heard throughout the classroom. With a sigh of relief with the end of the school day, the bell rings and at last, she skips out of the classroom with her baby robin unnoticed in her hands.

Humans have the capability to be cruel and this kind of behavior prepared me for man's potentiality in harming others. Some feel a sick satisfaction in watching the pain, isolation and confusion which they create between loved ones, even sometimes fooling and deceiving the outside world. Someone who may appear harmless and loving is only a wolf in disguise, engulfed in a sinister dark energy ready to attack when everyone and everything are lined up to his liking. I see this more clearly much later in life. But in elementary school, one particular boy won many hearts with his charming character traits as well as leadership qualities, while many of his classmates were oblivious or they just decided to overlook his cruel ways.

Nature became my best friend and supported me in its beauty and warmth. The rays of the sun on my head and the coolness of the morning dew upon my lips made its presence known to me without a doubt. Something as simple as this truth gave me comfort which has been lost to some weary travelers. Just the same, this knowledge is there for all to receive and can be found if you take time to listen.

We played in the creek barefoot, sometimes finding a pocket of deeper water to use as a swimming pool, especially if there was a hard rainfall the night before. Mud oozed between our toes as we climbed out onto the muddy embankment to inspect our toes and see if any slimy grayish slugs landed in between them. Laughing, we counted these critters to see who had the most! All of us together made a rather large group of children and we were so happy being together, living in a world that was made just for children. The memory of the fun and how it was created with eyes which found the magic and beauty in being has been an anchor moving me forward out of the darkness. Our minds were filled with important things such as aiding animals in distress, nursing baby birds that fell from their nests, taking care of mice that lost their mother and keeping baby opossums alive. Granted, we made many mistakes, but grew in knowledge because of what these mistakes taught us. We played, and were good at it, which many children today have forgotten because of being caught up in technology. Climbing every tree that was worthy of the challenge, we created a world of magic and flourished on Love.

There were occasions when we scratched our heads and wondered exactly what we were thinking about or if we were thinking at all! This happened quite a bit. On one such occasion, Pinky accompanied us into the small bathroom along with one of our little robin friends. Pinky was a little dog, mixed breed of sorts, which my Dad picked up from a farmer friend. Pinky contentedly watched as we tested our little patient's flying skills. Mairzy and I gently pushed the robin's body up, encouraging her to spread her wings. This little bird, being very eager to learn, began spreading her wings and to our surprise, this fledgling took flight and flew into the bathtub. Pinky ran to the bird eagerly, thinking it was a game of catch. Ultimately, the little bird's life ended—that is, in its body. Feeling shame-faced, it took awhile for us to fully come to terms, allowing ourselves to forgive our stupid, ignorant actions which were responsible for ending this innocent bird's life. It was such a horrible feeling to live with until the sweet release of forgiveness opened up the doors, allowing grace into our lives.

Dressed very fashionably, Thelma always looked happy when she was going out for a shopping spree or a church event. Dad became the designated babysitter with one responsibility: making sure our afternoon naps happened. During our nap time, we waited for a while and quietly peeked around the hallway, usually finding our dad sound asleep with the newspaper on his lap.

Quietly, we returned to Kay's bedroom where we were supposed to be taking our nap. This suited us just fine because her room made it a lot easier to make our escape. The windows in Kay's bedroom were lower and a lot easier to open than in our bedroom.

Now is the time to open the window and invite the fresh air into the bedroom. The summer air permeates throughout the room which includes the fresh fragrances of flowers in bloom, soothing the senses. Next, the screen window is easily slid open, and the two little girls climb out, landing in freedom on top of the shrubs outside the window. Quickly scattering onto the soft grass, they run as if horses just set free from their stalls. Neighbors quietly smile as they watch these two little girls skip around the yard waving their thin lanky arms, laughing and giggling. They enjoy their secret escape from a very boring nap. Clueless, Lester is sound asleep with the newspaper in his hand.

Our picture window was enormous, located in the TV room where Lester was found sleeping. Once in awhile, we checked in on him and peeked into the picture window finding him sound asleep. Outsmarting him every time, he never did find out how much fun we had while he took his nap. We figured he needed it a lot more than we.

Kay was gifted in many ways. Her smile radiated from within her and exploded outward, carrying with it such a great sense of humor but also a special softness. Kay and Lester loved to laugh together, enjoying each other in a very special way. When sitting together at the many restaurants our family frequented, the two of them could be often found in an intimate conversation together, having their own unique connection and special sense of humor. Their eyes became alive like diamonds as they looked at each other with some kind of deep knowing, having a deeper connection than most people experience. They had a heart connection.

The times she had the opportunity to watch over my sister and me when our parents went out, were very special. These times gave us the opportunity to have Kay's total attention. Retrieving a large container of the old fashioned Steinman potato chips from the kitchen or preparing popcorn for us, Kay made sure we had an ample amount of snacks while watching television. She gave us her full attention. Remaining with us until the sun set and the moon and stars came out to play; she read books to us as we snuggled close to her. She stayed with us until our eyelids slowly closed and our minds drifted off, creating dreams of mystical worlds beyond.

When we became older, we began to watch Alfred Hitchcock and Twilight Zone, which created havoc in our fragile psyches. One of the shows was about a mirror and if you looked into the mirror long enough, a person wearing a flowing white gown would beckon you to come and join them in another dimension. It was really creepy! For years, I was frightened and very nervous about looking into mirrors, especially if alone. I avoided it at all cost. Constantly worried, I would come across a figure in a white flowing robe beckoning me to come join them, which I was not at all interested in doing! Later, Kay decided maybe it was not such a good idea to watch Alfred Hitchcock while in her care, not wanting to be responsible for our mental torture!

In high school, Kay received permission to take Mairzy and me on a road trip to the Hershey swimming pool, about an hour's drive away. Departing for our excursion, the windows were rolled down, and my hair blew freely as I gazed dreamily out at the landscape. As summer's warm air gently kissed my cheeks, contentment encompassed my being, and my eyes glowed with happy anticipation for our adventure. When we reached our destination, towels, books and best of all a picnic basket filled with all kind of goodies were placed under the shade of a tall tree. This was not an ordinary pool, but very unique in its design. It had many granite steps built into the sides around its large oval-shaped frame. In the center of the pool was a glorious waterfall, making it a pleasant escape for participants to get away from the busy mayhem of the day. During Kay's college years, we were invited to stay with her in her dorm in Kentucky. Eight years old at the time, I recalled the experience of sleeping in the dorm as being in a very cold structure. I don't mean the temperature of the room, as much as the barren and dismal environment. But Kay's presence offset this fact and the room became alive, making it easy to overlook the contents of the room. I was so grateful to have a sister who was ten years older than I. She showed me how to change the energy from cold to warm simply by one's heart connection.

Growing up with my twin sister was a wonderful experience and I would never trade anything for it. It is difficult to put into words, but I knew it was a very special relationship to be relished. Always having each other, we could count on each other to stand in our favor, and support each other through life's journey. Mairzy was right-handed, while my left hand was my most dominant hand and because of this fact, our mother said that we were identical, mirror image twins, which is impossible. You are either one or the other, not both. Our dialogue was definitely unique to us and eventually speech lessons became a part of our schedule in elementary school. Later, we were separated into different classrooms to encourage us to exert our own unique individuality.

The development of truly identical twins versus mirror image twins comes down to timing. A single sperm will fertilize a single egg and begins development by splitting into more cells. If this group of cells now called blastocyst splits into two separate parts in the first 9-12 days, identical twins will be born. But if the split occurs after that, they will be mirror-images of each other. The literature stated the impossibility of being both identical and mirror-image. I really do not think anyone knew back then what we were, and it does not matter one way or the other to me.

It was not unusual to hear Lester singing or whistling during the day; it is what he loved to do. He believed in the power of positive thought. One of his favorite authors is Dr. Norman Vincent Peale who wrote, *The Power of Positive Thinking* which is unparalleled in its extraordinary capacity for restoring the faltering faith of people. He constantly reminded me of how important your attitude is in life and he gave me the book to read. I used the principles in my life and took this practice further by using positive thoughts in manifesting dreams. Go back in time and remember something in your life that made you so happy and free, and then bring that feeling forward to the present and into the future to associate this feeling with what you are looking to manifest. This generates a portal of energy to bring it into existence. As it comes to be, it is just like Christmas: you are not sure exactly how it is all going to work out but it does. It is a miracle waiting to blossom which pleasantly surprises you.

On the piano, songs from the soundtrack of the movie, '*The Sound of Music*' were practiced religiously. Thirteen years old at the time, my twin sister and I were ushered by our parents to see the Sound of Music at the movie theater. I just loved going to the movies with my parents and relished every minute of the experience. The grand finale of our night out was spent at Grader's Dairy. Lester joked about us all screaming for ice cream in a funny accent, as he directed the car into the parking lot. Once in the ice cream parlor, there were no limits to what we were allowed to purchase and sometimes we were there for hours just eating ice cream and socializing with friends. The owners of this ice cream parlor were very good friends of Thelma and Lester. They were also members of the Shady Pine Church. Lester loved ice-cream and it definitely was one of his weaknesses. Thelma's favorite story was how he used to take her to Mount Gretna to get a banana split. Lester would get two banana splits, one for him and one for Thelma, finish his and consume whatever was left of Mom's and then order a second banana split for himself. Although ice cream was a passion of Lester, he was of medium build with a body that was very muscular and lean.

The Cottage

The proud owners of this lovely cottage were Lovely and Ray, fine folks who were very active in the Shady Pine Church and very good friends of Lester and

Thelma. Our family often visited the cottage of these very good friends during our pre-adolescent years and teenage years. Becoming involved in the sport of water skiing, Lester and Ray challenged themselves with different tricks. Taking off from land, one-leg skiing, and underwater take offs were only a few of the many stunts attempted. Some of these stunts were accomplished, while in others they fell short. But their failed attempts gave good reason for hearty laughter from them, as well as their onlookers. The water near the shoreline also had loads of seaweed which came to good use.

Rising from the water, Lester presents the funniest picture. His best friend, a big slender man, gawks back at him with the biggest grin ever. He is the captain of the boat and is pulling Lester out of the bay water with just a thin rope attached to the tow ring on the stern of his boat. Covered from head to toe in wet greenish-brown seaweed, Lester gracefully skims over the top of the bay water. His silly smile brings his onlookers to tears. It is amazing how Lester can keep his balance with seaweed covering his eyes and face. His white teeth glisten and sparkle through the muck, making him look so comical and the sound of Ray's laughter reverberating over the bay waters raises their vibration as bliss visits them on that day. A beautiful feeling of peace came, as if nothing mattered than what was happening at that exact moment, and time stood still in a beautiful dream.

At the front door of this cottage sat a pan of cool water for those little dirty feet to step into and clean off the sand before entering the house. Once in awhile, the pan of water contained a couple of crabs which were caught early that morning. But the water's main purpose was to rinse any dirt residue from our feet. You just had to carefully avoid the little critters in the pan. Once in awhile, a pitiful scream could be heard from someone who became careless and had to be rescued from a crab which was latched onto a toe like its life depended upon it. A variety of different kinds of foods were found at this cottage, one being sugar cookies which Lovely stored in a huge old fashioned tin can. These cookies were one of Lovely's specialties, made especially for her visitors, and to quench your thirst she made homemade sun tea with freshly squeezed lemon decorated with sprigs of mint. Thelma brought homemade potato salad, macaroni salad, corn on the cob, and barbecue for the homemade potato rolls, celery, carrots and all kinds of salad munchies for the picnic feast. An old fashioned damp changing room with cement floor and walls was located below the cottage. It contained booths for changing from your wet bathing suit after playing in the bay waters. After you changed and climbed a few steps, the pan of water was waiting for you at the front door to use before entering the cottage to rinse the sand off your feet—an expected tradition. I loved Lovely.

Children crowd into the small patches of sand, thin angular limbs jutting in all directions, like a brilliant island of colorful shorts and t-shirts in a sea of pebbles. Brave swimmers pick their way down to the small, lightly breaking waves on tiptoe. Dogs run in and out of the spray, chasing sticks. In the glaring horizon you can barely see; but if you really look and are lucky, you might be able to spot children swimming and laughing, carefree during the lazy summer days. These children play on a barnacle-and-seaweed-covered wooden raft *which entertains them for hours, far out in the bay waters. Now they are rocking the wooden raft back and forth to see who can stay on it without falling off into the warm late afternoon water. A seaweed fight is providing plenty of entertainment for these children today, and throughout the hot summer days this raft is found garnished and decorated with greenish-brown seaweed. These sports exhilarate their souls and spirits. When twilight falls, the beach is tinted sepia, the sand more orange, the water darker, their skin soft to the eye. They sit there on the wooden raft, just taking in the evening and chatting in their happy characteristic pattern.*

Afterward, Lester's best friend had a hoot of fun, attaching an inner tube to a rope which was tied to the boat. He encouraged us to go with a partner, so we climbed onto the tube and held to the sides as if our lives depended upon it, receiving the wildest ride of our lives. Unsure if it was for our enjoyment or for their entertainment, we peered at them watching us with the biggest grins, as we held on with all our might so as not to be thrown into the waters. Soon the feel of the water splashing along the sides of the inner tube, and the sensation of being propelled through the water replaced any fear with a feeling of ecstasy, releasing my spirit to let go and soar. Another life lesson: let go and trust because the world is waiting inside you! Ray boasted how fit he was and bragged that with little effort, he was able to swim across the bay waters straight to the other side of the embankment. He stressed the importance of waving your hand if you saw a boat so the captain of the boat did not mistakenly run over you. I thought, "You've got to be kidding!" The possibility of such a tragedy happening became too real for me and therefore too dangerous. The decision was made not to attempt this challenge but later in my twenties I did so at Lake Winona, where my parents purchased a plot of land.

Our plot of land located at Lake Winona was inspired by a dream of Lester and Thelma to build a home there someday. Mairzy and I were in our teenage years by now and our interests had changed somewhat, but a wooden raft with an anchor provided much entertainment, somewhat like the cottage we visited frequently. This particular raft was a lot closer to shore than the wooden raft at our friend's cottage and had not a trace of seaweed. This is the lake I decided to swim across and then back, overcoming any of my fears of being run over by a boat. Brandy, our English sheepdog, loved to jump off the raft, fetching a stick or twig that was thrown into the cool still waters and at times followed me as I swam across the lake. By now our older sister was exhibiting very strange behavior but we left her be, as she danced on that raft to an invisible partner with a smile on her face.

My parents did not drink alcohol but we were told confidentially by our neighbor friends, that my Dad covertly went over to their home and asked for a shot or two of whiskey from Bart, their father. Quietly knocking on their door, Bart would meet and invite him in for a few shots of whiskey and, after a few laughs with Bart, Lester returned home without notice. He had the nickname *turkey neck* because at times the skin around his neck became a crimson red, and we laughed together, making all kinds of stories up with our dad which revolved around the silly subject of the turkey neck. We still connect to this day on this subject sometimes with our whole conversation revolving around turkey necks!

Chapter Three

Darkness

The awareness of dark entities came naturally to me. At times my body froze in fear as if rigor mortis set in, and I was unable to budge until my parents came home from one of their many outings to save me. Waiting is all I can do while the blackness comes and I pray that the light is not far behind. So I became frozen, feeling the frigid fear seep into my being. My heart could beat all it wanted to, but my body refused to move until my parents came home. I remained, waiting, breathing quietly. On one such occasion, I physically held my bedroom door shut for hours even with the ranting of my twin sister: "No one is there, Ember." "But Mairzy, please help me keep the door shut; they are coming!" Holding our bedroom door for hours, I peed right there on the carpet with my sister rolling her eyes at me. Appalled and clueless as to why my sister did not help me, I felt so alone and abandoned. I didn't realize at the time that I appeared crazy to others, understandably so. Was I confused about reality?

Practical jokes were not included in my mom's repertoire, but when she laughed it made me happy to see her sparkle with such life. One afternoon, as usual, my mom decided she needed something fun to create and on this particular time of day, she became involved in creating wax candles. At the time, I was very preoccupied dancing in our basement, pretending to be a ballerina. The basement had mirrors along the wall and I twirled, jumped and made up all kinds of unusual exotic rhythmic steps and movement. The furniture was moved to the sides of the room and what could not be moved was used as part of the routine, giving me the opportunity to stretch my creativity and still give me plenty of room for my performance. My mom stood at the basement steps, yelling cheerfully, "Ember, I made some whipped cream. If you want some, please come up now!" Wow, music to my ears as I ran up the steps. Whipped cream, made fresh from the cream that is separated from the milk and, better yet, unpasteurized, which made it tastier, not tainted by processing, truly a very special gourmet treat. A generous portion was found on a spoon and, wanting to savor it, I took it to the basement. As the spoonful of whipped cream entered my mouth, I found to my dismay that it was not whipped cream but whipped candle wax. The joke was on me! At the time I did not find it funny but she did. Her laughter could be heard radiating out and beyond the kitchen as I washed out my mouth in the basement sink.

Writing on the Wall

Deep seated issues haunted Thelma. Mairzy found the writing on the basement wall expressing Thelma's deep-seated feelings of being neglected by Lester. Unable to receive the attention she craved from Lester, she expressed her sadness that their twin girls got all of Lester's attention. As one can only guess, twins can be a handful and at the time they did not have a lot of extra money for a babysitter to get away alone. Just maybe, our father did not understand the importance of making sure to spend intimate time alone with our mother, away from the home. This message confused me at such a young age and I thought she did not like us, feeling hurt by what I read on the basement wall. I had no depth of understanding in my young mind as to the real reason our mother had written what she did. This message was a cry for help and particularly written for Lester to see. It was adjacent to where he took his showers, and most likely was only for him to read, not us. Hormones can wreak havoc on women, especially the huge fluctuation of hormones which comes with pregnancy and birth. Thelma was suffering from depression that hits some young mothers after having a baby. This made it very difficult for her to cope, particularly with twins. Eventually, our Dad painted over her writing, but then it was way too late.

Thelma was declared queen of a very royal dynasty very early in my life, which made it a lot easier to be in the same room and listen to her demands with a good attitude. Therefore, she got to be treated like a queen, receiving head massages and reflexology whenever she asked me, usually as she sat and watched television. It was so much easier to live in my fantasy world of waiting on and being in the company of a queen. Life flowed a lot easier in a world of make-believe, not exactly sure what spurred me into this kind of pretend play.

My sister and I circled around a tree singing, Ding Dong! The Witch is Dead, as Mom screamed relentlessly inside our home. We were so unaware of the fact that she suffered emotionally. Children can be cruel and we were definitely not immune to it. But we had no concept of what was going on, feeling as if she did not like us.

Something horrible was amiss with Mother. Desiring to grow up was definitely not on my priority list because adults appeared sad and so serious. Even the church became scary, lulling me into a deep sleep as I sat on the hard bench. In the winter months, Mother made us don earmuffs which squeezed my ears and made them hurt, making church all the more miserable. She also thought tiny feet were very important and anatomically correct, and admired the Chinese's tiny feet. Therefore, my shoes were purchased a couple sizes too small, believing if she did so, my feet would stop growing. My feet ached and hurt so bad, and in no time I began to despise shoes. My toes grew to become crooked.

Later sitting at a picnic table with one of my good friends at the Shady Pine Pool, she began laughing and pointing at my feet. Suddenly putting her hand over her mouth, she says, "Oh Ember, I am so sorry! I did not mean to make fun of your crippled feet!" thinking I had a birth defect. I reassured her that my feelings were not hurt, and no, I did not have a birth defect, but my shoes were bought way too small when I was younger.

One sunny afternoon, a young girl skips out of her bedroom only to find her mother lying in the hallway. She kneels down beside her mother, hugging her, and cries, "Wake up? Please talk to me!" When her mother remains limp and her eyes just stare into empty space, she cries, holding tightly on to her, not wanting to ever let go. Hysterically, she gropes her way back to her bedroom, wanting to hide from such a painful world. She puts her face into her pillow, as swells of water pour down her cheeks, drenching it. Her fears have come true, which creates such torment. Now she is living her own personal nightmare, the fear of death. Death always has been a huge worriment for her. She constantly reminds herself that even though she does not always agree with her mother and it appears to her as if her mother is at times mean to her, she must always find a way to overlook those mean behaviors. She knew death is inevitable and where there is life there always will be death. She knew there would come a time her mother would be taken from her but did not think it would happen so soon. Later, her mother enters the room while she is making a call for help, and she realizes it was just a horrible practical joke. While her green eyes turn the color of gray her emotional body remains in total shock.

I kept on asking, "Please God, show me where one goes when you die." Death scared me; even the thought of it terrified me. I never ever wanted to lose anyone to its grip, especially my mother. Again, my answer comes, but much later.

Chapter Four
Memories

I caught myself going back to childhood pictures that brought a smile to my face as I remembered what it meant to be free and to know that truly all was well.

Brandy was a surprise, a Christmas gift purchased just for Mairzy during her last year of high school while still living on Donegal Springs Road. Thelma smiled as she secretly hid Brandy, who was just a tiny puppy, in the big drawers in the laundry room at our ranch home. Pulling me aside, she asked me if I could be trusted with a secret. After going to great lengths in explaining why being trustworthy was an ingrained part of my character as a human being, she invited me to join her in the laundry room, and when opening one of the newly made bins for laundry out popped a puppy. Not like any usual puppy, she sported patches of black and white with long soft hair, an absolutely adorable female English sheepdog. So excited for my sister, I reassured my mom not to worry because it was our secret. So Christmas day, Brandy was placed in a big box wrapped in Christmas paper with a big red bow on top which I got to help wrap. Mairzy was so excited when she found such a cute little thing looking at her as she opened the package, and immediately she took out that puffball of a puppy and gave it a big hug. Eventually Brandy was secretly adopted by me and paved a very special place in my heart. Unfortunately, in her latter years she was one of the animals tortured and maimed by the shadow of lingering dark, evil energy and left unable to walk.

As my graduation from high school neared, Lester expressed a grave concern about Thelma. He informed me my mom was very sick and he did not see her getting better, but only worse. I didn't understand what he meant. She didn't look sick to me. Later, I had a greater understanding because her sickness could not be hidden anymore and slowly encompassed her whole being, devouring her.

A particular boy frightened me in elementary school, chasing me into the lavatory on more than one occasion. He successfully shoved me up against the wall a few times, but I always managed to wriggle out of his arms. With a sigh of relief, I sprinted to the entrance and removed myself as far as possible from him. He was very odd with a spooky soul and a quiet eerie darkness about him. He gave me a preview of what would come my way, which would change my life forever.

Later, following me into the girl's locker room in junior high, his taunts and teasing haunted me as he ranted about my horrible body. Mocking me, he pronounced my body as being horrendous, resembling a monkey with long limbs. I kept on imagining how that must appear and looked at my arms thinking they must be unusually long. At least they were not hairy! This teasing was not unusual because I experienced a lot of cruel criticism about my body in junior high school and throughout my young adulthood. Taunts about how my body did not develop like other girls made me sensitive about my body image and uncomfortable with my appearance. Children and young adults can be so cruel to their peers, oblivious to the suffering and pain they cause others with their words.

School was a very memorable experience and it is where many extracurricular activities captivated my interest and therefore the opportunity to expand as a young person. The upperclassmen sometimes intimidated me and at times made fun of my speech. This ranting brought back those uncomfortable familiar feelings, but engulfing my being in many school activities and sports, there was not much of an opportunity for me to think about my feelings. Therefore I hid and pushed my emotions into my body subconsciously, not knowing what else to do. Despite the mentioned challenges, I enjoyed school, had many friends and appeared rather well adjusted, excelling at many different sports. Taking much pride in my independence, there was a deep knowledge that each individual soul has something unique to offer to the world and I honored each person's individuality, popular or not. Sports and extracurricular school activities played a big part in my life, but academics were equally as important to me. My focus and hard work showed. My name appeared on the list acknowledging the students who acquired As and Bs for their grades that semester.

During my high school days, Lester had a balance beam made for me. He knew gymnastics was my passion and encouraged my goal to compete for my high school. I was constantly found on the balance beam at school trying to figure out how to stay on that narrow piece of wood without falling, which I found absolutely challenging. The coaches did not have much training as to how to help someone like me, so I taught myself by experimentation on my wooden beam. During this time I practiced the various stunts for competition. Lester's purchase was well worth the money he put into it because later my children used the same balance beam to practice.

Next, my dad decided to purchase a spotting belt for doing back flips. Before the belt was purchased, many afternoons were spent outside spotting me for back flips. Sprinting as fast as possible to gain momentum from a round-off, I flew through the air and brought my knees up to my chest which rotated me. I was so incredibly lucky that a bone was never broken. Sure, my Dad was somewhat apprehensive about my endeavors because he did not have a clue as to how to spot me, and he decided on his own to go out and look for a spotting belt. The mechanics of how to complete a back flip was never taught to me because there was never any kind of formal training at our school. Later, Lester came home grinning as he proudly held a spotting belt, giving him confidence that there would not be a catastrophe, at least when he was with me.

In time, I did go on to compete for my high school with my specialties being the balance beam and floor exercise. My parents attended my meets and were very proud of me. At one such meet, I decided two back walkovers were going to be part of my balance beam routine, and I performed this particular skill at whim because not much practice time was allotted to it. In fact, I do not recall being successful in the skill. The first back walkover was perfect and so in confidence, I decided to go right for a second back walkover but it was never totally completed. Plummeting to the floor, darkness encompassed me. The crowd sighed and while I lay in a heap on the floor my boyfriend's father hurried down from the crowd, being the school doctor. The gym became so still and quiet as everyone held their breath, at least that was what I was told. It seemed like an eternity, but finally my eyes opened and a long gasp of air entered willingly into my lungs. Later, a conscious decision was made to wipe my slate clean from any fear associated with that fall. Never looking back at that incident, I finished competing for balance beam and floor exercise up to and including my senior year in high school. During this time Mairzy also enjoyed gymnastics and focused on the uneven parallel bars but decided not to compete.

Deep green eyes shine in the night with anticipation and excitement for the challenge of what lies before her. This nightly adventure has been in the planning stages for quite some time and is now ready to be implemented.

The clock has struck twelve, timing it perfectly with the hope that everyone is sound asleep. In the afternoon, she shares her secret with her sister, inviting her to accompany her on this excursion. Mairzy looks at her, thinking her sister is a bit odd because she is not at all interested, having better things to do with her night—that being sleep. Finally, as she glanced over at her twin sister who is breathing softly, she arises from her bed and begins to creep slowly from her hot sticky bedroom, holding her cut-offs and t-shirt to don later. Just as her escape begins, the floorboards begin to creak. Stopping immediately, she carefully rearranges her feet to continue her journey. Practicing the night before to walk on the floor boards without a noise, she knew it was imperative to be as quiet as possible and it seems to take forever as she slowly moves along, very conscious of where to place her feet. Now it dawns on her that she is holding her breath, and she lets out a deep sigh, allowing another deep breath to follow, which creates more ease in her body as she approaches one step closer to freedom. Upon leaving her bedroom and entering the short hallway, she passes the piano on her left and next passes the TV; she enters the dining room and proceeds to tiptoe into the kitchen. Stealthily at a snail's pace, the kitchen door is opened, leading her outside. Quickly donning her cutoffs and t-shirt, her pajamas are left crumpled in front of the garage door to wait for her to hop into when arriving back home.

Taking a deep breath of the night air, she begins her stroll down the country road barefooted and directs her gaze up at the moon and winks at the twinkling stars. Dancing, jumping and kicking her legs together she laughs merrily, and begins the journey on Donegal Springs Road into Shady Pine, making frequent stops to visit friends on the way. Reaching her last stop, there is plenty of time to share secrets, talk and giggle way into the wee hours of the morning. Throughout the blackness of the nighttime sky, her green eyes sparkle like diamonds with fun and fervor of life but later she realizes her stay was far too long. Saying her goodbyes, she runs barefooted the whole way home from Shady Pine as the sky slowly turns into a beautiful kaleidoscope of purples, pinks and reds, painting the horizon into a glorious masterpiece. Concerned, because her dad will soon awaken, she hurries. Lester arises very early every morning to brew hot coffee and prepare a bowl of oatmeal before commencing his day of work. Knowing this, she has to be swift and not delay a moment. Finally, she reaches home with clothing totally drenched from sweat and her heart pounding as if it is ready to burst out of her chest. She changes hastily out of her cutoffs and tee shirt into her pajamas. The muggy heat presses in on her. Sweat trickles down her neck and back like warm soup. Her hair clings to her head like a thermal blanket, locking in the heat, frying her brain. Quickly she creeps into the kitchen, and gracefully glides through the living room, tiptoeing very quietly. As she approaches the short hallway she stops to get a breath, and listens for any sign of life in her parent's bedroom. Proceeding to her bedroom, she quickly slides under her cool sheets and consciously works on slowing her heavy breathing down.

Her mom comes in very soon after, looking rather concerned—unusual for her Mom to visit her bedroom. Hoping her secret will not be discovered, she gropes for a tall tale to keep her mother from her own investigation and detective work. Groaning and weeping, she cries that her body aches and feels as if it is on fire. Leaning down, her mother feels her hot sweaty forehead and believes her.

Sweaty street clothing is discovered in front of the garage door crumpled in a ball and her secret is out. Not a whole lot is said to her, but next time she would have to be a lot slicker if her nightly adventure would be successful and that she was!

Our sleepovers were very seldom just a sleepover; in fact, sleeping was rare at these parties. Many times during these escapades we explored the town of Shady Pine, laughing and spooking ourselves with all its shadows, giving the police something to do at night. They searched for us as we hid behind bushes. We never did anything really that bad, but the moon and stars fueled us and were our accomplices, filling us with so much mischievous fun and the excitement of being alive. The sleepovers gave us the opportunity to run free all night, climb water towers, tell stories and relax in the comradeship of friends. These gatherings became an extension of our younger napping days. Being energetic young teenagers, we quietly sneaked out of the small rectangular basement window and walked the country roads by the light of the moon. Such a feeling of freedom and excitement came over us as the ground under our feet brought life and energy to our bodies. Fresh milk was delivered by the milkman to the neighborhood homes' milk boxes in the wee hours of the morning. This made a great breakfast, along with the freshly baked bread. Being outside under the stars created many wholesome challenges for us. One of them was climbing the water tower. This created the space to discover that special connection of how amazing our world really was to us. We climbed the water tower numerous times to the top and each time, after finally crawling to the top, our bright curious eyes gazed down upon the landscape. Then we gazed up at the moon and stars and awareness crept into our souls as to the reality of how small our Earth really was in relationship to the huge galaxy in which it existed. The vastness of the universe with its endless galaxies compared to our Earth home boggled our minds. These thoughts made us stand to gaze in awe, giving Earth the reverence it so deserved.

Harmless pranks and mischievous fun were designed to help fill a void in my life, keeping me satisfied at least for a while. The Loop was a route in the small town of Columbia which fueled a big part of our mischief. We all piled into one of our cars and drove around the loop which seemed like it should have been boring and senseless, because of driving the same pattern in the streets of Columbia, but to a bunch of young teenage girls, it was splendid. On occasion boys drove the loop which later developed into flirting, a pastime which sometimes grew into infatuation and if we built up our nerve, maybe a sensible conversation resulted, which made our hearts flutter. These boys had beautiful dark skin, making them all the more alluring. They played basketball for Columbia High School. They were basketball stars! The loop inspired other teenagers, especially the girls that lived in Columbia. Pies, whipping cream and anything that was gooey became part of this fun, becoming a trademark of ours. When we got to a red light and a car of girls from Columbia pulled beside us, one of our specialties was secretly brought out; down came the window and like magic their car was decorated. Like a science, we timed it perfectly just before the light turned green. Delighted with the loop, we opened our windows and shouted for joy.

During these breathtaking days, chores were expected to be done. Scrubbing bathrooms, basements, cupboards, pulling weeds and sweeping were just a few of the chores which I was responsible for completing. Many were expected to be done without pay, but my favorite job was mowing the grass because this job gave me some money. After completing the mowing, my dad handed me a few dollars, which I tucked away to be used for the evening dance parties. Summer romance was always in the air and dance gave the opportunity to fantasize about love. Love was magical. The sparkling stars and the golden light of the moon coaxed it from hiding on those warm lazy summer days. Dance allowed expression of a whole new dimension to life, freeing the soul to experience the magic of love, embracing my power to rise. Summer was for romance or dreaming of romance and usually every summer, a new flame of love blossomed into a friendship.

Later, after graduating from college, I took the course at the YWCA to be a lifeguard; and, passing easily, different lifeguard positions were acquired without difficulty. Over the years, I obtained the position as a lifeguard for different apartment complexes, which gave me the opportunity to watch many pool parties. Realizing how much more fun it was to be a participant of these parties which had grown very rare and unusual, a longing in my soul developed for these magical times together.

My friends loved any opportunity that arose for an occasional practical joke. It was on this particular occasion that a door was opened and I became the unexpected recipient of their silly folly.

One sunny afternoon in the month of August which was in full blossom by now with only a few billowy clouds drifting up in the crisp bright blue sky, a group of teenagers is hanging out together on the road leading to Shady Pine. It is a motley crew of boys and girls from high school, some of whom are very popular. As the afternoon starts to peak, she leisurely gets into her dad's car and happily waves goodbye to her friends. It is unusual for her to spend so much time with these boys who somewhat intimidate her because of their popularity. But content in the day's events, she places her hands on the steering wheel to make a turn down the now warm country road toward home. Turning the radio on, she detects a hissing sound and her first inclination is that the sound is coming from the radio, and she doesn't give it much thought. But later, her eyes dart over to the passenger seat and to her dismay she discovers an unwanted companion, a rather large snake. She's thinking, "You've got to be kidding me?!" This creature displays its tongue proudly and gracefully moves toward her. Just the thought of it makes her become very hot and uneasy. An anxious feeling encompasses her whole being as it slowly begins to wrap its huge scaly body around the steering wheel, staring at her with its piercing beady black eyes. Coming even closer, it begins to acknowledge her with its slithering tongue. She stares at it in horror, not at all interested in befriending a snake, and panics at her predicament. She leaps swiftly out of her moving car. Holding her limbs close to her tucked body, she tumbles onto the road as her car keeps going on down the road. Eventually, the Dodge Challenger rolls to a stop but is absent a driver. Disheveled, she walks home with a few minor scrapes and bruises.

The prankster of this joke never did reveal himself, knowing the boundary had been crossed. Later, before dusk settles in, the car is retrieved with her father accompanying her and with a sigh of relief when no signs of a snake are evident. Her green eyes begin to relax and glow softly, and she smiles. What a practical joke.

The presence of a long, two-pointed, forked tongue helps you identify snakes. Snakes depend on their tongue for a great deal of information. They do not smell through their nostrils like mammals, rather they smell using their tongue to collect scents and then insert them into the roof of their mouth, where lies the Jacobson's organ. This organ helps interpret the different scents and guides snakes to potential food or mates, as well as away from potential danger. The tongue of a snake is not harmful. Snakes kill their prey in several different ways. Some species use venom, which they inject through their fangs. Other snakes use constriction, and squeeze their prey until it stops breathing. Also, many snakes simply grab their prey, overpower it and start swallowing. Snakes have jaws that are hinged and can expand in several places, allowing them to swallow prey bigger than their own head.

We had so much fun just hanging out and entertaining ourselves with the simplest things in life. Much of our time was spent at the parks talking, laughing and feeding the ducks with bread crumbs brought from home. Sharing stories about life in general, we relaxed in each other's company, sometimes gathering together at each other's homes. One particular friend, Bella Hunter, had a swimming pool where we skinny dipped quite often; swimming late into the evening, our laughter reverberating throughout the night. Also, the Shady Pine Pool gave us the opportunity to swim, opening the doors for countless summer activities. Volleyball, swimming and sunbathing occupied much of our time during the hot sweltering days. As the sun began to set, pool dances were held weekly, which offered the opportunity to dance and sway late into the evening. We enjoyed the enchantment of the summer breeze and the freedom it brought to our bodies and souls.

One summer evening, when the sun had set and the sky was lit by only the stars and the slit of the moon, a very good friend of mine unexpectedly entered my driveway in her red convertible. This was the most pleasant surprise to me but the most unusual visit. I was very happy to see her because we had grown to be very close. We spent endless hours in close comradeship and shared many laughs, living life as if every moment was precious. If the mood was just right, we were enticed to slip out of our clothing and run to her pool. Laughing and yelling we ran and jumped into the fresh cool water, and were able to experience freedom in our beings, as if children again. Skinny dipping became a rage, eventually extending out to all our friends who came to join us in the fun. Many days were spent together at the Shady Pine Pool. However, this particular evening was different; her look was very somber, which was opposite to what it was just a few weeks earlier.

It is such a wonderful surprise wedding shower. Food and drink are abundant at this festive event for Bella, with many beautifully wrapped gifts, with frills, pompoms, and ribbons, just waiting to be opened. What a gathering of people for such a wonderful occasion. Gaiety is in the air.

Bella had just come to a revelation. Absolutely unable to go through with this particular wedding, she already had made her mind up she would be absent. She just could not go against what every nerve in her body was telling her. Becoming conscious of her real feelings, she had to honor them. This particular night was the night before Bella's wedding and she was feeling pushed into making a commitment she was not ready to make, at least not yet. Will was her high school sweetheart. Therefore, never having the opportunity to date anyone else, Bella wanted to be able to open up the possibility of doing so. She wanted to spread her wings a bit and enjoy her independence. Her plans were shared with me, which involved driving to a remote town until the embarrassment wore off which she did. But she never did come back as she said she would. I praised her inwardly for standing up for herself, but missed her so. She spoke from her heart the truth, even if it meant hurting someone else. Love does not control others.

Having only seen her once since that time so long ago, we talked into the wee hours of the morning, so happy to see each other again, sharing our most intimate thoughts about life. Love shone through to connect once again. These years helped me tremendously to be able to find my way back home out of a terror that I thought could never exist in my wildest imagination.

I also loved my sister and never thought we would by any means ever part, supporting each other in every way possible. It became an unspoken truth that we were there for each other. She was gifted in art and made colors come alive on canvas as well as in my life. Later, when we went to college we shared a room. Though we shared each other's friends, we knew that we could depend on each other if all else failed.

Becoming more independent and rebellious, I began to become increasingly more confused and questioning "Why were my actions at times cruel and cold-hearted?" Why was I so spiteful, pushing my parents away?" I longed to be loved but pushed harder, which increased my isolation and depression. Many times, I just wanted to hug my parents, put my head on their shoulders and cry to release my burden. Darkness did not allow me to let go. There was one particular situation that made me vow to never let anyone hurt me again. At the age of fourteen, the feeling of betrayal and deep-seated hurt entered my being. It occurred during an absolutely typical afternoon. An enormous unbreakable hedge was consciously chosen to surround me for protection from any harm incurred upon me from the insensitivities of others. My parents were in the TV room at the time, and I was combing my hair in my bedroom. My mom yelled from the TV room, "Ember, please come and pick up your sweatshirt you laid on the floor." I boldly yelled from my room, "No, I will absolutely not pick it up!" I refused to do so, acting exceptionally defiant.

My parents were watching TV at that particular time of the evening, which was not unusual because during the evening that is what they often did, and that is when I heard my mom say, "Lester, settle her down!" I knew that did not sound very promising but oh well, what could he really do to me? My dad came into my bedroom and proceeded to beat me on my twin sister's bed, wrestling and pinning me down in a very aggressive manner. After he left my room, it took me some time to gather my wits but eventually I did and with my face flushed from the wrestling match began to leave my bedroom. I had to pass my mother who now stood at the other end of the small hallway which led to our bedrooms. She leered at me, saying, "Look what you made your dad do!"

Being so violated confused me. This particular act marked the turning point in my life and the feeling of betrayal became very familiar to me. I never in my wildest dreams thought my dad was capable of being so violent against me. This act created a deep hurt in my soul which later, unconsciously festered quietly. Ultimately, I was responsible for allowing it to do so, not understanding how it would affect my direction in life. After that particular horrible incident, I did not want to be left alone with him and if Thelma so happened to leave for an extravaganza or one of her meetings, I asked her to please tell Lester to stay downstairs in the basement, which was where his office was located. This suited her just fine because this attitude caused even a deeper rift between Dad and me which she sort of liked, since it fed a small cracked part of her psyche of not being enough. Therefore, she did not have to feel threatened that I was taking any of Lester's attention from her, at least for a while.

A Father shouts from the top of the basement steps, scolding his twin teenage daughters. Unleashing his temper, he tells them if they do not stop arguing he is coming down personally to take care of matters. Not giving them any time to resolve their argument, he proceeds out to the shed to get the whip used on their horse, King. Storming back in, he marches angrily down the basement steps.

The twin girls are so very frightened and, respecting their father's temper, have hidden. As he snaps the whip, loud whirring sounds can be heard throughout the basement, as he expresses the power of it. It is a very scary message, confusing them about how to use their voices in conflicts. Are we not humans that have a wide band of emotions and why do we not have the right to express these emotions, especially if this expression is done without hurting each other or losing the respect of ourselves? The wedge is being driven deeper.

After graduating from college, Kay moved straightway to Kentucky with Lerner, her college sweetheart. A teaching position had opened up to her in Kentucky and she willingly accepted the position and made Kentucky her home for awhile. Eventually, relocating back to Pennsylvania, she took advantage of a teaching opportunity in the Hempfield school district. It was during this time Kay and Lerner found a quaint farm home with a garden in the small town of Landisville. This home is where they entertained us with countless sleepovers, games and special dinners. The garden behind their home was rather large and in it grew many different vegetables which were used for their meals. My room was located in the back of the house with big windows which opened wide, making it quite cozy, and inviting me to a peaceful night's sleep. My bed was always adorned with fresh new sheets and pillowcases, which made me feel special. Looking forward to spending time with my sister, it felt as if Christmas arrived early when she decided to reside in Pennsylvania.

Mairzy was discovered in such a horrible state. It was late into the evening and I went into the bathroom to brush my teeth and perform my nightly ritual. I came across a sink full of long beautiful hair and immediately went looking for Mairzy. Finding her sitting on my bed with tears streaming down her bloody swollen face, I inquired what happened. Explaining between sobs, she was punished for staying out too late with her boyfriend. Whatever the reason for this punishment, it did not justify the force of such violence. Anger lodged deeper within me as I proceeded to help her clean up. This action reinforced my determination to build a wall around me, which ultimately sealed my fate of isolation. It was a deep-seated revolt that grew stronger throughout my being.

A bad temper was one of Lester's traits but as he got older he mellowed. Just maybe that temper would have helped him later, granting him the energy to change the outcome of what was to come later in his life. Is a temper good or bad or is it how and when you use it?

It is Sunday, the day after discovering Mairzy in our bedroom sobbing, and as usual everyone is sitting at the dining room table, which has been meticulously laid out with fine utensils and perfect place settings. We sit around the long rectangular table garnished with a bouquet of spring flowers which displayed a large variety of scrumptious edibles. Lerner inquires, "What happened to your face?" Bruised and swollen from the scuffle last night, Mairzy glared at him, not answering, and immediately excused herself from the table. Nothing was ever discussed, no apologies made, but one more thing was swept under the rug.

My dad had many fears after I started dating. At the time when it was happening it was horrifying but now looking back on it, I only find compassion and love for an overly anxious father. This particular date was very special, because I had been waiting for months for Lindy to notice me, and finally he did. He called and invited me to go to the movies.

That particular night we had our date, the time did get away from us and we became oblivious to the clock. However, my parents did not forget about the time and thought that I should have been home a lot sooner on this particular warm summer evening. Hence, my dad waited for us, hiding in the bushes located to the right of our property.

Timing it just as Lindy had begun to open up my car door; Lester sprang out like a cat after its prey and began to swing a baseball bat appearing as if he was extremely unhinged. When Lindy noticed him, he looked as if he had seen a ghost, and immediately jumped into his car and sped off. The sounds of the car tires squealing could be heard as he drove speedily down Donegal Springs Road. It was as if Lindy thought it was possible for Lester to run and catch up to him and jump on his car.

He never did call me again. Disappointment and frustration set in regarding my dad's impulsiveness. His total lack of respect for me as a person was embarrassing. Later as the years progressed, once in awhile Lindy and I ran into each other because of our professions. As a school counselor, he observed a few of the classes that I taught, but nothing more was said of that night.

Twitterpated

1942, apparently first attested in the Walt Disney movie "Bambi":

Thumper: Why are they acting that way?

Friend Owl: Why, don't you know? They're twitterpated.

Flower, Bambi, Thumper: Twitterpated?

Friend Owl: Yes. Nearly everybody gets twitterpated in the springtime.

For example: You're walking along, minding your own business. You're looking neither to the left, nor to the right, when all of a sudden you run smack into a pretty face. Woo-woo! You begin to get weak in the knees. Your head's in a whirl. And then you feel light as a feather, and before you know it, you're walking on air. And then you know what? You're knocked for a loop, and you completely lose your head!

Thumper: Gosh, that's awful.

My Dad did not know how to show his authority but deep down loved me very much. He was frustrated as to how to be a father and to be a good communicator, but many people in the world deal with this challenge. Communication is important, especially when it comes from the heart. This was only understood as I became much older.

Blind dates were not something that interested either my sister or me, and it is still a huge mystery exactly how we got ourselves in such a horrible predicament, because, this particular fine summer evening we were going on a double blind date. We were feeling rather distressed. When our dates finally pulled into the driveway, I went to get Mairzy who conveniently did a disappearing act. Not informing me that she had such a plan in the making, there was no way I was going to have this happen without her. As I looked everywhere in the home, it appeared as if she vanished into thin air. Wow, Mairzy created magic and willed herself to disappear, but eventually we decided to look one more time, and Thelma found her hiding under my bed. It took a long time to coax her out from underneath the bed on that particular hot summer evening, and it was also one of the worst dates we ever experienced. Very excited for it to be finished, we made a pact: no more blind dates!

In junior high school, switching classrooms became a fun pastime and the sheer act of confusing our teachers, or better yet getting away with our trick was definitely our reward. Only a few of the students knew about the switch but kept quiet in order not to blow our cover. A lot of amusement was created from these mischievous escapades, and a special bond was strengthened between us. We knew without a doubt that if life became too crazy we always had each other to depend upon. Separating ourselves from the world, we made our own world.

Later, in college we decided to switch dates. The young boys came to pick us up in the lobby of our dorm and since we lived together in the same dorm, it made the switch all the simpler. When hearing the name over the intercom, all we had to do was go down the steps and pretend we were the person with the name. They never noticed a thing out of sorts but thought they were with the twin they asked out and never were told differently! It was our secret!

Thelma had a part of her that was so much grounded in common sense but as time marched on, it became covered with darkness.

These memories and the feelings they brought, gave me something to grope onto as I brought them to my awareness again, assisting me In finding my way back home. In my mind's eye, I practiced reliving the positive feelings associated with the many pleasant pictures of growing up, which encouraged me to uncover that happy feeling again. Just the fact of how proud my parents were with their commitment to each other and the love they had for their children, as well as grandchildren, helped sustain me.

Maturing into young adults, we enjoyed long walks, jogging, swimming in the ocean waves. We truly laughed together, finding the secret of life. We discovered the nests of baby animals in the forest and explored the ocean waters for its many creatures. We enjoyed the art nature displayed on its sands with beautiful shells and marine life. Memories just as simple as these helped me to remember how life can be. Rehoboth created magic in our lives, allowing us to get to know each other and the opportunity to enjoy each other's company. It enabled our children to play and learn together.

Thelma loved to prepare meals for the family, and we stayed by her side helping her during this precious time together. Our children assisted in cleaning up after dinner by bringing the dirty dishes to the sink, stacking the dishwasher, then later shaking out the tablecloth, and eventually putting leftovers in their special containers to be placed into the refrigerator. Afterwards, they went upstairs to the attic to play games and later, growing in stature, they excitedly ventured out to have some fun on the boardwalk.

Alfrenzo was the tiniest little toy poodle. He would always come to visit me unexpectedly in my bedroom. He hurriedly turned around to leave after lifting his mighty leg and urinating on the post of our bed, smiling smugly as he left. Of course, it got cleaned up and he was disciplined. Later, making sure our bedroom door was shut, Marten and I laughed together at his boldness. It was paradise and I found my heart in these memories.

FIRE of LOVE by Aadil Palkhivala

Feeling is the essence of life. How can "twisting to the left" in yoga class help us make things right in the world? How can pressing your right shoulder blade down into your mat lift up this troubled world? In other words, is there a way that our yoga practice can reach beyond our mat, out into the world? It all begins with feeling.

Feeling is the essence of life. Without feeling, we are not quite human. The real value of our asana practice is that, as we do pose after pose with awareness, we are inviting more sensitivity into our bodies and our lives. We are learning to tune in and feel. So we not only feel better, but we are better.

When we are intensely sensitive, we taste the unique flavor of each moment. This makes our lives so much richer and more enjoyable. The more sensitive and aware we are, the more we instinctively know what to do, and make correct decisions that avert future pain and regret. We clearly feel what moves us toward our dharma, and what takes us away from it. Sensitivity simultaneously makes us more intensely focused and more expansively peaceful, and we are able to elegantly handle life's endless dilemmas without feeling overwhelmed or fearful. Yoga compels us always to become more conscious, more aware of ourselves—our bodies, minds, feelings, and our very nature. When we are feeling fully, we are finally living in the now.

Growing up was not on my priority list when I was little and the thought of being grown-up did not look like so much fun. Adults seemed so serious and unhappy, becoming confused as to how to have fun, losing their zest for life. Where did the magic of life go in adult life? It appeared as if it became covered up or just disappeared into a great abyss. But, of course, having no choice, I did grow up and graduated from college; but, instead of feeling empowered, I felt very confused. It was as if my life force was being snuffed out little by little. Where did I go? Is this what happens to adults?

Rebel

Just turning eighteen years old, to me the World seemed as one big playground and sparked my enthusiasm for adventure. Hitchhiking to a Grateful Dead event held at Kent State University with a few good friends from college was just one of these many adventures. This escapade began late in the evening with the full moon illuminating the night sky, fueling our excitement. Being that the universe had a great sense of humor, our first ride to the concert was in a hearse used for dead people. The last part of the trip to the concert was a wagon filled with hay, which was itchy but a welcome rest. The thrill of going to the concert was just as meaningful as being at the concert. Life was to be explored with movement.

Having developed our own distinct language and accent, Mairzy and I received speech lessons in elementary school. Nonetheless these lessons did not correct or change our accent, at least not mine. Opening my mouth to speak in a setting of a group of boys and girls in college was not a good thing because the boys made fun of my outrageous accent. Laughing, they inquired as to how it was acquired. I felt hurt, because I not only heard this one time but over and over again from my classmates, so receiving a phone call about my older sister's mental illness from Thelma just fed more fuel to my feeling of depression. Relaxing and stretching my lanky body on the dorm floor--contemplating what the news meant to me and how our family dynamics might be changed, I prayed.

Just as my college career began, our dad was in a really awful car accident. Deep in thought, with great sorrow in his heart, he was not focusing on the road; he took a turn too fast and rammed his car head first into a tree. The car was beyond repair and smoldered, threatening to catch fire as he sat wedged in between the steering wheel and seat, unconscious and unable to move. By divine appointment, a chiropractor drove by and stopped. Promptly, he called 911. Incapable of removing him, he stayed with Lester and within minutes an ambulance and help arrived on that remote country road. As spring was just peeking around the corner, Lester remained oblivious to it all as his car eventually became engulfed in flames.

Confined to bed in the hospital for a few months, he became very lethargic and bitter at God, entertaining thoughts of self destruction. But slowly, he was able to let go and the sweet release of sadness encompassed his whole being as tears flowed freely. Kay, the sparkle of laughter in his life, had disappeared.

Lester's favorite song was by the Beatles, *Let It Be* which he shared with me after I arrived home from college for my Christmas vacation at that simple beautiful ranch home on Donegal Springs Road.

Let It Be
Lyrics
When I find myself in times of trouble, Mother Mary comes to me
Speaking words of wisdom let it be
And in my hour of darkness she is standing right in front of me
Speaking words of wisdom let it be
Let it be, let it be, let it be, let it be
Whisper words of wisdom, let it be

And when the broken hearted people living in the world agree
There will be an answer, let it be
For though they may be parted, there is still a chance that they will see
There will be an answer, let it be
Let it be, let it be, let it be, let it be
There will be an answer, let it be
Let it be, let it be, let it be, let it be
Whisper words of wisdom, let it be
Let it be, let it be, let it be, let it be
Whisper words of wisdom, let it be
And when the night is cloudy there is still a light that shines on me
Shine until tomorrow, let it be
I wake up to the sound of music, Mother Mary comes to me
Speaking words of wisdom let it be
Let it be, let it be, let it be, yeah, let it be
There will be an answer, let it be
Let it be, let it be, let it be, yeah, let it be
Whisper words of wisdom, let it be

A young woman is excited about coming home from college to spend time with her parents and friends for Christmas. Finally arriving home, the next evening her dad invites her to go along on an errand into town. It is a very cold winter evening but she is happy to be able to spend time with her father, and quickly dons her heavy winter-hooded coat, scarf, gloves and boots.

As he begins to back his new Challenger onto the icy driveway, leaving the comfort of their warm garage, the car radio begins playing softly the song by The Beatles, 'Let it Be.' He sits quietly and pauses, staring out at the snow-laden dark skies of night. Tears glisten down his cheeks as he yearns for his older daughter, missing the special bond they had together which was taken from him forever.

My parents felt so guilty about my sister. They felt as if they were to blame and therefore responsible for her disease because of their lack of parenting skills. Reading too many articles that blamed the parents for this illness was way too much for them to bear. They were unable to understand that these were mere educated guesses. She was the apple of their eye, the shining daughter that made them so proud. Not that long ago she had graduated with a teaching degree, and immediately had landed a teaching position in Kentucky. Now she was gone. Just married, her husband was a bright young man who had the potential for a very successful career in psychiatry. She had everything she ever wanted and, with all of that, was also blessed with a beautiful voice. This voice bestowed joy and healing to those who listened to her sing. Involved in a Christian band, she had just cut her first record. Her album had a lovely cover, showing the pictures of the people in her group and on the back a list of their different songs. Thelma and Lester were so proud of her accomplishments as well as was my sister. She fostered a feeling of satisfaction and fulfillment, knowing she was heading toward her life goals, making her dreams manifest into reality.

Brandy had the honor of staying for a short span of time in our apartment while we lived in East Stroudsburg. This did not go over very well with our roommates, especially when Brandy went into heat.

Amidst a full blown ice and snow storm in the Poconos, one car can be seen traveling through the icy snow-drifted highway with two passengers aboard. At whim a decision is made to hop into their yellow bug to drive home. This is a very important mission because Brandy misses them, and plans have been made to rescue her and bring her back with them to their apartment at college, at least for awhile. This blizzard is not just an ordinary snowstorm in the Poconos, but is so icy it becomes extremely hazardous. Most people had enough common sense to stay home, not foolish enough to make a two and one half hour trip. Cautiously travelling through the snowstorm, they inch over many icy sections of the highway, singing loudly as the radio plays their favorite songs. Approaching closer to home, they notice that the storm lessens and the temperature rises above freezing and not a bit of snow or ice is found on the ground. Frustrated, they find the front door locked. It is a rare occurrence for their parents to lock the doors when leaving the home. So knocking again, but harder this time, the only response is the excited barking of Brandy, who by now is happily looking out the picture window fiercely wagging her tail. Realizing the home to be void of any human being, they proceed to the basement window. This window was used for many escapes during their teenage sleepovers and they are hoping that just maybe their parents forgot to lock it, but to their disgruntlement, they find it does not budge. Very soon a discussion is taking place as to which window might be the least expensive and easiest to break, and unanimously they decide to break the basement window. After much persistence this window eventually gives in to the force of the rock and cracks. They do not realize that this was the most expensive window to replace, just purchased for its shatter resistant properties.

Later that evening, their parents arrive home but by now they are on the road. Finding the window shattered and no Brandy, they promptly call the police. But a little later, with a few phone calls made, they realize their twin daughters are the culprits. Lester's face lightens up and he chuckles to himself, "By darn it, those girls have lots of spunk." He begins reminiscing about his younger days.

Tapping into the ocean's energy, we ran free as the soft caresses of nature released all our worries. Our senses became alive with our movement and we sang. Many magical memories were created by sleeping under the stars' gaze, each star having a unique vibration. Music choreographed by the ocean spirits lulled me into a deep sleep.

Allowing a feeling of freedom to envelop my body at whim, one late afternoon I hitched a ride with a young man and had the satisfaction of riding through Wildwood, a small beach town. My long hair blew way past my waist as a glorious feeling of exhilaration surged through my veins. It was a sublime feeling to be on such a huge machine which propelled me forward through the winding streets still lit with slits of the sun rays. The sparkle of the sun rays formed shadows from the tall buildings and in the horizon, soft splashes of pink, fuchsia and lavender could be seen dancing throughout the sky.

During college spring break in Florida, we slept outside under the stars on lounge chairs and peacefulness dribbled in, floating over our bodies as we remembered. But gradually the feeling of being connected to people seemed to slip away and loneliness and disconnection became my friends. By my third year of college, all sense of connection even to nature was gone. Therefore the divine spark of life within me became hidden, and there appeared only darkness and despair. The start of a new adventure had begun, but I did not realize it at the time. It was a battle which I had to fight alone.

My rebellious personality was just a way of coping and became my defense mechanism. But as I grew into maturity and wisdom, the ramifications and seriousness of my mom's issues were made known to me. Compassion developed within me for the human part of her that could no longer experience life and all its magic. Slowly, a conscious choice was made to relinquish the huge hedge around me, and this enabled me to find a greater love for my mom, seeing her spirit and not focusing on all the attachments that clung to her like lichens. Unfortunately, this happened much later in life. We are not here on Earth to find judgment unless we want others to judge us for our wrongdoing. We are not on this Earth because we are perfect but there is a bigger war that we need to focus on: a spiritual war. We are here to love. "If my people who are called by my name will humble themselves, and pray and seek my face, and turn from their wicked ways, then I will hear from heaven, and will forgive their sin and heal their land" (2 Chronicles 7:14, KJV).

A vision which definitely got my attention occurred in my early twenties at a hotel located in Wildwood, a quaint seaside town. A great weariness overcame me and I fell into a deep sleep. As I slept......

The door of the hotel room slowly opens, letting in the cool late-autumn breeze. The wind spirals into the room bringing with it a path of deep yellow leaves, circling and swirling throughout the room. An elderly woman dressed all in black, wearing a black cape stands just outside of the open door, letting in the cold air of late autumn. The night is dark with stormy clouds covering the stars and the New Moon. Grieving, the elderly woman slowly enters, as large brown leaves blow in through the doorway to lay a carpet for her entrance. The leaves stay suspended as if waiting for her to complete each step, showing that autumn is soon at its very end. Extremely hunched over, she hobbles toward the young woman who by now is sitting up on her bed waiting. Her laments can be heard piercing the night air as she slowly approaches the bed. Sitting down on its edge, she leans forward and her shoulders heave with grief.

A flood of such deep compassion flows into the young girl's heart and her soft green eyes look on consolingly. Reaching out to comfort her—

Startled, she awakes.

At the time of this particular vision, I was in my early twenties and thought maybe the lady in the vision was my mom. Later, told by a friend that maybe the woman represented me later in life. This was way too eerie for me to comprehend and I sure hoped not. Thelma was not hunched over and we lived in our ranch home at the time. Also, Lucas was not born as yet and life appeared grand. Thelma wrestled her own demons. But she kept very active, busy with friends, clubs and a strong connection with the church. It appeared as if she had won the fight with darkness. Having financial freedom, money was not even a concern for them by now. They both purchased a new car every year, and Thelma was lavished with jewelry, trips and nice things. Life was truly good to them and Lester's masonry business began to flourish. Quiet about their prosperity, still the signs were there, and it now had become a reality. Lester and Thelma were donating large amounts of money toward the expansion of the Church, extending the size and capacity of the church. Also, funds were created for a few of the children that were members of the church, so that they could obtain a college education. They were good people.

Loving my parents, I realized that they were doing the best that they knew how with all their filters developed to cope with the world. I had come to an awareness that we all have our filters and personalities, but love is what is needed and grace for all, including ourselves. Later, I protected both of them with the ferocity of a mother tiger protecting her cubs. They were my parents.

Receiving guidance from the counselor in high school, I was advised to become a physical education teacher. I did not seek out any other guidance or counsel, nor did I give my future much thought as to a career, or what really excited me. I felt lost. But I did not know any differently. It was as if my eyes had blinders on each of them, unconscious of my real desires in life. After graduating from high school a wall seemed to form over my psyche, blocking any vision for my life. At the time, I had only one great desire and that was to play girls' field hockey at East Stroudsburg University.

I became extremely involved with the varsity hockey team and excelled, but unfortunately a really bad case of mononucleosis forced me to pull out of sports and athletics. My face swelled up like a melon, my neck enlarged like the trunk of an elephant, and my sight became blurry, making my zest or any vision for life hide away. Therefore, forced to put aside my college education because there was no other option, I rested. Much later, after returning to school, my body was still chronically tired making it impossible to keep up with my full load, let alone walk the campus. My body was letting me down and I did not have a solution as to how to change its downward spiral. Eventually, admitting my body could not handle the rigorous physical education program, a change was made in majors, switching to elementary education.

Mairzy also attended East Stroudsburg University and became involved with classes for teacher education. Roommates, our desks were located opposite each other. Sometimes we studied together, enjoying each other's company. We were comforted in the fact that we knew each other in such a new and strange environment. There was a particular health class that we spent some time together studying for the class's final. After taking the test and receiving our papers back from the professor,

DAWN SINGLETON, PhD, DNM

both tests received failing grades. Baffled because we really knew our material, we thought why such a low grade? I talked to the professor and she said, of course, it was obvious that we copied off each other's paper. We had the same question wrong and she proceeded to give me a lecture about the value of honesty. She said she simply had no tolerance for dishonesty; so the decision was made to fail both of us. As I patiently listened to her accusations, my face became a beet red, I was defiant and hurt. "Absolutely not, we did not cheat, but studied together, which had to be the reason why we got the same question wrong!" I retorted. Reluctantly, she changed our grades but was not totally convinced of our innocence. She scowled at us the last few days of class.

Also, Mairzy played field hockey for the varsity team, but eventually she dropped out of East Stroudsburg University because she made the decision to marry her high school sweetheart. Therefore, she transferred to Elizabethtown University, a lot closer to our home, completing her education there. Her absence helped ignite the beginning of a dark depression which crept into my being. During this transition, it took root, growing strong and bold, impossible to shake. The following year any excitement or desire to go back to the university vanished. After being home for summer break that year, my parents stubbornly held to the idea of me finishing my education at East Stroudsburg University, making it my only option. Feeling coerced and as if the rug was swept from beneath me, I did not have the stamina, will or vision to confront my parents' decision. Therefore, I subjected myself to go without a struggle, even when my body and emotions said no. Now, it is important to listen to yourself because you are your best friend and if you do not listen, who really will?

My body literally fell apart the first day they dropped me off at the apartment. Grief and sadness overcame my body and shook me up in rebellion. My brain felt as if it exploded into tiny pieces and that evening my hair fell out in clumps. Nothing seemed to make sense to me anymore and I lost my way, spiraling downward into a bunny hole—a one-way road to hell. All sense of connection to my life and even to nature was lost. The divine spark of life within me, hid away and there was only darkness. Despair and pain forced me to let go; eventually, I could only look within for answers.

I am still unsure how my school was completed because my comprehension skills were obliterated. Making any kind of sense out of reading was literally impossible. Nothing around me was discernible. People were only globs of energy passing by. When I finally finished student

76

teaching with the teacher at the elementary school, she was pulling out her hair because of my lack of awareness. I graduated with a bachelor's degree, but before graduation, a psychiatrist was called in to see what was going on with me. Being aware enough to know they were observing me, I elaborated on a few reasons which were causing my disorientation, hoping it would be enough to get me off the hook. This person gave me the benefit of the doubt and allowed me to graduate, hoping that as time went on I would become a better teacher. They definitely gambled on me because my teaching abilities were nil. It took me many years until my brain and body recovered from what I believed was a stroke. The elementary students could have done a better job than I! I knew that I was a mess, but lacked awareness as to how to heal myself. I became embarrassed because of my lack of autonomy and independence.

I eventually asked for help, but realized very quickly that my searching was in the wrong direction. Ashamed, thinking that something was horribly wrong with me, I thought of myself as being defective and therefore unfixable. I hid, hoping no one, especially my friends, would discover my brokenness and judge me as crazy, I felt so alone, confused and in pain. It was years later that I was shown through my daughter, Roslyn, how to find my own unique connection.

In college, I had ultimately chosen a life path which took a huge toll on my body and brain. Slowly sports, church and wholesome activities fell from my life. Ultimately, I became involved with the wrong gang, which did not contribute to the growth of a healthy well-rounded person.

Shoplifting became a sport of my friends and I allowed myself to get caught up with their endeavors. Ellen, one very good friend of mine, became so involved with the sport and the challenge of shoplifting that all common sense left her. One afternoon while I spent time with Ellen, we decided to make the long hike into town to go shopping. On a whim, in one of the department stores, she decided to fill her bags with merchandise. It was almost comical to the point of being ridiculous because a feeling had come over her that she was invisible. Refusing to heed my warnings, she kept on plowing ahead in her endeavors and ultimately encountered two policemen with handcuffs, was put in the police cruiser and hauled off to jail. News got out of Ellen's capture and horrible plight, and enough money was gathered together from her friends attending East Stroudsburg University for her bail and she was allowed out of jail the next day.

When graduating from the university, a second-grade teaching position was waiting for Ellen at the school where her father was head principal. Ellen did a wonderful job motivating the children in her classroom and received high recognition for her teaching abilities, which tells you something about human nature. Some young adults do very foolish things in life before they become part of society, but that does not mean that they are rotten to the core—maybe just a bit mischievous. Talent is waiting to spring out of them when they mature, and after a few life lessons of sowing their wild oats, they blossom.

Many of the items stolen found their way to people's homes as Christmas gifts. Homeless people grinned as we handed them food on the streets. A turkey was carried proudly out of one of the grocery stores—one of the main items for our big Thanksgiving feast as well as some other food items to complement it. Our Thanksgiving party was definitely successful. It included many of the people who lived on the streets as well as students at the university that did not go home for Thanksgiving. Shoplifting got out of hand, especially the day a plan was set in motion regarding the robbery of a sports store in East Stroudsburg. We planned and mapped out how we would accomplish taking boxes of flannel shirts. Our friend from Long Island held a conversation with the clerk, getting her attention by asking questions, while boxes of flannel shirts were being taken from the store. This really seemed stupid because we did not have any need for all the flannel shirts. They found their way as gifts to the homeless people and were given to some of the students at the school who were not so well off.

Later, Mairzy and I had the opportunity and privilege to take a ride in a police cruiser. He lectured to us the many reasons why shoplifting was not cool, going on to say that if for some reason we were hungry we were to come to him, and he would provide the food. A kind and thoughtful young man, I surely appreciated his lesson of love and actually listened to him. His thoughtfulness was one of the deferring factors that changed my course in life.

One of the funniest pictures was not funny at all for my extremely nervous mom who just happened to pop in for a surprise visit to my apartment which I shared with five other girls in college. Arriving at 6:30 in the morning, Thelma rampaged into the kitchen and began her frenzied search for me, opening the doors of various bedrooms and finding a boy in a couple of my roommates' rooms. Finally arriving at my room, she yanked open the door and yelled, "What a rat house!" I think she meant Cat House! My friends found it humorous and lucky for me, I was alone.

My dad grinned about the weirdest happenings in my life—like for instance the evening I took my neighbor, Rex to go to a spaghetti dinner at the home of a friend, Janice. The dinner was held during mid-evening so the sky had seen its last rays of the sun and twilight had fallen. The sky turned to a light dusky purple littered with tiny silver stars. On our way to Janice's home, I succumbed to my craving for a soda at the old fashioned Tropical Treat. The Tropical Treat was not just some ordinary restaurant, but it was a place where you could park your car and order outside. Friends mingled at this location, a big meeting ground for school age and college teens. Proudly driving my dad's Challenger, just ready to make a left hand turn into the Tropical Treat, suddenly all the people in the cars outside started to honk their horns and yell. Thinking that they were excited to see me home from college, I started waving. But little did I know at the time, that the turn being attempted was not a road but the embankment. Not having any idea what exactly was going on, Lester's new Challenger bumped and bounced down the embankment, gathering lots of dirt under the front fender as it took on the challenge of a very steep hill. At the bottom, I glanced over at Rex to see how she fared in the whole ordeal, but not a word was said. She kept looking straight ahead without expression. So, very humiliated by my lack of awareness, I never did get my Coke but left immediately and kept on driving to Janice's spaghetti party as if nothing happened. My dad found out about the whole embarrassing mess from a few people at the Tropical Treat, and he chuckled as he asked me about it. I hoped my dad did not ever discuss this odd occurrence with my mom because I wanted to delete it out of my life as quickly as possible.

Later, Mairzy found herself back at East Stroudsburg to join me for my last years of college and to take a few courses to finish her degree in teaching. The marriage to a boyfriend in high school was short lived. Drugs and abusive behavior played an unbeatable part together, running wild. The tandem dissolved and cracked apart the marriage in a very short time. It was as if the marriage never happened. She became frightened of the abuser who happened to have too many toxins pass the blood brain barrier, upsetting his whole hormonal system.

After finishing at East Stroudsburg University, Mairzy married her best friend in college, residing in an apartment complex about fifteen minutes away from our parents' new home. Her wedding was held at the Roslyn Estate, which was perfect because it was her desire to have a very small intimate wedding with family and close friends. Not the usual home, it was a mansion which onlookers marveled at as they passed by in their cars. Joggers stopped to peer into the grounds, enjoying the beautiful shrubbery that was kept trimmed by hired landscapers. This home was on the outskirts of Lancaster, and within walking distance from President Buchanan's home. It is a historical site which pulls people from afar to see how President Buchanan lived.

Helen Keller said that it would be so much worse to be born with sight but no vision. When graduation came and went, there was no more spark left to my soul. The part of my skull that was removed is where many of the acupuncture meridians meet. This may well have had something to do with my compromised immune system. During this time of my life, any intelligent decisions were impossible to make and quick-witted conversation had escaped me.

A young girl is having problems getting a vision for her next step in life, masked by the muck of toxins in her lanky body and brain. So, searching through the ads in the newspaper for employment, she comes across a dishwasher position and immediately applies. Every day she drives to the Turkey Hill and loads and empties the dishwasher, clearing and cleaning tables all day long.

She has long brown hair to her hips with the darkest green eyes, but she is clueless to her beauty. She feels very uncomfortable with herself and is in pain, making it very difficult to relate to others which only increases her anxiety. At a very wearisome point in her life, she is well aware of her predicament but has not a clue how to make her body and brain work in sync again. The situation appears very grim.

I was confused regarding why I felt so horribly trapped in my body, but I hoped in time my brain would turn on again. My head ached constantly, which made my life miserable and my body was constantly wracked with pain. After coming home from school for summer break, I informed my mom of my dilemma. My parents thought a psychiatrist might be the answer. So, Lester supported me and transported me every week to the outpatient mental ward. They could very easily have said, "Ember, here is the car and the keys; you know how to get there," but they were very concerned, supporting me the best way possible. To them, it meant driving me there. This facility was a very sunny cheerful place but was not where I belonged.

My psychiatrist showed me different meditations, which he patiently guided me through, and I methodically agreed to the drugs which were prescribed, hoping to get some relief. But the medication made me feel very tired. It was adjusted accordingly but with no detectable difference in how I felt. Nothing seemed to work and in order to terminate my visits, and make everyone else feel better, including my parents, I feigned recovery. This trip was a complete waste of my dad's valuable time as well as mine. We were looking totally in the wrong direction, but I had no idea where to look or if there were any answers for my condition. My embarrassment increased because it was very difficult to have any kind of intelligent conversation with my old friends, let alone a casual conversation with anyone. It was impossible to hide from them, even though I tried.

Lester always prided himself in being a family man but his actions did not match his statement. As Kay's son grew into adulthood, Lester contradicted himself in his devotion to his family's welfare. He became unaware that his actions denied his statement, as his eyes were slowly deprived of sight. Their guilt about their beautiful daughter created a hole for this dark evil energy to seep into our family, which worked furtively and steadily, separating all that they loved. Slowly, my parents became ungrounded in the reality of the family dynamics, which led to their unrealistic obsession surrounding all and everything involving Lucas. Their eyes became blinded and warped, especially my mom's eyes. She could not see what was happening to her and where this darkness was taking her. It was a road of no return. Lester, in his own special way, loved and honored my mother, and toiled hard to keep her happy. Even if he did not always agree with her, he tolerated her obsession with this boy who eventually also became his warped, compulsive preoccupation. They were left unaware of the total disruption of a family that had once been full of fun, love and magic. Lucas was allowed to have the key to the lockbox of all their valuables, gold, jewelry and their precious will which had been changed numerous times. When death came to visit us, the sheet of paper was void of any value for Mairzy or me.

The Mansion

When first acquiring the property, Thelma was so excited to show me the house. Having just gotten home for spring break from college, it seemed odd not to go back to the home on Donegal Springs Road but Thelma's enthusiasm for this house carried me through the transition. She took my hand, discussing with me a vision of constructing a pool and a tennis court right in the front yard. This dream eventually became forgotten, smothered in other unworkable ideas.

Later, Lester showed me how to use the riding mower, which seemed massive compared to the push mower used at our ranch home. I'm sure I was comical to watch as I tried to befriend this massive piece of equipment. Dad looked on from a distance with a grin on his face. After graduating from East Stroudsburg University, my responsibility was to take care of this property: pulling weeds, collecting leaves in the autumn, using the sit down mower for the grounds in the warmer months, as well as keeping the grass outside the gated yard trimmed by our hand mower. I also manicured outside the gated area, pulling unwanted growth by hand along the sidewalk. This undertaking was a lot different from mowing the property of the home in which I grew up.

Other responsibilities that came with the bigger home included cleaning and painting the basement. This chore was not looked forward to because the basement was huge, gloomy and damp. Therefore, penetrating the murky place with paint brush and ladder really did not appeal to my senses.

Now, mind you, this home is not just an ordinary home, but a mansion and has a very special name. The woodwork of the home is exquisite, embedded with intricate carvings. Also, a huge stained glass window ascending the whole way up to the second floor invites light from the outside, and emits a prism of sparkling rainbow colors to caress the staircase leading to the second floor. Massive walk-in closets are big enough to be a bedroom, and there's an elevator in case you're not in the mood to climb steps. These are only a few of the items included in this home which make it very unique. The ceilings are very high, each having its own elegant artistic designs where the walls meet the ceiling. This added touch brings each room its own warmth and unique vibrancy. Hidden balconies for peace and solitude from the mayhem of the day are tucked conveniently out of sight. The outdoor landscaping is gorgeous, with a much smaller home called the carriage house setting in the distance. Attached under the carriage house is a quaint garage that has stalls used long ago for keeping the horses of visiting friends and, located to the side, hidden from the common observer, is a small pond with a vast array of flowers. In the middle of this small pond, a fountain of water explodes from a figurine of two young children blowing bubbles. This is where Mairzy worked diligently, pulling out the poison ivy and weeds from the pachysandra, which started to grow wildly out of control.

Another water feature, a beautiful intricately shaped koi pond is found in the front of the main home—a pond designed and constructed by a contractor hired by Lester. Drawing up a blueprint required much patience and time, a crucial part of the planning stages. Finally, coming to a consensus, they built this amazing water feature and transformed it into a work of art. Water lilies, turtles, fish, swans and koi were added to the pond, while many exotic flowers were planted meticulously around it, each having its own special place. Often found holding hands, Lester and Thelma gazed at the wonderful sight and soaked in the energy this feature generated, as the summer sun streamed through the trees and danced upon the pond's water. The dragonflies flitted to and fro, displaying iridescent wings and bodies, reflecting rainbow colors depending on the angle and polarization of light. This was a very old home which my parents bought when I was in my early twenties. Unlike the ranch home where blissful childhood memories were created, this was fit for a queen. At dawn, Lester looked forward to feeding the fish in the pond and observing all the wildlife it drew. Ducks and different wildlife traveled through, finding transient rest at this water feature, frolicking in the soft green grass.

This former P.T. Watt Home is named Roslyn. 1896—Historic Preservation Trust. It is a very well maintained carriage house with 2,000 SF apartments. Home offers beautiful woodwork (one of a kind), multiple fireplaces, and stained glass windows. "Roslyn" was built in 1896 by celebrated Lancaster architect, C. Emlen Urban. Mr. Urban who was also the designer of many city properties including, but not limited to, Central Market, the Griest Building, Watt & Shand (the soon-to-be convention center) and the theological seminary. This beautiful home is listed on the Lancaster County Historical Sites Register as a "Significant Level I" site, meaning the property is "exceptional" or of top importance. It was commissioned by Peter T. Watt, co-founder of Watt & Shand. Mr. Watt presented the property to his wife, Laura, on her birthday. The property remained owned by members of the Watt family for over 70 years. Lester and Thelma purchased the home in 1974.

There was definitely plenty of room for all the antiques my parents brought to this home and the landscaping of this property was just gorgeous with huge displays of flowers and shrubs which were elegantly and carefully taken care of by Lester and his groundskeeper. Lucas arrived in the picture later, and so we had the opportunity to enjoy our new home for a while, which did slowly change as Lucas grew into young adulthood. This is where our lives took a twisted turn down a bunny hole of dark smoky energy filled with phantoms, and places we had no idea existed. We were innocent bystanders that got caught in a web of lies, manipulation, and deceit with no knowledge of how to get out of its grip.

A huge hawk sets its talons into a little duck and flies off with its helpless victim. The duck quacks hopelessly as the hawk carries it off into the sky; its cry fades into the deep blue yonder, as if the little duck was saying, "Help me! Help me!" but it was way too late and the little duck's weeping goes on unheeded. Lester watches helplessly at the sad plight of this duck that had come to rest in the warmth of the sunshine of the pond.

Later

An old friend found me working at an apartment complex and invited me to go along with a bunch of his friends to Florida for Christmas. Eager for a change, I agreed. While they drove throughout the night, sleep came quickly to my tired body and when the sun was just peeking over the horizon, my friend woke me up gently, saying, "Look Ember! Arise, it is morning, we are soon to arrive at our destination."

What was really odd and downright unusual to an outsider, was the male female ratio. Only one female accompanied the five young men. One of the main reasons to drive to Florida was because Joe wanted to see his brother. Treated like a princess, I became a member of this happy family, and they made sure my needs were met.

Later, a very beautiful love letter from the brother that we visited landed in my mailbox. Extremely intelligent, and having an excellent position as a captain pilot for one of the major airlines, in his letter he expressed his deepest feelings for me and his willingness to commit to a relationship with the goal of marriage. Deeply flattered, not having any idea of his feelings for me at the time of the visit, regrettably I was not able to return the sincerity of his love. Searching for the person inside me, I had to learn to love me before love could radiate out to someone else in such a commitment. It would not have been fair to him. It was one of my most ethically correct decisions in life, because later, very hasty decisions were made out of sheer ignorance, pain, fear and unawareness.

While in Florida with my friends, monkeys came to visit me at night. As I slept on a lounge chair these little critters startled me awake. Many mornings they came and played with my hair and nose, waking me from a deep relaxed sleep. These sensations startled me and caught me by surprise as the creatures entertained themselves with my hair. Regaining my senses, I chuckled and thought what a peculiar opportunity it was to have monkeys with you at the crack of dawn. I found out later that their habitat was just next door. The thought of these cute monkeys sparked my sense of humor, guiding me on my journey to let go. Monkeys in some peculiar way seemed to be drawn to me, raising my energy and therefore my capacity to heal.

Scanning the beach, she checks to see if anyone is out for an evening walk. The beautiful sunsets often draw people down, but there is no one in sight. Skinny dipping is one of her favorite things to do, so quickly slipping out of her clothes; she makes a dash into the water. The feel of the water on her body is exhilarating and she swims out to where it's deep. Doing a few laps up and down the shoreline, she stops and lies back in the water, stretching her arms and legs and opens her palms and releases all bodily tension. Someone yells on the beach and quickly she drops her body below the surface. The young woman scans the shoreline and sees Little Joe's dog bounding into the water after an orange ball bobbing on the surface not far from her. "Wonderful! This is just what I need—to be naked in the water with a dog who wants to play." rolling her eyes, she tells him to turn around and she immediately swims to shallower water. Her feet touch bottom, and she quickly runs and fetchs her towel.

President Buchanan

Nearby my parents' home, located just a block away, was the Buchanan home. The Buchanan home was constructed in 1828 by William Jenkins, a local lawyer. It was sold to William M. Meredith in 1841. Wheatland changed hands again in 1848 when it was purchased by Buchanan. Buchanan occupied the house for the next two decades, except for several years during his ambassadorship in Great Britain and during his presidency. After his death in 1868, Wheatland was inherited by Buchanan's niece, Harriet Lane, who sold it in 1881 to George Willson. It was inherited by a relative of Wilson's in 1929. Wheatland was put up for sale again after the relative died in 1934 and was acquired by a group of people who set up a foundation for the purpose of preserving the house. Wheatland was designated a National Historic Landmark in 1961 and was added to the National Register of Historic Places in 1966. It was designated a contributing property in the Northeast Lancaster Township Historic District in 1980. The foundation and the adjacent historical society merged in 2009. So as you see, the Roslyn Home was in a nice section of town, with sidewalks that were great for jogging, bicycling and walking the dog.

The grounds were scrupulously kept just as meticulously as the inside of the home, which took days to clean. Choosing the housekeeper for this home took much time. Thelma scrutinized the applicants by having personal interviews with each of them, and then gave them the opportunity to show off their cleaning skills. Possible employees were given a few weeks to show how they worked. It was a big undertaking to find someone who measured up to her expectations. When one potential house cleaner was amidst her trial period, Thelma came home at an unforeseen time and found the woman on top of Thelma's step ladder, peering into the windows of one of the locked rooms with binoculars. Promptly, she was escorted out the front door, taking a hike, never to return. Another house cleaner on her trial period was discovered watching television happily with her feet propped up on one of their very expensive antiques, munching on popcorn. She was instantly fired. Thelma had countless candidates and many stories as to why they were not hired. Eventually, the perfect person for the job was found and became a very trusted member of the family. She incurred the responsibility of the laundry as well as keeping the home clean. Spending a lot of time in the home, she and her family were invited to use the bay house and were given permission to go swimming at Lake Winona.

The Stress of Mental Illness

My older sister was diagnosed with extreme paranoid schizophrenia. When I was a freshman living in the dorm at college, I received the most dreadful phone call from my mother informing me about Kay's condition. It rattled my whole being. At the time, being eighteen years old, I pondered, "Why Kay?" Thelma told me Kay was acting crazy and doing weird things. I had no idea what it meant to have a mental illness but did know it was a horrible mark of disgrace; a curse looked down upon by society.

Thelma and Lester had a huge problem in dealing with Kay's sickness. Because of the stigma, there was a lot of grief, anger and loss that was left unexpressed because they were too embarrassed to talk about it to any of their friends. Just maybe they did share their angst and heartache about their daughter to a few, but their friends did not know how to respond to their suffering. Therefore, not grieving the loss of Kay but squelching the heartache down deep within, ultimately was what created the poison in their lives.

Kay did many strange and desperate actions because of her pain, trying to kill herself on a multitude of occasions. Thelma and Lester felt helpless and were unable to search for help because of their severe confusion as to what was causing Kay to act out this bizarre behavior. Their embarrassment and guilt overrode all common sense. Unfortunately, people's lives can be ruined, stigmatized by this prognosis. What Lerner could not tolerate with the onset of her condition was when Kay accompanied a Mexican immigrant to live in New York City. He did not understand that most likely she did not have any recollection of her bizarre behavior.

It was very sad to watch. Furthermore, not given any help to develop tools in dealing with mental illness, they had not a clue how to cope with this heartbreaking situation. Lester went into a huge depression, trying to hide from the world, and Thelma felt condemned, a horrible mother, because of the various theories making the parents responsible for bringing this illness upon their children. Some claimed a contributing factor was a lack of parental skills, which drove her plain crazy. There was no question in their minds; they had failed as parents. Eventually, information came out that this illness was genetic or possibly caused by a chemistry imbalance, making them feel just as bad. In due course, Kay was seen as a misfit, judged for her actions, and a dishonor to her parents. This fact created a huge rift of pain and confusion between Thelma and Kay which progressively became worse, developing into a hedge. Their relationship became stormy, twisted and warped. Later, living upstairs before getting her own home from the State, Kay started to socialize with the wrong characters—individuals with evil intentions. Their intentions were to take advantage of her state and find information about her parents' home with the goal of entering the home and robbing them.

Nobody really knew for sure what caused this disease, not even the medical field. There were only educated guesses which the public took as the truth. Some new research which is on the frontier of science is helping people like Kay but very few are really receiving the help needed that can bring them back to a normal life. Please read *Brain on Fire* by Susannah Cahalan for a better understanding. There is a lot of misdiagnosis of mental illnesses, which most likely are related to autoimmune issues. Her book will help open your eyes to unlimited possibilities. She tells a simply amazing true story and she was fortunate to have the resources to find the right doctor who could help her, instead of accepting the diagnosis of schizophrenia.

Grace

Lester went through a deep depression as well as Thelma. They tried to hide her condition, because in their minds, mental illness was looked down on and frowned upon. They felt a horrible angst at the thought that they were to blame for their daughter's terrible plight in life. Confused as to how to help their daughter, they held on to the hope of a better life for Kay with the use of pharmaceuticals and the new drugs that were coming out constantly. These medications, she absolutely hated to take because they made her feel drugged. Kay lost her life as it crumpled before her. Her recording of albums was halted as well as her teaching career. Within no time, her husband left her. Kay's husband was a psychiatrist by profession. Confused and hurt by her odd behavior, ultimately he could not handle it. Separating from her, he began divorce proceedings immediately, which finally broke Kay's heart. When she became aware of what was occurring in her life, it was difficult for Kay to deal with the unprocessed emotions. The disease spirals down into your core, making it very difficult to come back, because not only do you have to deal with the disease itself but have to cope with what you created in your life by mental illness. Ultimately, it is hard not to feel accountable for the bizarre behavior and actions that occur partly because of the way they've affected your loved ones. Losing the love of her life to the disease, and also her bright future, Kay needed grace but, instead, was forgotten.

Some of her time she was committed to the Wernersville State Hospital, it appeared that most of the people in her section were dulled into a semi-stupor by the pharmaceuticals. Every day they lined up for their drugs which masked the pain. Something had to be changed in their lives. Therefore the messenger was stifled and unheeded. Later, becoming well enough, she attended a program at the State Hospital, which encouraged involvement in various activities which strengthened her sense of independence at Wernersville. This is when she appeared most stable.

I have witnessed amazing results in reducing the stressors using quantum biofeedback for various mental conditions, which can help people like Kay.

All this weird behavior started after taking diet pills which allowed one more toxic item into her system and, bingo, ended up passing the blood brain barrier. My parents were devastated. Kay was everything they had dreamt and hoped for in a daughter. Talented musically, she played the piano and organ with such ease and grace, she was gifted with a melodious voice, but most important of all she had a beautiful heart. As a young girl, I had the opportunity to visit the many tent revivals where Kay and her group performed. Her singing engulfed my whole spirit, bathing me in its vibration. Allowing her voice's vibration to flow throughout my body opened up the doors and made me more aware of my own spirituality, increasing the communication with the God of my heart. Therefore I was able to find more of God's love and grace in my life. The audience, too, became mesmerized by her soft melodious voice which created a dynamic stillness throughout the crowd, bringing with it the vibration of harmony.

As we lost her to the disease, I quietly watched her life self-destructing. I also watched the enemies, guilt and sorrow, became intertwined like a labyrinth rooting deep into Thelma and Lester's lives.

Later remarrying, she settled into the carriage house, but unfortunately the marriage was with someone who did not treat her with respect. She conceived a child while on heavy pharmaceuticals and it was while on this medication she gave birth to her only child, a baby boy named Lucas. Before she became pregnant, she lived in the home next door called the carriage house. But as her disease progressed, Thelma and Lester made an apartment on the third floor of the Roslyn Estate in which she and the new baby could reside.

Before Lucas's arrival, Kay was well enough to make a nice nursery. She took into consideration what Lucas would enjoy as a baby as he laid on his back looking up at the ceiling of his nursery. She painted colorful pictures of whimsical clouds, the sun and moon, sheep and winking stars for his eyes to explore. A flicker of happiness could be seen shining in Kay's eyes as she prepared and designed her art on the walls and ceiling of the nursery, but as time went on, her eyes faded to a grey. Finally, Lucas was born while she was still consuming heavy medication for her illness. Very ill during his birth, she exhibited symptoms of this horrible disease. Could she have been helped? I believe so. What kind of an effect did these drugs have on the newborn child, and the bigger question, why was she even allowed to take these drugs while pregnant?

Recognizably different in nature from the other nephew and nieces, Lucas fell off the swing on purpose when we pushed it. Also when we babysat him, he devised a way to place all the antique lamps on their side on the rug in the living room. He was rather smart because this was done exactly before his grandparents walked into their home. Finding this behavior extremely peculiar for such a young child, I did not realize he was already eliciting signs of what was to come. Although at first Kay took full control in raising her son, later Lucas's safety was jeopardized by her sickness. Thelma and Lester took more control in their care of Lucas, since Kay was not able to take care of herself.

Even though my older sister, Kay, played a big part in Lucas's arrival into the world, later Thelma tried to deny that part too. At first Lucas's care was a joint effort, but that eventually changed, becoming one-sided.

During pregnancy she consumes pharmaceuticals for her so-called diagnosis, 'schizophrenia' without any warning as to what side effects these pharmaceuticals would have on her unborn child. Finally, the day has arrived and Lucas is born. What should have been a happy day to rejoice is covered with deep dark ominous clouds.

Later, the father of this baby dissociates himself from the marriage because confusion sets in and he has no idea how to deal with his wife's weird behavior. She sees smoke coming out of the locks of doors, prances throughout the home claiming to be an angel from the heavens, and continues to act out her many other delusional states. Becoming a prisoner to her bizarre thoughts, Kay is totally incompetent to take care of a newborn child. Her sickness makes him feel so very uncomfortable.

Listening attentively to all the weird thoughts going through her older sister's head, she realizes that it was futile to convince her differently. Hopelessness and darkness appear to cover all, as her deep eyes of green become clouded.

Covertly the vengeful storm clouds brewed as the years progressed. Kay was beginning to lose all hope of ever finding a way to regain her health and was led down one bunny hole and then another. She became adrift in her mental torture and lost all desire to keep on living in that body. It was frustrating to watch and I had no idea what to say or do to help her find her way back and regain health. Her future looked very grim and futile.

A woman lies on her bed staring into space with blank eyes, quietly concealing a knife under her crisp clean sheets. Downstairs her mother frets because she has not yet come down the stairs for her usual late morning visitation. So without much thought, she decides to venture up the curving staircase now sparkling with the dancing colors of late-morning sun rays shining through the stained glass window. Opening the bedroom door, to the mother it appears as if all is well.

Later that afternoon, looking rather pale, her daughter walks slowly down the stairs. Walking towards her mom, blood drips from her wrists staining the tan living room rug. She faints. Her mother is terrified, as her father calls for an ambulance. Later, the blood-soaked sheets are removed from the bed and crisp new sheets now replace them. The rug is scrubbed clean and nothing much more is discussed. Life goes on as if nothing happened out of the ordinary. One more thing is swept under the rug. Only the unhealed cuts on the young woman's wrist are reminders of this event which gives the town criers plenty to gossip about, growing into the ugliest scars. Did anyone truly care or realize how she suffers?

When she finally landed with my parents, she stayed on the third floor of the home, and a nice room was prepared for Lucas. But slowly any peace she had in her being deserted her, and Kay was found often on the sixth floor for mental patients. Confusion set in, robbing her of any life and by now was taking a toll on her already taxed, very thin body. Shortly afterward is when Kay tried to commit suicide by slitting her wrists, not once but many times. Later she intentionally consumed too many pills and was taken often to the hospital by ambulance where her stomach was pumped frequently. The pain that created this urgency to snuff out her life must have been unbearable. Medication hid her emotions regarding her life and a multitude of emotions piled upon each other. She lost all movement, turning her to stone.

One sunny afternoon, Mairzy and I went upstairs to explore the Roslyn estate and found ourselves in Kay's living quarters. I noticed an ordinary small rustic-brown notebook on a solitary tableplaced in the corner of the sitting room. This small writing book was illuminated by rays of sunshine gleaming gold through the open window, my attention was straightaway drawn to it. With great deliberation and respect, I inquisitively opened it and was very surprised to find some of Kay's deepest thoughts. This diary had many pages which expressed her suffering. Becoming engulfed in her message, I gained a greater understanding, which developed into a mature compassion for my older sister's struggles. During this time, Kay was staying at the state mental institution.

Kay prided herself in her trinkets and jewelry, which were acquired while shopping at various antique shops and fairs. Therefore, many times Mairzy and I were invited to visit her upstairs, where she showed us many of her recent purchases. Much later, on several occasions, invitations were given to me to join her for a meal at her new home, acquired through and funded by the state. During this time, Lucas stayed with Thelma and Lester, having his own bedroom on the second floor of the mansion estate.

Life continues.............

When I was growing up, being barefoot was normal and I did not give much thought to where my pets squatted but after moving to a small suburb with my husband, I understood the importance of finding that hidden turf of grass for my dog away from neighboring homes and their surroundings. Being very naïve even after completing five years of college, I had a bit of sheer innocence in my psyche, making me at times very gullible. Baking was fun, and I made apple pies, pumpkin pies and blueberry pies from scratch, thinking nothing of it. I hoped in my heart and was determined that my brain would heal in time.

Giggles of delight can be heard as children romp and play in the big piles of vibrant autumn leaves. Piles of colorful leaves are found stacked up high under the thick branches of the massive oak trees which now reach into the sun rays, commemorating the wheel of life.

Finally, Mairzy's first child, McKenzie, arrived as summer finished its orchestra of music and wonderful menu of beautiful smells. Rains came, cleansing the earth, causing drifting clouds of steam on the driveway, generating a whole new scent and rainbows communicated the hope of miracles, enhancing our faith in life's goodness. Next, Lindsay came into the world with a head of dark brown curly hair. She was the wild child, full of adventure with big dark brown enticing eyes. The last of Mairzy's children, Layton, was so delightful at first we joked about his odd look but he blossomed into a very handsome man with a very refined look and great character. By now, my son, Justin, was born with the most beautiful eyebrows and a bald head. He gradually grew to be strong in stamina with a very adventuresome spirit. Later, he pursued his fascination involving airplanes, honoring his heart for exploration. Roslyn joined us a few years later with a beautiful head of curly hair and she was used for the baby model at the hospital for the new mothers. I was blessed to have two healthy children, a true miracle of life.

Unfortunately, at three months of age Roslyn became very sick and her tiny body became emaciated. Her milk did not just dribble down her chin but catapulted across the room like a rocket. When Roslyn accompanied me in her baby stroller in malls, shoppers came up to her because she was so adorable. I hoped and prayed that they would not get baptized in a horrible mess, because of not knowing when her body would decide to propel her food many feet through the air. At first, the doctors were unable to find the reason for this food repulsion, but eventually the root problem was discovered, which was the narrowing of the pylorus.

Pyloric stenosis is a condition that may affect the gastrointestinal tract during infancy. It causes your baby to vomit forcefully and often may cause other problems such as dehydration and salt and fluid imbalances. Immediate treatment for pyloric stenosis is extremely important.

Pyloric stenosis is a narrowing of the pylorus, the lower part of the stomach through which food and other stomach contents pass to enter the small intestine. When an infant has pyloric stenosis, the muscles in the pylorus have become enlarged and cause narrowing within the pyloric channel to the point where food is prevented from emptying out of the stomach. Subsequently, Roslyn had an operation to remove the blockage at three months of age. Post surgery, every strand of her beautiful hair fell out in patches and eventually grew back in a shade of red. At last she began to flourish and joined our wagon filled with bundles of joy.

Again my question to the medical community is, "Why surgery?"Is surgery the only way of avoiding the death of a baby with an abdominal blockage? Infant pyloric stenosis cases vary greatly in their severity; and the more slowly developing and milder cases can be, and in many countries are, corrected with a course of medication. It must be remembered that most doctors in English-speaking countries have been trained as scientists and to work for the best outcome from a narrowly scientific viewpoint. Treatment options other than the "established standard" of the pediatrician are often regarded with skepticism or dismissed with a list of factors which upset parents will be hard-pressed to question. Often the "established standard" (that is, surgery) is indeed the best way forward, but sometimes it will not be. From the considerable body of reports and other literature, many cases of pyloric stenosis can be treated without surgery, provided a few provisos are in place.

I believe if at all possible one should avoid surgery. Why create more stress in someone's life? Why are we not open to other ideas of helping patients in English-speaking countries? What supports this narrow way of thinking?

Easter was a time to celebrate and the traditional festivities were enjoyed by everyone. Thelma enjoyed hard-boiling dozens of eggs for Easter. These eggs were eagerly retrieved the next morning from the refrigerator by tiny hands.

Using an assortment of tinsel, paints, stickers, magic markers and glitter found on the kitchen table, the children chattered as they decorated their eggs. Smells of all kinds of delights radiated from the oven as streams of golden rays shone brightly into the kitchen from an open window. What a gala!

Arising at the crack of dawn, the sound of children's happy chattering can be heard outside as they search for Easter eggs. The many vibrant colorful eggs which are carefully hidden give clues of their whereabouts by bits of color peeking out from under the foliage. The children investigate in bushes which promise new life, they inspect flower gardens and look for bits of hidden color peeking out from the fresh new pachysandra. These are only a few of the places the children explore, hoping not to leave any eggs behind. Now bubbling gaily, they congregate together sitting in a full-sized circle. Sorting through their festive baskets on the soft parsley-green grass, monies are being collected from the plastic eggs which are put in a pile in the center to be later divided up among them.

Presently, inside the home, Easter baskets are being hidden by Thelma to be discovered later. Love was definitely in the air.

Having such a good heart, Thelma put so much time into ochestrating an array of different events for us, which included Dorney Park and Hershey Park. These outings were arranged and paid for by her. Also, she prepared food to take along for everyone which was put out and shared under the pavilion on one of the many long wooden tables. All the grandchildren were excited participants at these extravaganzas including Lucas, who usually had a friend or two accompany him.

Later Thelma grew to become obsessed with Lucas and felt compelled to sit with him for endless hours assisting him with his homework and sometimes doing it for him. Letters were found from teachers in Lester's office, opened on his desk. These letters expressed deep concerns for Lucas's struggles in learning and his disturbingly odd behavior which was acted out at the private school he attended. This further embarrassed Thelma and Lester. So, frustrated with his behavior, they hid their concerns from the rest of the family and world. They paid for a tutor for him but it was difficult and laborious for Lucas. He could not learn like normal children. His brain appeared to work much differently, very skewed from normal.

A volleyball net at the bay home was often used at Rehoboth by our children who came together to play volleyball. I held Lucas's hand and said, "We are going to play volleyball!" He could not comprehend or understand that there were two teams involved, appearing clueless even when the rules were explained to him many times. Therefore, he chose not to be a part of the game. He appeared very bright in many different areas of life—was he playing with my head or did he just not get it? Hoping Lucas would eventually work it out, I had no idea what was to come of this young boy.

Unable to see Kay's behavior as a cry for help, instead Thelma's mind made her accountable for the odd and at times unethical behavior. Thelma generated a lot of stress, produced dramas over silly happenings, and harassed Kay about things that were trivial. The energy of this behavior did not encourage Kay to get better, but only increased her frustration and stress level. Listening to this trite harassment of Kay made me squirm and feel quite uncomfortable. Lester too became increasingly distressed with how the relationship with Kay was slowly going sour with Thelma, not sure what his part was in this whole mess. He gave the impression of being powerless and afraid of Thelma, unable to assert his opinion, which made the whole situation worse because of not sharing his voice. Conversations with Thelma became one-sided. She screamed, had a temper tantrum or left the conversation if she did not like what she was hearing. Fear took root in her life and a hedge was put around her because of it.

As the sickness progressed, men who were thieves were permitted to enter the home. Many valuables vanished secretly from Thelma and Lester's home before they figured out what was going on and tried to put a stop to the thievery. Unaware of their goal to steal from the home at the time; Kay did not recognize what was happening as these men took advantage of her weakness.

Later, Lucas was guided to call Thelma, Mother, and his birth-mother, Kay, without Kay's consent or approval. A battle of wills went on and often Thelma wanted to exclude Kay, pushing her further away emotionally. Many times Thelma ignored her, increasing the distance in their relationship. The disease took my sister's life away and everything she had worked for, her goals and her aspirations all zapped dry as a desert, as well as her respect in society. So many people are uneducated regarding mental illness and what might be the root cause of this odd behavior. Again, please read, *Brain on Fire* by Susannah Cahalan; it will help open up your eyes. People similar to Kay are thought of as being defective and many are given pharmaceuticals for their odd behavior. These people have been kept away from society and are judged guilty as if they did something wrong and can be thought of as subhuman. A doctor told me, "Ember, karma created her sickness and karma cannot be changed, and therefore she will be pushed forward in life having no control of changing the outcome of her life or her health. She will have to learn how to deal with it." Now I know that is false, but at the time I trusted this doctor and what he said made me shudder.

No one has the authority to say something so callous. This kind of attitude does not allow any room for hope for the person with the disease or the loved ones of the person. It made her look as if she did something wrong and had to pay for it. Presently, any situation can be changed, all is possible and with a will, there is a way.

She spent much of her life on the sixth floor of the mental ward, locked in because of her mental condition. Later, the two-hour trip was made to visit her at Wernersville State Hospital, a place for her to abide out of sight from society. Oh boy! How I yearned for my older sister—to see her smile again. I yearned to see Kay's smile from the depth of her being, her soul. Kay was pampered at this somewhat scary place. She received manicures, pedicures and head massages. These weekly visits are where the most bizarre thoughts were expressed. Patiently, I listened to stories of a frontal lobotomy and many other disturbing stories which were never confirmed as true. The people she lived with were very sick and every day at the same time they lined up to get their drugs. Afterward, they would display the oddest behavior, which was very disturbing to the outside observer. They were all put together in the section of this hospital because of the severity of their mental confusion. The question persisted in the back of my mind, "How much was the medication really helping them?" This thought persisted until the answer was revealed to me after much research and study. What is the driving force behind the pharmaceutical companies? Is it love?

Prayer

Kay had the opportunity to attend a few of the Benny Hinn services which are free and open to the public. This is where people are encouraged to experience the anointed worship, ministry and healing power of God. We hoped that the energy of the worship would push her forward to create a spiritual, emotional and a body healing. Traveling together in the van with our children and their Aunt Kay, we arrived at our destination the night before and found rest at a hotel that evening. Early in the morning with great anticipation, we ventured off together for breakfast. After breakfast, we walked directly to the stadium and became part of the excitement of the long line of people who waited for hours until the doors opened. Kay, just as determined to get into the service, waited in the line which curved the whole way around the building. Hopeful souls from all around the world congregate here to receive their healing in an environment which creates a portal of positive energy conducive for the manifestation of miracles.

After taking our seats in the stadium, you could feel the energy of expectation and faith vibrating throughout the room. Usually, by this time, Kay became very sick and regurgitated the food that was consumed that morning into a napkin, which usually spilled out and over her. Our children became so grossed out for lack of better words and, immediately, she was accompanied to the bathroom and assisted in getting cleaned up. I was not aware at the time that healing of some sort was being started with Kay because many times the stomach is affected first. It is one of the physical organs that releases energy which might not be so appealing, but is a response that says "something here is being stirred up, whatever that might be for that person." At the time, I did not think of this physical response in that way because I was unaware of such things.

There are better ways of helping these people that have been labeled with a diagnosis which most likely is not really correct or the root cause. Now having become so angered, she has estranged herself from her twin sisters because of jealousy and confusion. Turning back the hands of time to go back and help her seems like a very tedious task but not impossible.

The Bay House

During the summer months, a special gathering place is frequented often. A meeting place for loved ones, named the bay house. As the sun begins to lower in the distant horizon, the silhouettes of small children can be seen from afar. Faint laughing is heard as they play in an old canoe along the bay waters. Later, when the night becomes pitch black with the twinkling light of the stars and the glow of the full moon peeking out beyond the clouds, the children meander inside. A warm sudsy bath waits for them with many water toys to occupy their busy minds. Playing happily in the bathtub, their innocent faces and hearts glow in the security of their parents' love. Consciousness observes with a sigh as the moon rays glow into the bathroom window.

Thelma purchased a myriad of inner tubes and flotation devices to be used in the warm waters of the bay. She was an important key player in giving us the space to have fun and enjoy each other. Elaborate meals were meticulously planned by her and enjoyed while dining together. Later when my parents decided that our family was growing, a bigger bay house was purchased with many bedrooms, an attic used as a playroom, and outside porches to sit and enjoy nature. A huge rectangular table used just for dining sat in a room containing many large windows which, cranked wide open, invited in the soft cool breezes of the bay. The spirit of laughter visited, reverberating throughout the home as we sat together in each other's company. I loved these times together.

Traveling to town, we spent much of our time in the hustle and bustle of the boardwalk where all the rides were found crammed into a tiny space with bright lights that twinkled and carnival music that blared loudly. Usually, the boardwalk was packed with many people in the evening during the summer months and the smell of cotton candy, pizza and hotdogs could be overwhelming. The boardwalk overlooked the bright blue ocean on one side with the white sand. It was where we sat on the wooden benches and watched as the waves came in, sweeping sand back out to the ocean. We contently listened as the waves hit the shoreline. The smell of salt was always in the air; it was a place where we absolutely loved to play together and were often found joining in the hustle and bustle with our children, entertained into the wee hours of the night on the many rides. Thelma loved to go off and play skeeball by herself, sometimes accompanied with a happy grandchild. It was heaven on earth!

The bay waters could be seen through my huge bedroom window, illuminated by the sparkle of the moon's rays, and the soothing sounds of its lapping water could be heard against the shoreline.

I absolutely adored my bedroom because it was located at the far end of the home away from everybody and because it had a very exceptional enormous window. The water danced and sparkled, coming alive with energy; it soothed my soul, setting the energy for a peaceful night's sleep.

Outside the window, she studies a bank of clouds that appear on the horizon, inching slowly across the sky, finally slipping across the moon and blocking out its radiant light.

Later, clicking off her night light, she turns her eyes one last time to the heavens. Outside, in the newly fallen darkness, the world has been transformed. The sky is now a glistening tapestry of stars. Sleep comes quickly, overtaking her whole being. The world is now made silver, transformed by the light of the moon, which is full, like a great luminous pearl in the heavens and the moon quietly glows in through her bedroom window as she sleeps. Awakened before dawn she is startled from a deep sleep by loud distressful cries. Her hair falls softly down to her hips as she sits up and squints, trying to focus in the darkness of night and notices a silhouette just outside her window. Arising, walking barefoot, she opens the screen window and to her pleasure finds a calico cat. Her stomach is swelling, ready to burst with little ones which are now eager and quite ready to be birthed into the world. The drapes blow gently with the soft ocean breeze, as she invites the mother cat to enter and she quickly runs to wake her daughter.

Cautiously, nudging thoroughly throughout the room, the mother cat makes an inspection of every nook and cranny. Finding the perfect spot, she births six tiny kittens in a drawer full of socks with the loving gaze of the full silver moon, emerald green eyes, and the brightest blue eyes. It was their secret.

Wet jets used for water skiing maneuvered along the coastline across the front of the bay home. Along the front of the property coming from the bay, children giggled as they were taught to water ski. Being onlookers, my parents were satisfied and happy to know they made such a beautiful playland. Bliss became a reality, created in love.

The boys became very adventuresome and bolder as they became older, maneuvering these massive machines through the rough channel which led out to the expansive ocean. Sometimes, they departed just as the sun began to rise and returned much later as the sun began to set. Thelma thought they were churning around the bay waters, having no idea where they really were. We came to an agreement that she did not need to know and waited patiently for their return to admonish them for being gone so long.

As the bay waters changed, so did the habitat and, sporadically, jellyfish mysteriously appeared, making it challenging to enter the salty waters. As the children became older, we took them out water skiing in the deeper bay waters and a game called dodge the jellyfish became a source of much entertainment. During this season of plenty, it was a very difficult game to win. Once in awhile one of the sticky travelers became adhered to and plastered across the chest of the skier. As the skier emerged from the murky bay waters with this creature stuck to their body, it created a heightened sense of amusement for the passengers of the boat. But humor was definitely lacking for the skier, whose eyes showed only terror, afraid to let go because of the mere thought of possibly landing on a bed of these creatures.

One lazy summer morning, ready for a challenge, they brazenly navigate through the channel. This channel can be very challenging because of rough waters but today has gone unusually smooth.

Sunbathers gaze out at them in admiration. It is a rare event to see wet jets in this part of the ocean. Extremely happy to be out in the ocean, they enjoy the sultry air and the morning rays of sunshine glistening on their faces. Soon this blissful feeling disappears for one of them because, out of nowhere, hands wrap around the older man's throat. As they begin to tighten around his throat he begins to panic, feeling as if any minute he will be yanked from his wet jet into the never-ending ocean waters and carried away by some hideous creature. Befuddled with his mishap, he realizes that around his throat are not hands or tentacles of a sea monster but only a fishing line.

Unexpectedly a fishing pole is jerked out from the sand where a fisherman has secured it for a blissful morning of fishing. Sitting oblivious to this mishap, he rests peacefully with his bright yellow cap over his face in the morning rays of light. Lulled to sleep by the gentle sounds of the sea gulls and waves against the coastline, he is left unaware that his pole is now being dragged along the sandy coastline.

Hauling the line, still around his throat, the wet-jetter finally reacts and releases one of the handles of his wet jet. Mustering enough strength to lift the fishing line, he yanks it from around his neck while still traveling full speed ahead. Lucky for him it works; he was very close to getting caught with the razor-sharp hook. Finally coming to a stop, he searches for his companion, oblivious to the angry fisherman who is now running along the shoreline shaking his fist at him. Looking at each other, the riders shrug their shoulders and laughing, speed off.

Learning to be more observant for obstacles along the way, he grins as the story is retold. The energy of panic can create very stupid decisions and reactions. It is much later in his life that he finally understands the lesson that the universe was forcing him to pay deep attention to inside.

Mighty love

Playing with the binoculars, Jackson saw something far in the distance, an object that appeared as if it was moving toward the boat. As it floated closer, he became very fascinated as to what appeared to be now paddling through the bay water, heading in the direction of the boat. As this moving object came closer, it became more easily recognizable and he clearly realized it was some kind of tiny animal, possibly a rat or wild animal caught at sea. As it advanced steadily and its form materialized, we could hardly believe what we saw.

Very soon realizing it was Alfrenso, Mairzy's toy poodle, we were so amazed at his brave spirit. He decided to venture out into the deep waters of the bay searching for us! It is simply an astounding story. No matter how little you seem, if you focus and be true to your heart, anything can be accomplished. Mairzy pulled his wet soaking body up into the boat as his tail wagged fiercely with joy in finding his beloved owner. Believing he was mighty in this huge ocean, Alfrenso did not see the massiveness of the ocean but only sought after his goal of being with the ones he loved. Love is powerful and you can do great things with it, and Alfrenso was our amazing teacher.

Thelma invited her card buddies to Rehoboth once or twice a year which was her time with no men or family involved. The honor of witnessing that side of her was refreshing and just plain lovely to see, I imagined her barefoot and dancing free from any cares of the world.

If only you could envisage all living in harmony where no one suffers and the awareness that all is truly well, only imagine where love prevails to create life in harmony.

On this particular occasion, she had guests and when she answered the phone, it was with much gaiety, catching me by surprise. This attitude was very enlivening and much unanticipated. Hearing the joyous laughter of her friends in the background was refreshing and this side of her was very unusual to catch but delightful to experience. Able to find joy, happiness and the capability of releasing the cares of the world, her spirit soared wild and free.

When visiting the bay house, a recurring feeling visited me, which was weird and ominous. Lingering, it felt as if some kind of entity was threatening to take it all away. When packing to go back home, this same feeling came over me the next time even stronger. I thought maybe it was just me, overreacting to these feelings which for whatever reasons my psychic dreamt up. After saying our goodbyes with lots of hugs and kisses, Thelma and Lester followed us out of the home and waved as we departed in our van with all our children aboard. Everyone put their heads out the windows of the van and waved fervently until Thelma and Lester disappeared into the distance. Such an isolated, lonely feeling struck the pit of my stomach as we left the bay house, and a strong knowledge came over me as to how important it was to relish each moment with my parents. This strange feeling appeared time and time again for many years.

Our children were in their teens when Thelma indicated casually that she was not going to give the bay house to us or even grant us the opportunity to buy it. But instead, she informed me flippantly that it would be sold to someone outside the family. She declared boldly that Lovely and Ray had given their bay home to their children but that was not going to happen in our case. A horrible feeling came as the realization how very sick my mom had become. I retorted, "Really, is that really what you want to do? Why not give it to Mairzy and me?" Thelma then went on to say that there were other people in the family that would want to use it. Trying to appease her, I told her everyone was welcome to use it and that Mairzy and I would gladly split any of the expenses it incurred. Not answering me, I thought for sure she would eventually change her mind.

Taking my mom to Franklin and Marshall University, which was within walking distance, she had her first tennis lesson. This became a weekly occurrence that went on for a couple of years. Thelma was a willing and eager student as well as a good sport. She enjoyed playing tennis at the age of eighty and impressed me with her great attitude. Thanking me for taking time out of my schedule to teach her, I knew the time together was much more valuable than the lesson taught.

Excitement radiated from our beings when spring came and fresh buds peeked from the earth, promising new life, showing off the majestic masterpiece of God's creation. We became mesmerized by it all, spurring faith and hope in a divine plan.

The Roslyn estate and its property became Lester's pride and joy. Every time we visited the home, weather permitting, my husband and I usually walked the grounds with Lester. As we walked, he pointed out various plants and named each one of them, and every week proudly showed us the new foliage which had been added to the gardens. He was so refreshing to listen to as he shared his knowledge of different plants. Jokingly, Lester gave various leafy plants very odd and long names and with a serious stare said, "Now I want you to repeat it." I looked at him and said, "Are you for real or just kidding me?" He glanced over at me with a blue twinkle in his eye and said, "What do you think?" and I knew.

Lester's heart softened in time and he evolved into a truly kind man. Often in the latter years, he was found sitting outside. After searching for him on the property, we found him sitting on one of the white hard metal benches that were hidden from view. Usually, he was taking a nap with his cap over his face, sometimes with his devoted companion patiently waiting by his side. Sitting down next to him on the soft grass, I tickled his chin mischievously with a branch until he woke up, making us both laugh. After waking, he usually enticed his companion to play tootsie with him, which involved him removing his shoes. Moving his stocking feet back and forth across the lush grass made it irresistible for his devoted companion. Laughing with blue sparkles in his eyes, he exclaimed, "Look, he just loves to play with my feet!" Weather permitting, before venturing inside the home, our usual walk was made through the bamboo forest. Creating his own humor, he loved to laugh, laughing heartily throughout most of his life and he still does.

Lester primed up the grill for our cookouts, proudly acquiring the ability to grill steaks to perfection. Leaving him outside with the grill, my sister and I usually proceeded inside to the large quaint kitchen to see what still needed to be done to help out with dinner. During the warmer summer months, we sat outside on the patio to eat and engaged in a boisterous conversation amid much laughter while the children played with all the assorted tricycles, wagons and balls. Good friends, they knew how to play and have fun together, with only one missing who came later from a faraway land. Not even born as yet, her spirit was being coached to set the plan in motion, playing out the role of the witness.

As the children grew into their teenage years, we played the game of hide-and-seek, which evolved with many variations. The countless places to hide outside made it all the more stimulating and, as we quietly hid, anticipation grew as to where the person who was designated 'it' might be stalking. At night under the gaze of the gleaming and glittering stars, it seemed like a large hand had tossed diamond dust into the sky. It gave the game a whole different flair and meaning. It was fun to play this game in the dark under the gaze of the shimmering stars, but we always had to be mindful as to where we hid, especially in the pachysandra that Brandy frequented quite often.

Cooking was Thelma's specialty. She enjoyed cooking and everyone loved eating her food. The satisfaction of seeing our happy faces enjoy her cooking was the reward in preparing her delicacies. All kinds of goodies were masterfully concocted by Thelma. Christmas cookies, potato rolls, apple dumplings and corn fritters were only a few of them. The many different recipes handed down from her mother were endless and very unusual because Thelma came from the sect of the old Brethren. Her mother taught her how to make many fine delectables such as cow tongue, pickled pig's feet, rabbit, duck, heart, liver and stuffed pig stomach (which were not at all unusual to find on the dinner table). Every kind of pastry imaginable was prepared, created from the recipes given to her from the old Brethren including the many recipes handed down to her from her mother. Apple dumplings, sugar cookies, shoo fly pie; apple, peach, raspberry, mincemeat, strawberry, and lemon meringue pie were only some of the many desserts. The list was endless, with many more fine foods not mentioned, all made from scratch and definitely not from yucky cans.

Thelma loved to entertain company with her food and was very good natured about allowing us to bring guests over for a meal. Thelma was a very happy spirit when she could be a service to others and, looking at her, one was truly amazed at such a beautiful being whose light shone so brightly. One of the coaches from Lanco Gymnastics training center was invited for dinner. Knowing that he was from Russia, she researched and found a dish made in Russia. History says that borscht was and is one of the most popular dishes in Russia. He absolutely loved it. Borscht appeared at the end of the eighteenth to the nineteenth centuries. The main ingredients are red beets and broths made from meat or fish, or mushrooms, or smoked sausages. Plus, many people add cabbage, onions, carrots, potatoes, tomatoes, spinach, and sorrel. The sour taste it can have is caused by the vinegar which is one of the ingredients. Our ancestors ate borscht with pancakes, different porridges and pies. Poor people made borscht without meat, only with vegetables.

Because my parents had different bouts of broken bones and health issues, we brought many meals to the home. Various entrees made at home were brought from our car and the children headed into the dining room to set the table for our feast. This became a common occurrence on many Sunday afternoons. We made it a point to show Thelma and Lester extra attention, and made them feel special and loved with birthday cakes and takeout from restaurants, preparing many special meals for the holidays.

Classical music is playing softly throughout the ranch home as happy whistling is coming from the bedroom. Always whistling or singing, Lester enjoys music and loves how it makes him feel. Today, the choir is going to be practicing for the church's Christmas concert. The energy of celebration is in the air. Lester is very dedicated to the church and its choir. He and his wife became members when they were teenagers. Now they are in their middle-age years and they love being part of the church which represents a family to them.

Later the sounds of happy festive bustling are heard resonating in the kitchen as they prepare for a women's Christmas party. No men are allowed to this party but regardless Lester looks forward to helping his wife prepare for this festive occasion. Gaiety is in the air as they work happily together.

These fine folks have lots of common sense, with very high personal and work ethics, but also know how to have fun. They love to entertain. 'Card game night' is held once a month at their home on Donegal Springs Road which eventually graduates to the home in Lancaster where laughter and small talk can be heard reverberating throughout the many rooms. Getting together with their friends often, they have a wonderfully rich fun social life inside, as well as outside the home which encompasses a vast array of activities. Riding mopeds, waterskiing, boating, and flying are only a few of them. Now they're full of enthusiasm for life, but as time marches on, these fine folks outlive all their good friends and darkness comes knocking at their door.

Chapter Five
The Devil

When my children were in their teen years, my mom asked me, "Where do you think children come from, Ember?" It caught me off guard because it seemed like such a stupid question, and I thought what is up with her? Going along with the question, I said children come from the love of two people. Later, she shared with me that she thought they came from Satan. Never hearing something so odd from her, this statement sounded so unlike my mom!

Denial

"Lucas is so great. He would never mark your vehicles, hurt your animals, steal your Christmas gifts or steal money out of your pocketbooks. And he never took our credit card for personal use. No, Ember, he is not doing heroin! How dare you say that and you have no right to talk that way!" The phone is quietly placed on the receiver while she keeps on screaming.

It was bizarre to think that his addictions and abusive behavior were permitted in the home. Lucas could drink in the home, smoke cigarettes, shoot heroin, stare me down, swear at me, hurt our loved ones and create mayhem and pandemonium by staging dramas thoughtfully planned out for every special occasion held at the home. It was acceptable to my parents that Lucas and his wife lived there without any kind of contribution to rent, household duties, or groceries. Also, Lester and Thelma took care of his fraternal financial responsibility from his first marriage, while Lucas and his wife stayed up into the wee hours of the morning partying.

My dad's forewarning about my mom's health started to reveal itself as true. Her mental health was declining and she became less rational, which was getting in the way of the love she had for her twin daughters. Now, I was beginning to understand what Lester meant about my mother when he indicated that Thelma was not well. Not making much sense to me at the time, he had glumly told me of my mom's illness right after my graduation from high school. At the time I thought my mother was physically ill, not realizing he meant a mental illness. The tip of the iceberg was now being observed, and there was a lot more concealed that would be emerging shortly.

Chapter Six
Motherhood

I had to love my parents and realize that they were doing their best with all the filters and distortions that developed in their ways of coping with the world. We all have our filters and personalities, but love is needed and grace for all, which begins with ourselves. They were my parents, precious and irreplaceable. This understanding about people came later in life. The awareness of my mom's psychological issues which attracted lower energies vibrationally, cultivated a compassion for that part of her which could not have the life that was waiting for her to claim. I loved her dearly, but not the attachments that smothered her essence.

Much later even a deeper level of understanding and compassion were discovered, coming from parts of me that I never knew existed. I mourned.

A rebellious angry young woman is confused with life in general. Her body is falling apart from the toxic environment of life—some ingested out of ignorance and others shot into her veins in the name of health. Regardless of the reason, her immune system is failing and the magic of life hides from the lanky green-eyed young lady.

Eventually, discovering the art of yoga and meditation, she connects to a higher consciousness bringing in answers for her own healing as well as her daughter's. Introduced to a healing modality called quantum biofeedback, she is carried and led by an army of angels in this science. Fueling her intense desire to find answers, this enables her to ultimately earn her doctorate in energetic medicine.

The Quantum Biofeedback System harnesses the power of quantum physics, fractal mathematics, and subtle energy for medicine by addressing the deep and subtle issues underlying health problems—fundamental issues that western medicine is not designed to detect or treat. With over 250 computer programs for stress reduction, relaxation, pain management, brainwave training, muscle re-education and more, the Indigo can empower the innate wisdom of the mind-body connection and restore the body's natural ability to balance, heal and cure itself.

Watching as she finishes her near perfect balance beam routine, her green eyes dance, celebrating such an impeccable routine. Unexpectedly while in mid-air, Roslyn crumples to the floor unable to complete her dismount. Later, Roslyn's coach informs her parents that the pin juggled out from the balance beam used for adjusting the height of the beam. It must not have been pushed in properly for whatever reason. This oversight, in turn, caused the balance beam to drop just as the push was executed for her dismount, not giving her enough thrust to finish her rotation in her double twisting back flip. Instead of landing on her feet, she fell to the mat after her forehead caught the end of the beam.

Later, she realizes that big changes have to be made within her in order to help her daughter. Society says it is impossible for her to accomplish or say she is just plain crazy. A reconnection to that childlike innocence and to the power within to create whatever she wants is imperative. With fierce determination, she only looks forward.

What makes someone keep on trudging onward until they are totally exhausted, frustrated, at their wit's end, depleting all resources, but still pushing forward to produce another life that they just do not have enough fuel to create?

A young woman looks onward with confusion encompassing her green eyes. Her first child is now ready to be born. Having premature labor pains for some time now, she lies on the steel cot in the silence of her room. Suddenly, she perks up recognizing the voice of her mother outside her doorway. Her heart lightens to think that someone cares enough to be with her. But instead of staying, she takes a couple steps into the cold room only to glance at her and proceeds to quickly turn, weeping.

As the gas mask is placed over her face she enters a dream-like state. The group Iron Butterfly performs 'IN A GADDA DA VIDA' as she feels her son's body enter into the world. A cyst is discovered on his sack which steals his food supply. Ultimately, it is the reason why this little life is snuffed out right before entering the world. Her doctor tells her to stop crying. He was really ugly and for that reason, had made the decision to throw his lifeless body into the incinerator. "You really wouldn't have wanted to see him, he was ugly, so skinny and not much to look at." he informs her.

Young and naïve, she can't grasp that her firstborn son's lifeless body came into the cold world where the human soul is not honored, and she feels very alone, abandoned in her grief.

During the end of my pregnancy, premature labor pains began about the sixth month and my doctor prescribed paregoric medicine to alleviate the contractions. Naïve, believing that doctors knew what was best for their patients; I was in for a huge awakening. Jonathan made his mind up that he no longer could live in that environment and wanted to be born, but did not have the energy to make his appearance into the outside world. Not having the energy to live, he ended up in an incinerator without my permission. I was deemed never to see his precious body, and scolded by the doctor, "Please stop crying, and get over it, Ember! He was ugly, not much to look at. "I became more withdrawn.

A professor at the university had a smile which appeared as if it had become frozen on his face and I often wondered, "Did he also become lost and just want to fit into his body and society?" One day while sitting in the faculty room during lunch break, I was told, "Please stop smiling; there is nothing to smile about!" and I knew the teacher was right. I just wanted to fit in some way with that group but how can you, when you cannot connect with who you are? I sat there in the faculty room on a chair along the wall as the other teachers sat at a table together, lost deep in their conversation. As I listened to their interesting tales of life, I didn't realize my smile also became frozen on my face as if on a clown. At this time in my life, my first child named Jonathan, a beautiful baby boy was stillborn.

With great enthusiasm, a small boy is searching for crickets under rocks or in the tall grass. He is going to put them into a box to later be a meal for one of his exotic reptiles. Wilbur has joined him and his mother on this very special walk, and is exuberantly found bounding throughout the tall grass.

A few years later, his sister will join them, absolutely adoring her big brother. She has the bluest eyes; her name is Roslyn.

Wilbur had a bad habit of visiting the farmer's henhouse and it happened one morning that his leash wiggled loose from the skinny tree where he had been tied. He succumbed to his weakness. This was the tree we always stopped at after my morning run so I could do my pushups on the grass. Glancing up, I caught him dashing in front of me headed for the field of threshed corn at least a mile or more away. Very concerned, I had a good hunch exactly where his nose was leading him, to a very largely populated farm with chickens, roosters, and peeps. This farm was located on the other side of the corn field, next to the country road which could be quite busy early in the morning with buses full of children going to school. To Wilbur, this was like a child having full access to a candy store. Well aware that his visit to the hen house would be very unwelcome and dangerous, I sprinted after him with all my might across that barren field and yelled, "Come, Wilbur, come!" Lucky for me he still had the leash hanging from his neck which eventually became his downfall.

Running as fast as possible to catch up to his powerful gait, there was no way I was any competition for him. Wilbur was so big and powerful; he reached the chicken pen much quicker than I could ever have. With my face by now a scarlet red from my crazed dash across the field, I finally arrived at the barn and madly searched around the corner of one of the stalls. I was happy when I finally got my first glimpse of him but, unfortunately, by now, Wilbur already had a flustered hen in his mouth. So immediately charging him, I did a long stretched-out dive. This dive resembled a racer's dive but instead of gliding across the smooth water, I landed on my stomach face-first in the oozing mud. Desperately, I reached out for the end of the leash as my face smacked down into the gooey mess and by sheer determination, as my hand reached out, it was just enough to catch the tail end of the leash. That day was this chicken's lucky day because Wilbur opened his mouth and the escape was made. The chicken's feathers were all in disarray and its psyche a little frazzled, but she remained unharmed.

Lack

Life keeps on going forward but if your physical body cannot handle the abuse and lack of love, it starts to wear down little by little. My body was letting me down and I was often found in a hospital room with an IV hooked into my arm, looking very lethargic. These many medical tests became a common occurrence for a day or two after landing in the hospital every month. The medical community could never figure out what exactly was wrong with me. I even became a VIP, acquiring my own special pass to bypass the emergency sign in procedure. I knew hours before my body showed the signs of going out of control, shaking with a fever that soared high as my body became wracked and smitten with pain. Wearing my woolen hat, I curled up on the bathroom floor, alone.

One afternoon in the Poconos, while visiting Mairzy, the same particular odd feeling began to come over me, now very familiar to me. This feeling was an urgent message screaming "Mayday," letting me know it was most imperative to find help as soon as possible. Experiencing this feeling several times by now, I knew most likely what the outcome would be, which was not going to be much fun. Therefore, immediately gathering up my few belongings and my children, I headed to Lancaster driving a two and one-half hour stretch and as soon as I arrived home and everyone was unloaded, exhaustion overcame me. Definitely relieved to be home, I fell onto the couch with a fever that was skyrocketing and later landed on the bathroom floor with the commode as my best friend. Finishing the nursing school was not physically possible. The faculty tried to talk me out of leaving; commending me on my hard work which produced high grades, but an inner voice told me my decision, no matter how difficult, was correct. I was now running on empty. Roslyn was born when I was enrolled in nursing school and it was three years later that the decision to give up the nursing school was made.

Later, when my health began to stabilize, I decided to begin a gymnastic facility.

In the beginning of my journey of substituting, I could only imagine the teachers coming back the next day, gritting their teeth and making a note not to ask the weird chick back ever again. Everything around me appeared foggy, nothing made sense in my world and my brain decided to go out for lunch and never come back, at least for a long time. It went on strike! Gym class made a bit more sense to me because blowing my magic whistle was somewhat familiar to me. Therefore, teaching physical education went a lot better than being a teacher in a classroom because I did have an understanding of what a race was and knew how to make teams.

Eventually, after getting the hang of coping with substituting, the art of teaching gymnastics was pursued with a passion. I watched a multitude of videos on how to break down the most advanced skills of gymnastics in order to teach with safety in mind for the student as well as the instructor. Various studios began to recognize me for my coaching skills and I could be found working late into the evening at different studios, usually after spending time substituting for the school district. Doing both jobs was strenuous, and finding enough energy was difficult at times. The headaches became habitual, sometimes developing into migraines, and learning to work around the pain took much patience and perseverance.

Driving up to the gymnastics facility on Clay Street, lines upon lines of people are seen waiting at the door to register for classes. Her eyes dance a light green, shining with delight as she looks out at all the people. It is the gym's first day of registration,

Later, thoughts went through my head about how exciting and gratifying it would be to have my own studio, which brought into being an old warehouse perfect for the project. This warehouse flowered into a gymnastics facility with two young beings part of this adventure! All kinds of gymnastic equipment such as; mats, ropes, inclines and octagons were purchased, making it perfect for a top notch gymnastic facility. Terri, a dear friend, stenciled gymnastics figures on the freshly painted walls, while Mairzy enlivened the party room using vibrant colors and sparkling gloss. She sketched and painted a big bear holding balloons sporting a colorful party hat, perfect for a birthday celebration!

The party room exploded with festivity and danced in the energy of celebration. It was where children enjoyed pizza and cake. And of course, they opened gifts. But before settling in this room the party participants had the opportunity to participate in many different fun activities. Parachute games, pin the tail on the donkey, obstacle courses, trampoline games and, of course, gymnastics led by trained instructors--all activities included for a bunch of energetic partygoers. There became quite a following for this small gym which ran on love, blooming with creativity.

The new gym took much time to get ready for the new students. It was located on Clay Street, a very quaint side street of Lancaster. There were all sorts of activities devised by our children to entertain themselves as the gym was in its planning stages: roller-skating, obstacle courses, tumbling, swinging from a rope to travel over the trampoline and then releasing the rope to bounce high into the air.

Justin and his sister walked together to Turkey Hill where he bought a hot dog for them before he was driven to afternoon Kindergarten and later when the freedom of summer came, giggles were heard in the adjacent room while I taught classes in the morning. They loved devising different obstacle courses for each other to do and Roslyn sometimes would appear from nowhere at the oddest times and participate in a class that was taking place. She had the demeanor of a famous star but looked more like a class clown; and I smiled quietly because my only desire for my children was that they have fun and be truly happy.

After the gym was broken into, a stereo was stolen, we received some odd notes, and, lastly, were given a tip that the warehouse was going to go up in flames, I thought it might just be a good idea to move the gym.

Every piece of equipment was brought over to a very large empty warehouse and that was the start of a masterpiece. When we graduated to a larger warehouse its name was changed from Lanco Gymnastics Studio to Lanco Gymnastics Training Center. There was much work to do which entailed transporting and purchasing more balance beams, uneven parallel bars and many trampolines of all different sizes and shapes. We hired men to operate bulldozers to excavate a huge pit which was later manually filled with foam. An in-ground trampoline was designed over the pit with a spotting belt attached from the ceiling, making it an overhead spotting belt used for spotting back flips, front flips, back handsprings and front as well as back layouts. The large long pit, running the whole width of the back of this building was designed with safety in mind and in due course a section of the pit was used for a set of uneven parallel bars for the team girls to train for giants. This pit had plenty of room for the in-ground trampoline and a thirty-foot long trampoline running along the far right hand wall. This very long trampoline was used for more advanced gymnastics skills which most of the time took a running round-off to lead into a more difficult skill. Class students loved this long trampoline just for the sheer fun of jumping off the end into the pit. Also, one of the vaulting horses was strategically placed next to the pit so that the gymnast landed in the soft foam of the pit, making more difficult vaults easier to learn or for the recreational gymnast to have fun by exploring movement.

A year later, just as the caller said, the location of the first gym did burn to the ground only to become rubbish.

The new gym provided a multitude of activities for the public. Dance for preschool children through adult, a tumble bear program for the preschool age child which encompassed gymnastic lessons and many other activities specific for that age group, a parent and toddler program, birthday parties, cheerleading, Special Olympics gymnastic classes, karate, judo training, just-tumbling classes, slumber parties and adult gymnastics lessons with open gym held every Saturday evening as well as Sunday afternoon. These were only some of the wide selection of programs offered. Eventually team programs came into being and flourished, which included the best staff from China, Romania, and Russia, with one coach being an Olympian.

Whenever the opportunity arose, birthday parties were held for my children, as well as for my nephew and nieces. Justin and Roslyn became very involved in this facility, which helped shape them into who they are today. Eventually, the boy's team became a significant part of Justin's life, which he continued while attending Eastern Michigan. Roslyn was offered six different scholarships from six different universities for her gymnastics' ability.

Every weekend our family cleaned the gym, which took hours to complete. Keeping the gym clean was imperative: we vacuumed, mopped up any excess chalk around the equipment, sanitized the mats, shined up the mirrors as well as cleaned the dance room. The gym definitely kept us busy.

As he matured, Justin became responsible for the open gym held on Saturday evenings as well as Sunday afternoons. Roslyn helped in the pro shop, giving guidance to shoppers on purchasing the proper size gymnastic slippers and the right pieces of apparel which suited their unique body type. Definitely, Lanco Gymnastics Training Center was a family project.

Camping, hiking, swimming, tennis, sledding and any other activity which created a feeling of exploration and was fun to do, we did it. We went camping all through the year up to the end of November. Camping was definitely a passion of ours and a great way to spend time out away from technology. First, we used a big tent and eventually bought a camper. Whichever way it was done, it was so much fun!

Every evening at home when it was time to shut those eyes that did not always want to shut so easily, we read a book. Our reading time alternated between bedrooms and was time spent where we snuggled close together on the bed.

Each grandchild was given the opportunity to have a birthday party at Chuck E. Cheese, a grand and very festive environment. With radiant and happy smiles, Thelma and Lester greeted the birthday girl or boy with bags of birthday gifts all wrapped beautifully with ribbon and bows. It was a perfect place to join together, as performers dressed up as animals danced on the stage, singing festive birthday songs accompanied by an old-fashioned band. The birthday child had a chance to go on stage with the characters as they sang happy birthday and, before leaving the stage, the child received a big hug! During the entertainment, the party participants sat at a long rectangular table filled with party favors and balloons, ate pizza, soda and ice cream cake with candles glowing. It was a child's heaven. We were innocent and pure of heart, unaware of the storm clouds that were slowly building.

Hershey Park, Dorney Park, and the different water parks at Rehoboth were exciting occasions. An array of scrumptious, delightful arrangements of foods and fine delectables were brought by my mom to these parks. Most of these goodies were prepared from scratch the night before, which Lester loaded into the trunk right before leaving. Thelma always accompanied her grandchildren by herself, while Lester stayed home. She merrily drove off as Lester stood out on the driveway waving goodbye, with a few of the lucky grandchildren who managed to find an empty seat in her car, in the company of Lucas and maybe one of his friends. They were her happy passengers for that day. Later, meeting the rest of us at the amusement park, Thelma would be found waving her arms as we approached the parking lot. Her eyes sparkled with excitement just as happy to be there as we were.

The Christmas party for the women's group of the Shady Pine Church was held at our home on Donegal Springs Road every year. The ranch home burst at the seams with this festive party and continued on at their new home in Lancaster, the Roslyn Estate, which gave everyone plenty of space to enjoy each other's company.

Later in Lancaster, Thelma and Lester invited many of their friends from the church as well as outside the church to attend a formal Christmas party where everyone came, donning their best evening attire. The adults gathered together in the many different quarters of the Roslyn Estate which were exquisitely decorated just for the season. These parties gave their guests the opportunity to enjoy the interior of their home which was embellished with unique antiques, crystal chandeliers, and paintings on the walls, making the rooms come alive with color and imagery. Some of these paintings involved scenes with one or more of our family members in them, painted and signed by Mairzy, truly a work of outstanding artistry. She did not have any idea how talented she really had become.

Later, our children accompanied us to these parties and played with Lucas down in the mammoth basement. Chairs were garnished with balloons and a long table decorated with a festive table cloth, holiday cups, napkins and special party favors prepared just for them! A Christmas party!

Park City was visited often with an excited traveler by Thelma's side. At the crack of dawn, Thelma came to pick up the lucky child, and after hours of shopping, they departed for home after the sun had set and the sky turned dark, with only the light of the moon and stars. The shopping extravaganza totally petered out the grandchild but it appeared as if Thelma could have gone on for a couple more hours, bubbling with excitement as she shared information about the different bargains going on in the various department stores!

With the intention of showing the purchases that night, newly purchased items were laid out on the shopper's bed, but usually, the content shopper was found sprawled out beside them fast asleep.

One weekend before Thelma and Lester's situation became too crazy; Roslyn had the opportunity to sleep over at her grandparents' home. Roslyn was watching a Disney show in the TV room while Thelma and Lester were in the kitchen. She overheard Lucas demanding money for cigarettes from Lester. His voice increased in strength becoming very loud and threatening which terrified Roslyn, and therefore she ran upstairs to hide under Grandma's bed. She stayed put for hours as her body trembled, enveloped in an intense fear for her life as well as for her grandparents. Later, noticing Roslyn was missing, Thelma went to look for her and found her softly sobbing under the bed.

He was turning into a monster that was gaining more and more strength; his dislike and eventual hate for us and our parents took over his life.

Feeling drugged, because of accidentally ingesting one of Kay's pills. Lester sits down and puts his head in his hands, baffled, "Oh no, why is this happening again?"

Picking my parents up at their home to go to a school picnic at Lucas's Christian private school, we could see Lester was not feeling very well. During the whole function, he felt very strange and dizzy and had to sit down, putting his head in his hands. He shared with us that there were many times he took Kay's medication which somehow ended up in his vitamins, and so it happened again that afternoon. He was baffled as to how this happened yet again, not only occurring this day but many other times. At the time, I did not give it much thought, but I did find it strange that these drugs ended up in his vitamins. Looking back at this, the question is who did this and why, and how could it have been an accident? The drugs did not have little legs and jump into Lester's vitamins. Lucas was nowhere to be found at this function held at his school which we attended just for him.

One afternoon, while checking his home on Donegal Springs Road, Lester stands at the basement steps and feels pressure from a hand placed on his shoulder. Startled he loses his balance. Falling out of control down the whole flight of wooden steps to the concrete floor, he blames this fall on vertigo. Crawling back up to the top, he feels the same pressure on his shoulder which sends him catapulting back down to the hard basement floor. Confused as to what had just happened, he lay on the cement floor in bewilderment.

As he tried to piece it together later, he believed he fell down the third time and that is when he blacked out. The story goes that finally Lucas got him up, loaded him in the car and drove home. Was it an accident? We will never know but the occurrence seems very suspicious in nature. Much later in his life, Lester was given four times the amount of his medicine and went into a coma, almost dying from the overdose. Our names were removed from the list of people to notify in case of an emergency; therefore this information was discovered after he pulled through a near death experience. Lucas was responsible for administering the overdose that nearly killed him. Thelma did not want me to know how he got an overdose but, later, Lester confided in me.

These are only the incidents I found out about; were there others?

The Shady Pine Church is where many good memories were cultivated. The Sunday school class and the church service which followed were faithfully attended by this devoted family, attending every Sunday morning. The church represented a place to reach out to in times of need.

Now growing into young adulthood, my children had attended the Shady Pine Church for a good portion of their childhood. Many special events were held at the church, one being church camp. Every year we loaded up our children and attended the week long family church camp. It was here that we sang songs, created many different crafts, played all kinds of board games, had ping pong tournaments, enjoyed hiking, ice skating, sledding and attempted crazy obstacle courses. We enjoyed this camp as a family, becoming part of the different Bible classes and we ate really good food.

Lucas rarely attended this particular church but Lester and Thelma paid for a private church school called Riverview Christian Day School, so Lucas would have a Christian background and interestingly enough, he had the Bible memorized, reciting verses at whim.

Was this really Lucas or some dark evil covert energy unleashed that overtook him and/or some outside structure working through the weakened, sending out evil vibrations which keep the population unaware, fighting against each other, unable to succeed in life? Why do wars exist and terrorism? What is the motivating factor that propels these events forward to play out the evil forces? What happened to all the Jews and the horrible way they were led to their deaths? Why did that go on for so long? The questions go on and on.

Later, Clifford was added to our family, a beautiful golden setter blessed with a very out of the ordinary personality. Clifford absolutely loved to run in the fields and very early in the wee hours, we ventured out with the sky still lit by the moon, and we ran. Usually, he was kept on the leash the first half of the run but was given his freedom halfway through the run so he could soar and enjoy being a dog. Knowing he would always return to me along the forest at the top of the hill, I gave him the freedom he so loved.

During a season of our running days, red-tailed foxes were seen in the far distance, frolicking on the top of the hill along the forest where Clifford and I met at the end of our run. This hill also served as my sanctuary where hours were spent meditating during the day, alone and undisturbed, while my children were in school. The promise of hope came with the rains and beautiful rainbows. It was here on many mornings that these youngsters were seen frolicking and wrestling together, enjoying the first light of day with their mother. I considered myself very fortunate to have the opportunity to witness this phenomenon as frequently as I did. Today these youngsters were made more visible. This particular time of the morning it was pitch black and the globe of the full moon was cloaked in velvety darkness. It peered out of the hazy mist, and bathed the trees in a filmy shimmering light, making their silhouettes even more defined, and I looked on in awe and reverence at their magnificence.

Later grown red tail foxes were only seen once in awhile scurrying into the forest and as time went on, they seemed to disappear.

One early morning showing promise of a beautiful summer day, just as the sun began to peek above the horizon painting the sky with color, a skunk emerges from the tall grass. This little creature looks at her visitors with curiosity.

Clifford and I had just finished our run and were meeting, as usual, at the top of the hill along the forest where the foxes used to be seen tumbling and playing. The sun was just beginning to peek over the horizon, and I was getting ready to put Clifford's leash on to travel home across the school property. Before I could get his leash on, out of the tall grass emerged a creature of some sort. Very dark outside, it was hard to discern what exactly it was. Therefore becoming sidetracked, Clifford had his own agenda and chose not to stop to allow me to leash him, but instead became very mystified by this little animal. Curiosity got the best of him and he went up real close to sniff this now very visible skunk. The skunk turned her back, snubbing Clifford and that is when I yelled, "Clifford! Please, please come to me!" It was too late. Clifford's curiosity again outweighed any listening skills he had and this little creature seemed in no hurry to run off. She lifted her tail and did what she knew best, that is sprayed him. She sprayed him as he stood there dumbfounded, appearing clueless to what was going on. The damage was done. He got to wear a very special perfume scent. Not understanding why I did not let him come near me, he ran home alone, looking very confused as I said, "Get away, Clifford. Stay away from me!"

Clifford's kennel was connected to the garage which could be entered at his convenience using a dog hole. A cozy arrangement for sleeping was prepared for him and Wilbur during the cold winter months. A heater was set up which made the garage warm and comfortable with big fluffy beds for them to lounge on. The special skunk perfume he acquired that morning could be smelled throughout the garage, and at times a whiff was caught leaking into our home, which took a coon's age to disappear.

Both dogs loved sledding and running through the snow drifts. Their strength was put to good use and occasionally they were used to pull the sleds through the snow with a few giggling passengers. At times a little white cockapoo was lucky enough to be on board. Taking long walks in the huge drifts entertained us during the cold frosty winter days and the school hill at the tennis courts provided us a grand sledding hill.

Even the moon was beautiful. Each crater on its bright face was visible. The moon, the stars, the streaming clouds, everything glowed with its own auspicious light. Everything was perfect, at least for now.

Shadowy, ribbon-like clouds flowed around the full moon. Late into the wee hours of the night, you could find us sledding as the moon played peek-a-boo, weaving in and out of ribbons of black clouds scudding across the sky. Many times the sky opened up, offering a gift of snowflakes appearing like soft shimmering sparkles caressing our bodies. Stoked by the glistening falling snow, it was the most spectacular time of our lives. Razzle, our cute little cockapoo, accompanied us as well as Wilbur, with their snow boots, coats, and hats. These furry friends loved to chase the children up and down the frosty slippery hill as the children laughed and shouted, sliding down the hill on tubes, toboggans, and sleds. Sometimes, Razzle had the privilege of sitting on the lap of a child who allowed her to enjoy her wish of becoming a passenger. Her eyelashes glistened with frost and it looked as if she was smiling as she went down the sledding slope with her friends. Sometimes we do not realize or appreciate these very special times but adversity can create a different outlook on life and a whole different sense of appreciation. We were so blessed to have the company of the moon and this big hill within walking distance, making sledding very convenient!

At the young age of three years, Clifford made his next step. He had just been out with me for a walk, enjoying his run through the snowy landscape. He went back to his kennel to eat and decided to take a nap. When he was found later that morning, his teeth were wrapped around the wire of his metal home, because of the misfortune of a ruptured aneurysm in his brain which ultimately took his life.

That evening reclining in my bed, I felt him bound into my room and jump up on my bed. Licking my face with his ears flopping back, he had the biggest grin on his face, saying, "Thank you for such a grand time, I am so very happy." Calmness came over my being, allowing dreams to come of our times together.

Life is precious. Birds found on the road appearing as if they are dead may only be stunned. They catch my attention and if possible, we turn back to rescue them. Helpless creatures are left in my car with open windows until they get their wits back to fly off to the blue sky. Life is precious on Earth and when it is our time, we do move on to another state of being which is hard for most of us to comprehend. At the time, it was almost impossible for me to imagine, because death frightened me.

Justin was very inquisitive about the Earth and its inhabitants. His desire to explore outdoors was strong, which contributed to his happiness and his very core of being, shaping him into the young man he has become. The first thing he did on summer mornings when old enough to crawl, was to find the door and crawl outside. This is where he discovered a whole new world just waiting for him to explore. He became fascinated with sticks, rocks, stones, and many other items nature provided for play within this enchanted place called Earth. As he became older he became drawn to creating challenges, and while I was teaching at the second location of the gymnastics facility, Justin pretended to be a daredevil. He enjoyed the challenge of jumping ravines with his bicycle, and it was on one of these occasions when he was preoccupied with pretending he was a famous stunt performer, that he totaled his bicycle. One of the students who had been watching him came frantically running into the gym searching for me, shouting, "Justin just demolished his bicycle and is lying in a clump of grass because he couldn't jump a ravine."

For some reason, not being too alarmed, I gave ice to the young girl to take to him. His bike was irreparable, but his body recovered completely.

Eventually, becoming much more focused on performing gymnastics, he developed his talent in the sport and received a scholarship for gymnastics. He went on to participate on the University of Michigan men's gymnastics team. Justin excelled while attending Michigan University and received a degree in aviation and aviation management which later he pursued as his career and passion.

Later, I studied aviation and finally got my pilot's license. We flew the blue skies together, laughing as we made some really cool landings on grass runways. Life was so perfect with him.

The celebration of Halloween was full of fun with never a dull moment. The season made us giggle and laugh at the most outrageous costumes and decorations, which were fun, cute, spooky and at times just plain freaky.

Scream in the Dark is a fun-filled, scary seasonal event where people are loaded up on tractor-drawn wagons filled with crunchy soft hay. These people have paid good money to be frightened and are taken by a wagon through a farmer's field. They are entertained with all kinds of scary characters, scattered and hidden in the tall brush or found in the trees with thick gnarled branches which camouflaged many hiding phantoms and goblins in their crooks and twists. Occasionally, phantoms ran after the wagon or swung from one of the rough branches and jumped into the wagon, taking the passengers' breath away.

As the wagons progressed deeper into the woods, screams are heard throughout the dark eerie night, while the moon chuckled and gazed down with love through the branches of fiery autumn trees dressed in brilliant colors celebrating the season of fall.

Next, the second part of this ghostly event is ready to begin as eager participants wait patiently to enter a barn filled with all kinds of ghouls, goblins, eerie sounds and deep breathing.

On a cold Halloween night, laughter is heard in the frigid air as a motley crew huddles together waiting in line, enjoying the festivities of the night. Accompanying the group this evening is an elderly man, very excited to be part of the Halloween festivities. A teenage boy and his younger sister, who gazes up at her brother with the biggest blue eyes, are laughing because they just completed their ghostly wagon ride through the farmer's field and are soon ready to enter the barn of screams!

……Progressing deeper into the drama this barn has to offer, all sense of reality is forgotten. Imaginations go wild. They walk very carefully; only

the creaking of the old wooden floorboards is heard as they cautiously peer around each of the corners, their eyes luminous in the darkness.

Suddenly, a hysterical scream is heard in the night air causing panic and scrambling. Quickly running around the corner, they laugh smugly as they enter an empty open room. But to their dismay, out of nowhere a horrible ghastly creature pops into the room with unkempt dark hair flying like a rag broom being shaken. Running and tumbling on to each other, they shift their eyes, hoping to find the escape route—anxious for this barn of tortures to be finished.

Walking away from the building, an exhale of deep relief is heard. Secretly glad that this particular ordeal is over, their eyes look to the oldest member of the group who was forgotten in all of the excitement. Waiting patiently for that perfect moment and with a twinkle in his eye, he reveals from his coat pocket the wig, the ghastly creature's hair.

Wishing to add himself as a character, he had covertly taken one of his wife's old wigs at home, stuffing it into his jacket to be worn in the dark old barn.

This was only one of his many boyish tricks. When Lester was taken back home, we were so excited to share the story with Thelma, describing how facetious Lester was at the event. We never realized that our Halloween fun with him would come to a halt. He never came with us again.

During this time a very special secret was being kept, which was becoming more difficult to hide. Left unnoticed, the tiny bump which expanded under my over-sized jacket promised new life, my fourth child named Alexandra.

During my last full term pregnancy, I was very careful. For my peace of mind, an amniocentesis was scheduled to make sure the baby was okay. It was during this procedure that Alexandra's tiny hand reached for the object that was used for this exam, and the technician informed us, "Feisty healthy little girl." After being reassured, we went on a family vacation to Canada to celebrate. It was a road trip with our children and cute little cock-a-poo, Razzle. Enjoying the beautiful scenery and, of course, the majestic Niagara Falls, we walked a lot. At night, Razzle had the leisure of being put in a blanket and carefully taken up the steps to the hotel room where a very comfortable bed waited for her.

When I arrived home, I was now in the fifth month of pregnancy. Alexandra's heartbeat and vitals were checked. The heartbeat could not be found and the most horrible feeling came over me. All my dreams and expectations came to a halt for this lifeless body. They were squelched to nothing. The deepest, darkest, depression crept into my being. The bad news of her demise was given to me on a Wednesday, which meant I had to carry her for three days, knowing her lifeless body was in my womb. This knowledge tore and tugged at my whole being. I'd never realized that life could be so painful and morbid. Agonizing soulful cries came from within me, chilling the air as they vibrated unheard throughout the long lonely nights. The blue moon illuminated the tenebrous, starless sky as if the stars knowingly ensconced themselves behind dim, gray clouds.

Before Alexandra, many miscarriages came into my path of life which seemed like a never ending nightmare. Unrelenting sorrow stayed with me and I was unable to let go. On many occasions, I was detained at the hospital because of uncontrollable hysteria, which by now easily seemed to envelop me. Was this a tragedy or was I being led or pushed to make another step in a different direction?

When Alexandra came into the world, she came with a beautiful head full of thick dark brown hair, but unfortunately, the umbilical cord was wrapped around her neck, making her active body become stillborn. During this induction of labor, there was a student observing and I felt as if my life and privacy was invaded for others to learn. I tried to make myself numb to the world and its insensitivities.

New Promise—The witness

As time moved forward, the fifth child already was paving the way, becoming part of our family. Our family attended a camp for families that adopted children from India. There was an array of activities for the attendee to enjoy. Games, arts, crafts and food all unique to India were found at this camp and even the attire the children wore the last day of their stay was made in India. Camp Lotus acquainted adoptee families with the many customs of India and helped to bring a greater awareness to India's diverse culture. Many of the children were adopted at an older age, and this camp helped create a sense of belonging, so they felt special about where they came from. It honored their roots and all of India's unique traditions. Our family attended this camp for several years before our new family member arrived. This is where we discovered much of our information about The Holi festival.

The Holi festival commemorates the victory of good over evil, brought about by the burning and destruction of the demoness named Holika. This was enabled through unwavering devotion to the Hindu god of preservation, Lord Vishnu. Holi got its name as the "Festival of Colors" from Lord Krishna, a reincarnation of Lord Vishnu, who liked to play pranks on the village girls by drenching them in water and colors. The festival marks the end of winter and the abundance of the upcoming spring harvest season. Holi, the colorful festival of spring, is a time for fun and pranks. It is a festival to let your hair down and do what you like, say what you like, meet, tease and play with colors with the people around you. The festival is celebrated on the full-moon day of Phalguna in North India, while it is stretched up to a week in some parts of Northeast India, typically Manipur. According to the traditions of Holi, the people gather around on a day before the festival as we know it, which is the evening of bonfires. People light up bonfires of dead leaves, twigs and wooden sticks, dance and sing around it to welcome the spring season, commemorate the saving of Prahlad, a mythical character and the burning of his wicked aunt Holika. People take embers from this holy fire to kindle their own domestic fires. In some communities, barley seeds are roasted in the fire to eat. It is believed that the yield of the upcoming harvest season can be predicted by reading the direction of the flames or the state of the roasted barley seeds. The ashes of the Holi fire are believed to have some medicinal properties. Next morning, it is 'Dhuledi' or the main festival of colors, when adults and kids smear colored powder on each other and splash water jets known as 'pichkaris.' Traditionally, only natural colors prepared from flowers and herbal products were used. However, today, artificial colors have taken over the herbal counterparts. The color frenzy of oranges and reds, greens and blues and purples soon wash away all the enmity and hatred among folks at the festival and serves to bring the community closer.

Memories of Love

Later, my parents joined the festivities of Halloween at Rehoboth. Throughout the streets of Rehoboth and on to the creaky boardwalk, all sorts of dogs paraded in line, sporting various costumes with their proud owners by their side. The audience clapped and encouraged every cute critter of all different sizes and shapes, dressed in their elaborate or not-so-elaborate costumes. Like proud grandparents, Lester and Thelma smiled as tiny Razzle, a cute white cockapoo and her friend Wilbur;

a big black Gordon setter, walked side by side displaying their festive costumes. Memories like these are precious, created with the ones you love so dear; and we created many of them. My parents were in their eighties during these parades. Thelma and Lester invited us out to dine for special occasions such as Easter, Mother's Day, Children's Day, our birthdays and just get-together days. These outings included everyone in our family. Lucas came in the beginning when he was a young boy, but as he matured into a teenager and became a young adult it became very difficult for him to come around and join in the festivities, later avoiding us all together. Every Sunday at Rehoboth and usually after church, we joined together at the Rusty Rudder for breakfast, a grand restaurant which had the best breakfast. They offered a grand smorgasbord of fruits and vegetables with fresh omelets and eggs prepared any style, made just to your liking as you watched. Later, sitting at a very large round table which accommodated all of us, we were served plenty of coffee and any beverage our hearts desired as we engaged in hearty conversation. Lester's face beamed during these occasions, enjoying everyone together.

Chapter Seven
The Picture Window

It was not unusual to wake to the moonlight shining on my body. Playfulness was in the air, sometimes awakening me gently from a restful night's sleep. The excitement of the day's events of crab-trapping, enjoyable long walks, in-depth conversations, boat rides, water skiing and laughter coaxed me to arise with happy anticipation. This was a safe haven, a place to enjoy each other and to develop stronger relationships, a place where our children had the opportunity to play and grow together. But on this particular evening, an intense weariness came over me. Therefore, very early that evening the sound of the gentle ocean waves and the soft cool salt breeze on my face from my open window lulled me gently to sleep. The light of the full moon later lovingly visited me through my window as the most unusual vision arrived.

The night has rolled in over the beach, bringing with it a threat of a summer thunderstorm. The air is still, and heavy thick clouds blot out the stars. The once blue sky transforms into a vast expanse of jet-black. The picture window to the bay water is shown in full view and it is nighttime but unusually pitch-black. Peering out into the night with a dark wicked storm brewing, she hears only the harsh sounds of the rain pelting against the window pane. Her green eyes reflect concern as the rains raise bay waters to overflow. To her surprise, a full grown lion comes into view and as quickly as the lion appears, it vanishes. As the rain continues, the sky brightens with a flash of light from a lightning bolt, creating streaks throughout the sky. The sounds of thunder crack above ushering into view a lone graceful deer. Suddenly blackness covers all for what seems like an eternity—

A picture of the lion again comes into view, roaring powerfully while shaking its head, lit up by the bright flashes of electricity in the night sky. For a while, the night becomes pitch black as coal. Later, after a long lingering stillness, a flash of lightning and fireworks boom, again illuminating the deer but this time, it is bleating timidly. With another abrupt flash of jagged light clipped by another oppressive boom, *the Lion is exposed, which now appears to be hiding, concealed in the dark. All these pictures come in instantly, with a breath of surprise but vanish abruptly and the scene becomes very silent, giving an eerie feeling of ominous foreboding. As she peers out the picture window, her piercing green eyes become mesmerized by what seems a deep endless chasm of blackness. In suspense, she listens as the quiet rumble of thunder is heard in the distance. It seems to go on for quite some time until a loud boom is heard far away. The heavens are about to let down a deluge. The thunder seems to crack the air as if the very heavens might split apart. It rolls like the ash cloud of a volcano, becoming a rolling booming rumble. It declares to all the raw power of nature and gives fair warning of the wrath that is to come. Following, a line of red electrifying energy* ushers in the *Lion that magically materializes, not alone this time but with the deer. What she sees disturbs her greatly because the lion is clutching tightly onto the deer's neck which is distorted at an unnatural angle. Scarlet blood oozes down his jaw, as his fangs dig deep into the deer's flesh.*

Awakening with a gasp, she looks around frantically. This vision is conveying a message to her but she does not understand.

The old bay house, the home just up the street and within walking distance from the new bay home, was located in a gated community complex which was a cozy smaller home. It was where we had resided before our family expanded and outgrew it, needing a bigger place to accommodate everyone. This is when Mairzy approached the issue as tactfully as possible about Lucas's intense aggression toward her children. Lucas, the son of our older sister, was being very nasty and hateful to the other children, aggressively engaging in throwing sticks and stones at them, which made the children fearful of him. I also was apprehensive with his behavior because he wanted to take showers with my son which gave me a very uneasy feeling. There was hearsay from a secret observer of his odd meetings with boys down in the basement of my parents' home, and if true, he was definitely not somebody I wanted my son spending time with alone. Were these gatherings just a figment of an over-stimulated imagination? Rows of candles were lit in an otherwise darkened room in the basement, where various kinds of obscene activities were observed being performed while kneeling at a makeshift altar.

His mother, not knowing how to handle the situation, believed he was involved with some kind of satanic worship. My parents were also scared of him but did not want help from the outside world, so they hid. Lucas was much older than Justin, who was still a child, and I became very uneasy but needed to be careful regarding how I handled the situation. Thelma would be furious and dissociate herself from me.

This particular day Thelma just stared into space as Mairzy commenced to convey a message of concern about Lucas's aggressive nature toward her children. Thelma dissociated herself from Mairzy and the situation. Her face became void of all expression as if Mairzy was not there. It was strange and disturbing to see Mairzy's pleas ignored as if she was a ghost. Usually Thelma would be eager to talk to us but when it concerned Lucas, she put up a fence around herself which made it impossible for anyone to reach her. Once in awhile you thought you found a way over, but suddenly to your surprise found yourself outside the fence which was fortified stronger and towered higher each time.

Layton became very ill when vacationing at the old bay house and was covered head to toe with chickenpox. He looked like a burn victim with not an inch of normal-looking skin on his back. Being in such excruciating pain, it was only worsened by the weather which was sweltering hot, sticky and humid, making him even more miserable.

Common sense told us to keep the switch turned on for the air conditioner. Therefore, making sure Layton was comfortable, we left for a trip to the grocery store down the road and were gone for about an hour. Upon arrival back with groceries in hand, as we opened the front door we were struck with a wall of stifling hot air, making us feel as if we were entering a sauna. We were baffled because Mairzy made sure the air conditioning was turned on before we departed for the store; hence the house should be cool. Soon we discovered that the air conditioning was turned off while we were gone, and the heat was turned on as high as possible. At the time the only one home was Lucas.

Mairzy had a big heart but it got stomped on too many times and in due course, she took a detour, walking through life as if she had blinders on, slowly becoming oblivious to the love that waited for her. This ultimately broke my heart.

Traveling from the Poconos where she and Jackson now resided, Mairzy visited the Roslyn Estate for a few weeks. Lester and Thelma used to travel around the world, enjoying their time together and sightseeing, but when Lucas came into the world it was almost impossible to continue with their travels because Thelma had a hard time letting go of Lucas. Therefore Mairzy offered to watch over the home and Lucas so they could get away and travel together. Surprisingly, Thelma took up my sister's offer. Mairzy tended to the animals, played chauffeur, and cooked meals, making sure Lucas got to bed at a decent time. She even took on the job of removing the poison ivy which had impacted the pachysandra near the carriage house.

Knowing that she had just arrived, I went to visit her after working at Lanco Gymnastics and found her diligently working outside pulling the vile poison ivy plant out from the ground. The poison ivy was becoming very thick, spreading its deeply embedded roots and creating nasty poisonous leaves all around the carriage house. Meticulously, Mairzy removed the roots from the earth. Thrilled that Mairzy was in Lancaster, I visited her each day after finishing work at the gymnastics' facility, and long deep conversations came naturally while spending time together at the home. Wearing thick gloves for protection, she placed all the poison ivy in big white buckets to be discarded safely in garbage bags, but unfortunately, the poison that was creating roots secretly in our family was left unnoticed. We had no idea what was in store for us.

About a month later, I casually mentioned to our mom how nice it was of Mairzy to take the time out of her schedule to take care of Lucas and their animals while they were gone. Furiously Thelma replied, "No, Mairzy never played a part in our being able to go away. Mairzy did not come over to weed and clear poison Ivy from the pachysandra and no, she did not visit. Please stop talking, Ember, because you do not know what you are talking about!" An odd knowing came over me that something was terribly wrong with my mom and the thought frightened me.

Razzle

Often staying with Mom overnight to be a companion and friend, Razzle absolutely adored Thelma. When visiting my parents, she became so excited and could hardly wait to get into the home to run and greet her. They had a special bond and it shone over both of them. On occasion, if we were going to be gone for a family vacation and Razzle could not accompany us, Razzle would stay with Thelma. I noticed when Razzle came home she often became sick. I assumed that maybe she was spoilt with too many snacks and food, and she always got better in a few days. I mentioned to my Mom that just maybe she was feeding her too much because we noticed Razzle did not feel so well after her visits, I suggested fewer snacks.

On Razzle's last visit with Thelma and Lester, she assured me she was going to keep Razzle by her side. Not allowing anyone else to feed her; she would keep an eye on her. After being gone for about a week, I drove into the driveway and parked. No one came out to greet me as they usually did. Their cars were in the driveway and it seemed so strange not to see Razzle anywhere on the grounds or in the house. I searched the grounds to look for Lester who I thought might have Razzle by his side. Suddenly, I caught a glimpse of her running toward me from behind the carriage house and just knew something horrible had happened to her. It is funny how a feeling can come over you, a light bulb clicks on and with it comes a strong knowing. Realizing that she was left in the hands of someone evil, I quickly picked her up and carefully put her in the back seat to take her home.

She had to be carried up the steps into our bedroom. She was hurting so much she appeared crippled and was unable to walk for weeks. She hid under my bed, not wanting to be bothered.

What was really out of sorts that day is the absence of Thelma and Lester. Their cars were parked in the driveway. They were always eager to greet me with Razzle but I never received an explanation from them.

As the roots of evil became visibly present, I gave Thelma and Lester a call. Pleased to have both on the phone, I pleaded, "Please understand, my heart is breaking." Lester sensed the urgency in my voice and encouraged Thelma to give me the courtesy to at least listen. I went on to say, "I do not understand the hold Lucas has on you! I am concerned and believe that he is potentially dangerous. Information has been given to me that he was observed injuring and mutilating animals. He was seen torturing a cat, using a broken coke bottle to push up its anus, smiling as it screamed. How many other animals had fallen prey to him? Many animals which had perfect bodies were found on the property mutilated and they usually died. Razzle had much difficulty in walking after we brought her home. Razzle loves you, Mom, but I cannot let her come over without me. Why do you let Lucas and his wife live upstairs in our home? You encouraged us to find our own place to live, to assert our own unique independence. Lucas is allowed to stay at the home to watch us like a hawk, being hateful toward us while creating horrible dramas every time we come to visit. I do not understand. My heart cries for all the people involved. Please consider paying for a place for them away from the home so we do not have to be afraid when we come over to visit. If you choose not to listen to my suggestions, I will not be able to visit the home. It is not fair to me or my children to put ourselves in an abusive situation. Just remember, we love you and never forget it. The memories of enjoying my childhood will always be relished and will never be forgotten. I have only the highest respect for both of you but if you choose not to listen to me, please consider getting outside help and counsel. I am very concerned for your safety."

My dad replied, "Thelma, we need to pay close attention to what she is saying; can't you hear her?" She closed her ears.

Thelma and Lester love Christmas. Venturing out into the cold brisk air of winter donned with heavy coats, boots, hats and gloves, they climb into their pickup truck with a mission to find the perfect Christmas tree for their home. Visiting the tree farm, the most beautiful Douglas fir is chosen which is perfect for their home and, with a bit of help, they manage to cut the tree down. This tree is beloved for its evergreen fragrance, soft needles and dense shape— definitely, the quintessential Christmas tree. Loading it into their pickup truck, they arrive back early afternoon with the biggest tree their home can accommodate. Later that afternoon, Lester is happily standing on the ladder to receive decorations from Thelma to hang from the tallest part of the beautiful pine tree. They love Christmas and what the season brings with its many festivities and parties. Happily, they garland as a team all day long and toward late afternoon, Thelma excitedly retrieves her many beautiful shiny manger scenes. All of the figures are set out except the Baby Jesus; the nativity scene itself is left empty until Christmas Eve when Baby Jesus arrives at midnight.

Porcelain Christmas decorations, angels, magical tinsel, shiny stars and the many Santas and elves are also all carefully removed from their boxes, which she arranges throughout the home. Meanwhile, Lester is busy outside, hanging a multitude of festive lights. Their eyes shine with anticipation to see happy faces sparkle on Christmas Day. Love is in the air.

Christmas was always a very special time in our families' lives. Spending time together and enjoying the holiday season was important to us. Christmas Eve service at the Shady Pine Church was special to us because it was during this time that we sang Christmas songs while holding a candle which was lit by just one candle in the whole congregation. Everyone's candle shared the single flame of a lone candle lit in the darkened sanctuary. As all the candles began to share this one flame of light the congregation stood in unison, singing Christmas songs of Christ's love for mankind. The candle of light is represented by verses found in the Bible which have been of great significance in my life.

"Let your light so shine before men, that they may see your good works, and glorify your Father which is in heaven" (Matthew 5:16, KJV). "No man, when he hath lighted a candle, putteth it in a secret place, neither under a bushel, but on a candlestick, that they which come in may see the light" (Luke 11:33, KJV). "Ye are the light of the world. A city that is set on an hill cannot be hid" (Matthew 5:14, KJV). "Neither do men light a candle, and put it under a bushel, but on a candlestick; and it giveth light unto all that are in the house" (Matthew 5:15, KJV). "Let your light so shine before men, that they may see your good works, and glorify your Father which is in heaven" (Matthew 5:16, KJV).

The smell of Christmas is wonderfully tantalizing. As the aroma of the pine needles permeates the air, fragrant candles burn, ushering in the festive occasion. Each child's gifts are lying in a neat pile with each individual's name written on festive tags under the Christmas tree. Now it is becoming a family tradition for everyone to be involved in decorating the tree. Many handmade ornaments made by the grandchildren are proudly displayed, hanging on the tree's massive fragrant pine branches.

Merrily, the children begin to remove the wrapping paper and bows from their Christmas gifts to discover the surprise that awaits them as they sit in a circle chatting carefree. Taking turns, they open their gifts and afterwards the gifts are put in individual piles in the corner of the room to be taken home that evening. Later that evening, as they begin to gather their belongings, they realize a few of their gifts are missing—even the cards filled with money which Santa signed himself.

Lester was a good guy and desired only the best for his twins but, for lack of better words, Thelma somehow lost her love for us in that special kind of motherly way. Her love became twisted and full of holes of dark energy which snuck into her life in deep secret places, creating her own personal torture. Her love was covered by darkness; she forgot how to love.

Mairzy and I were brought together for a meeting with our father's financial planner to talk about a trust he began for us and his grandchildren. Happy about this meeting, we had no idea Thelma was against it, and never entertained thoughts that she would ever want to put a stop to it. Thelma was not at that meeting but within months brought the trust to a standstill, managing to dissolve it all. She said she had no intention of us reaping financial benefit from a trust. A form of cancer was secretly wrapping around the roots of their finances, slowly rotting them, exposing the branches which became bare and bleak.

As they enter the home, Lester is found in his favorite leather chair, sitting behind his desk finishing up some morning business. Rising with a warm smile, he greets everyone as Brandy; the English sheepdog looks on, wagging her tail excitedly. Thelma is found in the kitchen finishing the last loose ends for the feast. Working together, the girls take many different dishes of food prepared for this family gathering to the dining room. Kay is doing what she loves to do, which is making the mashed potatoes. Later everyone is called to the table and Lester gives a blessing for the food being served. As they pass the food, the conversation begins.—

"Why does she keep looking at me with those mean eyes? What did I do for her to hate me so? Is Kay in there or has an entity occupied her body that does not want me around? What makes people go crazy? Why, God, did you choose her—such a bright beautiful soul, and my sister? Will she leave forever?" Her deep green eyes flicker as she thinks quietly to herself.

The Blessing

Ten years later, after Lanco Gymnastics Training Center was founded, the blessing came. A beautiful baby girl, traveling across the ocean on a plane from India arrived with five other babies with only a smock and diaper to her name. Her name is Sakshi meaning 'witness'.

Waiting patiently for her at Dulles Airport, as the other Indian babies were being taken to their new prospective adoptive parents, my son spotted Sakshi right away. He knew it was her from a little picture and a video mailed from the orphanage in Gujarat to us. This video was viewed together quite often; we stopped it when the video came to Linnea and focused on her sweet face and tiny body. Moving the video very slowly, we watched every minute gesture of Sakshi. At first I did not believe him, but he was so certain and confident, knowing it was her. I was not yet convinced. About a week before going to Dulles, doubts and negative thoughts came into my mind. We had no idea about her parents. What if they were druggies? What kind of genetic make-up does she have? Now much older, maybe I did not have the energy to deal with a baby. But my husband reassured me that we were going in the right direction and he held firm with the vision for this tiny baby. This one particular barefooted baby was crying fiercely in the distance and, as they came closer to us, they looked at me and smiled. The caretaker outstretched her arms toward me with a precious baby girl in her hands. Graciously, I accepted the gift as her arms wrapped around my neck. Clinging to me, she snuggled her curly head into my neck and immediately stopped crying.. That mop of curly hair created Heaven on Earth and my face turned a beet red as if someone etched scarlet red magic marker on it. Having the honor, I experienced love at first sight.

Found as a newborn in the gutter of the streets in Gujarat by a kind soul, Linnea was immediately taken to an orphanage in Gujarat and acquired the Indian name, Sakshi. This is where she stayed until she was seventeen months old when she was taken to the United States to her adoptive parents.

Justin, Roslyn and I piled into the van and headed to the back seat. Sitting together on the wide back seat, we took turns holding her while Marten played chauffeur, transporting us out of Dulles parking lot and safely back home. He was such a good sport. This adoption required piles of endless paperwork from him and many phone calls in order to manifest this bundle of joy. Playing such a big part in bringing this miracle into our lives, he prepared the path, making it become a reality. Knowing the outcome would be worth all the work fueled him forward.

So proud to be our chauffeur, he departed from the airport while our new little newcomer was enjoyed by her family in the back seat of the van. First stopping at a restaurant on our way home, we had one more detour before arriving home. Seventeen months old at the time, she stared at us with the biggest brown wide eyes occasionally lifting them up to the ceiling as she ate. It appeared as if she was shy, but not when it came to eating. A big bowl of fish chowder was consumed with gusto. She shoveled the chowder into her mouth with her spoon as if she had not seen food for a long time. Later, Sakshi was taken outside to see if she could walk. She could only take a few steps, appearing rather weak.

She was adorable with her curly black hair which brought travelers from India. These hitchhikers were very difficult to get rid of. Eventually, they settled in all of our heads, making it very uncomfortable and lots of work to remove. This project took a lot of perseverance and a ton of patience, but with a fine toothed comb, it eventually became possible. Because of India's unsanitary water, a disease called giardia entered her tiny body which created her huge appetite, these little critters fed on the food she consumed and created a feeling as if she had to keep on eating to nourish her body. Giardia is a living thing that lives in, or on, another living organism. It is a parasite which can infect the bowels of both humans and animals. An infected individual will pass out the giardia in their stools. If water, food or drinks are contaminated by the infected feces, giardia can be passed on to others. Transmission is often via contaminated drinking water containing the parasite. Giardia is not killed by standard chlorination of drinking water. If there are deficiencies in water filtration, or if there is sewage contamination of water, giardial infection can be transmitted.

Eventually all this was eliminated. She became the blessing which became a gift in the suffering. We spent an enormous amount of time reading books together, but by now the other two children had other agendas on their minds. We rocked, read and sang together. She was so special because she came from Gujarat, India to become a part of our family. Sakshi means witness and she has lived up to that beautiful Indian name, demonstrating to our family what joy, peace, love and enthusiasm truly is by her life.

The camp we attended loved the Holi Festival. It was the wildest thing to watch all the children run by, covered from head to toe in all different colors of dry powder and colored water. Some of the children carried water guns and colored water-filled balloons used for their water fight. Anyone and everyone were fair game, friend or stranger, rich or poor, man or woman, children, and elders. We kept involved with this camp as a family, but now had an extra member to accompany us. As she grew into a little girl, she absolutely loved the Holi Festival and, since moving to Hawaii, still keeps in contact with some of the children that faithfully had attended the camp every year.

By now the gym had moved and was thriving in the new warehouse which we converted to a first class gymnastic school. With the anticipation of our new family member, we knew miracles were in the air. When this new family member came along, she needed a lot of my attention and eventually the gymnastic facility was sold to Roslyn's coach and it still flourishes today.

Points of Interest about India

The people of Gujarat or the Gujaratis are known as a successful business community. Some of the famous businessmen and industrialists can be seen operating hotels and motels in California, running stores in Australia and New Zealand and newspaper kiosks in England.

The women in Gujarat are rated as the third most abused by husbands and the state itself, rating the fifth highest in crimes against women with the police complicit in the crime, making money on the side or showing indifference.

Through the ages in India, women have been treated as the sole property of their father, brother or husband, not given any choice or freedom of their own. One more reason for the decline in the status of women and their freedom was that original Indians wanted to shield their women folk from the barbarous Muslim invaders. As polygamy was a norm for these invaders they picked up any women they wanted and kept them in their "harems." In order to protect them, Indian women started using 'Purdah', (a veil which covers the body) and it was due to this reason that their freedom also became affected. They were not allowed to move freely and this led to the further deterioration of their status. These problems related with women resulted in a changed public mindset and they began to consider a girl as misery and a burden who must be shielded from the eyes of intruders, needing extra care. They believed a boy child did not need such extra care and instead would be helpful as an earning hand. Thus a vicious circle started in which women were at the receiving end. All this gave rise to some new evils such as child marriage, Sati, Jauhar and restriction on girls' education

Sati: The ritual of dying on the funeral pyre of the husband is known as "Sati" or "Sahagaman." According to some of the Hindu scriptures, women dying on the funeral pyre of their husbands go straight to heaven so it's good to practice this ritual. Initially, it was not obligatory for the woman but if she practiced such a custom she was highly respected by the society. Sati was considered to be the better option than living as a widow as the plight of widows in Hindu society was even worse. Some of the scriptures like 'Medhatiti' had different views, saying that Sati is like committing suicide so it should be avoided.

Jauhar is also more or less similar to Sati but it is a mass suicide. Jauhar was prevalent in ancient Rajput societies. In this custom, wives immolated themselves while their husbands went to perform Saka. They had to face the larger army of the enemy, knowing that they would be killed since they were outnumbered. When people of the Rajput clan became sure that they were going to die at the hands of their enemy, then all the women arranged a large pyre and set themselves afire, while their husbands were used to fight the last decisive battle with the enemy, thus protecting the honor of the women and the whole clan.

Child Marriage was a norm in medieval India. They tried to get girls married at the age of 8-10. They were not allowed access to education and were trained in housework instead. Child marriage had its own share of problems such as increased birth rate, poor health of women due to repeated childbearing and high mortality rate of women and children. There was a restriction on widow remarriage.

The status of widows in medieval India was very poor. They were not treated as equals and were subjected to a lot of restrictions. They were supposed to live a pious life after their husband died and were not allowed entry into any celebration. Their presence in any good work was considered to be a bad omen. Many widows also had to have their hair shaved off as a mark of mourning and were not allowed to remarry. Any woman remarrying was looked down upon by the society.

This cruelty against widows was one of the main reasons for a large number of women committing Sati. In medieval India living as a Hindu widow was nothing short of a curse.

Purdah System~The veil or the 'Purdah' system was widely prevalent in medieval Indian society. It was used to protect the women folk from the eyes of foreign rulers who invaded India during the medieval period. But this system curtailed the freedom of women.

The girls of medieval India and especially Hindu society were not given formal education. They were given education related to household chores. But a famous Indian philosopher, 'Vatsyayana,' wrote that women were supposed to be perfect in sixty-four arts which included cooking, spinning, grinding, knowledge of medicine, recitation and much more.

The status of women in Southern India was better than in Northern India. While in Northern India there were not many women administrators, in Southern India we can find some names that made women of that time proud. Priyaketaladevi, queen of Chalukya Vikramaditya, ruled three villages. Another woman named Jakkiabbe used to rule seventy villages. In South India, women had representation in each and every field. Domingo Paes, the famous Portuguese traveler, testifies to it. He has written in his account that in Vijaynagar kingdom, women were present in each and every field. He says that women could wrestle, blow the trumpet and handle the sword with equal perfection. Nuniz, another famous traveler to the South also agrees to it and says that women were employed in writing accounts of expenses and recording the affairs of the kingdom, which shows that they were educated.

There is no evidence of any public school in northern India but according to famous historian Ibn Batuta, there were thirteen schools for girls and twenty-four for boys in Honavar.

There was one major evil present in South India of medieval time. It was the custom of Devadasis which was a custom prevalent in Southern India. In this system, girls were dedicated to temples in the name of gods and goddesses. The girls were from then onwards known as 'Devadasis' meaning servant of god. These Devadasis were supposed to live the life of celibacy. All the requirements of Devadasis were fulfilled by the grants given to the temples. In the temple, they were used to spending their time in worship of god and by singing and dancing for the god. Some kings invited temple dancers to perform at their court for the pleasure of courtiers and thus some Devadasis converted to Rajadasis (palace dancers) prevalent in some tribes of South India like the Yellamma cult. During the colonial times, social reformers started working toward the removal of the Devadasi practice on the grounds that it supported prostitution.

The status of women in modern India is a sort of a paradox. If on one hand, she is at the peak of the ladder of success, on the other hand, she is mutely suffering the violence inflicted on her by her own family members. As compared with the past, women in modern times have achieved a lot but in reality, they still have a long way to travel. Women have left the secured domain of their home and are now in the battlefield of life, fully armored with their talent. They have proven themselves. But in India, they are yet to get their due. The sex ratio of India shows that the Indian society is still prejudiced against the female. There are 917 females per thousand males in India according to the census of 2011, which is much below the world average of 990 females.

There are many problems which women in India have to go through daily. One is malnutrition. One of the major causes of malnutrition among Indian women is gender inequality. In many parts of India, especially rural India, women are the ones who eat last and least in the whole family. This means they eat whatever is left after the men folk are satiated. As a result, most of the time their food intake does not contain the nutritional value required in maintaining a healthy body. In villages, sometimes women do not get to eat a whole meal due to poverty. This nutritional deficiency has two major consequences for women: first, they become anemic and second they never achieve their full growth, which leads to an unending cycle of undergrowth as malnourished women cannot give birth to healthy children. Malnutrition results in poor female health. The women of India are prejudiced against from birth itself. They are not breastfed for long. In their desire for a son, they get pregnant as soon as possible, which decreases the nurturing period for the girl child, whereas male members get adequate care and nutrition.

Women are not given the right to free movement which means that they cannot go anywhere on their own. They have to receive permission from a male member of their family to take them along. This means that women miss visiting doctors even when they should go, which adds to their poor health. The maternal mortality rate in India is among the highest in the world. Since females are not given proper attention, this results in the malnutrition and then they are married at an early age which leads to pregnancies at a younger age when the body is not ready to bear the burden of a child. Complications can occur, which can lead to gynecological problems and become serious with time, sometimes leading to death.

In India women's education never received its due share of attention. From medieval India, women were barred from the educational field. According to medieval perception, women need only a household education and this perception of medieval India still persists in villages of India even today. Girls are supposed to fulfill domestic duties and education becomes secondary for them, whereas it is considered to be important for boys. Although the scenario in urban areas has changed a lot and women are opting for higher education, a majority of Indian populations residing in villages still live in medieval times. The people of villages consider girls to be a curse and they do not want to waste money and time on them, as they think that women should be wedded off as soon as possible.

The main reason for not sending girls to school is the poor economic conditions. Another reason is the far off location of schools. In Indian society virginity and purity is given utmost importance during marriage and people are afraid to send their female child to far off schools where male teachers teach them along with boys. The lack of education is the root cause for many other problems. An uneducated mother cannot look after her children properly because she is not aware of the deadly diseases and their cures, which leads to the poor health of children. An uneducated person does not know about hygiene. This lack of knowledge of hygiene may lead to poor health for the whole family.

In India violence against women is a common evil. Not just in remote parts, but even in cities, women bear the brunt. They are subjected to physical and mental violence. They are the ones who work the hardest but are not given their due. Every hour one woman is raped in India and every ninety-three minutes approximately one woman is burnt to death due to dowry problems. There are many laws such as The Hindu

Marriage Act of 1955, The Hindu Succession Act of 1956, The Hindu Widow Remarriage Act of 1856, The Hindu Women's Right to Property Act of 1937, The Dowry Prohibition Act of 1961, to protect women and punishment is severe but the conviction rate of crime against women is very low in India. These numbers have changed but this gives you an idea of the seriousness of this problem during our adoption. Indian women work more than men of India but their work is hardly recognized as they mainly do unskilled work. Their household chores are never counted as work; if a woman is working in a field to help her husband, it will also not be counted as work.

In India, a large percentage of women do not have power. They cannot make decisions independently, not even those related to their own lives. They have to ask permission from male members for each and every issue. They don't have any say in important household matters and not even in matters of their own marriage. The family mainly arranges the marriages in India. The scenario in villages is very bad. The girl is not consulted but is told to marry a groom whom her family has chosen for her. They are taught to abide by the whims and fancies of their husbands. Going against the wishes of a husband is considered to be a sin. In marriage, the husband always has the upper hand. The groom and his parents act as if they are obliging the girl by marrying her and in return, they demand a hefty dowry which is another serious issue in modern India. Courts are flooded with cases related to death due to dowry harassment by husband and in-laws. In ancient times women were given 'Stridhan' when they departed from the house of their parents. This amount of money was given to her as a gift which she could use on her and her children but her in-laws did not have any right to that amount. This amount was supposed to help the girl in a time of need. Slowly this tradition became obligatory and took the form of dowry. Nowadays parents have to give hefty amounts in dowry, the in-laws of their girl are not concerned whether they can afford it or not. If a girl brings a large amount of dowry she is given respect and is treated well in her new home and if she does not bring dowry according to expectations of her in-laws, then she has to suffer harassment. Due to this evil practice, many newlywed women of India lose their lives. Women were supposed to be, and in some areas of India are still, considered to be cursed by some strata of society and their birth was taken as a burden. So in past times they were killed as soon as they were born. In some of the Rajput clans newly born girl children are dropped in a large bowl of milk and killed. Today, with the help of technology, the sex of the unborn baby is determined and if it is a girl child then it is aborted. In all this procedure women do not have any say and have to do according to the wish of their husbands. Even if she does not want an abortion, she has no choice. The divorce rate in India is not so high compared to Western countries but that does not mean that marriages are more successful. The reason behind the low divorce rate is that it is looked down upon by the society. It is regarded as the sign of a failure of the marriage, especially of the woman. She is treated as if she has committed some crime by divorcing her husband.

In some communities, like Muslims, women did not have the right to divorce their husbands. They were divorced at just the pronouncement of "I divorce you" by their husband thrice and they could not do anything except to be the mute spectator. Recently Muslim Law Board has given right of divorce to women. After a divorce, women are entitled to get their "Mehr" for themselves and their children's sustenance. In Hindu society, women get maintenance for themselves and their children after divorce. Please take time if you have an interest in the women in India. These statistics were based on material written in 2011 but relevant at the time of our adoption of Linnea.

Finally, the last grandchild arrives April 10, 1998. The story goes that she was found as a newborn in a side gutter on November 27, 1996. Lying there she was very weak not making a sound but the Spirit of Love comes to fight for this precious baby's life and immediately carries her to an orphanage in Gujarat, which will be her home for the first seventeen months of her life.

Then, carried in the arms of the wind she travels fiercely across the sea with five other babies and now is ready to meet her excited family at Dulles Airport. The eyes of her adoptive mother glow a deep emerald green as the caretaker comes closer to her. The caretaker adorns a beautiful deep purple sarong. Looking into the caretaker's beautiful dark eyes, Ember opens her arms to receive Sakshi. This small baby and her mother's heart immediately connect and beat as one, which is meant to be and the connection they were waiting for. At last, it is finished.

Not allowing Thelma to bog herself down with fears of the unknown, I decided why not address it from the beginning and give her some relief? I headed straight over to my parents' home in Lancaster after leaving the restaurant. At first Thelma was out of sight but eventually appeared to see this wonderful little being.

Linnea in Monet's Garden is a unique blend of imagination and education, teaching children about the art and life of one of the most important painters of the 20th century.

Roslyn loved reading *Linnea in Monet's Garden*. The book is about Linnea's visit to Claude Monet's garden! In Paris, she gets to see many of his actual paintings and understands what it means for a painter to be called an Impressionist. This innovative art book for children contains full-color photos of many of Monet's famous paintings and a doll created just for the book which inspired her first name, Linnea! A charming tale of a little girl's love affair with Impressionist Claude Monet's paintings, she discovers the real places which served as inspiration for their favorite paintings.

Shortly after Linnea arrived from India, Thelma expressed an interest in taking care of Linnea so she could play with her. Together they could be seen outside playing many games together. I smiled, watching from a distance. She kept to her word and did so with vigor, proving her statement true. She absolutely adored Linnea.

Justin is the first to leave home to attend the University of Michigan and a few years later Roslyn follows him, accepting a full scholarship from the University of Pittsburgh.

After graduating from the University of Michigan and receiving my blessing, Justin loads up his car to travel west using his car, which he also uses for sleeping arrangements. Desiring the freedom to be able to see the beauty of places never traveled yet, he lives his dream to travel without any attachments holding him captive. After some time, Justin lands a summer job in the Grand Tetons.

Roslyn decided to visit her brother during her summer break at the University of Pittsburgh. Planting herself there for the summer she decided to work with him right through the summer at the resort lodge. It was during this time she was exhibiting confusion in her life journey and struggled significantly. With counsel from Marten and me, the painful decision was made to give up her well-earned scholarship with the University of Pittsburgh. Having no idea at that time what was to occur in her life, Roslyn eventually did a free fall, descending into a black chasm of no return and her spirit soared downward, broken, and unable to thrive. Not realizing at the time what was the cause of her collapse, we definitely knew something was not right with Roslyn.

Stopped at an intersection in his new Ferrari, a doctor by profession enjoys the heat of the morning sun. Entranced in his thoughts, he remains very unaware of a young man commencing to make a left turn on his motorcycle. Traveling forward, the Ferrari strikes forcibly into the side of the motorcycle, sending the passenger catapulting at great speed, hitting his skull on the windshield. The young boy's body eventually skids to a stop in the middle of the intersection. The doctor looks on horrified as he listens to the helmet hitting his windshield. The cracking sound of the impact of the helmet contacting the glass overcomes him with such angst that he panics at the realization that he might be responsible for snuffing out this young man's life.

Soon the screeching echo of the siren is heard in the distance. The red flashing ambulance is coming; he makes out its blurred shape through his weeping eyes as he kneels next to the lifeless body, pale and limp lying in the intersection. Suddenly burly hands pull him back into the blinding light of the ambulance and he watches as paramedics channel the young man's body onto a stretcher and carefully place him into the ambulance. He never felt so horrible in his whole life and he grieves. As the keening wail of the siren goes on and off, they head together to the emergency room.

The tone of his voice on the telephone conveyed a distinct urgency. He was in terrible trouble and immediately I purchased a plane ticket. This was a very challenging flight because the connecting flight allowed only a short amount of time to physically get to the gate. Sprinting with my bags, I pushed forward and made it just seconds before the gate was closed. Waiting for me at the gate, the attendants could see the urgency in my flushed face as beads of sweat poured from my worried forehead. After helping me onto the plane, taking care of my bags, and making sure I had plenty of water, the door was closed and off we went into the blue skies.

After arriving at Albuquerque Airport, where Justin was well known because he worked there, straightaway I was met by one of his pilot friends. I was transported to Justin's house where he was found in great distress looking very helpless. Still in shock from the impact, his body trembled and became very chilled at night--so hot that pearls of sweat beaded from his skin, drenching his sheets and mattress. It did not make any sense as to why his doctor released him from the hospital so soon. Living alone with his spirit so broken, it appeared to an outside observer a very unfeasible task for anyone to flourish in that state. Why didn't the health care providers ask him some personal questions? They would have found that his family lived in Pennsylvania and he lived alone in Albuquerque. It was difficult watching him and at times I felt powerless. However, I did know the importance of keeping him hydrated and made sure the dressings on his deep wounds were clean. With the power of touch, massage, and good food, he slowly regained his strength with patience and rest.

Time heals the weary and Justin's body gained enough energy to venture home to Pennsylvania with his companion, Charlie. The fact that Justin was on crutches did not hold us back but up we went into the blue skies and soared. Time stood still and we laughed as we traveled through promising rainbows and watched the big fluffy clouds float by, catching the sparkling rainbow dew drops in the sky. Exploring the skies, we were in awe. It was such an amazing journey connected with a special glow of love.

Later, Roslyn came to join him in Albuquerque with high hopes that being around people her age would encourage her to come out of her terrible funk. It was during this time that she took a turn for the worse. She spiraled downward, becoming catatonic.

At the bay house, Kay accompanied Marten, Linnea and me on a late afternoon stroll to the golf course. We had a mission and that was to fly a kite. This was out of the ordinary and the first time Kay spent time with me at the bay house. Lately, it was very rare to find Kay at the bay house at all. Therefore since it was such a noteworthy day and on top of that a gorgeous summer day, we went to watch Linnea fly her brand new kite. At the golf course, Marten helped Linnea set her kite free to soar as the sun played peek-a-boo behind the white fluffy cumulus clouds which floated lazily in the peacock blue sky. Performing an occasional cartwheel as her kite ascended high into the sky, happy bubbles of laughter poured out from the depth of Linnea's being. It was during this time that Kay and I had a chance to talk together. Reminiscing warmly, she recounted our many different episodes of life together. She fondly remembered how she always looked forward to spending time with her little sister. She utterly touched my heart.

Later, piling up into the van we headed to the boardwalk and when climbing in to sit down, Linnea proudly showed her Aunt Kay the charm bracelet she received from her friends. Kay smiled in acknowledgment as she held the bracelet, admiring the shining ornaments hanging from it.

The faint lingering lilac sky fades into the shadow. Soon, the shimmering sparkling stars brilliantly silhouette the darkness. A trembling gush of wind inaudibly drifts across the skyline, as the day comes to an end. The time to unwind fills the shadow-emitted sky with a pleasant silence.

After we spent many hours at the boardwalk, the sun had started to set in the midsummer sky, and we sat patiently watching its descent as the seagulls took flight for the evening. Deciding it was getting late; we piled into the van and headed back home. Just before climbing out of the van, Kay stated proudly that she had a birthday gift for Linnea, a charm bracelet which she would give to her in the morning.

A brown-eyed girl looks up at her mother. She is very distraught, having just lost her charm bracelet, not understanding where it could have gotten to. She remembered for sure she took it off in the van, placing it on a napkin while returning home from Rehoboth. Her mother assuages her, saying that it did not develop tiny legs and run off. Stubbornly, she insists that the charm bracelet was carefully laid on the brown rug in the van wrapped in a tissue.

The following day, the charm bracelet that was lost was returned wrapped in birthday paper. Kay gave Linnea back her charm bracelet as a gift. I did not deal with the situation in a positive way and became angry and hurt, not understanding how someone could be capable of being so cruel to deceive an eight-year-old girl. My ego got in the way, crippling me. Therefore incapable of handling the situation, I became blinded by judgment. Confused and hurt, Kay was not included in any of our family activities that day or the rest of my stay at Rehoboth. It was unusual for Kay to come to Rehoboth to spend time with me, and it became the last time we had to enjoy each other. I was a fool blinded by my own attachments. So hurt, I became very impetuous in dealing with the bracelet. Kay absolutely denied the fact that the charm bracelet was the bracelet Linnea had on the day before, saying she bought it at Macy's.

The situation pushed all of my buttons and I reacted recklessly. Many live in this world oblivious to the suffering of others, wearing blinders, unable to find their hearts in consciousness. Aunt Ida fervently prayed with Kay asking for divine intervention. Was God listening or was he smiling gently, saying there was a bigger lesson in all this which was way beyond our comprehension at that moment in time?

The Wildest Ride

One sunny summer afternoon, my father had just invited me to go out water skiing, and, running on his suggestion, I grabbed at the opportunity to spend time with him—

Out across the bay waters toward the cooler ocean waters, the boat named Thelma Jane comes to a standstill. A lone passenger sits on the edge of her father's boat, her back to the hot noon sun rays and her feet dangling in the cooler summer waters. She kicks lazily at the swelling waves until they fall below her toes again. She prepares her body for the idea of skiing. It would be something to do and would be fun, a break from the sweltering heat. Her head felt hot, the heat sinking into her brown hair. She slides to her side and dangles her arm down to catch the briny water with her fingertips. The side of the boat is uncomfortably warm and so she sits. This far out, the waves have no white crest, no foam spray; instead, they roll in as if lazy arcs like the back of a giant cobra. She gets abruptly to her feet and without calling out a warning to her dad, she dives right in. The sultry air is immediately replaced with the cool water of the ocean. Soon her lungs clamor for air and she kicks for the top, quite unaware that the boat has moved... The rope used for skiing is thrown to her and, feeling quite lucky, her fingers catch the end of the handle. Nodding to the captain, off they go for the wildest ride ever on skis. She skims over the water with her two skis snuggly secure on her feet. Time stands still as she glides on top of the shiny crystalline ocean waters, creating such a feeling of ecstasy. Looking up into the sky, she sees seagulls above her, darting to and fro, following her, looking for a possible snack.

Later, veering around one of the marina poles, she realizes the corner is taken way too sharp by the captain, she has no choice other than letting go of the ski handle, preventing the ski rope from wrapping around the pole like a yo-yo. Letting go, she sails across the cool waters and then slowly sinks into the deep waters of the bay, disappointed her fun has ended so abruptly. But very shortly, Lester makes the biggest u-turn and heads back to pick her up, skimming right beside her. Being the Captain, with a grin and a sparkle in his sea blue eyes, he implores kiddingly, "Why did you let go, didn't the Captain do his job?" and they both laugh at his silly steering and funny voice.

With her green eyes in deep thought, she made up her mind that a change was desperately needed in her life. But before making that huge step, she would bring her parents to the place that would eventually be her home. She'd let her parents know that she would be just fine, and also have an understanding as to where their daughter would probably land for some time in her life. Little did they know that her passion for writing would be found at this new home or that she would be helping her daughter recover from such a horrible traumatic brain injury. Her parents are very excited to join her on her voyage, where they will be shown the place she fondly calls the 'coffee shack'.

Lester and Thelma are helped to board the plane from Harrisburg and given assistance on the connecting flights. Finally, after the long journey, they arrive at their destination. Immediately upon landing, they retrieve their luggage and head to a very quaint town by taxi. Continuing up a long curvy rough road filled with potholes, they happily arrive at their destination. Exhausted from their travels Thelma and Lester are later taken to the inn for accommodations, where prior provisions have been made and immediately fall in love with this clean very comfortable rustic place at the bottom of the hill.

Thelma and Lester, being spunky people in their late eighties, arise early and hearing the rooster's crow are ready for a new day. Heading down the hill to pick his grandparents up from the inn, Justin brings them back up the hill to have breakfast. Marten is found preparing fine delectables in the kitchen and freshly brewed coffee is waiting for them. There is a hum of excitement in the air for the day, surely a great day to be alive as they laugh together. Even the size of this home is easily overlooked because a magnificent energy of love radiates from within, extending far beyond the five acres of this sacred space.

The next day, Lester and Thelma walk the property with their daughter, enjoying the fresh fragrance of the various fruit trees. The trees are now bearing luscious fruit along the edge of the property. Lilikoi, starfruit, oranges, lemons and bananas are only a few.

Other fruits of Hawaii, some of them found on our property are: 1. Rambutan, also known as lychee. This sweet fruit comes in many shapes and colors with the most recognizable being round, covered in soft hair-like spikes being bright scarlet in color. While seemingly uninviting, the inside offers a sweet and subtle white flesh, reminiscent of grapes or cantaloupe. 2. Egg fruit, not exactly shaped like an egg, this fruit's texture is exactly that of a hard-boiled egg yolk which has a sweet and savory meat, smooth and creamy with a slight crumble. It is deemed the "pumpkin pie" fruit. The taste resembles both that seasonal dessert as well as sweet potatoes. 3. Pitaya "dragon fruit" This otherworldly fruit looks as though it has just been lit on fire with hot pink and green flames which lick up around the sides, giving it its mythical nickname of Dragon Fruit. The inside, even more baffling, is a transparent white gel-like meat like a kiwi freckled with tiny seeds. The taste is something between a tangy pear and a melon. 4. Poha berry peppers are found along the lush green trails in the mountains of Kaua. Poha comes pre-wrapped in their whimsical paper lantern-looking shell like a tomato. The berries contain numerous small seeds. Ripe poha characteristically have a mildly tart flavor, making it ideal for fruit salads, jam or homemade pies. 5. Papaya, a better-known fruit, is usually enjoyed sliced in half, hollowed and sprinkled with lime. This tasty melon-like fruit grows all around the island and can be found throughout the year. 6. Strawberry guavas are a sweet and refreshing treat after a long hike. They are considered a mix between the two flavors: strawberry and guava. As the name implies these dainty fruits are filled with crunchy seeds and tart, mouthwatering insides—bright orange, round berries that resemble cherry tomatoes. 7. Star fruit is a bright yellow fruit having a waxy exterior and a sweet, pear-like interior. You can eat the whole thing, skin and all and when sliced in half you'll find out exactly why the fruit has earned its out-of-this-world name 8. The cherimoya has been known to taste like the perfect mix of banana, strawberry and pear. An oddly shaped fruit, it almost appears as though it were a melon and artichoke hybrid. 9. Breadfruit has a name which is derived from the texture of the cooked fruit, having a potato-like flavor, similar to freshly baked bread. Locals substitute the fruit for bread, creating new fun dishes like breadfruit pizza or even nachos! "Ancestors of the Polynesians found the trees growing in the northwest New Guinea area around 3,500 years ago. 10. Also growing in popularity is the passion fruit found growing wild. This fragrant fruit is "round to oval, either yellow or dark purple at maturity, with a soft to firm, juicy interior filled with numerous seeds. The fruit is both eaten and juiced. Passion fruit juice is often added to other fruit juices to enhance the aroma.

Having so much fun together during their stay in Hawaii, they check out the coffee plantations, joining a tour explaining how coffee is made from the berries of the coffee trees. They also visit many beaches, dine at numerous restaurants, and of course visit the famous volcanoes.

Little did I know what was brewing on the horizon. It is amazing what the human soul/body can endure in the name of love. Suffering seemed to become a very familiar but unwelcome friend of mine, which forced me to find a deeper understanding of the possibilities and strength of my own body-soul connection, pushing me to limits that I did not know were possible.

Eventually, our family occasions were halted by Lucas, because of his jealous rampages and anger toward our close relationship with my parents. Becoming older he gained strength, his power increased, and my parents secretly became afraid of him. Dramas were devised to make it as uncomfortable for everyone as possible. At first, it was little things, but as time went on, the energy got scarier and weirder, building like a snowball rolling down a steep hill increasing in size, becoming so big it appeared immovable. Some of the little things that happened at first were quite subtle, such as: the grill being secretly turned off for family picnics, the air conditioning turned off at the bay house, Christmas gifts disappearing, as well as money from our purses. Parked out in the driveway our cars became marked or scratched, pets were found dead mysteriously or maimed for life. Computers suddenly stopped working and Mairzy and I were blamed for it, even though we never touched the computer. The lights suddenly went off in the whole house while having a family get-together. This became an all too familiar theme and the list is long. At the end of all the horrible mishaps, magically Mr. Fix It would be the savior, the one who magically fixed the problem. If you needed anything fixed, all you had to do was call on his name, Mr. Fix It, and he was there just like Superman!

Every Father's day, the guys religiously attended a Father's Day dinner celebration held at the Shady Pine Church. On this special occasion, Lester and Lucas usually arrived together in one car. But as the years went by, the celebration they had together came to a halt because Lucas no longer desired to be part of the celebration. When receiving the phone call from Thelma about the event being canceled, I asked, "Why? Why should this social event be ended because one person does not want to attend? Dad always enjoys this so much; why take it from him? This does not make sense to keep them from enjoying this special family tradition." Thelma became irate.

That same evening, Thelma fell or was she pushed because she confronted Lucas? Or was the energy from my anger somehow responsible for her fall? She was immobilized for two months with a broken hip.

A dark sinister energy of evil was in the background doing its sweltering work, helping to stir the cauldron, and placing its hateful spell upon the innocent, squelching the love shared during this beautiful celebration between Lester, his sons-in-law, and grandsons.

One beautiful sunny Christmas day, as usual we were invited over for a Christmas celebration and had just arrived to find Thelma very bothered and worried. She was very frustrated about not being able to locate her ornaments which were gifts from past Christmases. "They have been tucked away in a special drawer designated just for the ornaments you bought me, Ember," she said in a worried voice. "The ornaments are missing and I cannot imagine what happened to them?" Having a good hunch what happened to my gifts, I stayed silent. My attention was immediately diverted to Kay, who seemed to want to engage in a conversation with me. This is unusual for Kay and, wanting to take advantage of her friendly mood, I was truly in high spirits to be able to spend time with her during this Christmas, and I listened attentively to her. But suddenly, doing a total 180 in a shrill voice, Kay began to quiz me as to the whereabouts of her pocketbook. Not giving me any time to respond, she began to accuse me viciously of confiscating it. A feeling came over me that I was in some kind of crazy house. Knowing that it was imperative to stay calm so her fury did not escalate, I reassured her that her pocketbook must be close by and certainly did not run off with tiny legs. "We will find it, no need to be upset and please remember our family just arrived," I said, "so it really was not physically possible for any of us to have taken it, even if we wanted to." This comment did not convince her or assuage her anger.

Later, everyone, as well as the children, was being accused viciously, singled out individually and called horrible names. When she started to attack Linnea, the youngest child, we escorted everyone out of the house and loaded the children into one of the cars, gave them money for food and had the oldest cousin drive them away from the vicinity. The situation was just escalating and anything could happen at this point. Mairzy and I stayed until the energy simmered down because we were concerned for our parents' emotional well-being and safety. It was just horrible to say this was my family. The pain pierced and tugged at my heart. The situation was wicked. The children's excitement for Christmas and innocent expectation of magic was totally ruined, making everything go ugly. I recalled the Sunday school song:

This little light of mine
I'm going to let it shine
Oh, this little light of mine
I'm going to let it shine
This little light of mine
I'm going to let it shine
Let it shine, all the time, let it shine
Don't let Satan [blow] it out!
I'm going to let it shine
Don't let Satan [blow] it out!
I'm going to let it shine
Don't let Satan [blow] it out! I'm going to let it shine
Let it shine, all the time, let it shine

Satan won; he blew the light from Christmas that sad and sorrowful day. They never did unwrap and open their Christmas gifts or enjoy our traditional Christmas dinner.

After the grandchildren left the home, Layton did a bit of detective work, hanging out in the vicinity of the location of his grandparent's home. During the early evening, he watched as Kay got into her car, and travelling only a short distance, parked her car around the block. This is where she was seen meeting Lucas, who handed her an unspecified medium-sized object wrapped in a blanket which was immediately put in her car. He watched unnoticed and in luck, because Lucas now walked off with Kay, leaving her parked car along the curb unoccupied. Waiting until they were out of sight and careful not to be seen, he walked up to Kay's car and shone his flashlight into the car revealing what he thought might be the lost pocketbook. A pocket book was located on the back seat barely visible; peeking out from what appeared a light cloth of some sort. Was this the lost pocketbook? Either Lucas gave Kay her pocketbook or maybe Kay had it all along, just misplacing it. There was always that possibility that maybe she had known from the beginning of the saga the whereabouts of her pocketbook. What a crazy mess and drama for what should have been a happy time shared with those you love. Was there a conspiracy between them? This began to become a common occurrence for each holiday.

Later we were informed that Lucas did find the lost pocketbook late Christmas evening. He fixed the problem of the walking pocket book, the true savior of our family

As the years go on, she questions as to whether anything of value should be given to her parents for Christmas. Very special expensive glass tree ornaments are all missing which Thelma had lovingly placed in a special spot waiting for the next Christmas. The tree becomes barren of any of the gifts which were so carefully picked out for her mother. They were gone and her dark green eyes become frustrated, not knowing what to do.

Christmas was a time to carol and to spread good cheer for a motley group of friends who gather together every year, consisting of all ages. Finally, after walking what seems for quite a while on the snow-covered streets, they arrive at their first destination all bundled up in sweaters, scarves, coats, and boots. Welcomed at the door with smiles, they are invited out of the cold and given a place for all their cold weather clothing.

Now ready with sincere focus after tuning their instruments, they line up to perform and, holding saxophones, flutes, trumpets and violins, begin to play. The residents' faces explode with happiness as the melodious music vibrates throughout their hallways. Afterwards, enlivened by the music the residents begin to chatter happily, enjoying the festivities of Christmas with hot apple cider, nuts and cookies, remembering bits and pieces of their lives which had been forgotten from long ago. These memories make them come alive inside and their hearts open, setting their spirits free at least for awhile, connecting with their own unique light.

Invited back to perform next year, this group of musicians believes wholeheartedly that Christmas represents, 'Peace on Earth and Joy to Men.'

The next visit is the 'The Roslyn Estate.' Lining up on the beautiful carved wooden balcony of this home and with a one two three, making sure they are all in pitch, they begin their warm up. The notes reverberate throughout the home as they prepare to perform a Christmas concert. Bubbling and oozing with Christmas cheer, the one participant at this event looks down from the balcony to see her parents grinning from ear to ear, making it all the more worthwhile. Excited to have the music brought to their home, they have the opportunity to hear their grandson play his saxophone, making bold, clear notes as his sister plays her violin beside him, warming their hearts. With her finespun eyelashes glistening with Christmas magic and her bright green eyes glowing, Ember sits down at the piano, bringing the room to life with harmony as all her friends join in with a multitude of instruments making a mighty orchestra, and creating a dream come true for this elderly couple who are singing along melodiously with the group as they perform. It is a perfect winter day, cold outside but warm and full of love inside. Later, as everyone is bubbling with good cheer, Thelma serves cookies and hot chocolate while they congregate together in the dining room and kitchen. Bustling with excitement, they enjoy each other's company by sharing old stories from long ago.

As the seasons cycled and years passed, they have not been welcomed anymore and when this group enters the driveway reluctantly, Lester locks the doors, eventually letting them in but telling them not to come back ever again. Along the driveway, the trees bow their heads in mourning as the cars depart one by one never to return again. Pools of salty tears flow from deep sea- green eyes.

Lucas did not want us to perform at the home and therefore his wish was granted.

For years Lucas hid when we visited my parents. Searching for him, we retrieved him and encouraged him to be part of the festive occasion. He remained for a while, but an excuse was always found to leave and later, as he became older, he found a place to hide or left the home, avoiding us altogether. One evening as I took a picture of Lucas, he just went berserk and ran from me as Thelma and Lester encouraged him to come back so Aunt Ember could get a picture of him.

Later our time at the home became even more difficult because his behavior became very aggressive and in the final few years, he made it a point to be around, making it very difficult, if not impossible for us to have an enjoyable time with my parents. Eventually, we were locked out of our parents' home. But I think what was most disheartening, was the final year when he planted himself next to his grandparents and stared at us with frigid eyes, two merciless pools of caldron-black, while we had a conversation together, making it literally impossible to enjoy one another. He was focused on ruining any kind of communication between Lester and Thelma and their daughters, absolutely not wanting us around at all.

Love is a pond full with water lilies, wedding chimes in the distant, a whisper in the night and tender steps in a home, a couple of fireflies in the total darkness and sacrifice against all common sense.

Grace and compassion for my parents became important ingredients and aided the establishment of a greater love, growing deeper than thought possible. An understanding and awareness were developed over time that these people were doing their best with what they knew how—the many filters developed in their ways of coping with the world, distorting their vision.

Farmed out at the mere age of nine, Lester worked on various farms and in return received board and meals. Not one time in his childhood did he get to go home, not even for special occasions or holidays. He longed to be like other boys and girls who were included in the festivities of each year and to just be a child. If only they could see his suffering or did they really care? Christmas was one of the hardest holidays for Lester. His eyes glistened with tears as he witnessed from afar the family he worked for exchange and open up their gifts.

Stories about his job of cleaning the stalls of the animals on this farm were abundant and his eyes lit up as he remembered back to when he was ten years old. —"One brisk cold winter morning, I had gone out to clean the stalls of the barn animals. It was late afternoon and tiredness was creeping into my body because of being up since dawn and I was wearily looking forward to finishing my last task, the mule's stall..."

Beams of sunshine are streaming in the open window of the stall as sounds of belabored breathing are heard from inside. In the barn is a young boy cleaning out the stall with a pitchfork. He stops looking at the open window and, leaning on his pitchfork, he thinks. Being away from home seems so odd to him and he still does not understand why staying with his family was not an option. Jostled from his thinking by the sounds of the animals in the barn, there is no time to think and feel abandoned as yet.

Not lingering lest he get into trouble, he quickly wipes away the sweat of his brow and, in the mule's stall, starts to pile up the manure in a mound, which would be used later for fertilizer.

This feisty mule is not used to someone standing right behind him and decides to buck. Kicking at a very inopportune moment, he lands his hoofs right into the young boy's stomach knocking the wind right out of him. He is thrown onto his back into the pile of manure, and the lights dim, flickering out for awhile. Later, he wakes up very startled not knowing exactly what happened and why he is lying in manure. As his wits slowly come back to him, he realizes that he has been lying there for hours because the sun has now set and the barn is dark. Groggily, he slowly pushes himself up from the manure and hobbles to the old farmhouse where the moon hangs smoky and yellow behind thin scudding clouds. It has no brilliance to offer him in his excruciating pain. His only desire is to find a little help and comfort.

Admonished for being gone so long, he slowly gets ready for bed to get a good night's sleep so that he is well rested for tomorrow's long list of chores. The next morning, rising before the sun comes out to play; he looks forward to finding breakfast before his daily chores.

A soft smile enveloped his face when telling this story. He said, "It was a hard way to learn a lesson." Never stand behind a horse, donkey, mule or any large four-legged creature, because you never know when they will kick!" Lester's father became ill during the flu outbreak. Lester was three years old at the time of his death. His grandpa, I was told, prepared a hefty amount of money for my dad set up as a trust which he received when he was a lot older. His grandfather stayed in the background of his life, never having a lot of physical contact with him. The fact that he was given to a farmer, where he was expected to perform chores in exchange for a bed at the farmhouse, gave me a whole different respect for my father. His tales of his life living on the farm and how he coped still keeps a captive audience.

When reaching his middle teenage years, just before becoming a young adult, Lester does run away. Leaving secretly, he entertains himself by hitching rides on trains, exploring the world while playing a banjo. (Even at the age of 99 he still enjoys the sound of trains). Tales of adventures that he experienced while growing up, about his daredevil days of jumping trains as a stowaway, and being a member of a band can easily hold a captive audience. He loves to talk about how he followed

Frank Sinatra, who was born in Hoboken, New Jersey, on December 12, 1915. Frank Sinatra rose to fame singing big band numbers and Lester had the opportunity to watch the women cry when they heard Frank sing. He said that even the men cried. "People became crazy." He laughed when he recalled watching one young man jump through a window head first because of being so thrilled to be able to listen to Frank sing. Unfortunately for the enthusiastic young man, the window was shut and he shattered the window pane, but lucky for him he acquired only a few bruises. Lester laughed fondly as he recalled this guy's befuddlement as to who closed the window. Such a funny picture of how people can be so impulsive!

Of course, since he loves to eat, the good food prepared by the women on Sundays at the farm is still a focus of many of his conversations. My dad went through changes and metamorphosed into a kind, gentle being, becoming much softer in his ways.

As the sun just begins to peek out from the horizon, a glow shines upon the Earth, softly waking slumbering beings from a deep sleep, warming their hearts, and impregnating the day with a multitude of possibilities. This particular morning a young girl is working hard in the kitchen to help prepare breakfast for her brothers and sisters. She has taken much of the responsibility in caring for her siblings because her mom's energy is being zapped by slow-spreading cancer in her pelvic area. Thelma massages her mother's aching back, alleviating the pain caused by the ruthless disease which has one mission, to take her mother's life. Assuming the responsibility for most of the daily household chores, it is a very difficult time for her and she can be heard crying sorrowfully at times throughout the cold night, not wanting to ever lose her precious mother.

But this morning at the sound of the bell, a motley group of children run to the rectangular wooden table where breakfast is being served. Sitting down, her mother has a renewed eagerness for the fresh new day with high hopes and expectations; she lifts her eyes up in gratitude at each of her beautiful children.

The school Lester and Thelma knew was not at all like the school I had the opportunity to attend. Instead, their school was surrounded by farmland in the country, called the one-room school house. This school included all the different ages in one classroom, where only one teacher was assigned. It was a time where your education was often regarded by your family as secondary to helping out on the farmstead. There was no electricity or plumbing, so the drinking water had to be brought from a neighboring farm. The washroom was a hole in the ground in a shed across the schoolyard. A classroom contained students of all ages, with brothers, sisters, and cousins. Classes were taught year after year by the same teacher. Definitely different from the modern school world of today, but as recently as fifty years ago it was the reality of the rural pioneer education system, which was so dependent upon the one-room schoolhouse.

When Thelma's mother was getting ready to graduate, Lester, Thelma and one other male friend supported her in making that next step in life, a very important gala in one's life and not to be ignored or hidden. The last half hour of her life on Earth, she appeared so present and kept on mentioning how beautiful her son was dressed in a white robe.

Passing on at a very young age in his life on Earth, he explained to her that he was waiting to take her with him through the tunnel of light. The last hour the bedroom became very dark, except for a bright beam of light which gradually grew larger and eventually so far-reaching, the light illuminated all around my grandma. As the light surrounded her body, her face glowed and with her last breath she exclaimed, "Isn't he so beautiful!" and then she was gone. This story was retold to me many years later by another male person present with her in the bedroom. He wanted to let me know how special my grandma's passing had been to those few who stayed with her that evening, and that her passing was definitely a testimony of the reality of the spiritual world. They kept on looking around to see how the light was coming in through all the blinds but this was not light from our physical world. It was coming from another plane of existence.

Thelma's biological father passed away while I attended college. She was silent about her father but slowly bits and pieces of information trickled in about him. One piece was that he loved his booze and left his family because of other women. Portraying her father as a lousy cheating bastard, absent from their household because he had more interest in booze and other women, she chose to have no contact with him. At least that is what I was told. But when my sister and I arrived from the hospital, after our few days' entry to our Earth home, my mom informed me that my grandpa wanted to see us in the worst way. Stopping in for a visit uninvited, he requested permission to see the babies. Thelma confided that he looked at us with amazement and said, "Wow, two perfect beautiful baby girls." He could not stop gawking at us. This story was shared with me a couple times and one of those times was when I was hanging out at my favorite place, the basement of our home on Donegal Springs Road becoming a famous danseuse.

Most of my relatives dressed in plainclothes, usually in solid, normally dark colors. The women wore white bonnets and the men wore dark plain clothing and worshiped in simple structures.

They had a utilitarian view of technology, similar to the precautionary principle of technology in that unknowns should be avoided, but the emphasis was on the results in the eyes of God. If they were unsure of how God would look upon a technology, the leaders of the church would determine whether it was to be avoided or not. The degree to which this principle was supported varied among the congregations.

We piled up in our black car and traveled the country roads to visit my grandma's old farm home for a social event. This is where my many relatives congregated and socialized together for dinner. The door designated for entering this old farm house led directly to the kitchen, where women were found working busily in the quaint old fashioned kitchen preparing food together. A few would be doing the finishing touches to the huge long table. The scene was recollected in my young mind and I still remember the wonderful smells permeating the air and vibrant shades of blue in this kitchen. The sounds of many happy conversations in the kitchen are vague and hazy. As I watched my grandma work, I became fascinated with her attire. She wore a head covering and dressed in old brethren attire, with a simple dark colored dress that appeared to have an apron attached to it. A long wooden rectangular table was used for dining, set meticulously by the young children who were guided by the older women. These people were pleasant of nature and appeared hard workers. Many were step and half brothers and sisters of my father, whom I really never got to know personally. There was one full-blooded sister on Lester's side: Aunt Ida, a kind woman full of love and faith in her heart, enabling me to trust and relax in her company.

The children at this social event often ventured out to the barn to gather eggs from the roosting boxes. Walking gaily on the dusty path to the barn, my step grandpa could be heard bellowing in the background. His nerves became a bit frazzled with all the children's energy and even as we gathered eggs, we heard his shouting in the far off distance, "Please don't let those darn kids go out into the barn!" I could only imagine him running down the dusty lane waving his cane at us, which created a somewhat comical image in my mind, allowing my fears to dissipate. I learned at a very young age that humor changes energy.

Grandma took care of us at the big old country farmhouse which was horribly boring. After being dropped off by our parents, immediately we were given a piece of paper with a list of chores to complete before dusk. Dusting, sweeping the porch and the tedious job of pulling weeds lasted into the early evening. Finally, dinner time came and we had the privilege of watching Grandpa eat corn on the cob. First, using a very sharp knife to cut off the kernels from the cob, he proceeded to carefully line all the kernels in a row on a dull knife, slowly and deliberately arranging them to his liking. The conversation was very minimal at dinner or maybe it was because shyness came over me, not allowing me the opportunity to really get to know them. He seemed so proud that he could line up the corn kernels and then proceeded to lift the knife to his mouth without dropping a kernel. He looked at us and said, "Why are you staring? Didn't you ever see someone eat their corn off of a knife before?"

After her husband passed to better pastures, she moved to a smaller apartment and our visits became more frequent but increasingly brief. I usually walked outside to explore, or meandered to the basement to look at the coal stove which heated Grandma's tiny apartment. Staring into the hot embers, my imagination became vivid and stories of in-depth fantasies came alive. However, it seemed these fantasies were never completed because Lester appeared anxious to leave, keeping our visits brief.

On occasion, we gathered together with a bunch of people at a park who were all sitting under a huge pavilion. Somehow, I was related to these people but exactly how confused me, not making any sense in my brain. Not close to them on a personal level, unlike my friendship with our neighbors, the Kentin family, these meetings became dull and colorless. There were all kinds of games, relays and water games for the children which I participated in because of feeling obligated to at least try to fit in. Most of the people at this social event donned bonnets, old fashioned dresses and black tie up shoes, being very nice, happy people.

On several occasions Grandma came to visit our home and took care of me and my twin sister for the evening. She combed our hair and put curlers in it, so when we took them out the next morning our hair had extremely tight ringlets which I absolutely abhorred. Embarrassed to go to school looking so different, I begged my mom to allow me to take the curls out. They made me look like Shirley Temple, except that my ringlets were twice as tight. She never verbally gave me permission to take the curls out, but she never said to keep them in either. So as soon as the bus dropped me off in front of the school, I dashed to the lavatory and proceeded to wet and comb my hair. Usually I was successful in removing the tightness of the so-carefully-wrapped spirals.

On Thelma's side of the family, her sister, Aunt Mae, was the most important person in my life, being very modern in her ways. I loved Aunt Mae. She had a genuine love for me which radiated out from her, and unlike the other relatives she dressed very fashionably. Dancing and laughing with a bright twinkle in her eye, she charmed me with her cheerfulness. Later she visited my gymnastic facility even though she was going blind. Nevertheless her desire and love was stronger, outweighing her disability.

Seeing her one last time, we hugged goodbye and shortly after that visit she passed. Information on her passing was not shared with me until later. Therefore I was absent from her funeral. There are no boundaries with love; in death we are not parted. Touch, human touch, that is, was not something that was familiar to me. When Thelma drove and Aunt Mae sat in the back seat with me, she would have me lay my head on her lap. As she softly stroked my hair away from my temples, I absolutely loved the feel of her touch and would put my hair back over my face so that she would repeat her stroking. I simply adored Aunt Mae and her soft energy of love.

Love is Eternal

I can never get her back again in her human body, but her spirit lives on. She is everywhere and her spirit is set free—the spirit she showed me later in a magnificent display of power! Love is strong. I only knew the meanings of these visions after the event occurred, not ever knowing if I could have done anything to prevent the horrible disaster that was brewing in the darkness.

Sometimes we do not want to consider that it is impossible for another person to have the same love to reciprocate. It is like expecting a cripple or someone with no legs to walk and then judging them for not being able to. At times, we make excuses for the other people we love in our lives or feel for them the terrible loss of love that they cannot experience and the devastation caused on other hearts and relationships. We take it into our own bodies, which can only create sickness for ourselves and does not serve anyone. You cannot take material things with you. Ultimately without love, they are useless and greed can set in, ruining relationships, putting what is important in life out of perspective and damaging the outcome and quality of life. Greed can branch out to the extent of not wanting others to flourish on their own, which is exactly what my mom did. She did not want nor could not fathom the idea that Mairzy or I would get any of her money and definitely not an inheritance to enjoy. She did not always feel that way. Her thinking became warped because of sickness and depression; therefore it is not for me to judge.

She wanted us to remember how they had a lot of money and how we got to benefit from it while they were alive but not to personally have anything when they were gone. It was a sickness that overtook her.

Lester was setting up a trust for us but when Thelma got wind of it, she put a stop to it. She made sure we would not have anything, which ultimately included her. In her own sick distorted mind, she allowed her stalker to take her money so that there would be none for anyone else. She needed help but did not know that help was out there for her in her sickness. If she was well, she would never have wanted to be what she became and not in her deepest dreams would she have imagined what her life was to become. Her disappointment and confusion with my older sister's illness, and her attempt to cover up the sickness of Lucas, made her all the more susceptible to allowing stubbornness and denial to take control of her life. She was not given the opportunity to express the lower form emotions that she was experiencing to a close friend who could have been used as her sounding board. Just maybe she could have observed how horrible she sounded and would have had a better chance of turning from her course of destruction. Grief, guilt, and betrayal were a few of the lower form emotions that needed to be expressed and released. They were sapping the very life from her.

It takes a special person to be a sounding board and allow a friend to express her deepest, darkest thoughts without judgment. Friends are like rare gemstones shining their light on the darkness.

There were so many clues that something was wreaking havoc with Thelma's mind. It became obvious simply through her responses to us, and this energy ate at her for years and progressively worsened as she became older, finally devouring all of her. My dad told me when I was a young teenage girl that Mother was not well, and he saw her only getting worse as time went on. I did not understand what he meant by this statement, not having any concept of the depth of her sickness. The stress of trying to raise a child like Lucas just took her further down the rabbit hole. She appeared as if she was getting better, but this responsibility was too much for her. Lucas was in desperate need of very expert medical help and should never have been living with elderly people.

When Lucas was a young child, he purposely fell off the playground swing. At first, we thought we pushed him too hard, but realized later that only his back had to be touched and down he fell to the ground below. Arriving home, he cried to Thelma and Lester as to how he was hurt because of being pushed off the swing at the park, receiving their full attention. On occasion, every lamp in the home was secretly overturned when he was left in our care. This scene was upstaged to portray us as being responsible for the lamps lying on their sides. This strange occurrence happened precisely as Lester and Thelma were pulling into the driveway returning from a social event—strange bizarre behavior for such a young child. Our family situation was a bit different before he came into our world but the fact of imperfection is why we are in the World to learn, but it grew even odder, like a story found in a good psychodrama movie.

Later stolen items were found stored in the carriage house. The police knew of Lucas's involvement in heroin but just had to catch him in the act. Keeping an eye on him with the information given to them, they eventually caught him in the act of buying heroin, and therefore found him a new home for a year. This was so healthy for everyone in our family, including Lucas. We took advantage of that year and everything seemed back to normal, and we laughed and played together as before. We could breathe deeply again.

They created a monster and were oblivious to it. Thelma could not see the heart which was breaking or the love for her which held no bitterness but only wanted to start a new beginning. Time is valuable; every minute is important and never can be regained. Enjoy and honor each other. Do not focus on each other's faults but find an attribute that you can love about that person.

Back then everyone believed what the medical doctors said to be absolutely true. We did not realize they just did not have enough information to make a proper prognosis. Now discipline and dedication are needed for Kay to become healthy, and tough emotions would have to be faced. She is loaded with so many toxic drugs. That has to be removed one by one in order to set her free and with that comes stuck emotions which have become easily attached to the many toxins. Kay would need to be brought to an awareness of feelings not yet expressed and find skills to allow them to dissipate by consciously observing them. She hides behind all this, not knowing there is a different world waiting, full of light and color. She remains living in a world of whites, grays, and black.

Stress retraining is of utmost importance. Biofeedback has been scientifically proven to help reduce stress and hypertension that may be related to illness, injury or emotional trauma. With the ability to provide virtually instant information through a comfortable and relaxing non-invasive process, biofeedback professionals are able to address their clients' stress in a sophisticated and finely tuned way. Quantum biofeedback promises to play a significant role in the future of increasing health through relaxation for stress and pain management. For more information see *The Power of the Entangled Hierarchy*—a true story. More information on quantum biofeedback can be found also at http://www.thequantumalliance.eu/

Getting in touch with your breath by meditation and brain entrainment is invaluable for all of us. Terry Hodgkinson has many excellent short meditation sessions in Brain Tap Technologies which are easy to follow, guiding the participant into deep relaxation to open the doors for their own unique healing. We have forgotten how to breathe and breath is needed to move your lymph system. This, in turn, increases the capability of the body to remove toxins and prevent disease. .

Information is being brought into the light about autism, dementia, Alzheimer's and other brain diseases. Just like Kay, Thelma had a poor immune system and this was part of the piece that played in the intricate puzzle of her illness as well, (please see *Brain On Fire* by Susannah Cahalan). Other energetic parasites came into play with her condition, which disabled her from being able to function in the world in which we live. Eventually, the darkness devoured Thelma until the only way life was possible for her was through death. Slowly, Thelma's life was sucked from her.

At first, as a young boy, Lucas was a part of all our family gatherings and we were happy to see him, but as time went on he started to create havoc with our family, taking every opportunity to do so. In due course, he attended none of our family functions but his only interest was to create dramas. Sometimes spying on us, he lurked in the shadows. The last few months, he stuck around, gluing himself usually to Thelma or Lester, staring at us with the most vicious eyes, monitoring every word we had with each other. Once in awhile, we strove to entice him to engage in the conversation but we became very apprehensive in doing so. Because of his unpredictable and erratic behavior, we never knew what to expect. This behavior squelched all the joy and desire for our families to visit Thelma and Lester. If only they would agree to receive professional help, but they thought that was only admitting defeat and another screw up in their lives.

Precious Memory

It is a tapestry of autumn; trees are dressed in the colors of fall: golden hues, vivid pinks, red, crispy earthen browns. The leaves lie crunchy underfoot.

Falling leaves tumble, pirouette in midair and cascade to the earth below. Layton, Lindsay, and McKenzie throw leaves in the air, making a wild chaotic fountain, a shower of colors. They're excited to play with their newly arriving cousins.

Vibrant colors explode in brilliance as the sunlight draws out each leaf's own uniqueness and dynamic color. The trees look upon this family invitingly, joyfully reaching to the heavens as they drive up the long driveway. On this particular day, their cousins have arrived early and are eager to play.

These family gatherings have become a weekly occurrence. Each feast is, by its own merits, a masterpiece created by Thelma. A huge chandelier sparkles as it creates dancing flickering lights from the clear crystals dangling from it. This chandelier is attached to a rope of gold from the high cathedral ceiling found hanging in the dining room above a long rectangular wooden table which is meticulously decorated, adorned with an exquisite tablecloth and naturally scented candles containing essential oils. The candles softly glow, making the silverware sparkle invitingly and focusing attention to the centerpiece made from a beautiful array of various summer flowers picked and arranged the night before. This magical space is created for family and friends to find the true beauty each person offered.

As Lucas grew in stature he was allowed to put a halt to these gatherings in the home. We became even more determined to keep our connection to my parents. Nothing was going to keep us apart and we improvised, but he became stronger in his intentions. The darkness tugged and frayed the rope that tied us as a family unit until it became so worn there was only a strand of thread that hid from his eyes.

Maneuvering a machine through the sky exhilarates, liberates and sets her spirit free. Many fears are faced flying such a little Mickey Mouse plane, which reminds her of being in a comic strip plane bounced around by the wind. Takeoffs and landings in themselves are a pleasant challenge. She knows it is imperative to be at your best physically, mentally and emotionally. Flexibility in your thinking is also an important ingredient to maneuver this piece of machinery which is vulnerable to the changing weather conditions. It is her first step in making changes within her and she knows they will have to be drastic, but, most important, patience and kindness will be needed for this rather long journey. Now, watching poles and wires go by as she carefully maneuvers the big flying bird, she is mindful to keep it a safe distance from any obstacles along the way. Taking a long deep breath as Smoketown comes into sight; she exults that her long distance solo is finally finished. Upon landing, she calls her son to include him in her personal celebration and journey to freedom.

It was one of the happiest days of my life and one of my oddest. Already having done my cross country trek the week before, it was now time to do my check ride. After talking for a long time with the elderly gentleman who was responsible for my check ride, we finally got into the Cessna. Extremely nervous, I left my pilot bag sitting where the plane was parked. It was a rather important item, containing maps and the glasses that were needed for a very important procedure during my check ride. When coming to the part of the check ride where I covered my eyes and relied just on my instruments, I realized neither the glasses nor my pilot bag was anywhere in sight. Informed that we would just have to finish the check ride later, I felt rather unhinged, not wanting to have to go through this again. Making some quick decisions, I grabbed a piece of paper and tore tiny holes in it so my eyes could just barely see the instruments and luckily I found a rubber band. Securing the paper around my head with the large rubber band, I looked very comical wearing my homemade contraption but I passed the test!

The week before, a cross-country trek was accomplished of over 100 nm total distance. This trek entailed having to land at three airports. My first destination from Smoketown, Pennsylvania was to Georgetown, Delaware which was a big challenge for me because my first reaction when beginning the flight was panic. Panic is definitely not what you want to experience when it comes to being a pilot. Nothing looked familiar to me in the sky after taking off from Smoke town. My initial thoughts were that I was crazy to be attempting such a flight and must have some kind of subconscious death wish. But after calming myself down and getting a grip on where my location was in the sky, my body began to relax a bit.

Approaching Georgetown, I radioed for help to locate the airport and very shortly thereafter, a pilot was personally escorting me to the runway. I was happy to be down on the ground, but still faced the challenge of landing at one more airport before I navigated back to Smoketown. Concerned about my time, I hoped to arrive at Smoketown airport before dusk. The second airport was located quite effortlessly. After landing, I quickly ran into the office to use the restroom and talked to the office personnel, who made sure my logbook was signed and dated. Not staying very long, the Cessna was maneuvered to take off into the now darkening blue indigo skies and not too much later the Cessna was seen approaching the Smoketown runway.

Tears of joy caressed my cheeks, as the descent began.

Later, taking the oral exam and checkride at Harrisburg Airport, she receives her pilot's license, January 28, 2005. A celebration is in the air, creating glitters of light exploding throughout the limitless sky.

Appreciation

As my parents became older and less energetic, it was increasingly difficult to visit them without being harassed by Lucas. Instead of never being around, he was always at the home ready and waiting. So we decided to improvise and we spoiled them, joining them in many events, knowing it was imperative that a strong connection be kept.

Thelma and Lester waited excitedly out front for us, and when our van arrived they greeted us with enthusiasm, they clambered in to find their favorite seat, and off we went to gymnastics meets, restaurants, Longwood Gardens, musicals, American Music Theatre, Sight and Sound Theatre and any other kind of event imaginable. Mount Gretna was one of our favorite places which we visited often. It is a beautiful lake town with many cottage type homes in the woods. My first swimming lesson was taken with my parents as my teachers at the Mount Gretna Lake. This community is quite different than most communities with many cottages built close together in the woods. Mount Gretna is a laid back community hosting many arts, craft and jewelry shows throughout the year. A huge covered pavilion still brings people from afar to take part in or be the audience for plays and musicals. Within walking distance is also a very frequently visited place called the Jigger Shop. Lester esorted Thelma to this place when they were in their teens for banana splits!

Thelma's face beams with bubbles of excitement and leads them to where she was courted by Lester at the Jigger Shop. Sharing the story which was heard many times before, she says, "Lester loved ice cream when we were dating and still does!" Without thinking, she sits down at the exact place where they had sat together eating banana splits while he was courting her and proudly begins to describe in detail how Lester bought both of them banana splits, eating his and then went and ordered another one for himself. Later, he finished her banana split as well.

She glows as she looks at Lester and exclaims that Lester truly amazes her with his appetite for ice cream and the fact that he never gains a pound, but is so lean, handsome and muscular! Lester gazes into her eyes and smiles as they all begin to order, having now joined Thelma sitting at the round table. Later, Lester is seen enjoying a banana split as the stars twinkle and rays of the lights above them shine through the mist in the air, creating rainbows as an avalanche of star dust spews forth, creating magic.

The community in Mount Gretna is a close-knit group of people and is considered an artsy community, having all kinds of art shows for people to attend, endless walking trails and biking trails are found in the woods, where horses can be brought for riding. The trails are endless and wind throughout the forest joining other trails like a maze. Some travelers take refuge overnight on the trail, revitalizing their spirits to rise early and travel under the canopy of trees as the sunlight infiltrates and sparkles on the morning dew of daybreak.

The Playhouse in Mount Gretna introduced the opportunity to enjoy many different art forms including plays and musicals. The Playhouse is an open air theater in one of the most beautiful and unique settings imaginable. Joining the Chautauqua movement in the 1890s, Mt. Gretna is a haven of charming cottages, art, culture, music and theater in the middle of a lovely and tranquil mountain forest. The Playhouse provides a wide variety of shows. The seats are comfortable, and high-tech fans keep the audience comfortable on all but the most stifling days.

n amazing ice cream shop, the Jigger Shop, is a short walk away, as is the fascinating gift Emporium. But best of all are the streets of the town, lined with delightful cottages, filled porches, and a feel for another very friendly world. But there are many other places in Gretna hidden in nooks and crannies. One of these special places is Timbers Dinner Theatre which serves a lovely meal. After the meal, tables and chairs are set up outside, protected from the elements, for after-dinner entertainment, usually involving music. Performers traveling the world come here to entertain and then like gypsies move to another location. The last few years' these social events were visited often, with my parents celebrating their birthdays and anniversaries. The performers sang happy birthday to them and on their anniversary shone the spotlight on Thelma and Lester, performing a special song just for them. Thelma and Lester grinned from ear to ear, loving all of the attention. They were pampered with all kinds of activities that we thought would inspire them, many times involving music and of course ice cream.

Mt. Gretna was born in a forest of chestnut trees that for more than a century provided charcoal to the Cornwall Furnace that once forged cannons for George Washington's army. The site was discovered in 1883 as a pleasant place to spend a summer day along the extinct Cornwall and Lebanon Railroad linking the Reading Railroad in Lebanon with the Pennsylvania Railroad near Elizabethtown. Originally you could travel here by rail from any point in the country. President Benjamin Harrison actually did. He and thousands of picnickers detrained at a small station, walked down a tree-lined corridor past a stone fountain (that still exists) and spent the day in a woodland park that expanded each year as the number of visitors grew, eventually sporting an elaborate carousel, a primitive roller coaster called a "switch-back," a dancing pavilion, and other attractions of an early amusement park. In 1885 the Pennsylvania National Guard began a 50-year annual encampment at Mt. Gretna. That year Conewago Creek was dammed to form Lake Conewago, more aptly called a pond, but ideal for swimming and canoeing.

In 1889 iron-foundry heir and generous owner of most of Mt. Gretna's original land, Robert Coleman, built a narrow gauge railroad to carry visitors from the park, around the lake and up to the top of Governor Dick Hill where they could see as far as Lancaster and Harrisburg. A loving history of Mt. Gretna can be found in Gretna historian, Jack Bitner's book: "Mt. Gretna, a Coleman Legacy." In 1892 Methodists identified Mt. Gretna as a good location for a Chautauqua. Mt. Gretna's "Pennsylvania Chautauqua" was modeled after the original Chautauqua Institution, established in 1874 in New York State. Within a few years they drew up a plan for lots and began constructing, according to a popular plan of the day, a vaulted conical-roofed outdoor auditorium for lectures, religious services and concerts. The first "Chautauquans" built summer cottages around it, a "Hall of Philosophy" for meetings, and a small wooden Greed temple for the "Chautauqua Literary and Scientific Circle." Both buildings are still used today. That same year the United Brethren moved in across Pinch Road from Chautauqua and hired the same builder, John Cilley from Lebanon, to build a Tabernacle for religious services and Bible meetings. The Tabernacle, a smaller version of the Playhouse (23 chestnut supporting posts around the perimeter vs. 26) still stands in the Camp Meeting, (the Playhouse collapsed in 1994 under a heavy load of snow and ice.) The Brethren mapped out plots for tents around the Tabernacle, but by the first summer Bible Conference, 100 cottages had already been built by worshipers on the tent plots. Tents appeared only around the immediate perimeter of the Tabernacle, each sparsely furnished with a table, chairs, a lamp, a Bible and a box-like bed with straw sheets. The success of Mt. Gretna as a summer retreat led to the construction of restaurants and hotels, including the Chautauqua Inn, the Jigger Shop Ice Cream Parlor, the Conewago Hotel, Kaufman's Store and Hotel, and others. Through the first two decades of the 20th century, Mt. Gretna teemed with summer visitors who attended concerts, lectures, trade shows and Bible meetings and relaxed in the park, lake and on porches. Built in 1909, the 125-room Conewago Hotel was one of the first in the country to offer private baths and telephones in the rooms and an elevator, as well as "servants in uniform… and chefs from New York." Guests could enjoy the terraced tennis courts overlooking the lake and parade grounds by day a "ladies orchestra" in the dining room at night for dinner and dancing. It thrived for only two decades. A casualty of the new mobility made possible by the automobile, it was already vacant when the Depression dealt it a second blow. It was finally dismantled in 1940. The Chautauqua Inn, once standing near the Playhouse, had a longer life. It was more rustic and lacked private baths, but its dining room remained legendary well into the second half of the century. Even so, modern fire codes and liability insurance rates forced its closing and demolition in 1970. For a short time the small Kaufman Hotel across from the current Mt. Gretna Inn, completed a trio of Gretna hotels, but it too no longer exists. No longer being an obligatory destination of captive railroad passengers, many of Mt. Gretna's attractions languished in the 1920s as vacationers began to drive their cars to the Atlantic shore and other more distant points, and students found summer education at colleges.

The Depression, departure of the National Guard in 1933, and finally World War II diminished Mt. Gretna's popularity. The amusement park closed, hotels lay empty, and the narrow gauge was abandoned. Even the chestnut trees fell victim to a nationwide blight and were replaced by oaks and evergreens. Some Gretna institutions continued: a long tradition of theater in the Playhouse, the Camp Meeting Bible Conference, Chautauqua programs in the Community Building, the Jigger Shop, swimming and boating in the lake, a Roller Rink in a remaining building of the amusement park, and, of course, the long tradition of lingering on the porches. The Timber Restaurant was built in the 1960s on the gentle rise that had been the site of the National Guard headquarters. A growing population of permanent residents began occupying the homes. Some date Mt. Gretna's modern revival to 1976 and the First Annual Outdoor Art Show, the creation of Gretna artists, Bruce Johnson, Reed Dixon and John Wenzler, then Director of Summer Programs for the

Chautauqua. In its distinctive setting, the show almost immediately became one of the most successful in the state. In the next two years, a new Gretna resident, physician, and musician, Carl Ellenberger, again at the suggestion of John Wenzler, began inviting musician friends to perform in the Playhouse and longtime Gretna resident, Mary Hoffman, revived the theater productions in the Playhouse after a year when the theater was dark. Both Gretna Theater and music flourished, attracted government, foundation and corporate grants as well as new visitors and residents. Mt. Gretna became known in the region as a center for arts and culture and increasingly as a desirable place to live, especially for those who wanted to participate in its artistic activities, but also those who had discovered its other virtues during a visit to the Playhouse or the Art Show. Many Gretna residents serve on one or more of the boards that guide each section of the community and the performing groups, and most volunteer to help at the Art Show which brings thousands of visitors and vital economic support to Mt. Gretna. Whether or not Gretna residents enjoy the artistic activities of Mt. Gretna, they mostly agree that these activities give the community an identity far stronger than most other communities of similar size and make it a desirable place to live.

The American Musical Theater and Sight and Sound were a few of the many other events we visited. The festive shows were enjoyed tremendously and of course, why not? Thelma loved to dress up, showing all her classy purchases and jewelry—gifts from her beloved! During this time of their lives they were in their eighties. The spirit of the holiday season overflows at Longwood Gardens with a Christmas-fountain-inspired display. Filling the Conservatory are blue and white twinkling lights, whirling fountain features, thousands of seasonal plants, and a bounty of trees with shimmering icicles and fountain-inspired colorful glass ornaments. Outside, a magical world waits. From the Italian Water Garden illuminated with a 20-foot tree form, to a maple tree with its roots aglow with twinkling lights near the Meadow Boardwalk, to the colorful fountains of the open air theater, there is holiday magic everywhere!

During Christmas season, we loaded into the van and went to Longwood Gardens for their Christmas display of lights. It was glorious to be outside with all the beautiful display of lights throughout the gardens. It was magical. Displays were found inside as well as outside and when we opened the huge massive doors to go outside, Roslyn ran outside, took her coat off and flung it, exclaiming, "I feel so good,"

She spun and did circles, looking up into the night sky as an avalanche of snowflakes spewed forth, shimmering down from the sky onto her face. We laughed and were so happy during those times. Roslyn at the time was only five years old and we continued this tradition of visiting Longwood Gardens during their display of Christmas lights for many more years!

As an offer by Mairzy and Jackson was put in motion for the purchase of the bay home, we all eagerly awaited the outcome. Everyone wanted to keep the beloved bay home. Holding so many beautiful memories, it was Lester's desire to keep it within the family. Lester's excitement about the proposal showed all over his face, if only he could get Thelma to agree to this transaction. Her only desire was to sell the bay house to an outsider. This notion upset him because he knew once it was sold; it would be gone for good. Distraught, not knowing how to get around Thelma's crazy notions, he fretted and worried.

Thelma and Lester would be able to live at the bay home after the mansion was sold and any needs or concerns would be paid for and taken care of by us. We hoped Thelma would agree with our proposition, so patiently we waited and prayed for a divine intervention. "Yes," never happened and, shaking our heads, we asked, "Why?" The "Roslyn" Mansion was already paid for in cash a long time ago, so it definitely looked like a very good choice to sell this home, and it was already on the market with some potential buyers interested in it. Not interested in listening to anyone, Thelma looked past and through us, her face turning blank as if we did not exist.

Little did we know that Lucas had already been stealing large sums of money from my parents, running up the debt on all their major credit cards. Most of their money already had been siphoned from their bank account with very little left. They did not reveal any information about this horrible situation; instead, they hid it from us. Thelma was very distraught about something, you could see it. We knew something was going on but they would not reach out to us about what was troubling them; therefore this isolation became their downfall. Lucas was responsible for showing their home to potential buyers and later the sale sign was removed with no one knowing exactly what happened to it.

Previously, we kept on warning our parents of our concerns about the possibility of Lucas taking advantage of them as they become older and more vulnerable, but had no idea how bad it already had become.

Years later confiding to Marten—

A conversation can be very challenging since his stroke, but this particular day, he becomes very quiet for what seems like an eternity and then begins. "Held at gunpoint, I was forced to hand over all of my money and credit cards by a very bad guy. As I reached out to grab the barrel shotgun that was being pointed at me, there was a big scuffle." Lester goes on describing the best he could, "Holding on to the shotgun with all my might, realizing I'm no match for the culprit, I let go. That son of a bitch tried to shoot me!"

During this ruckus Lester falls to his knees and weeps. All his money, everything that he has ever worked for is taken from him.

"Everything is gone. What can ever be done? I guess he will just get away with it, and this evil event will be forgotten because nothing can be done about it. The dirty scoundrel will run free, Mr. Marten! I am scared he is going to find me and hurt me. Please don't let him hurt me! Please listen. I am frightened." Previously, he brought this subject forth but now he is sharing it again, but in more depth. Earlier, this conversation received much attention from his daughter. He informs her as to what happened to him the best he could with his messed up brain, and calls the perpetrator a stinky bastard. It was a very amazing testimony because making sense of his life was very difficult for him since the stroke, but bits and pieces of what exactly happened to him started to be remembered and he shared them with his son-in-law. Prepared this time, he records his conversation for the detective now assigned to the case by the hospital staff.

This abusive behavior was going on for a while because when I saw my dad, he looked as if things were not right and something was bothering him terribly. Again, he didn't tell me what was going on nor did he reach out for help from the police, who were waiting to help. He chose to live in isolation. Darkness kept seeping in like a quiet killer stalking its prey, waiting to attack. My hands were tied because the Chief of Police informed me that they could not do anything to help my parents until they asked.

Chapter Eight
The Great Manipulator

No one would listen to our horrible dilemma as we cried out for help. They too were flattered by the psychopath and could not possibly believe the things we said about him. He won their hearts, flattering them with his words.

My parents wanted us to include Lucas, but he, in turn, did not want any part of us and his wife, Abbey, followed suit, which frustrated my parents, who blamed us. Gradually jealousy overtook Kay, squelching any remaining love for me in her heart and making our Sunday visits increasingly uncomfortable. The holidays were turned upside down, except for the rare times when Lucas was not in our company because of travel, extracurricular activities, or drug dealing. Then there was a longer period of time which was about a year when he spent his time in jail for the use of heroin. It is in jail where he actually did some labor, eventually working himself up to the position of the chef in the kitchen, but in no time, after being released from jail, he resorted to becoming increasingly dangerous to our family. It is during this time his maliciousness increased, and he schemed and deliberately planned family disruptions with his accomplice. It was during one of the last Christmases spent together that Kay went into the frantic drama and accused the family of stealing her pocketbook. She screamed viciously at each grandchild, as my parents watched in frustration, not knowing how to handle this drama. Flustered, they wrung their hands as the Christmas spirit spiraled down like a jet with broken wings and crashed, becoming totally unfixable. What was interesting, Lucas was always the savior in these horrible incidents. He found the purse much later in the evening when most of the family had left, only after the whole holiday was destroyed. Yes, he was our 'Mr. Fix it!'

Thelma invited Justin, Roslyn and Linnea over for a special birthday celebration for Justin. They had the opportunity to enjoy one of her wonderful birthday meals and watch Justin open his neatly wrapped birthday gifts. Marten and I were going to be away. Therefore Thelma thought it would be fun to celebrate Justin's birthday.

Kay and Lucas glared at each other during the whole meal while sitting at the dining room table. It looked as if they were up to something which was reported back to me later. Darkness had settled in as Justin said goodbye and hugged his grandparents, thanking them for having him over. Roslyn and Linnea followed suit and out the door they went to travel home. Finally arriving home they used the automatic garage opener and drove directly into the garage. They didn't notice the thick mud on the driver's car door because it was very late and they were dog-tired. They headed straight to their bedrooms.

When getting into my car for the first time since returning home, the thick smudge of mud on my car door was very noticeable in the light of day. Not thinking much about it, I quickly retrieved a cloth to wipe it off and found deeply embedded carved Xs, rather large in size. Furious and very frustrated, a phone call was made immediately to my parents. At first, they seemed disturbed about it but later did not take what happened very seriously, choosing only to laugh it off. Lester accused everyone else, excluding Lucas. He said, " Boys will be boys," retaliating by accusing Justin and Layton, who are much younger than Lucas, for minor petty things done when they were toddlers, such as putting stones down the outside drain pipe. This did not even make sense that he used this incident to defend Lucas who by now was in his twenties. It was not just what Lucas did but the attitude of hate and spite in which it was done. My dad refused to believe me, and my mom had no comment. Later, I had the opportunity to talk to them in person which did not make any difference. The only comment from Lester was again, "Boys will be boys." I felt like the scary movie Twilight Zone was becoming very real in my life. From then on we parked along the sidewalk outside the gated area and walked to my parent's home.

Later that year, while visiting, we were invited to stay for dinner. Hesitating and feeling a bit awkward, I conceded. Wilbur, our Gordon setter, was in my car so instead of parking outside the gated area, I parked the car in the driveway under the cool shade of an oak tree, for his comfort. Wilbur, Linnea and I had just returned from a long hike in Mount Gretna. While sitting at the table, Kay stared blankly at me, making me feel all the more awkward. Thelma kept offering us more food, which made Kay glare all the more. Later, going outside to enjoy the fresh summer air, I found Kay walking around my car and asked her what she was doing. Appearing as if everything was okay, she said that she was looking at the beautiful markings on Wilbur. I thought it seemed to be a plausible reason for being near my car because Wilbur was a Gordon setter and his markings were exceptional but something still seemed strange or off. After saying thank-you and my goodbyes, I drove out of the driveway and made a stop at K-Mart on the way home. After getting out of my car, light scratch marks were made very visible now by the light of the sun, as if someone had taken keys or something similar to scratch my Cadillac. That is when I knew without a doubt, she was also a part of some of the weird dramas.

These acts did not represent the real Kay but the medication dulled her essence. In the beginning, I became well aware of the indifference that Thelma started to show Kay in not wanting to recognize Lucas as Kay's son. Doing my best with what I knew at the time to support Kay, my support was not what she was seeking but only her mother's love and acceptance. It was a difficult situation because Thelma had no idea why Kay exhibited such bizarre and odd behavior which Kay many times did not recall. Clueless about mental illness, I just wanted to fix Kay. Thelma wanted Lucas to address her as mommy and call Kay by her name. They eventually fought over the silliest things and Thelma became annoyed by Kay, provoking her and taking advantage of my sister's weakness. It was difficult to be around Thelma when she picked on someone weaker and broken. Definitely, this situation was way too complex for me to fix and ultimately too much for Thelma to handle, who became worn from all of the responsibility.

For a long time, Kay lived with Thelma and Lester, staying on the third floor with Lucas when he was an infant. But as he became older, he eventually ended up staying on the second floor with his grandparents and later his mother moved to a small apartment. The extra responsibility of raising Lucas was way too much stress upon Thelma's psyche. She was unable to dissociate from the mess around her and became consumed by it, ultimately causing her own demise. During these times, Lester became confused and very unhappy with all the bickering, not knowing how to handle the madness or even get beyond it. He confided in me often, but my hands were tied because he was not willing to get outside assistance without Thelma's consent.

Finally, Kay was able to move into her own home funded by the State, receiving much attention and many visits from her caseworker. Also, a lot of outside social workers were assigned to her case. Occasionally, I was invited over for a light dinner, and we had wonderful conversations during this time of her life. It was on these specific occasions when she appeared much healthier. Her house was filled with all her antique relics which were neatly arranged in her home each with a specific spot designated for it. Kay enjoyed pruning and tending her garden which contributed to the many delicious fresh vegetables found on the table, complementing her many dinners. But the disease was very strange how it affected her personality and it was confusing to the people that loved her. A better understanding of the disease would have helped us to be more understanding and compassionate for her strange behavior. During this time period, it appeared as if she was improving or at least holding her own, receiving food stamps and receiving some money for her disability which gave her a feeling of independence. Different people that followed Kay's case history stopped at the house, keeping in touch with her, taking her shopping or transporting her to different appointments. Kay was happy for the comfort found in her new friends and newly found independence, still visiting my parents often. Later, it is not totally clear why she had to move from the apartment. My parents bought her a house located a few blocks from their home.

Much later, Kay became increasingly more malicious against me. She frightened me as her anger arose from nowhere and there was always the dreaded fear of saying the wrong thing to her. On one such incident, she had stopped in to visit Thelma and Lester unanticipated while Marten, Linnea, Roslyn and I so happened to be visiting. During our gathering in the kitchen to have tea and light conversation, Kay became very hateful toward me. It took me off guard when she began spewing much hateful verbiage with such a vengeance directed solely at me. Her vicious attitude culminated as she waved a knife around and near me which ultimately was one of my last times ever spent with Kay. Every second was crucial; every movement made was as if I was in slow motion. Life slowed down, making me super aware of the importance of every split second and in a monotone voice, I asked my family to please leave the kitchen and call 911. Inwardly I kept on asking myself over and over again, "How am I responsible for this?"

The Journey

In the beginning of this journey, my husband and our children spent a couple of our Christmases together at the little coffee shack with its five acres of macadamia trees and, even before that, rented an inexpensive rental on Oahu. It was the week we spent on Oahu that enticed our appetite for a new adventure. It inspired our purchase of our macadamia orchard and vacation home. We put a bid in for it and like magic it was ours. Later that year, flying to Hawaii to meet the real-estate agent, we followed her up the windy narrow road to our new purchase and turning into the gravel driveway, I immediately fell in love. It was perfect.

Right before the time of this purchase, our home in Pennsylvania had just been remodeled. The interior walls were removed to open up a great room used for a lot of socializing. Rugs were replaced with wooden floors, the walls were painted with fresh vibrant colors and wallpaper was purchased which had many shades of deep reds. The vibrant colors of this wallpaper were the first thing people saw as they entered the front door. In the back of the home, windows were put in that opened with a switch and were able to close on their own if it rained. These windows were built into the newly designed room where relaxation was encouraged by an enticing, newly purchased hot tub. Complementing this energy of leisure, many skylights shone from a high ceiling, complete with a beautiful water feature hanging from the wall which was discovered and purchased at Rehoboth. Outside, a playful backyard was created with an above-ground heated swimming pool, complete with deck and winding stairs. It was a perfect place to have family fun. Each dog had its own personal raft to float upon in the warm water. Wilbur used flotation devices to help him swim because of old age setting in. Many late nights we ran to this pool even if it was cold or raining and jumped into the warm water which had a mist rising magically from it created from the cooler outside air. We truly laughed. It was so exhilarating to swim at night.

Flowers grew along the stone path leading to a splendid fountain found on the right hand side at the back of the property. This home, as well as its property, was laid out Feng Shui appropriate, and stone was used to create a beautiful appearance on the outside of the home, laid by the best craftsmen in our masonry business. Knowing Roslyn was soon to be born, spurred this move to a different location because our home needed more space. A gift of money from my parents was responsible for us being able to acquire this bigger home. It was not unusual for them to do so and very much in their nature of helping others in need.

Our home located near the school and within walking distance for our children made it very convenient for everyone. Only one straggler did not go to this public school but went to a school associated with the Worship Center, a church we fell in love with later. This decision for Linnea to attend a smaller private school was unanimously agreed upon by our family, believing it might be less overwhelming for her to go to a smaller Christian school. Linnea attended preschool at the public school which was within walking distance of our home, but afterwards she attended Living Word Academy. We joined a carpool for transporting the children attending this private school, which was about a thirty minute drive.

Our home was conveniently positioned in reference to the paved path that extended from the development's sidewalk. This path was traveled frequently, which led to the school but then curved and circled around below a wooded area, which provided us with a lot of entertainment for walking, jogging and bicycling. This curvy path brought beautiful memories which changed, as the seasons came and went. The bike path curved right below the hill along the woods where I often sat enjoying the serenity amidst the bustling activities of the day, meditating before it was time to meet Linnea.

From out beyond the nimbus cloud, the mighty sun overlooks the woods with bright golden beams and awakens her soul like beautiful chords of a harp. Sitting alone in this forest is where the sunshine and the soft breezes clear her mind as she has the luxury to watch the whimsical clouds float in the sky. Time stands still and there is a whole other world found basking in this amazing vibrant energy. Deer and redtail fox dart by and once in awhile a beautiful rainbow appears after rains come to cleanse the earth, giving her hope of a new plan and future on the horizon. The years go by as the children grow up but this hill supports her throughout their childhood days, a time to regroup, rest and strengthen her being.

In the garage, I was getting the dogs ready for a nice late afternoon walk on the bike path, when Marten shouted from the basement. I was not excited to hear what he was saying because by now I was anxious to get out the door so I could enjoy some free time before Linnea was dismissed from preschool.

"Ember, I just found a home for sale on a five-acre farm of macadamia nut trees!" The statement stops her in her tracks and shivers run up and down her spine. Standing there in the garage with dog leashes in her hands, she knew what they had to do.

The bike path brought forth many good memories. A place where my children and I spent a lot of time taking walks, collecting crickets, going sledding and riding our bikes together. Justin and Roslyn were pushed in a stroller on the bike path as I ran to get exercise. Later a bugger was attached to the back of our bikes where they sat with seat belts safely securing them. This enabled us to bike very long distances, venturing as far as the grocery store ten miles away to do shopping, or just for a leisurely bike ride. One of our favorite rides was to the airport. This is where we watched the planes land and take off. Loads full of magical memories were made on this path and I knew this path would be missed, but another path was gradually being carved. This particular day when Marten got my attention, he had been playing around online for homes in Hawaii.

—Our previous dream was being brought alive from the grave. It had been forgotten and was by now covered with darkness. During a visit with a good doctor friend of mine practicing the art of acupuncture, she flippantly shared with me about their recent purchase of a home in Kauai. She said jokingly, "Ember, buy a home in Hawaii so we can be neighbors!" A light flickered in my eyes and I remembered our dream to move to one of the Hawaii Islands after we had visited the island of Oahu. This dream was squelched very quickly by a proposal made to us after I had excitedly informed my parents that we were preparing to live in Hawaii. We were ready to leave everything and move at that time, but immediately a proposal was offered that was irresistible. Grabbing the bait I became hooked, but unfortunately, this proposal was not upheld by Thelma and Lester and the deal fizzled out as well as our dream. But this particular day while getting the dogs ready for our walk, Marten shouted excitedly from the basement. (He spent a lot of time down in the basement, which was made into an office for him). "Ember, I found this plot of land which is considered agricultural, a macadamia orchard which comes with a small house. The plot of land is five acres; what do you think?!" A knowing came over me that we were to purchase that plot of land and so it happened.

When visiting the Island to see our purchase, my husband pointed out free aura healings with the Clairvoyant Center and said let's go in and we did. That was when my journey started with being a student at the Clairvoyant Center. During this purchase, Justin was getting ready to graduate from the University of Michigan and Roslyn was attending the University of Pittsburgh engrossed in gymnastics, becoming a star.

What makes people mean? The pain felt in my soul was indescribable as the family dynamics played out, and hopelessness engulfed me. My whole family was being destroyed right in front of me; all the ties were being stretched and strained with the people I most cherished, until they broke. Holding in so much grief was destructive, but I was hopeful that somehow this mess could be turned around; I worked around the sensitive issues that were presented in our family, an impossible feat which caused much angst in my being. As each holiday came and went, it became only odder. Dramas and events happened that were staged to ruin our holiday cheer. It appeared that Lucas gained an accomplice in helping to stage these dramas. My family loved visiting Thelma and Lester, but our visits seemed to cause so much tension, making it very stressful. The grandchildren were extremely uncomfortable going over to visit, feeling very disturbed and frightened of the situation. We encouraged Thelma and Lester to get outside help but it appeared as if they were mesmerized by the part of Lucas that was so charming and they chose to overlook everything else. They were not willing to admit that his issues affected everyone concerned because, if they admitted that Lucas needed help, they would have been admitting failure again as they did with his mother, which of course was not true. Later, fear and stubbornness cemented the situation. Numerous times in the beginning, they admitted that Lucas was getting out of line and were open for outside help but they were afraid of society and the stigma they believed they would receive, and they became stuck. They could not follow through with the plan of action. Instead Thelma and Lester rationalized and used denial and projection as their shield of protection.

Puppy

Today is a particularly beautiful spring day; diamonds of nature glisten on the leaves, then drop down and evaporate quickly, representing the start of a new day. Frivolous fun is in the air. Eyes shine with sparkles of green light, she is happy to be able to spend time with her twin sister and brother-in-law. Enjoying the property, they stroll, looking at the beautiful fresh flowers of spring. Being outside with nature makes life so much better. It is mid-morning and while enjoying the sun's rays, they converse without a care, engaging in fun conversation.

Approaching the edge of the property grounds, they spot freshly upturned dirt peeking out from a flowering shrub just visible enough to get their attention. Going over to check it, they discover a large rectangular hole located close to the boundaries of the property, behind the carriage house, the perfect size for a coffin. Thinking it odd, they stand to look at it and ponder about theories as to why the hole was dug and who did it. As they stand reflecting, something odd catches their attention to the right. An object is detected floating in the fountain's pool of water. Pointing it out, they walk over curiously and find a puppy floating in the water with its head totally submerged under the water. This puppy would have grown to be a fine golden retriever, a larger type dog.

A quaint iron post fence surrounds the whole property, making it very difficult for this dog to have gotten into the grounds of this home. Oddly weird occurrences materialize around these happenings. Secretive peculiar meetings are reportedly held down in the basement of the Roslyn home with candles burning, as bizarre religious ceremonies take place. Later old photos are found of the twin sisters on the floor of the basement. Beginning to realize Lucas' intentions were warped and evil, she had no idea of the power in what he is worshipping.

> *The dark, black Angel of Chaos*
> *Time after time experienced loss*
> *Planning the absolute annihilation*
> *Of those whose hearts are full of sin*
> *Wrathful Angel from above*
> *Dead set on destroying love*
> *Full of hate and full of rage*
> *You'll never want to be engaged*
> *Beautiful Angel of Insanity*
> *The angel people want to be*
> *Pained by the darkest grey chains*
> *Your blood washed by the summer rains*
> *Crying Angel of Misery*
> *Full of sorrow and agony*
> *Left behind and all alone*
> *In the eyes, warmth not shown*
> *Chaos Angel brings annihilation*
> *Wrathful Angel desolation*
> *Insane Angel revocation*
> *Miserable Angel obliteration*
> *Poem by Blackness Rose*

These odd gatherings were observed by a member of our family several times and brought to my awareness. Strange behavior was happening downstairs which involved warped sexual acts and cutting each other's wrists in some kind of ritual while bowing and praying at an altar. All these activities occurred while they were being observed by the messenger. The basement was not like a normal basement but had many rooms with concrete walls and hallways, making it easy to hide. No one ever said anything to him because ultimately we needed the support of Thelma and Lester and inwardly fearful of what he could do to us, making life even more difficult.

That afternoon during my visit, one of my questions to Lucas was, "What are your plans for the future? Do you ever have dreams and aspirations of having your own home for you and Abbey?"

"Absolutely not," he retorted, "my plans are to only take care of my grandparents."

The lion taking care of the deer; little did I realize the Lion was already in motion and was stalking its prey.

Becoming bolder, he stole Lester's credit card, using it at whim. Marten received many calls from various stores about a young boy with Lester's credit card who was exhibiting very disturbing, rude and obnoxious behavior in the store. We were told Lucas drew out a switchblade and threatened the clerk as he stole condoms at one of the stores.

It was becoming more difficult to communicate with Lucas; and most of the time, he disappeared when we visited. If he chose to hang out for awhile he appeared higher than a kite and in another world. Later, needles were found lying around the home and the carriage house, setting off red alarm lights, screeching and blinking saying, "Mayday, mayday."

Thelma and Lester were constantly looking for their valuables and money. We also became very vigilant in keeping our pocketbooks nearby, staying on guard and protecting our valuables the best we knew how. Psychological counseling helped him stay on course for a year after he left jail, but later he returned to his bad habits of selling and using heroin. Lucas was taken to the bay house by Lester and Thelma to help him terminate this horrible addiction and they watched over him as he went off of heroin cold turkey. But before this was all completed, he sobbed and ranted, begging to be taken back home to Lancaster and as his body shook and trembled, they returned home.

In the beginning, Lucas bragged about his big bank account with his captive audience, who by chance just happened to be in the kitchen. We were confused as to what he meant by his big bank account because everyone knew that it was hard for him to lift a finger around the home for his grandparents, let alone hold a job away from the home. Humoring him we listened, mused on exactly what he could mean. My brother-in-law, Jackson, chuckled and told me he probably meant my parents' bank account, joking quite often about this young man's boastful claim of his gigantic bank account. This was rather bizarre because it was nearly impossible for Lucas to get up in the morning to help with maintaining Thelma and Lester's property. Lucas was into drugs. That is what he was involved with and we all knew it. Jackson, my brother-in-law was absolutely correct because Lucas made sure he drained their bank account by the time he was done with them. His energy was like a vampire draining the life out of the weak who allowed him to do so because they were hypnotized and did not notice. Little by little their very essence which made them so unique was zapped dry.

Conversations with the police of Lancaster were lengthy; they knew of Lucas and his shady goings on but explained to me that their hands were tied unless he was caught in the unlawful acts. Also, Thelma and Lester had to ask them for help, not hide what was going on behind closed doors. They repeated that they were only able to do so much in this type of situation. Lucas was put in jail for a year because of his involvement with drugs but not nearly long enough. Later after his release, he became more empowered, and the situation increased in intensity with his actions becoming more dangerous.

His imprisonment occurred shortly after my one phone call which brought a secret smile to my face.During his absence I lived as if every moment was precious and could never be lived again, visiting the home without any harassment. During this time, Lester and Thelma did not let anyone know of Lucas's whereabouts, but all kinds of things can be found out using the internet, and Mairzy was curious enough to do so. We smiled to ourselves in our secret.

In time, a great compassion came into my being for Thelma, as well as frustration in knowing how our family was being affected by her irrational decisions. I realized there was nothing at the time which could be done to stop her. I never felt so lonely, embarrassed and depressed to see our family ties slowly disintegrate before my very eyes.

Covering up for Thelma so my children did not see her weaknesses, I hoped for them to see only the best in her so that they would give her the love she so desperately needed. Life is precious and if you can find a way to love someone, it is far better than despising. Love shines on the darkness and loosens its grip, bringing forth freedom and forgiveness in your heart. Emptiness began to engulf me, as time marched on and my heart started to freeze from all the backed-up unprocessed emotions. Becoming very ill, I felt as if my days were numbered. The people that were part of my life turned their backs on me and my love was not reciprocated. My magical world disappeared over and over again. What was my reason to live? Caught in a web, unable to get loose, I seemed to always be in the wrong, but I was never offered concrete ways that I was annoying others. Despite all the other family dynamics taking place, at least we could lift each other above it. But that closeness from a relationship was not the route I was to travel. Something had to change.

Mairzy followed me one day to pay a visit with Lucas. Keeping her presence unknown, she parked her car along the sidewalk as I brazenly drove into the driveway. This particular morning, knowing that Thelma and Lester were not home, but most likely Lucas would be found upstairs in his bedroom or close by, I scurried up the steps and knocked on his bedroom door. Mairzy waited behind the carriage house. Since Lucas was going to be encouraged to come outside to meet me, she would be able to hear my cries for help.

Hurriedly, not giving it much thought after a rigorous Bikram class, she runs up the steps to the second floor and knocks, quietly calling his name, "Lucas, are you there?" Surprising her, he answers and asks, "What do you want, Aunt Ember?" Taking a deep breath to liberate the overwhelming anxious feeling which was building quickly, she replies, "Lucas, would you please come downstairs, preferably outside on the patio? I don't wish to bother you but something has been haunting my mind for such a long time. I truly need to talk to you,"......

Outside, fumbling for the correct words, she begins to talk about his mother and her respect for Kay as well as him, realizing it must be difficult at times to watch or even understand his mother's behavior which the sickness has created.

Fondly recalling memories with her sister, she reminisces, "Kay has a unique personality which creates a beautiful space around her. When I was a little girl, I admired your mother and her talent in singing. Her energy had a softness that made you want to be in her company, making me feel as if I was walking on clouds of love, and could rise above any adversity." Working on opening up the doors of communication, she softens her eyes while looking at him. They glow a soft jasper-green, inviting him to relax. Openly, she shares her love and respect for his mother regarding her challenges and, at times, stormy relationship with Thelma. Having nothing to say, he listens. She encourages him to share what his future plans and goals are in life. "Did you ever think how fun it might be to have your own place with Abbey?"Lucas expresses great disdain at the notion of claiming his independence and says his only desire is to stay with his grandparents, helping them as they age. She reminds herself to take slow calm breaths, hoping not to show any of her feelings of annoyance or frustration, but only acceptance of him at this moment in time.

Exhaling, she shares her disappointment of discovering Xs carved into the left hand front door of her car. These marks were found the morning after getting back from traveling which baffles her because her car remained parked in the garage. The car was driven to visit grandma and used for traveling to Berks Gymnastics Academy. "Remember you and your mother were at the celebration grandma had for Justin?" she said. Leaving that subject, she inquires about Razzle. "Razzle could not walk for a month when I brought her home after being taken care of by grandma. What do you think happened to her? If she was hurt on purpose, the person responsible is in need of counseling. We need to talk to that person to encourage them to find help." She was not blaming him for anything but was looking for information. She explains, "When my car was marked, I did not care because it is just a car, but when an injury comes to an animal, that is where the line is drawn." He becomes offended, and again she quickly reminds him that he is not being accused. "It takes a strong person to admit that they need help and many successful people receive guidance from a counselor, psychiatrist or psychologist throughout their lives. Was anyone else at the home that possibly could have hurt Razzle?" Lucas suggests that maybe Razzle got caught in between doors as they were being shut and her green eyes dim. His pair of glacial eyes stared back at her coldly.

She is aware of information shared by someone who watched Lucas ram broken coke bottles up the anuses of innocent pets. Having no idea that he was being watched attentively from afar as he performed these heinous acts, most of his pets died early or were maimed.

Staring at her, he says, "How dare you accuse me of doing this?" and she repeats, "I am not accusing you, I am only asking if you have any information on the subject. Do you have any idea who was responsible for these acts? Maybe it was Kay?" Lucas said that his mother would never do any harm to an animal. Before leaving, she wishes him the best in life and hugs him as her eyes glow a soft green.

Fireworks

Visiting my nephew backfired on me. At that point, visits to Thelma and Lester became more miserable, almost to the point of being unbearable. Approached with the truth made him furious; nobody had ever messed with him before. Absolutely despising me after that visit, he made my life more miserable than I could have ever imagined. Not wanting to hear the truth and not able to handle the love that it was given in; he turned on me with a vengeance, taking me off guard. He frightened me. This was the turning point in my life and drastic changes needed to be made. There was no other choice but to leave; there was nothing left for me to look forward to in this situation. The magic of life was no more to be found, but a vision of a faraway land was quietly beckoning me in grace. After talking to Lucas, my cell phone rang constantly. Nasty threats were found on my phone that night as we drove to Rehoboth. Who gave him my phone number?

The next week when we visited Thelma and Lester, he made his presence well known. Instead of hiding, his behavior was very rude and disrespectful. He planted himself right next to them and stared at me scornfully, not saying a word, making an intimate conversation literally impossible.

Breaking the long silence, he speaks his eyes flaming with hatred.. Angrily he taunts her and tries to engage her in an argument which does not at all interest her. Rapidly, he begins to talk about the Christmas fiasco regarding the lost pocketbook. His verbiage leads to a whirlwind of dark energy that explodes from him as he lashes out at her and other members of their family not present. His language is crude and detestable, culminating in speed like a roller coaster ride going down a steep hill, but out of control and off its tracks.

Keeping her voice calm, she relaxes her eyes, asking inquisitively what he thought might have happened Christmas day. And then in a soft voice, she professes her love for him and the love of the other people in their family, making him all the angrier. Rage devours his body destroying any common sense and he spews vehemently, saying horrible things that should never have been spoken. This seems to go on forever as he accuses her to be demonic from the deep recesses of hell, telling her that she will burn eternally.

It was very strange and eerie, as Thelma and Lester held each other's hands pleading, "Please leave, Ember. Get out of here now!" In shock and unable to comprehend that it actually had gotten this bad. My husband, Linnea, and Roslyn followed me to the van and as we left, the trees bowed their heads in prayer. Roslyn by now was showing symptoms from a traumatic brain injury but we were not aware. Out of that dysfunction, she had made the painful decision of giving up her scholarship. Heaviness in my heart surrounded me and a conscious decision was made that evening. I never felt so lonely and unloved.

What happens in a person's mind to trigger uncontrolled hatred? Kill innocent animals, mark visitor's cars for spite, steal from those that love you, make up dramas to destroy a family get-together, isolate and threaten the elderly and then turn around and look like the savior--the savior of the drama he created to terrorize the family but in turn appearing magically to fix the problem.

Later, sharing my most intimate thoughts and emotions with my parents, my mother listened because Lester encouraged her..... "Why do you protect Lucas as if he does no wrong?" I said. "Why not be honest about it so we can devise a plan together for our family? I do not feel comfortable or safe around him or comfortable with allowing my children to be part of this situation which is abusive in nature. It is not fair to them! How can we make this so our family can remain intact? Maybe it would be possible to help pay for an apartment for Lucas and his wife to live in until they will support themselves? Just remember, I love you and have only the utmost respect for both of you and will always relish the good memories of my childhood days as well as our wonderful times together at this beautiful home. But this family is not working out at all for me. Please hear my heart, it is breaking. Let's make this work for everyone concerned."

Abbey, Lucas's wife, developed a grudge that ate at her heart. My son went to high school with her and knew her, but drugs took a toll on her life and she began to appear waif-like and very fragile.

Having left for a while to live in the Poconos, Mairzy and Jackson eventually came back, settling into a beautiful home in Lancaster. So while Thelma and Lester visited Rehoboth, Mairzy and I made a date to meet at the home. She wanted to take the time to point out each of her pictures given as gifts to Thelma and Lester. These took countless hours to paint. She used various mediums to create each masterpiece, and at times she surprised the viewer with a totally different style.

"There are a variety of ways in which to approach creating art, none of which is better or more correct than another," Mairzy said. "Which approach you take will to some extent be influenced by your painting style and personality." She talked about different styles of painting, listing, "Photorealism, super realism, sharp focus realism, hyperrealism—you can call it whichever of these labels you prefer and argue about the minute details between the styles, but ultimately they're all art styles where the illusion of reality is created through paint, so the result looks more like a large, sharply focused photo than anything else." She explained to me that photorealism is a style which often seems more real than reality, with detail down to the last grain of sand and wrinkle on someone's face. Nothing is left out; nothing is too insignificant or unimportant to be included in the painting. She was fluid in her speech and very knowledgeable on the subject matter. "Acrylics, pastels, watercolor, crayon, color pencils, oil paints are a few of the different painting categories," she added, "and, of course, they all need their own special paper."

Very open to trying different approaches in many of her paintings, she didn't think only one style should be used in a painting but explained that she mix 'n matched approaches whenever she felt like it. As we entered each room, a shadow of a person was caught darting out the doorway, and when we moved to a different room, this shadow darted to the next. Darting from each room and avoiding us at all cost. We found out later it was Abbey, which did not surprise us. She really had no reason to dislike us, and I questioned what horrible stories were made up which plagued her mind. Later, our parents changed the locks on the doors because Lucas told them that while they were gone Ember and Mairzy came over to antagonize him and Abbey. Also, he did not like Aunt Ember going up the steps and knocking on his door, asking him to please come outside on the patio to talk with her.

Thelma and Lester explained to me the "real" reason the locks to the home were actually changed; they held onto a false story that the locks had been changed because the original key had been found by someone who might be a potential burglar. I had no reason at the time to doubt my parents as to why the locks were changed, but I found it strange that a replicate of the new key was never given to me. They appeared uneasy as they gave me a lame excuse as to why they did not have the key. This same occurrence also happened with the key to the boat at Rehoboth. The key could never be found in the later years at Rehoboth and when we visited the bay house the key was always missing. Therefore we could not enjoy the use of the boat.

Eventually, the real truth came out about why the locks were changed. They were changed because of Lucas's dislike of us in the home, especially when Lester and Thelma were away. His story was that when we came into the home we wanted to pick a fight. At first, it was difficult to comprehend, but later, after I thought about it for a while, it made sense to me that he would say this to them. Regardless, soon after the confession, they gave me the key to the home, making me feel a lot better, because if something happened to my parents, we'd be able to get into the home.

Lester and Thelma had two lives. They had one life with my sister and me and our families, and then a whole other world with Lucas and his wife. They began to keep us separated but that was because Lucas hated us. It was the easiest solution to containing his dislike so in a way they felt forced to. They could not see any other way of solving the problem. It looked as if he was working himself more and more into their lives, deceiving them and creating a weird sense of blindness to the love we had for them. There were very few family functions that he and Abbey attended by now. Tactfully approaching Abbey on the subject, I told her we would love to be able to spend more time with her and that she was very welcome at any of our gatherings. She stared right through me, appearing quite aloof and stormed away with the attitude of 'how dare you to talk to me?'

Marten, Roslyn, Linnea and I (Justin, by now, was off having his own adventures), were all sitting together at the kitchen table eating dinner at the new bay home at Rehoboth. Out of nowhere, Thelma glared at Marten, demanding to know when he was going to remove his horrible beard which at the moment amused me. Her eyes simmered with spite as she informed him that she could very easily take his position away in the business and bring Lucas into it because he was entitled to the business and Abbey would then have the responsibility of taking care of the billing.

Lester was absent during this conversation because it seemed as if he was made to stay home and did not come to the bay home nearly as frequently as he used to. Marten and I could not tolerate the thought of Thelma being able to do so and questioned the soundness of her mind with her outrageous thoughts. At the time, I was the one responsible for all the billings in the business and had been doing a wonderful job with it, always very prompt. The comments by her hurt our feelings tremendously and fueled our desire to break away from the business to establish a masonry business of our own. Later Marten did so by forming a company of his own and became very successful in building many beautiful schools and large corporate buildings.

By now, it was unusual for Lester to be at the bay house when I visited. Feeling disappointed, I asked where he was because I knew he absolutely loved socializing with his family. Thelma always had some excuse for him as to why he was not going to come. So encouraging him to join us we were happy to have an opportunity to transport him to Rehoboth. Stopping along our route, we ate at a restaurant, enjoying light conversation and each other's company, therefore arriving at the bay home late morning.

Thelma was furious and berated us for being so late, telling us we would never be allowed to take Lester with us again to Rehoboth. My sights were already directed toward Hawaii, being pushed by some unknown force. Support in Pennsylvania was dry as bones in a desert and my fading spirit knew that in order for my dying body to live and eventually flourish, it had to carry me away. Taking me away it did, definitely getting its way. It was going to be a long time before I wanted to or was able to land back in that broken body. Grief and despair became constant companions, which caused my body to become heavily burdened.

Before bringing my family over to Hawaii, I spent time alone for six months, mourning the loss of the family I grew up with and the loss of my daughter. The Clairvoyant Center was a huge help in this process, holding the space for my personal journey. I am grateful for the Yoga Center which gave me a space to breathe and reconnect, and for the beautiful Islands of Hawaii which set the energy of acceptance and for rediscovering the love and the power in the name of Jesus. Returning to Pennsylvania one more time to help prepare the way for my family to come with me, it was during this time that Mr. Marten's Grill opened.

Chapter Nine
The Inward Journey

It was our last flight to a vacation in Hawaii for Christmas—spending time together as a family unit for Christmas; I decided to stay, spending over a half a year alone to find answers before Mr. Marten's Grill opened in Pennsylvania.

I meditated and spent most of my time at the Clairvoyant Center of Hawaii. They said, "We are not here to help you to solve your problems but are holding space for you to find your own answers." Not exactly what I wanted to hear but I knew it was true. I did find answers and, with a lot of growing pains, became stronger. I began to find the light within. This light gave me the means to find that place of forgiveness for myself and my imperfections, which in turn made it easier to forgive the atrocities, abuse, ignorance and blindness of others. It is energy and I looked at it as energy, knowing it also will pass in time. This energy is connected to wrong mental meanings and thought forms. Consciousness lined up events in my life that I was not yet capable of understanding. This changed me and molded me into a totally different person. It was not an easy situation; it felt as if I was in an eye of a storm, being tossed and turned, not able to get out. It too would pass because now was the time to claim my sovereignty.

Synonyms of sovereignty according to http://www.merriam-webster. com/dictionary/sovereignty autonomy, independence, independency, liberty, self-determination, self-governance, self-government, freedom

I like to think of it as an awakening. It is as if I had to get through all those nasty pictures, fears, and experiences in order to find the beauty within me, coming to terms with the fact that my life is not determined by all the exterior people, events or what other people think. I am free of them and in order to discover this beauty, had to go through the experiences which forced me to look inward and trust. Feeling unsupported by the people I loved, I still felt supported by the universe and the Great Spirit of Love. I worked with fierce determination on changing me, so I could help my daughter, Roslyn. Roslyn gave me the perseverance to find my light regardless of the storm which fueled me forward to find answers.

The Dreamer

"The medical world is telling you that it is not possible, so why can't you accept the fact and their advice. Please medicate her, Ember. You fool, you need to medicate her. Your head is in the clouds of dreamers, not reality." Not listening to the world, my eyes were focused on what I needed to do or believed had to be done. First I had to change myself and, in exchange, open my higher consciousness to answers. It was difficult to release all the attachments, genetic tendencies, and stuck emotions without getting caught up in the muck but if I did, Roslyn's spirit surely could mirror me. Becoming involved with the Clairvoyant Center of Hawaii, I had the opportunity to sit in the luxury of my own home and take the class by telephone as a long distance class. The clairvoyant classes were offered in Pennsylvania, which made them long distance but when my family went to Hawaii for Christmas, I remained and immersed myself with these classes at the center for six months. Changes had to be made and the first change was with me. I was determined nothing was stopping me, absolutely nothing.

Spending the majority of my time meditating on the word and attending classes at the center offered a place where acceptance was created with support for my own unique journey. Any additional time was used for swimming in the magnificent ocean, which invited me to release and surrender in its softness.

One afternoon, after a luxurious dip in the mighty ocean and later visiting the little grocery store at the bottom of our hill, my car proceeded up the curvy and bumpy road. I was the happy driver. The first interesting sight that occurred as I entered our gravel driveway was the sight of our whole backyard filled with a multitude of various shapes and sizes of wild pigs. It appeared as if they were holding a town hall meeting. At dusk, our property was always the central meeting ground for wild boars, which enjoyed snacking happily on our succulent macadamia nuts. However, I'd never seen such a large congregation of wild pigs in the middle of the afternoon. Their rummaging was done at night time. Our home, which is less than 1000 square feet, is complete with five acres of macadamia nut trees which attract droves of wild pigs that keep on multiplying. Tiny babies could be seen scampering to and fro looking for their mothers because at times they became lost—accidentally separated from their mothers because curiosity got them into trouble. Our property pulled all the wild pigs from the island because it contained the best nuts on the Island. Since the pigs have the highest of standards, they savored every crunchy morsel and it was not unusual to hear pig squeals and grunts throughout the night as they dug up the yard to find these tasty nuts to eat. They knew they'd found a safe haven.

On one occasion, close to our catchment tank, the long grass started moving a lot, so I decided to check it out. Maybe a mongoose found a nest in the long grass and was having a picnic on our chicken eggs which did not sit with me quite right. Mind you, Molly, Gertrude and Henrietta had a special hen house with roosting boxes away from the home to lay their eggs, or when nature called close by the house, they had the option of using the cat stand on our porch. The cat wasn't so keen on the idea but the chickens always won. They had a choice, but they did not always do what we wanted them to do and sometimes the biggest nest was found hidden away with dozens of eggs quietly incubating. Not wanting to share our chicken eggs with a mongoose, I bravely went to check on what the rustling grass was all about. Creeping to the grass slowly, I heard a weird noise like low grunts emerging from the swaying grass. Suddenly a mother pig appeared from the grass and looked right into my eyes. Bellowing a loud grunt, she began running but not alone. Her babies scampered after her to the front of the property. These mother pigs can be very ferocious when it comes to protecting their babies and will go to all lengths in doing so. They have been known to bite very hard and dogs have lost limbs in the battle. Therefore, this mother pig was given the highest of respect from me as I backed away.

A catchment tank is also called rain harvesting. These simple systems connect downspouts (gutters) to a central water tank capable of holding about 100,000 liters of water or more. Often, in African countries, the issue is not that it never rains, but rather that when it does, most of the runoff is lost. These water systems make the best use of what little rain there is. Rainwater harvesting has been around for hundreds of years. It is in use in developed and underdeveloped nations alike. In Australia, for instance, many homes away from the cities use it as a primary source of water. These simple systems are cost-effective and last for a long time. In communities that have medical clinics, schools, and other larger-roofed structures, these roofs can do a great job of collecting much-needed water to use throughout the year.

At night on previous Christmases, the children and Marten went out with Hondas searching for the pigs to scare them off our property. Various sizes of pigs could be seen and sometimes babies that were small and fragile were seen running beside their mother. Of course, cute little piglets being frightened did not go over with me at all and when they saw my concerned face, they gave it some thought, deciding to end the sport. Eventually, we fenced in our property and that solved the pig problem. These feral pigs are descendants of the small Asiatic domestic pigs introduced by Polynesians during the early colonization period (400 AD) and the larger European domestic pigs first introduced by Captain James Cook in 1778.

This was my first day alone in Hawaii since my family left to go home after Christmas, and I was so excited. Having just gone for a swim in the ocean and coming up the hill with a couple bags of groceries, I turned into our driveway. I found herds of pigs back in our backyard. This was unheard of during broad daylight because they usually hid until night came and then did their scavenging as the sky grew darker. Painted blue on blue, one stroke at a time, into deeper and deeper shades of night, the sky opened, creating a multitude of beautiful stars above or was hidden by the black clouds of night.

Well, after being startled by these wall to wall pigs, I closed the gate that was around the home to keep the pigs from entering and proceeded into our humble abode with bags of groceries in hand. Opening up the refrigerator door to put the groceries away, I was suddenly caught off balance, with the weirdest sensation that the refrigerator was going to fall on me. My first reaction was to put my hands up to keep it from crushing my body. The home kept on rattling as if it was going to fall apart and there was this bizarre sense of disconnect and total lack of control in my whereabouts. It was the oddest feeling not knowing where the ground was under my feet. Since Hawaii is known for many earthquakes, it was not rare to experience an earthquake but that day was my first time to experience something so strong. It totally rattled me.

Earthquakes in Hawaii are closely linked to volcanism. They are an important part of the island-building processes that have shaped the Island of Hawaii and the other Hawaiian Islands. Thousands of earthquakes occur every year beneath the Island of Hawaii.

Eruptions and magma movement within the presently active volcanoes Kilauea, Mauna Loa and Loihi are usually accompanied by numerous small earthquakes. They originate in regions of magma storage or along the paths that magma follows as it rises and moves prior to eruption. These are loosely termed volcanic earthquakes. Many other earthquakes, including the largest ones, occur in areas of structural weakness at the base of Hawaii's volcanoes or deep within the Earth's crust beneath the island. These are referred to as tectonic earthquakes. In the past 150 years, several strong tectonic earthquakes (magnitude 6 to 8) caused extensive damage to roads, buildings, and homes, triggered a local tsunami, and resulted in the loss of life. The most destructive earthquake in Hawaii's history occurred on April 2, 1868, when 81 people lost their lives. With a magnitude of 7.9 and a maximum intensity of XII, this destructive earthquake destroyed more than a hundred homes and generated a high tsunami along Kilauea's south coast.

Later that evening I decided to divert my attention to a comedy on TV, choosing to keep my mind off the odd experiences. Just as I began feeling cozy and involved in the movie, rain began to pour down on our tin roof creating a deafening roar. Rising, I turned the volume up and sat back down to relax and munch on my popcorn. About the time I became totally engrossed in the plot of the old time movie, the home lights decided to turn off and only pitch blackness filled the room. Sitting on my bean bag chair for a few minutes, waiting for the electricity to switch back on again, the notion came to me to pull out the book that I started at the airport. Groping my way to the closet, I felt really lucky because the brightest and the biggest flashlight was found sitting on the floor right in front of me. It was usually used for spotting wildlife at night time. In good spirits, I thought, "Ember, let's make the best of this situation." But within a half an hour, the light from this particular flashlight grew dim and eventually petered out, leaving me sitting in darkness once again, but this time with my book in hand. Although not fearful of the night that was shrouding the world in front of me in pitch-black darkness, I finally gave up and found my way by literally groping and crawling to my bedroom where the sweet release of sleep came rapidly.

Painted blue on blue, one stroke at a time, the sky that night turned into deeper and deeper shades of night. Then the sky opened, creating a multitude of beautiful stars above or was hidden by the black clouds of night.

In the morning, with the sun shining down upon our home, batteries and flashlights were purchased at the hardware store down at the bottom of the hill, procuring plenty of ammunition for the possibility of a similar dilemma. Therefore, our home, fondly referred to as 'The Coffee Shack,' would be better equipped for the darkness that might come again. Eventually, the sun willingly gave its energy for light protecting it from the darkness, and nowadays our home is very self-sufficient and we take much pride in the installment of solar panels.

This point in time gave me the opportunity to get to know and love myself and created a healing space to release all the emotions squished and pent up inside me. I made a conscious choice to let go of the family known as a child. Letting go enables love to shine from within—that is unconditional love which is rare in the world as we know it. Usually, love has a price, but true love does not; it just is. I also had to release Roslyn, who by now needed to be pried from me with a crowbar. My grief was insurmountable but it was of paramount importance to let go of her. Through the misfortune of having a traumatic brain injury, not a trace of Roslyn was found inside that body. We didn't know at the time that this injury would eventually become a gift.

Trying to make things work with the family that I knew as a child, gave me the insight that somehow there was a lesson needed which was: all you really need is your best friend, yourself and a strong connection to a higher consciousness with spirit beings working for your paramount interest. You merely have to ask for their help and wait for answers and be willing to act.

I stayed alone to receive answers throughout the winter, which brought frigid air coming from Mauna Loa's cold, icy slopes. I donned hat and gloves to go to bed and ultimately resorted to turning on our oven for the comfort of its heat throughout the night. Shivering as the morning came; my breath could be seen in the cold air of the home as I waited patiently for the sun to take out the morning chill. Now a wood stove warms the frigid air, keeping us cozy and comfortable in our home.

The snow laden volcanoes, Mauna Loa and Mauna Kea, are responsible for the winter in Hawaii which is especially colder for those at a higher elevation where the cold air loves to linger. These volcanoes' powers are able to create total opposites in the weather. The volcanoes' hot magma creates hot water springs coming from the floor of the ocean, giving swimming a whole new meaning. The senses awaken with the splendor of the colorful textures and the beautiful reef activity of coral, fish, turtles, rock formations and the sounds of ocean life. This in combination with the cool fresh water from the cold springs, combined with the taste of the salt water of the ocean awakens the spirit, bringing beauty to a whole different level. Beauty is multidimensional on the Hawaiian islands, bringing the observer to awe and giving this land the reverence it so deserves.

It rains quite a lot on the windward (East) side, up to 300 inches (10 meters) per year. Most of this water does not flow directly to the ocean but sinks down into the ground until it hits a barrier. This barrier is composed of salt water, which is heavier than fresh water. The water in this layer then slowly dissipates to the edge of the island and flows into the ocean. In the volcanic areas, the water flows through rocks that are heated by magma. This heat is absorbed by the water and taken along to the coast. As the water moves away from the magma it cools down a bit, especially if the cold water mixes with it, but the water stays warm enough to give visitors a comfortable warm bath!

The Island captivates her soul; its beauty too alluring, grandeur too inspiring, the enchantment…too intoxicating. The wind's gentle whisper beckons to visit, to explore this place—to walk and live in its magic. Laughter is heard radiating from the kitchen. It is a time to celebrate this gift of life.

Finally coming home after being gone for a half of a year, we were enjoying the best cold pressed coffee. We usually sat around the kitchen bar on high stools in the morning and, engaged in a lively conversation before it was time to go to the dining room. Streams of sunshine streamed through the windows, bringing the kitchen alive with the promise of a new day. Lester and Thelma chattered excitedly in the kitchen, so happy to be visiting for our very special time together.

The dining room was where all kinds of breakfast goodies were found waiting, prepared in the early morning by Marten. The dining room was an extension of the great room, with its high ceiling and large windows, beginning on the first floor and extending to the second floor of the balcony. On the balcony, comfortable chairs sat for enjoying the view from a different part of the home or just for reflection. Relishing this very special time together in the great room, Razzle, our little white cockapoo, was always in our company. When you looked at her face you could swear she was smiling as she watched the colors of love in the air.

My parents looked forward to their excursion to our home and it is on this one particular morning after breakfast, while sitting on the big red couch next to our piano, they said, "We are not used to being treated with such great respect and love. People are treating us horribly."

We tried to pursue this subject matter further, but they were not willing to disclose any more details.

Thelma and Lester stayed until it was time for my mom to go to her hair appointment which was the same time every week. Following them out to their car hugs and kisses were exchanged before they climbed into their sports car. As we stood waving, they pulled out of the driveway. My mom's hair appointments were very important to her and my dad enjoyed driving her to them in their latter years. By now, we'd made a conscious choice not to go to Lester and Thelma's home, but arranged time together at different locations, usually opening Martens Grill every Saturday morning.

This last home in Pennsylvania was surrounded by Amish farmland and this was where much of my long distance training was done with the Clairvoyant Center. We traveled back and forth from Hawaii quite a bit while living at the home on Aver hill Road and it was on one of our later trips to Hawaii that Lester and Thelma accompanied us. But it was afterward when we moved to the home in the country when I came across the Clairvoyant Center and became totally engrossed in the program, living alone to find answers for half of a year.

Classes were done in progression: meditation one, meditation two, clairvoyant one, clairvoyant two, which eventually led to the teacher program. These classes took a lot of dedication and much time to complete. The teaching program was done after the move to Hawaii but many of the other classes were attended long distance with a few of them attended while I stayed the six months in Hawaii. As we increased in our competence, readings were done and the first reading was to look at each other's aura. These readings were exchanged by using a conference line which was dialed into with a room full of students living in various places around the world. When my turn came to receive a reading, the readers saw all kinds of colors and began to share what they saw. As they took turns sharing, tears began to pour from my eyes because my heart was touched deeply. I cried quietly, having never heard such nice things said about me. My tears came out acidic, which burnt my cheeks, creating bright red streaks going down my face, and my throat ached as if it was on fire. Almost immediately, my tongue turned black, which lasted for months, and about six months after moving to Hawaii my bath water started changing to midnight black, which continued for many years.

I do attribute the removal of this horrible fungus from my body to using a box which we attached to our water supply to change its frequency and therefore increase the water's properties to nourish the cells. We had this box at our last home in Pennsylvania, drinking this water as well as bathing with it. I experimented in other locations and got baths at friends' homes or hotels and my bath water did not turn black but when going back home to Hawaii my bath water became a midnight black, disturbing but good to remove from my body. Our good friend, John, is the founder of the Talya Water Home System. The lower energies that had crept into my body could no longer stay because gradually my will to live grew stronger. Having a choice to live or die, I chose life. It was during this time while in Pennsylvania that my long distant entrainments of quantum biofeedback were being received by a practitioner residing in Hawaii. This played a big part in my own personal journey. You can find more information about quantum biofeedback by reading: *The Power of the Entangled Hierarchy.*

Feigning happiness, I never felt so alone. Thelma had an intimate send off party for me and Linnea. Marten and Roslyn were also present at the home for this send off party. Again the all-too-familiar feeling came to me of depression. There was no life in Pennsylvania: no joy, no movement and no hope. This discomfort is what had always been, and will always be here and I finally accepted my profound inability to "will" change in either the behaviors or mood of my immediate family. The next morning, Linnea and I boarded a plane to Hawaii.

Having flashbacks, she remembers sitting in her beautiful home surrounded by Amish farms, recalling the conversation in the dining room with her father.

"Why do you have to leave, why not stay with us?" And with a heavy heart, she says, "No, I cannot live in this kind of situation. I already discussed it with you and Mother." She is surprised, how straightforwardly the answer came not knowing where else to go with this question. Her mind is made up. He looks at her with imploring eyes. She begins to think why not let your parents stay in this big home with you? A bedroom could be arranged for them out of the adjoining office which already has a small kitchen to cook their meals. This section of the home has an extra entrance and exit door with separate living quarters with a complete bathroom designed for an elderly woman. But the thoughts come around with all the solutions to one main deterring point. Lucas and his wife would tag along, eventually making their lives miserable and they'd be strangers in their own home. Unable to find any remedies for the situation, her thoughts churn and spew in her head just like a hamster wheel caught in a cycle of agonizing energy. She explores different solutions, only coming to what ultimately daunted them: Lucas would come to live with Thelma and Lester and would be able to come into their home at whim. He would figure something out even with a restraining order.

Material Things

When the decision to leave Pennsylvania and come to Hawaii was made, that's when my real journey began. Our last home was my dream home. It was so beautiful, with huge windows looking out into the country landscape and forest, with a balcony inside our home where you could sit quietly looking out those windows observing nature. I was able to do my laundry in a spacious room just dedicated for laundry. This laundry room was on the second floor, complete with sink, drawers, and bins where laundry could be sorted, and our downstairs basement was huge—with a large area to play darts, Ping-Pong, pool or watch movies—complete with its own bathroom. The home movie system had a huge screen complete with surround sound, making you feel you were at the movie theatre. An old fashioned popcorn maker went along with the gaiety, and eating hot fresh popcorn on a big comfy couch or a fluffy chair completed the experience. The basement had plenty of room for my personal gymnastics equipment which we could get out at whim. Upstairs, our bedroom's adjoining bathroom had a huge whirlpool used for a bathtub. It had different jets which massaged your tired muscles, releasing the tensions of the day. It also had its own private room to watch television. Our bed was in a separate room away from the hustle and bustle of any noise and was only used for sleeping. Large windows were opened at night, and we were serenaded by the nighttime creatures. The kitchen floor was heated by hot water pipes that lay under it, joining the great room and the dining room. This home was complete inside as well as outside and proudly showed off its gorgeous landscaping, complete with a swing set and trampoline.

Surrounded by Amish farms, we were visited by Amish children selling their items pulled in an old-fashioned wagon. They entered our home timidly, wearing bonnets and sporting bare feet and looked up at me with those big champagne-brown eyes. Demurely, they showed me what they were selling. It was nearly impossible to turn them away; usually, they departed with a smile on their faces and a skip in their step because of making one more sale.

When walking to the neighboring farm to buy raw milk and to shop at an old-fashioned country store nearby, it was not unusual for us to see a couple of horses and buggies pull up into the parking lot so Amish could do their shopping. Sunday evenings while walking the country road, we saw continuous lines of Amish buggies pass by in single file pulled by their loyal horses, proudly trotting down the road. All were heading to the same destination, a Sunday evening gathering. Babies and children peeked out from the buggies curiously to see what was about them, often waving as they went by. These functions had a huge variety of different foods prepared by the women, which enticed the men to come to these long drawn out meetings.

The young men have parties called hoedowns in a barn which is where they "sow all their wild oats" as my dad would say. On a few occasions as a young girl, I had the privilege of witnessing a couple of these hoedowns with a good friend of mine named 'Little Joe' who was friends with some of the Amish young men who attended these get-togethers. Lots of music, beer and dancing were part of these parties. The hay was stacked very high in a part of the barn which was used for a landing by some of the brave souls. Jumping from the rafters, they yelled and hollered as they landed atop the lofty mountain of hay. Some boys were seen swinging from the wooden beams using a thick rope to hold onto which oscillated back and forth as the band played. These parties were definitely vibrant and alive.

While parents and church leaders might feel embarrassed when the Amish youth violate the strict teachings of the Amish church, it is usually tolerated to a large extent because it offers young Amish adults the opportunities to explore the outside world before they commit themselves fully to the strict regulations of the church. Before their adult baptism, they are generally free to experiment without fear of excommunication or shunning. In other words, by having an opportunity to "sow their wild oats," Amish youths are granted the choice of whether or not they want to be Amish and follow the rigid regulations which that decision entails. A large proportion of those young Amish adults who rebel eventually choose to remain Amish.

Leaving my new home behind for awhile was a must in order to make this new journey untraveled yet, not realizing it was my last time to spend time in it. Since leaving Pennsylvania, our good friend, Atticus, keeps our grand piano in his home. Very gifted in music and trustworthy, he enjoys our piano, tuning it and making it sound glorious. When making that long trip to visit my dad, Atticus graciously opens his second home for us to reside in and the use of his red truck for travel. If we're lucky, he invites us to his home where he plays music on the piano that rocks our soul.

Coming to rest at the coffee shack, not for one moment did I believe that this would become our new home. Dreams of either building a home from scratch on our land or buying a new home were in the making, that is, if we decided to stay in Hawaii. But consciousness had its own plan.

The coffee shack was built for the people that worked in its majestic macadamia orchard. Surrounded by five acres of these very fragrant trees, this home beckons its new owners to come and rest. First, a little girl from India named Linnea with the most inquisitive big brown eyes accompanies her mother, being drawn by its soft caresses of beauty. With school soon starting she travels with her mother, knowing her father and sister, Roslyn, will follow them later in October.

Gazing out the window, while sitting on the plane gave me plenty of time to go within. Knowing that my husband would be bringing Roslyn later, I knew my life was going to be changing but had no idea as to how much that would be.

Toxic

A young woman with fiery green eyes decides life is not working out at all for her and her heart is heavy with many burdens. Hitting rock bottom, there is nothing left to keep her in Pennsylvania, only a gorgeous home, and her devoted animals. Estrangement from her family grows stronger and more intense with walls being built up to keep her out. She has to come to her senses and stop trying to change that which is impossible for her to make different. Therefore, she decides to leave the toxic environment which reminds her of her deep sorrow. She has a choice of trying to tear down the impossible wall, running a hamster wheel of memories around in her battered psyche which eventually would drag her down a rabbit hole of no return or a decision that it is enough. Not wanting to sit in the stormy stew anymore, she refuses to allow this energy any more opportunity to penetrate further into her already tired body. Removing herself from the abuse, she leaves everything behind.

Finally, the enchanted island that has grown to love her gets its wish and she listens as it beckons her home, where grace is found. On this particular trip, Linnea Sakshi is her companion and arriving at the quiet quaint airport, they find traveling accommodations to their small home where they prepare a plan together for the next morning. To onlookers, they are an unusual motley team. Linnea has beautiful deep brown skin, the deepest dark chocolate-brown eyes and long midnight black hair, shiny and thick.

Eventually, the rest of their fans came circling and trickling in to land, being guided by love. In a few years her brother arrives, landing a captain position for an airline carrier. The Universe has worked it out, making it possible for this family to come together and thrive.

Linnea had a good attitude about going through the open door to a new adventure in Hawaii. Searching and visiting the different schools the year before, we came across a Christian school, which seemed to be the perfect fit for Linnea, since she was already attending a smaller Christian school. Linnea thrived in this smaller school, making many friends but after two years of attending, she was forced to leave because we were struggling financially as a family. Reluctantly, she enrolled in the public school system but before that change was made, I personally talked to the head of her school, asking if she was willing to give us a break with tuition. But realizing it still was not feasible to pay the lowered tuition for this school because of the many other bills that needed to be attended, we felt as if we let Linnea down. She could not stay with the school she had grown to love.

Since then she'd graduated from a public school where good friends were found who rocked her soul. These friends shared many common interests with her. She became involved in sports, the student leadership program, trained and worked as a teller for the Community Bank, an opportunity provided by the school, attended youth meetings as well as receiving very good grades. Later, she found financial support for her university of choice, by searching for and applying for a variety of grants to pay for her education. At the present time, she attends and is part of many worship activities, outreach programs and has become involved in the opportunity of mission work. She is a spirit/soul body in creation, enjoying the many choices of the smorgasbord of life, living up to her name 'the witness'.

My childhood days gave me something to look back at to catch that memory of feeling free. My life experience was deeply transformational and I am not the same person, having been forced to transform dramatically. There were times that I was not sure that one more step could be taken forward. Old friends had gone but new friends came into my life. People I believed in left me. My family I grew up with, everything and everybody I relied on, including most of the people in the medical field were unreliable and there was nowhere to turn but to look up. So that is what I did. Meditating, I connected to my divine essence to create a different me and therefore create a different life. My heart was breaking and every emotion was covered up. But in order to be strong, I had to address each emotion or simply let them go. I kept on changing and so did my body which began to detoxify, making my bath water black. Black fungus invaded my immune system because of the huge emotional toll put on my body. My lymphatic and immune systems gave up and became overloaded, unable to do their job the way they were designed.

It was definitely a journey, a journey to freedom and, as time went on, my nervous system slowly started to heal. Communicating became more fluid, and my brain began to work better as I broke free. My studies for my doctorate began in Hawaii and progressively, I became more focused while working with Roslyn. She was rejected by the medical field which forced me to look elsewhere, but I had faith there was something out there that would help her, instead of heavy medication and a psychiatric ward. When quantum biofeedback was introduced to me by a Naturopath doctor in Hawaii, that's when the real healing journey began. This journey fueled me with the desire to fight for myself and in turn be able to help my daughter. My children were my inspiration to choose life. I had no other choice.

Last Visit

Visiting Thelma and Lester after moving to Hawaii occurred only one time while they were able and well. We met early morning for breakfast. After meeting them at our favorite quaint restaurant for breakfast, I handed a gorgeous plant full of blooms to my mom as she was getting into their car to travel back home. Happening to glance over at my father and mother as they began to pull out from their parking space, I noticed my mom's shoulders heaving with grief. Seeing her sobbing relentlessly made it so difficult to leave her in that condition. So, convincing Marten to come with me to visit my parents at their home before returning to Hawaii, we drove over to visit them in the late afternoon.

Circumstances had not changed and it felt eerie and odd as Lucas stood to stare from afar with his mother, who came out only to glare at us. If only my parents would ask for help in this odd situation, life could be so different and fulfilling, but they chose not to. Circumstances were not going to change:nothing stirred, nothing sounded, and nothing sang. It was so difficult to make that conscious choice to let go, but I went back home to Hawaii the next morning, as tears streamed down my face, never feeling so alone or gloomy.

> What have I got to do to make you love me?
> What have I got to do to make you care?
> What do I do when lightning strikes me?
> And I wake to find that you're not there
> What do I do to make you want me?
> What have I got to do to be heard?
> What do I say when it's all over
> And sorry seems to be the hardest word
> It's sad, so sad
> It's a sad, sad situation

And it's getting more and more absurd
It's sad, so sad
Why can't we talk it over?
Oh it seems to me
That sorry seems to be the hardest word
What do I do to make you love me?
What have I got to do to be heard?
What do I do when lightning strikes me?
What have I got to do?
What have I got to do?
When sorry seems to be the hardest word
By Elton John

See the truth and it will set you free. Change those thoughts of, "What do I have to do to make you love me—what do I have to do to make you care?" I knew how it felt to be like a dog eager for love after the neglect and abuse of its owner, though I was certainly not a dog or any kind of animal. If we are led by the Holy Spirit we think it will always be peaceful, which is not always necessarily true. Jesus was led into the desert for a long and difficult time of testing, and we also may be led into difficult situations. Many a time temptation will come to keep us off course and also our self-doubt can come to rob us.

"Judge not, and ye shall not be judged: condemn not, and ye shall not be condemned: forgive, and ye shall be forgiven" (Luke 6:37, KJV).

When caught in the storms of life, it is easy to think that God has lost control and that we are at the mercy of the winds of fate. In reality, there is a much bigger picture in our own personal evolvement. About two years after leaving to make a home in Hawaii, we lost our family business which we relied on for our income. All was gone and in order to be happy, detachment from any material or human connection was necessary to discover my own connection with the divine. Learning how to live in the light without fighting the darkness became my life lesson.

Meetings in Pennsylvania

In the hope of saving his business and bringing security to the people who depend on upon it, he books his flight. Formerly, he made this business into a very lucrative enterprise; therefore in confidence, he now boards a plane to Pennsylvania to fly throughout the night to meet with some of the top executives of Northwest Bank. As he flies over the ocean, his mind races with high hopes and expectations that the people he is meeting will be receptive to him. Sleep comes but is fleeting. After landing at the airport, renting a car and arriving at his destination, he quickly tries to make himself presentable for the meeting which should be held shortly. Little does he know they are already waiting comfortably for his arrival, sporting suits and ties while drinking coffee and savoring sweet pastries.

Led to the room by the receptionist, the door opens slowly, revealing a roomful of executives waiting for his arrival. Introductions immediately begin and after shaking everyone's hand, he takes a seat and begins to outline his ideas on changing the business plan to keep it within or below the credit line. Also, statements are shown proving that revenues are soon to come in from a job almost completed. He explains to this group of people that payments for this job are received in increments, meaning his business receives monies only as the project is finished in stages and the last stage was almost finished. There would be more than enough monies to pay the line of credit.

These top executives had no idea how his family suffered and depended upon this family business to find and purchase therapies for their oldest daughter. It was such a distressful time in their lives. The line of credit was used for materials and any other unforeseen issues and for now, he needed that line of credit to survive until approved changes were made within the business structure. His father-in-law, who is very well known in the community, relies on a line of credit and is very successful with his business. They listen and he leaves with hope, proceeding to his next destination.

At Thelma and Lester's home, he shares his difficulty with the business and humbly asks to borrow money, promising to pay it back little by little. This financial predicament is very humiliating to him and he hates to ask them for money. His father-in-law hearing the urgency in Marten's voice immediately writes out a check, not aware that there was someone lurking around the corner in the shadows listening. As Marten begins to extend his arm in acceptance, a hand that seems to come out of nowhere snatches the check from Lester's hand. Ripping it into tiny pieces, a young man with sandy blond hair glares at him with hateful eyes, saying, "Leave my grandpa alone."

The next day in Pennsylvania a secret meeting is held at a restaurant and this time a check exchanges hands. These elderly people's greatest desire is to help their granddaughter.

Previously, they had received a phone call from their hysterical daughter who is worried about losing their business. This business is needed for Roslyn, who needs intensive care and therapy, now living at their home with her sister who is still in elementary school. This was a very important check.

False Hope

Content in believing it was all going to work out and anxious to get home, he looks out into the blue sky over the deep ocean believing his trip was well worth it. He would have more than enough to pay the line of credit with the money received from the completed job which is coming very soon. He did not want to let his family down.

Several trips were made to attend meetings with the top executives from the Northwest Bank in Pennsylvania. These trips were made as brief as possible and made for only one reason and that was to save the business. Marten knew he was needed back home with us, knowing the grave situation with our daughter. It was imperative that he return as soon as possible. Thinking for sure they were going to give us a second chance, he felt good after coming home, particularly after the last trip. Hope was fueled with optimism, but later this proved to be false because the bank was ruthless. The top representative did not follow through with the plan they had projected for the business. Instead, the top executives disregarded the plan of action, not taking into consideration the horrible plight of this small business and the many families that depended upon it. The bank had no mercy even when the money for the line of credit was promised to be paid back shortly and a change of business structure was already being implemented. It appeared as if the top executive had already made up his mind. The line of credit was going to be pulled and down would fall the corporation.

Would the result have been different if I had accompanied my husband? But at the time it was not an option, nothing was going to keep me from our home because of the urgency to be there with Roslyn. Terribly saddened by the turn of events, we mourned the loss of our business and did not know how we were going to manage to keep our home.

> Humpty-Dumpty had a great fall;
> All the king's horses, and all the king's men,
> Cannot put Humpty-Dumpty together again.
> *Source: Smith, the Little Mother Goose (1912)*

The earliest recorded publication of "Humpty Dumpty" dates back to 1810. The rhyme is thought to be an allegorical reference to an enormous cannon used during the siege of Colchester in 1648. After Parliament opened fire at the city wall supporting "Humpty Dumpty," the large weapon fell to the ground. The Royalists, or "all the King's men," tried to lift "Humpty dumpty" on to another part of the wall, but failed to do so due to the cannon's massive weight. "All the King's horses and all the King's men couldn't put Humpty together again." Alternately, Robert L. Ripley theorized that the original Humpty Dumpty was Richard III, the last of the Plantagenet dynasty, who fell at the Battle of Bosworth in 1485. Humpty Dumpty is also a prominent character in Lewis Carroll's "Through the Looking-Glass."

Material things lost their importance in my life. Marten ended up having a trusted friend in the business sell most of the equipment and received tens of thousands for it. At first, in the beginning, the stage with the intentions of filing for bankruptcy, an attorney advised that all monies needed to be accounted for. So deciding to trust a friend of mine, we invested some money into a start-up business she had proposed to us. With part of the monies we invested and entrusted with Melinda, she stated that she would bring us in as her partner as well as be the majority shareholder. She would follow up and forward us the partnership agreement after her cruise. Melinda and her husband boarded a cruise to write up this partnership agreement as advised by her accountant. The agreement was later sent to us to look at and sign, but she never signed and returned the documents and most of the money was used for her personal needs while the balance was used for bad business decisions. We were horrified. Details were found out later by contacting the inventor who was working on our behalf to upstart this project. We learned that the project was not completed because she did not honor the financial agreement towards the development of the quantum chair. We realized she depleted the funds through her own personal greed. The contract became void and null with the inventor who she blamed for this and Melinda was in total denial of her mistake. We were convinced that she displayed the utmost quality of character but found a wolf in disguise hiding behind religion.

Graciously, she had opened her home to the members of our group who needed provisions for rest, sleep and food during the span of time our group worked at a booth in Las Vegas. Elaborate meals were made for us every evening after getting back from a long day of work and in the morning breakfast was served before we went off to work. After breakfast, we congregated at a very prestigious convention center, preparing our booth to promote quantum biofeedback. Our equipment was set up for curious attendees who were potential customers so that they were able to see and experience the technology of quantum biofeedback.

While going to the convention center, I received the phone call from my sister. She was hysterical, trying to find words to let me know what was happening within our family. Intense out-of-control drama had infiltrated the family, and later I received a phone call from Thelma, confirming the legitimacy of Mairzy's hysteria. I was informed not to come to the house, and if I did so, I would be met by a policeman to escort me off to jail. So, my friends knew that things were looking grim for me and patiently listened to my concerns for my parents and their safety. We prayed together for them the evening of my mother's phone call. Of course, we definitely were foolish in trusting her with our money but the stress was a huge player in this decision which made us unable to think rationally or think at all. Stress had a stranglehold on us by now and we thought it sounded like a good idea to keep our money hidden in the business enterprise suggested. This business involved the development of a special quantum chair built to connect with the body energetic.

The bankruptcy attorney preached like the old time preachers who could cause the hairs on your arms stand up, making you feel that if you did not bare your soul and reveal every dime and nickel to your name the pit of hell was your destiny. Burning eternally, pushed into the flaming pit, our lives would never be the same again. Many of our personal items would be confiscated, including our furniture, cars, as well as anything else we possessed such as extra cash and even the clothing we wore could be taken from us. Our lives were already stressed like a rubber band threatening to break because of what was beginning to unfold in my parents' lives, and our battle for our daughter's life. Life, in general, had gone haywire and just plain crazy.

Right about this time, my husband received a contract for a commercial project with a general contractor. But at the early stage of construction, they heard about our masonry company being stressed and set up a dinner meeting with Marten. They discussed different strategies and reviewed our financial statements to devise a plan to bring both businesses together, and later decided it was too risky to incur the debt load. Showing him pictures of his multi-millionaire home and sharing the many personal items he had purchased because of the wealth he acquired through his business, he led Marten to believe there was a future working with this company. But later, our job contract was abruptly terminated and our equipment was secretly hidden by this company. We did not create any hardship or debt to him and the masonry job we had an agreement on was being completed in a timely manner, using our best men. Not answering his phone or returning any of the messages which Marten left, his intentions were obviously dishonorable. He scammed Marten into believing he was there to be his friend but instead stole the company's equipment.

By now we were renting our new home to a family. A letter had been received from them while we were residing in Hawaii, stating that they absolutely loved our home and would love to be renters if we were open to the idea. Agreeing, after some background checks, we thought what a great idea and were happy to have the extra income. Later these renters got incoming warped information from the town criers. News of bits and pieces of our dilemma began to run rampant throughout the community. Scavengers came out of hiding and began to sharpen their knives and forks, licking their chops to get ready for the plucking. They became like those animals that peck on a bird that is still in the game of life which is still fumbling, just wanting to stand up in the worst way. They were without conscience. Men can revert to their animal brain, the lower part of their brain which lacks consciousness and does horrible acts, unthinkable things against others. The bank did not own our home because we were working on a strategy to keep our home, but instead of paying the rent we had agreed upon, these people took it upon themselves to reduce the rent, complaining about everything regarding the home.

This home was pristine, built from scratch, meticulously constructed by the best contractor, and featured on the cover of one of the editions of *Home and Garden* magazine. We knew they were just taking advantage of our weakened state. Unfortunately, the people that lived in our home did not honor their rental agreement adding extra bills on to it, therefore paying very little to us. They constantly nickel and dimed us looking for every expense, using us as their scapegoat for their own personal gain and they took advantage of our dilemma as an excuse to do so. They did not care and their attitude disappointed me; anger ran rampant for their inconsideration.

Friends

Gathering quite a bit of information about people through life experience, the realization dawned on me that there are very few people that you can call your friends—people you can really trust and depend upon, who truly desire the best for you. Consider yourself fortunate if you stumble upon one and, if lucky, a few on your life path.

It was in Pennsylvania that a very good friend of ours named John Albright heard our conversation about a form which needed to be filled out by our accountant to prove our taxes were paid in order to save one of our properties. Our funds were so tight at the time the money was just not there to pay the accountant for doing our tax work and therefore she was not going to sign the form. It was a very embarrassing and humbling time in our lives. Overhearing our worried conversation, he asked us how much we needed and immediately began to write a check out without blinking an eye. At that time I was unable to look at John because of an overwhelming flood of emotions that came over me, leaving me speechless. There were no words in my vocabulary that could have expressed the gratitude and thankfulness I felt from this gesture of love which came through so unexpectedly. That day, a spark of light was ignited within me, creating hope.

Little did I know that consciousness had another plan for me, one that I could not see as yet. It was a better plan which was already being set in motion and taking root, becoming established in a very strong way. Meeting us on one of our later trips to Pennsylvania, John spent hours with us, sharing information about all of the projects he had on the burner. The three of us laughed together sitting in a booth, dreaming and knowing one day his hard work would pay off.

In Pennsylvania, Marten and I focused on making doctor appointments for Roslyn. They were clueless how to really help her, but it appeared as if I stumbled onto a key player while staying alone in Hawaii, a doctor that so happen to see Roslyn. Roslyn was definitely on my priority list and my main focus, the reason why the Clairvoyant classes and Quantum University were attended. She is the one that pushed me forward; inspiring me to learn as much as was humanly possible using quantum biofeedback, obtaining my doctorate in Natural Medicine and a Ph.D. She was my inspiration and the star that guided me through the pitch black night.

The remaining last bit of money from the business revenue was used in purchasing a hyperbaric oxygen tank. We acted on a recommendation by a doctor whose specialty was with traumatic brain injuries, and with a little research of our own, we were convinced it was definitely an item needed.

Nothing seemed to make sense anymore. The world familiar to me was falling out of control, which forced me to trust and fortified my faith in a higher power, believing that these events had to be created for an important reason. Everything that happened was molding me, as painful as it seemed at the time, and I am so much wiser. I have come to a greater depth of understanding about life and human behavior, with a greater compassion for myself and therefore others. Detaching myself from wanting anything but allowing it to manifest in a natural way, I chose to let go. Before, my happiness depended on spending time with the family I grew up with and enjoying each other's company but I was forced to look elsewhere, finding my own happiness through a new door of being. A different path supported me and therefore the God of my heart was honored, nurturing me with what did serve me, not running after that which was empty. Happiness comes from within.

The Key

Graduating from the clairvoyant teacher's program, which has become a focused passion of this young woman for many years, eventually, the title reverend is acquired, her eyes radiate a green light as she focuses on the goal of complete healing, the so-called impossible.

With patience, answers did come in and with those answers came the responsibility to go forward connecting with more answers on this journey for Roslyn and her unique healing, as well as mine. Now Roslyn had gone into a catatonic state. While spending time with her brother in New Mexico, a plan was set in motion. At first, there were no answers in sight, only rejection from the medical community but answers did slowly trickle in and that was when a flicker of hope arrived, spurring me onward to a frontier that no one had ever traveled before.

A naturopath doctor saw Roslyn and she was the key that opened the door to a whole other dimension of healing. It was imperative not to let the drama that was going on with my parents, Lucas, and the loss of our business take me off course. Also, staying neutral to the dramas that came up as Roslyn's healing journey began was the most difficult task for me as her mother. It was paramount to keep a focused intention with the outcome of my daughter's miracle, her full recovery, therefore detaching from any other outside distractions. This was not going to be an easy task and some professionals thought it impossible at the onset of this unique journey never before traveled. Understanding the importance of being neutral with what was being released from her body which had occupied it while she was gone, I did not give it the energy that it wanted from me but became trained to be neutral to it. It was only energy, feeding on and depleting her life essence.

Roslyn incurred a head injury but the mainstream doctors did not see it as so. Instead, they thought she had psychological issues. Yes, she appeared as if she had psychological issues but they stemmed from head injuries. One of the injuries happened at a gymnastics training center and another had to do with faulty equipment at a university meet which my family had the opportunity to watch. A pin had begun to jiggle out of the end of the balance beam unnoticed. This pin was used in adjusting its height for practice. Just as Roslyn performed her dismount from the end of the balance beam, the pin jostled just enough to allow the beam to drop, which made it not possible to get enough propulsion for the rotation of her twisting flip. Roslyn fell forward, striking the front of her forehead, catching the end of the balance beam. Marten, my parents, Linnea and I watched in horror as Roslyn's body crumbled to the mat below.

It was this particular accident which put the brain in total overload and slowly in time she became very sick.

Bright Future

Choosing Pittsburgh after visiting five other universities was a difficult decision for Roslyn, but finally, after much thought, she chose the University of Pittsburgh. Before Roslyn made her decision the women's gymnastics' coach from the University of Pittsburgh traveled by car across Pennsylvania to meet with her, while we lived in our older home. While visiting, Debbie was invited to our home for a spaghetti dinner and it was during dinner that our white cockatoo, who resided in her huge green bird cage, kept bobbing up and down yelling, "Oh shit," and various other special phrases that were picked up and heard. Marten really needed to be more careful with his language which was heard drifting from his office, an offset room of our home. These phrases were heard and learned by Packi easily because my husband said them very loud and at times quite often with a lot of enthusiasm and emotion. Apparently, the bird was doing his studying and decided to show us what he knew at a very inconvenient time. Packi could not be quieted and kept on repeating a huge repertoire of vocabulary words including, "Jesus loves me, Oh shit," and, "Where is Lester!" Eventually, his cage had a blanket put over it in hopes of soothing him, but out from under the blanket, you could hear his cries, "What happened to the Lights? Oh no, lights out! Oh shit! Help me, Jesus!"

Looking back at this particular time in our lives these memories were very precious and refreshing and important for me to remember and connect to again. This helped strengthen and fortify my belief in the human spirit as being fresh and innocent. Humor has a high vibration and encourages the healing process.

It was a huge accomplishment to be able to say that six universities wanted to give her a full scholarship, but later Roslyn could not make simple decisions and with much agonizing, chose to relinquish her scholarship with

Pittsburgh, eventually becoming catatonic and losing touch with reality as she knew it. I had to come to a greater awareness of myself in order to help her, which was going to be a huge undertaking. There was no other choice but to do so because the medical community did not give me any answers. Believing all was possible, I looked onward.

Losing the business was huge and we had no idea how things would work out. How could we help Roslyn? How could our mortgage bill be paid? I started to think about how homeless people might feel, fancied myself as being homeless and understood that times can get really rough. What is the history of those living on the streets? Granted, many have become involved with drugs but what led them down that path? Talking to people living off the streets gave me an appreciation for these people and their lives. Many of their stories do not involve drugs of any sort but horrible sorrows that devastated their spirits bringing them down to their knees. They gave up.

"How can this get much worse, God? Is this some kind of sick joke putting me here on planet Earth; please beam me up now! I am so done!"

This absolutely can't get any worse but little did I know. Horrible muck thick like cement sucked me down like quicksand. At other times it was hard as a rock, not allowing me to take another step forward in everyday life and it felt as if I barely existed.

Thelma and Lester became increasingly aloof in a multitude of ways and it began to feel like a losing battle. Thelma started to forget our birthdays or was she not allowed to honor our birthdays? She was losing the battle to the psychopath who was slowly taking her soul in order to separate her from the family. He was responsible for ultimately creating her demise. Horribly troubled and isolated with Lucas, they became overwhelmed. They outlived their friends and lost the support of the church. Lucas said many times that there was no way that he was going to move away from his grandparents' home because his role was to take care of them. He was like a leech that would not let go. What did he mean by taking care of? We had Lester over for dinner years ago at our home because Thelma was with her friends at Rehoboth or travelling at the time. Lucas drove up to the house. He sat and stared at us, demanding that his grandpa come home. Lucas was welcomed to eat dinner with us but refused. Lester never came over again alone.

On a bright cheery Sunday, the phone rings. Relaxing on the lanai and sipping good organic Hawaiian coffee, a woman with jade-green eyes deep in thought slowly arises, wondering who could possibly be calling so early on a

Sunday morning. Answering, she is pleasantly surprised to find her father on the line. He says it has been a while since he has taken the time to call her, and wants to let her know how grateful he is for all the time she spent with him using quantum biofeedback.

Chuckling he says how good he feels, in fact so good he plans on being around for a long time. As he shares this with her, she can only imagine his deep blue eyes sparkling with happiness, and her heart beams inside, extending out into space.

Many healings have been witnessed in the use of subspace in the quantum world, creating miracles in people's lives. Lester had been diagnosed with bladder cancer. The prognosis was not that promising and he was not given much more time to live on Earth.

The Quantum World

Being able to scan an individual from anywhere in the world is one of the most unfathomable ideas imaginable.. But time after time, it has been shown to work with great accuracy. When an individual is born they have a very specific energy about them which makes them truly distinct in the quantum world. Inputing the person's full name, date of birth and place of birth, distant therapy can begin. This amazing technology connects to an individual anywhere in the quantum world. Similar to dialing up a friend on a mobile phone, subspace allows you to dial into any individual at any time, with their permission.

Mathematicians describe subspace as a multidimensional set of possible geographic space superimposed under our universe. There are multiple dimensions in our universe-with one dimension still contacting and uniting all things. This dimension is called subspace or the fundamental glue of the consciousness of the universe.

Long Distance Healing is done through quantum physics principles. In scientific circles, this is known as non-local healing. It is a proven scientific fact that this method of healing is extremely effective. Harvard University holds seminars in non-local healing. The medical establishment has performed many double-blind studies that also prove the effectiveness of this type of therapy.

Was Lucas listening to that conversation? This was common practice by him and if he heard that remark, it would have made him very angry.I can only imagine his cold eyes glittering with hostility. Very strange how one day Lester was sharing happily how fantastic he felt and then the next day had a massive stroke leaving him incoherent. We were not informed about his horrible state of affairs until three days later after he was hospitalized. This information was discovered accidentally by Mairzy who called me immediately. My other question is, was this the time span when he was threatened to hand over his bank account and all his earnings with someone standing pointing a shotgun at him and his wife? The information he shared quite a bit later with Marten. Did the struggle cause the stroke or was he pushed? These are questions that haunt my mind.

The Phone

For years, when calling the home of Thelma and Lester, deep breathing could be heard on the line throughout our many conversations. At first, it began in a subtle way. It seemed as if someone was on the phone listening but you were never quite sure. Later, this bizarre behavior became increasingly noticeable while we lived in Pennsylvania. But it was when I moved to Hawaii it appeared stronger and more controlling. The awareness of how insecure he had become to feel so compelled to listen to our phone conversations was eerie. This behavior had been going on for years and escalated, becoming habitual. At first, Thelma or Lester would ask him to please hang up the receiver, but gradually the odd behavior was reluctantly ignored and because of tiredness creeping into their spirits, eventually it was accepted. During the last year and a half, the phone line wires were tampered with so when Mairzy or I did call, a busy signal was always heard. The last time we conversed with Thelma was right after Lester was brought home early from rehabilitation for a major stroke. Thelma called me and expressed her fear of being in their home, confiding in me that she was just pushed and was frightened. She indicated to me that she was being terrorized in her home which only harbored evil. This disturbing phone call was received while I attended a workshop for Yoga. Immediately after Thelma talked to me, I called Mairzy. Expediently, Mairzy and Jackson drove to the home and found Thelma huddled in the kitchen against the wall with remnants of fresh smoke from a cigarette lingering in the air, but Lucas was nowhere to be found.

Mairzy almost convinced Thelma to come with them, but just as they began to push Lester's wheelchair out the door, she changed her mind and was not able to leave the home. Adamantly refusing their help, it appeared as if she was crying out for help, but just could not step over that line.

When I called her the next day, she informed me that everything was going to be okay because Lucas gave her a pill for her headache. This statement made my hairs stand up on my arm, and my body cringed in anguish. Later, I called to see how she was doing and Thelma talked as if she had a mouth full of marbles, not making sense at all. My pleas were heard too late because the pill had already been ingested. "Please do not take anything from Lucas because you do not know what it really is or consists of."

She went over the edge that day, her voice lacked meaning and after that episode, the phone was always busy and it was impossible to get through. The police were informed immediately after she expressed her fear of being alone and being pushed in her home. Again the next day, they were informed of the garbled conversation with Thelma. The police and I had a very good relationship, and they gladly listened over the years of my concerns for my parents well being and immediately went to visit Thelma on both of these occasions. They were met at the door by Thelma telling them that all was well, as Lucas lurked in the shadows. Thelma needed to ask for help or their hands were tied. This situation looked like a losing battle and by now he had full charge of Thelma who was scared and fearful of him, frightened of life in general. She hid behind the evil one and allowed him to take full control of her.

Knowing it was extremely crucial to arrive home as fast as possible, I booked a ticket to Las Vegas to work for a few days and then planned on heading to Pennsylvania. But it was in Las Vegas that the message came from my mom for me to turn around. Everything seemed to go sour and I felt extremely helpless, angry and frustrated with the turn of events. A horrible black nightmare of rejection, despair and abandonment had a strong foothold on my psyche. Everything known was backfiring on me.

During this time Thelma lost her strong other half, Lester, who had a massive cerebral hemorrhage. A cerebral hemorrhage is a type of intracranial hemorrhage (intracranial hematoma) that occurs within the brain tissue. It is alternatively called intracerebral hemorrhage. It can be caused by brain trauma, or it can occur spontaneously in hemorrhagic stroke. Non-traumatic intracerebral hemorrhage is a spontaneous bleeding into the brain tissue. Non-traumatic can refer to increased exertion, tension or stress. More common in adults than in children, intraparenchymal bleeds are usually due to penetrating head trauma. A few months before, Lester had been overmedicated, which had left him in a coma-like state. Eventually, he pulled through and the details of his narrow escape from death were shared later with us. Lester was so distraught that Lucas gave him way too much medicine. No one in their right mind would have taken such a high dosage, but then I do not understand why my parents trusted him with all their medications. It still does not make sense to me. Lester was disappointed that neither one of us called him when he was overmedicated, not understanding why he was abandoned in his time of need. We explained to him that no one informed us of his precarious predicament; therefore we were clueless of the situation. He was very fortunate to have survived and he shared his feelings of isolation and neglect. Later, he confided that the person responsible for giving his medicine was Lucas.

Mairzy discovered the news of Lester having a stroke only a few days after the stroke happened and immediately called me with the horrible news of our dad's dilemma.

Just maybe, help was possible with quantum biofeedback using subspace. A small hope lingered, help could be given to him from afar. Doctors are still amazed at his recovery. Is it possible that Lester tapped into his own healing energy? The human body has great healing capabilities if we get out of the way.

Only concern can be seen in the eyes of a woman, reflecting hues of flickering green light—concern that the people who occupy Lester's and Thelma's home are tolerated. But toleration slowly changes to fear for the lives of her parent and her eyes become dark with storm clouds. Lester was just taken out of the rehabilitation center prematurely, where he was resting and receiving therapy after a major stroke. Jealousy and hate run rampant, fueling this foolish decision.

The nurses and doctors' develop a grave concern for Lester in the center after witnessing the manipulative warped relationship between this young man and his elderly grandparents. Urgently, they discuss their concerns with Mairzy, sharing their frustration regarding this seemingly out of control situation. She is concerned about how the rippling effect of this abrupt change in Lester's care has the potentiality of creating a setback for him. Their hands are tied as Thelma agrees with Lester's early release, and removes the names of her twin daughters from the list of people for the hospital to contact.

The nurses and doctors suggest getting help from the Office of the Aging.

The Hotel

At the rehabilitation center, Lester loved Mairzy, looking forward to his back and head massages. He also loved being washed and fed by her. He thought he was in some kind of hotel and thanked her for not letting the bad guys get him. He could talk, but had extreme difficulty in making sense of the world around him. Thelma stuck up for Mairzy that day before Lester came home early from the rehabilitation center. She told Lucas, "Stop being so jealous!" The next day her hysterical phone call was made to me, stating she was scared because someone pushed her.

Mairzy and I came to the conclusion that we needed professional outside help and agreed on the agency called The Office of the Aging. We acted upon the recommendation of the nursing staff and doctors where Lester was admitted for rehabilitation because Lucas's behavior was so odd and unusual it disturbed the hospital staff, making them afraid for this elderly couple's safety.

Lucas's possessiveness and sick obsession with our parents alarmed us and now we believed their lives were in danger. By now, Mairzy was worn down and fearful of Lucas, and so we decided to receive outside assistance to deal with the financial part and someone outside the family who could be the guardian for our parents. We requested a person to take care of our parent's finances because we had a good hunch that Lucas already had a tight hold on their bank account.

Not knowing what else to do and extremely frustrated, because we were barely putting food on the table for our own family, we definitely did not have the resources to hire a lawyer. So we thought, why not use Lester and Thelma's money to pay a guardian and financial advisor? This seemed the most logical idea to us at the time. Before the Office of the Aging became involved, Lucas had full charge of the mansion, making sure that the phone never worked. Therefore calls were not received by me or my sister. After the Office of Aging became involved, we still got a busy signal or if it rang nobody picked up when calling to the home. Theri, the representative from this agency, ignored our pleas to fix the phone, informing us that the phone was working perfectly because Lucas checked the phone lines while she was visiting. The lion is hiding behind a façade.

We requested and permitted an outside agency to come into this situation because we needed someone outside the family to deal with the complex problem. Our parent's safety was of utmost concern but this agency did not have the skills, nor did they take the time to know the background of this situation. Nobody seemed to listen to our pleas and emails, which were recorded and kept a record of seriously. The one woman who was in charge of our case befriended the perpetrator.

Was the guardian who was appointed by this agency made aware of how important it was for him to become familiar with this grave complexity? Did he take the time to look at the e-mails sent to the Office of the Aging and listen to the many phone conversations that were taped before becoming involved? Just maybe there was a sheer possibility they decided the importance of doing so, but by then it was way too late and when that shift happened, darkness already arrived as predicted. Even the church had no clue as to what Thelma and Lester were dealing with in their paralyzed state. They did not want the church to judge them about their inadequacies or failure as grandparents, which was wrong thinking but very real to them. All they had to do was express their need for help. Their pride kept them from reaching out to the community or to the police for protection which in turn helped to create the separation, making the job of their grandson all the easier.

This dark energy took every opportunity to bore into and take root like a weed. Gradually this young man strategically planned his plot of hate to tear them apart and feast on the winnings.

The plot was already set in motion, catapulting at great speed. Only after it was too late, death brought the attention they were asking for and a few began to open their ears and eyes, seeing that there might be some truth in their mournful cries for help which society left ignored. The "caretakers" didn't need to worry because they were not the ones in pain. It seemed easier to look the other way.

The innocent watched in disbelief as the demonic plan was put into action. Extreme pain, shock, and anguish encompassed and gripped at their bodies, and they were unable to get away from its strong clutch.

How could the Office of the Aging let this go on for so long? Didn't they see that Lucas could not take care of himself and to expect him to take care of my parents was crazy, absolutely bizarre! I do not understand how they just ignored our pleas for help in this case. They were conned into believing that we were the bad guys but what about common sense? Where did that go?

The picture was being put together slowly, as bits and pieces were discovered for this puzzle. Though we reached out for help to those that were trusted, they turned their backs on our cries, unaware of the extreme danger. Pertinent information was discovered by asking for help from those that I believed trustworthy, finding out later that these people were innocent victims, which became a part of the scheme ultimately responsible for creating our mother's death. Unconscious of the fact that they aided the psychopath in the labyrinth of evil, some of these victims were: the representatives of the church, a few cousins, and the head of this scheme: the Office of the Aging. We reached out to the Office of the Aging thinking they could help Thelma and Lester, but these people ended up supporting Lucas in not allowing their twin daughters on the property where we had played such a big part in loving and caring for them. Previously, Lucas had a meeting with these people to have them support Thelma in her decision to keep Mairzy and Ember at bay, away from the property. Was Thelma coerced to sign the no trespassing order?

The Call

In travel to the convention center, a phone call is received from her hysterical sister. After arriving at the home to take care of their father, Mairzy is greeted at the door by Lucas who adamantly demands that she immediately remove herself from the property, stating that the next time she sets a foot on the property she will be arrested and put in jail. She has to remain outside the property perimeters beyond the iron fence.

Shock sets in as well as disbelief, listening to her sister's frustration. It is literally impossible to process the whole rotten mess. After saying goodbye to her sister and pondering this odd predicament, she receives the call. Happy to hear her mother's voice, Ember soon realizes that this call is not for good cheer but for only one reason. Her life is turned sour and upside down from the hurtful message and her mind runs like a wheel in a hamster cage. Arrested if I touch the property? The property where many good memories in my life were made! It is where I mowed the grass and painted the basement during summer breaks. We played hide and seek, laughing as we hid in the pachysandra with our children and it is here where Easter eggs were meticulously hidden, a home where I spent much of my time alone in solitude, sunbathing out on the balcony catching the soft summer breeze.

She remembers the precious times making pumpkin pies with her mother and actually laughing together. Many memories were made at this home. The children played in a big pile of leaves which they piled up high with the mower, and she took Brandy running and went for long walks in the cool autumn air. These are only a few thoughts that run rampant through her head as tears flood her eyes. Furious and frustrated in not being allowed to touch the property, she thinks "my parents are in danger!" The phone is now always busy when she calls the home. Heavy clouds of rejection and frustration fill her stormy-green eyes which bind her and her eyes become darkly frustrated as the demonic plan unfolds. A horrible feeling comes over her as if she is tumbling in the air out of control, plummeting into a deep hole, as a spinning dark funnel continues to pull her toward a nightmare of no return. After turning around from her travels to Pennsylvania, immediately she decides to call the church and with renewed confidence makes her request, "Please help my parents! My dad is totally incapacitated from a stroke and my mom has expressed to me her fear of being in the home alone, informing me she was pushed. I know for sure they would appreciate food as well as some attention from the church." The pastor literally scolds her and retorts, "The church is not going to take sides on this matter."

"I am not asking anyone to take sides. Please visit them, it would mean so much to them. Check in on them once in awhile," she pleads. What did he mean when he said he was not going to take sides? Her eyes emit intense fiery green rays.

The no trespassing notice kept us at bay for several months, which seemed forever, and waiting brought with it insurmountable angst and worry for Lester's and Thelma's health and safety. What was actually going on in that home? How were they being treated? Were they frightened for their lives? How were they being fed and how was Lester being dressed? What about Thelma's mental health. The last time I heard from her she had been in such an alarmed state about her husband's misfortune of a stroke. Her world was tumbling and cracking around her to unfixable pieces. Lester was deserted in a dysfunctional state, unable to take care of his needs or even to know exactly what his needs were. Who was really taking care of him? Informed about the no trespassing halfway through my journey to Lancaster, I was directed to turn around because I was not welcome. This came to me as a huge blow.

The phone call I received from Thelma occurred while I drove to the convention center to work. Theri who represented the Office of the Aging stood behind Thelma, guiding her in what to say, tying the knot to my mother's fate while aiding the continued abuse of Lester. These people were supporting and encouraging her decision because of being misinformed about my intent. They were made to believe my arrival in Pennsylvania was in the energy to fight and create a scene. They all sat in the same room with my incoherent dad and troubled mom while she made that disturbing phone call.

This information is revealed to me later by a clergyman from the church, also present at this meeting. Having no idea that all these people were visiting the Roslyn Estate while Thelma made the phone call, I did not realize how complex the situation had become. Were threats made to my mom? I was pondering, how did Lucas become so close to my cousins? Was this the reason my sister and I were excluded from and never given information on any of the parties they had together with my parents until after the event occurred? Betrayal became a well-known word as we entered a portal of a nightmare.

There is much that will never be revealed, but Lester has shared information that has been very informative as to what might have been going on before his stroke.

Chapter Ten
Blinders

The Painted Doll

Since we were not able to set foot on the property, McKenzie visited her grandparents and reported back to us and also on one occasion gave us the opportunity to talk with Thelma by using her cell phone. McKenzie's father, Jackson, did the same when visiting. Unfortunately, visitors had to check with Lucas to set up a time to visit, which had to suit his busy schedule. Frustrated, particularly at first because it seemed absurd that we had to get permission to visit our parents, it was also difficult to find a time that suited Lucas. When McKenzie visited, on a few occasions she found Thelma waiting upstairs with her face painted up like a porcelain doll. Planted next to her, Lucas glared with piercing-glacial eyes which made it very awkward and nearly impossible for her to have an intimate conversation with her beloved grandma. Was he anxious as to what Thelma was going to share with McKenzie because they were very close? The prey is within reach of the Lion. Finding Grandma's hair looking very unkempt and matted, McKenzie described the scene in the upstairs bedroom as very weird and eerie. Someone had painted ruby lips and dark eyebrows on Grandma that looked fake and unreal. McKenzie kept on calling the Office of the Aging with her concerns but they seemed to shrug them off, not taking what she said seriously. Also Jackson found the visits disturbing, describing it as a very pitiful situation which was being left unnoticed by the world. Thelma looked to Lucas for approval for each and every word that was shared with Jackson. Leaving each time very distraught, he reported to this agency his horrible feelings on how odd the situation had become. Thelma had bruises all around her face which made him all the more suspicious as to what was going on. Reporting these suspicions, he demanded round the clock care not just the three hours in the evening which Lucas had agreed upon, because of Lucas's busy schedule of night activity. Jackson reported that he believed that they were not being fed breakfast and believed their hygiene was not being addressed, especially Lester, who needed help to get out of bed, dressed, toileted and fed. The home began to look barren as if many of their valuables were being stolen. His pleas were ignored.

Rent

Lester loves to share how their home was made from scratch with his friend Big Red, a school teacher by profession. "Any extra time was put to good use laboring on our new home, while I was still working full time at the shoe factory. Now mind you," he said, chuckling, "Big Red was a big man with luxurious thick red hair that any girl would have loved on her own head and a pale complexion that turned red with any kind of intense emotion."

This home is the source of so many happy childhood memories for his twin daughters which later become deeply buried under the weight of life.

At a very late hour, Lucas went to the home located on Donegal Springs Road to collect the rent money; a discount would be given if the renters paid cash. The renters felt very uneasy about Lucas's threatening demeanor. He appeared agitated and angry at their hesitation in giving him the money. The month before, they witnessed Thelma running out the front door of her home in Lancaster to retrieve the rent money and noticed that her forehead was bleeding. Prior to visiting, they had called the residence and inquired if it was okay to drop the rent money off at their home in Lancaster, and gladly Thelma agreed. She said she would look for them and as their car entered the driveway, keeping to her word, she promptly came out of the front door to meet them—

Trailing right behind Thelma is Lucas, looking very obtrusive. They cannot help but notice her forehead is bleeding from what appears to be a freshly opened wound. Looking appalled as Lucas edges closer and towers over her, she can sense their concern and informs the renters that she is fine. Her bruise was caused from a small mishap of falling. Upset, and not feeling quite right about everything, they reluctantly hand her the envelope of money, while Lucas stares on with an attitude of gnarly deep oppression. Very uneasy about the whole scene they had just experienced, they believe something bizarre is going on and immediately the next morning they mention their concerns to the neighboring family, the Kentins. These neighbors are very upset because they have a long history together with this family. They played together as children from morning to night and their friendships grow stronger as young adults. Mairzy's telephone number is given to the renters and that is when they voice their many deep concerns to her and their fears for her parents' well being and safety.

Letters given to the authorities

I just got a phone call from Rachael who is my parent's tenant at their house on Donegal Springs Road. Lucas is coming to her house to collect the rent. Sometimes he wants cash for rent installments. She does not feel comfortable giving him money. Rachael believes Lucas is using the money for himself. Rachael says she will be calling you. She is very frightened by his rude demeanor. She has also witnessed the grandson's controlling behavior as Thelma walked out from her home in Lancaster to collect the rent check. He appeared as if he was hovering over her and her face had bruises on it. Something weird appears to be going on. She is afraid for the family and their safety. She thinks he looks capable and is scared he might hurt her. Her number is— She will be sending me the rent check. Please advise me as to what I should be doing with it.

Sincerely,
Mairzy

Before my father had a stroke, I talked to my mother or dad every other day, seeing them at least once a week. I invited them over for family dinners, which included special occasions such as birthdays and holidays. When my father was in rehabilitation, I spent many hours with him each day, including time during breakfast, dinner and many of his therapy sessions. Since July 30th, the only time I get to talk with him is when my husband travels to the home and is let in by Lucas. Jackson then calls with his cell phone and lets me talk to my father. He does the same for my sister, Ember. Lucas is hovering. During the week, the phone is off the hook. If by chance it is not, when I say hello the phone is hung up, and then remains busy afterward. On one occasion, my mother picked up and I could hear in the background Lucas asking her who was on the other end. He then directed her in what to say and after a while, there was no conversation, and the phone was hung up. On August the 20th, Lucas spent a lot of time talking about the prospect of getting the power of attorney. I am also very worried that Lucas will be selling my parents' valuables for money. In the past, he has stolen from them when he needed money for drugs.

Sincerely,

Hi Edmond,

I wanted to inform you that Marten shared the information of the dynamics of this family, so you have an understanding of what has been going on for some time. To help make any kind of judgment, we feel it is important that you know

Thelma is very scared of Lucas. This type of behavior started long ago because of Thelma's mental illness. In some sick way, she believes she is protecting him from us. Lucas and his wife, Abbey, do not like it when we come into the home and we have not done so for a long time. Lucas would hurt our animals, steal Christmas gifts and make it a point to take time setting up scenarios to ruin our holidays. I used to go over at Christmas time and carol at their home, taking saxophones, flutes, and many other musical instruments. My children, friends and I were eventually not allowed to do so because it bothered Lucas and his wife. One of the last times at the home, we dropped Easter flowers off to give to my mom. Marten went to shake Lucas's hand and Lucas at that point freaked out and he was ready to beat my husband outside with our two daughters watching in horror. I made a decision that I could not subject my children to this kind of abuse, let alone myself. He can torture animals; he can do the same to humans—mentally, emotionally and physically. I had talked to my parents about my decision, thinking that maybe they just might come to their senses. My dad seems very willing and receptive but my mom wants to protect Lucas's interest. Brokenhearted, I decided to move away and make a new life without abuse of this type. I also knew I had to reconnect to love and the compassionate arms of those that accept me, which is our birthright. As hard as it is to believe for an outsider who has no idea of the pain caused to the grandchildren and children, I can understand where you are standing in regard to my parents' happiness but I feel that you need to know a bit of the history so you have an awareness of what has been transpiring. We love our parents and always try to make Lucas feel wanted and a part of our family, but he is not interested in any kind of healthy relationship. He appears to want to take control of our parents. He has stolen from them and dislikes us being involved in a relationship with our parents. I believe Lester is very unhappy because of his lack of control of what is taking place. Before, if we talked with Thelma she became more rational in her thinking but it looks as if she has gone around the corner and is not returning, at least for awhile. I love my dad and I only want the best for him. I am very scared that Lucas could hurt him because of how he tortured his pets and our animals. I do not trust him. The first time my dad was in the hospital he was overmedicated. They were allowing Lucas to give Dad and Mom their medication. My dad had been given too much and almost died from the overdose. I was not called until he became conscious. He could not understand why I did not call him. He felt abandoned and alone and I don't blame him.

Lucas was so jealous of my sister taking care of Lester when he was in the hospital this last time that he somehow figured out how to get Mairzy's name off the list of people to be notified and also took him home early before his therapy was over. Thelma did say to Lucas the afternoon before he was removed from rehabilitation, "Quit being so jealous, Lucas." That evening she called me to tell me someone pushed her. I believe it is possible that Lucas pushed her. She told me she was scared and I called my sister to go check on Thelma.. I kept trying to call her and she would not answer the phone, so I had the police check with her later just to make sure she was okay. I think it was the next day that I talked to her, and she said Lucas gave her a pill for her headache. I told her not to take any pills from anyone but to get them herself, so she knew exactly what she was putting into her body. Later, I tried talking to her and her words were all garbled as if she was drugged. After that incident, I never got to talk to my mom. I believe that might have helped with her total chemistry imbalance. I can't say for sure, but do think it very possible.

The day before my dad went into the hospital he talked to me after he returned from taking my mom to church and expressed his love for me. He appreciated a letter he had received from me that I had written to him reminiscing fondly of different events in my life growing up as a child. He told me he was feeling so good, he planned on being around for a good amount of time, also crediting his good health to the quantum biofeedback that I previously had done with him when in Pennsylvania. If Lucas was eavesdropping, which he did frequently, and heard Lester talking to me, expressing his love to me, I worried that he took it out on him and do believe he is quite capable of doing so. That was how scared I was of him. In fact, it got to the point that my mom was told to get off the phone if she was talking to me.

I talked to the chief of police about different goings on: stolen products coming into our home that were brought in by Lucas, his involvement with heroin, stealing from my parents and the calls received from different businesses regarding him using my dad's lost credit card.

My sister and I were guided to talk to the Office of the Aging to get some help because the nurses and doctors at the rehabilitation center saw what was taking place. They felt very uneasy about the situation.

With all that being said, I am coming to PA the 12th and would like to be able to visit with both parents if possible. If not, I would like to visit with my dad. I do energetic medicine and would like to run an appointment with him which I have done many times before with both of them. I believe it will help him. I am hoping to get to talk to my mom and believe she will want to see me which might help her come to her senses. I am in the process of achieving my doctorate in this kind of medicine; I will be in PA at least a week if not longer to help them. I plan on seeing them every day starting with the afternoon of the 13th. Please do not make decisions on my mom's erratic behavior. She will get worse if you go with her behavior. Do not give in. I believe with love and frequent visits, she will eventually concede and come around. She needs support but firm guidance of what is for her own well-being and to realize that we only have love for her and not jeopardize my father's grieving to see his twin daughters.

Sincerely,
Ember

Edmond wrote:

Happy Thanksgiving, Mairzy,

I can certainly appreciate how you must feel about your mother and father. On Tuesday I sent an e-mail and had a brief discussion with you about my desire to ascertain what your parents wish. At that time I had indicated that the Wednesday visit (yesterday) was fine and that I would communicate with you about Friday and Sunday. I believe we all want what is best for your mother and father. Additionally, we must be mindful of how to best support them while they live in their home.

Last week you and I had a conversation about outings with your father. You had expressed some reservations about taking your father out, which is understandable. However, I believe that this will be the best way to satisfy your father's desire to see family and mitigate opportunities for your mother to be anxious and angry. I think that you and your father will do well out and about, which can be very therapeutic. Just over the span of three weeks I see your father's strength and stamina improving. Furthermore, with the impending Christmas visit of your sister and her family, going out with your father now will help develop a routine for both of your parents, which will help to alleviate further anxiety.

May you and your family have a nice holiday.

Edmond

Sent:	Wednesday, November 23, 2011 6:54 PM
To:	Edmond Levine
Cc:	McKenzie
Subject:	visits

Edmond,

This is unacceptable. I have a limited amount of time to see my father and I need to see him as much as possible. For over three months I have been forbidden access to my father entirely. We had to end up before a judge to gain access to my father and now a week into it, I am being told that I am allowed to see my dad for just one hour each week on a Sunday. I do not believe that what you are proposing is in the true spirit of what the judge was saying that day.

Sincerely,
Mairzy

From: Edmond Levine
Sent: Wednesday, November 23, 2011, 4:48 PM
Subject: visits

Good afternoon everyone,

Mairzy, I met with your parents and in keeping with their wishes, it is difficult to develop a balance between your father's desire for visits and your mother's desire for no visits. You are able to visit Sunday. However, a Friday visit cannot occur. Your mother was visibly upset and made it quite known how angry she is that there were three visits in one week.

Here is what I was able to work out with your parents

One visit a week on Sundays at 1pm

Visits with your father would occur in his office

Your mother does not want to see anyone other than McKenzie. I know that this can be extremely difficult to reconcile; it is not uncommon to see in people. I am hopeful that with time this will get easier for your parents and your mother will become more open to visits.

I hope you have a wonderful Thanksgiving.

There were so many more cries for help from us as well as their grandchildren. These were only a few letters of the many that were sent to the authorities responsible for this case.

Good evening, Detective Leon

Just to note, my yellow book advertising on line was tampered with. Lucas's phone number was put in place of my company's phone number. Yellow Book did some research regarding how the phone number was changed. The only information so far is that it was changed this past March.

Also, comments by an anonymous person slandered Ember and me. Ember asked the newspaper to remove the comments; the content of the slandering remarks make us very suspicious that it was Lucas. The below article is where I found the slandering remarks.

I also get frequent phone calls with the caller ID as private. They stay on the line for a while without saying anything and then hang up.

Sincerely,
Mairzy

The church, the Office of the Aging, and our very distant relatives, were all misinformed. Mairzy and I were made to look responsible for dissension and fighting. Did they understand that this weird sort of family dynamics started to play out a long time ago and appeared that it was building in speed and strength, fueled and contorted by evil? Coming only in peace and love, our only desire was for the safety of Lester and Thelma.

What did the church represent? We pled with the church, "Please go visit my parents, make sure they are okay," but they chose not to take sides. What does the body of the Church represent, is it love? Is it helping others in need or is it questioning whose side they are on? I thought the church represented a love that is a pure love that Jesus represented to mankind. My parents donated financially to this particular Church because they loved what it represented to them--a family.

As a young girl, the Church made such an impression on my fragile psyche. A signup sheet was found on the bulletin board and every day of the week it was filled with people's names that were willing to bring meals into the homes of those church members that needed help, usually because of sickness. So, a different person prepared a meal for the respective person chosen from the church, and they had a meal arranged for each day of the week. This service was called meals on wheels. Respecting the Shady Pine Church for helping people out in their times of hardship, I took note of it as a young girl and believed that this church represented ideas that inspired me.

My parents donated much of their time to the church and also their money, giving huge amounts to the church. Unfortunately, the church did not reciprocate or take an active part to help my parents in their greatest time of need. My parent's lives were wrapped around the church and this extra effort would have tremendously boosted their morale in knowing the church they supported and grew up in still cared for them in their weakened state. Despite their age, they were just as important and mattered.

The pastors of the church did not have any faith in our integrity but acted as if they did not know us. Gravely concerned about the situation, immediately the Shady Pine Church was contacted after turning my course of travel, having no idea that my mom was being supported by all these people.

"Ember, we are not taking sides," the clergyman exclaimed adamantly witha voice as lifeless as a burial chamber. Immediately, I dialed Mairzy's cell phone, so she could listen to the conversation which was really blowing my mind, making a stressful situation even more difficult, very grim and dark. I asked him politely to please repeat what he said to me and Mairzy went off like exploding buckshot.

A little girl with eyes of jade looks up to the face of her cousin. She likes him despite their age difference, so full of fun and loved his boyish ways. The sparkles in his eyes shine with mischievous fun.

Oddly enough, after returning from my travels, a message was found on my cell phone from a particular cousin named Will. I had not heard or seen from him for forty years but he was chosen to be the bearer of good news in this awful situation and left a voice message for me to call him. "I have an important and most urgent message from your mom." He was one of the cousins who attended the meeting while my mom was being coached on that particular peculiar day. Immediately giving him a call, I gave him my name and he abruptly hung up. Thinking that the call was cut off accidently, I called back but he did not answer and never did connect with me after leaving his message to call him.

Aunt Ida was a dear soul but, looking back, it appears as if Mairzy and I had been purposely excluded from the family functions involving her and her children. My parents were always there and my mom once in awhile would fill me in a bit after the event occurred and how wonderful the event had been, praising Aunt Ida's children, saying how delightful they were to be around. Again Aunt Ida's passing was not shared with me until after the funeral. I was told how beautiful the funeral had been and how Aunt Ida's children are so wonderful. I pondered quietly why we were not informed of our Aunt Ida's passing. But now the question is was I not invited because Lucas attended these events and therefore we were excluded to keep him comfortable? They were my cousins from my dad's sister, Ida. Why was this information about these events heard about after they occurred? Attempting another angle in reaching my cousin, Marten called with his cell phone and left a message but the phone call was never returned. Weird, like I had cooties or something was terribly wrong with me. What false information was being put out there?

He also informed Mairzy he had a message for Ember from her mother but was too cowardly to share the message which was found out later to be, "I love you, Ember." Love does not exclude.

Already having the opportunity to relay the message to Mairzy, she gave him a piece of her mind and I am sure he definitely was not ready to be surprised by what her sister had to say. He was just an innocent bystander who got caught in the web.

"*You* need to be at the hearing, Ember." So, I purchased a ticket but decided to cancel my flight when I was told not to come. "Please do not come, you absolutely are not needed." At the time it was imperative to help my daughter find her way back to health and there is only so much one person can do in life without cutting themselves into halves or quarters.

They changed their mind the evening before the hearing and told me to be there, which is impossible when flying from Hawaii. It is not that easy just to jump on a plane and get to Pennsylvania from Hawaii. That is not how it works. You have to make sure there is a flight out and many times they are full. Looking at all the options for different possibilities to get off the island it just would not have worked out because with the flights that still had seats, I would have missed the hearing.

Mairzy and Jackson sat in the courtroom feeling unsupported and downtrodden about the whole mess. Lucas and our parents' lawyer sat on the other side of the room. This situation was not just an ordinary family spat. It was way deeper, dark and scary to the bone. He had succeeded in separating Thelma and Lester from their loved ones for a rather long time, stripping them of all their belongings, their assets, money, savings, jewelry, beautiful clothing and dignity because of his deep-seated disdain of their twin daughters. Thelma was not getting the support needed in something as simple as a hair appointment nor did Theri understand until it was way too late that she was dealing with a totally different can of worms. We pleaded for twenty-four-hour around-the-clock care for my parent, which was ignored

Warped reality-Court

When the case did go to court, the judge decided to lift the no trespassing in lieu that Lucas is his grandparents' caretaker, which meant he was responsible for attending to all their needs such as toiletry, meals, food bought for the refrigerator, and transporting them to their appointments. Also, he is warned not to steal from his grandparents and if he did so, there would be grave consequences. What were those consequences? Slaps on the hand, bad boy for stealing other people's things, please do not do it again? How would they know if he was stealing or not? We questioned if the judge listened to any of our recorded conversations with Theri, the person responsible for our case and if so, we could not imagine in our wildest dreams why he treated the case as so trivial. Did they really care or was this just about padding their own pocketbooks? After the no trespassing was lifted, Lucas still had full control of when our visits took place and all guests had to get permission from him regarding the day and time of their visits. But refusing to be caught in this game, I told the guardian firmly but cordially, "I am flying from Hawaii and expect to see my parents." At the time, a few favorite words for these people involving this nasty situation enriched my vocabulary which will not be shared at this time, but I think you might get the drift.

Chapter Eleven
Retaliation

Lucas brought Lester's lawyer to the court that day and he demanded answers. Lucas asked Mairzy who gave the information about him to the Office of the Aging. When she said that she had no idea, he stared at her with his dark beady eyes and said, "Ember will pay for this."

At the time, I hated Lucas and forgiveness was not even a word in my dictionary for what had been done. He destroyed our family. If this agency had taken into account what was being said they would never have put out a generic letter for all to read regarding Lucas's bizarre behavior. He was informed by the guardian the exact day and time we were to arrive in Pennsylvania. What was being planned to make me pay for informing the Office of the Aging of his odd behavior? The world was oblivious to the depth of his conniving and his sick desire to snuff out the life of the 'deer,' fulfilling his sick obsession to torture.

After the no trespassing was lifted, Mairzy was granted permission to visit with Lester, keeping her visits short and, of course, when they suited Lucas's schedule. Thelma was very adamant in not wanting to have anything to do with Mairzy, even after the trespassing notice was lifted. Within a few months' time, a plane ticket was arranged for us to visit Thelma and Lester and I knew as soon as I had a chance to visit with my mom, her heart of love would shine through the darkness. Later, the guardian mentions her desire to see me, and I knew without a doubt this information was what I was waiting for.

The day I arrived from Hawaii after the no trespassing was lifted was like heading dead smack into a horror movie. The guardian, who was appointed with our approval, revealed that my mom was looking forward to my visit, unlike her refusal to see Mairzy which did not make sense. This warped sense of distaste toward Mairzy involved a letter she had written and mailed to Thelma and Lester. Did they know this letter was the expression of her deepest thoughts involving her desire to purchase the bay home? Somehow Lucas got a hold of that letter, warped and twisted the message into something horrible, hateful and mean which my mom surmised as being true. He used this letter to portray Mairzy as a monster to the clergy, our cousins and Office of the Aging but they were never given the opportunity to read it, consequently never realizing its true content.

The True Letter

Later, Mairzy mailed me the letter to read the contents. The letter revealed Mairzy's sadness about the direction our family had gone. She did not understand why her noble attempt to keep the Bay Home in the family was left void and not given any consideration. The letter stated that the whole family would have full use of the home and, of course, Thelma and Lester would be able to live there rent free. This, in turn, would free up the Roslyn Estate and they could pursue what was already in motion, the selling of this beautiful estate. My parents by now were feeling a financial strain and did not share with us the real reason why they struggled, revealed later to us.

Subsequently, Thelma began to say they were having financial problems, but by then we did not know what to believe because of the many games which were being played with our heads. Lester just smiled, saying nothing; therefore we did not take what Thelma said seriously. All they had to do was stand together and tell us Lucas was stealing them blind. This information would have gotten our attention. Not informing us of what was going on in their lives, they kept their secrets quiet.

Looking forward to my visit with her, I thought it might just be what Thelma needed to help her wake up from the severe delusional mind which imprisoned her, but that opportunity never came.

Boarding, she sits down and sighs a breath of relief because finally she is going to be able to visit her mother. The events unfolding around her are rather odd and unbelievable, only found in a good psychodrama mystery movie. However they are true and they bring shame to her. Her dark green eyes are tired, but on this very long flight it is hard for her to be comforted in rest. Sleep evades her as she flies over the vast ocean during the darkness of night. The crescent moon comes out once in awhile playing peek-a-boo behind stormy jet ink clouds in the rain squalls of the turbulent skies

The Arrival

As the red truck drives up the driveway, the brown leaves blow and twirl as if they are paving a path to the home. The trees bow, grieving the fate of these two souls. Tired, sliding out of the seat of her friend's truck, she stops and takes a deep breath, looking lovingly at her home. But soon her eyes become clouded with deep emotion and sorrow. The guardian comes out of the home informing her that her mother was recently found upstairs unconscious and has left the home, transported via ambulance to Lancaster General. The nightmare begins. She enters the home to find her dad. Now frail, frightened and skinny without a trace of a smile, so unlike the last time she visited him, he says, "Please, I beg you! Oh please do not push me!" His bone-thin arm reaches up to protect himself, his hand shaking in fear. It appears as if her father is in shock and obviously, should still be under the care of professional help. The evil plot has all been set in motion and is almost finished. Just one more item for now on the agenda, but then it, too, will soon be done. This woman remembers visions she had as a teenager and a vision later in life and it was all starting to come together. She pauses at the steps to the balcony and turns and enters the TV room, setting out her device to help her father. She connects him with head straps wrist and leg straps. She is a Doctor of Natural Medicine and has seen profound results and miracles through the use of quantum medicine in helping others.

Lucas threatens her, saying that if she wants to see her mother alive she'd better go this instant to visit her. He is very disturbed that she is working with Lester. Wild-eyed and crazy, he says, "What are you doing, Aunt Ember! Stop it, leave him alone, now!" She becomes fearful of what he might do to her. He then calls his mother, informing her he can meet her to make the exchange. What did he mean by that call? She feels as if she is zooming down a rollercoaster that has no brakes.

Imploring, with fear reflected in his gray-blue eyes, he says, "Please, be careful do not push me!" and she reassures him she only came to help him.

Our pleas for twenty-four-hour care, which were previously ignored, got their attention only after Thelma was found unconscious upstairs. It backfired when we asked this agency to become involved. We had to go to court to get the no trespassing lifted and in turn this young man and his wife were to take care of my parents? Lucas convinced them he was the good guy. They'd never dealt with a full blown psychopath that delighted in ruining relationships. They were not equipped or educated to deal with this situation. It was the most unusual and bizarre family dynamics that had grown full bloom and they were clueless regarding how to deal with it. This situation was just not a minor family scrap but involved a deadly killer who looked like the savior.

Heading to the hospital, she finds her mother hooked up to life support and a very disturbed doctor, baffled as to why Thelma was left for such a long time without anyone noticing her precarious predicament.

Seeing my mom for the first time on life support brought so much angst into my being. Her hair was all gnarly and knotted looking as if it hadn't been combed for days. Her face looked stressed with so much angst and pain. The Office of the Aging was informed many times about my mom's hair and her daily spa treatment but obviously, they did not follow through with this request. "Please, Father; help me to find forgiveness in my heart for them that sinned against me and my loved ones." Forgiveness was not found.

On that first visit to the hospital, a deep sadness settled down upon me and an expression of my most intimate feelings of love for her came freely. Reminiscing with my mom about our special times together, pictures came to me of teaching my mom the game of tennis at Franklin and Marshall University tennis courts, travelling together to the many pedicure and manicure appointments, baking our fresh pumpkin pies, sharing our many good times at Rehoboth, being passengers on the boat "Thelma Jane," and reminding her of the many piano concerts she watched me perform, our Easter egg hunts planned together, and as the pictures kept on coming, the tears flowed. They were like a fresh surging river unleashed from a dam as every special moment was relived with my mom.

Expressing how grim the prognosis looked for Thelma's recovery, the doctor appeared very agitated. Numbness set into my being as I stepped outside the emergency room and waited in the hallway, giving my mother and the nurses their privacy, as they helped her change. Lucas and Abbey mysteriously appeared outside the room and stood to the right of the hallway, away from Marten and me. As the guardian came out of the room he walked over to stand with Lucas and preceded to hand jewelry to Abbey that was removed from Thelma's thin body. This "guardian" totally, disregarded me on my first day from Hawaii to visit with my mom. I cringed. How this clueless outsider could dare decipher who received Thelma's jewelry. This item of jewelry given to Abbey was never found, disappearing very conveniently. Why did all these people decide to go to the hospital when I was there? It seemed so strange; they did not give me space or time to be alone with my mother.

I was in extreme shock, only able to see her thin strained body on life support struggling to stay alive with a huge blood clot enveloping most of her brain. The doctors were very concerned about how a person such as my mother was left in such a condition for such a lengthy time. It was obvious she was not properly taken care of because of blood clot and her general condition. One particular doctor was very grave and appeared disturbed as he conversed with me. He was unable to comprehend how this could have happened to her as he noticed all of the bruises on her thin body. At this initial visit, as I gazed at her face, to me she appeared stressed and in severe angst, not ever imagining that something so horrible could have happened to her.

A doctor exclaimed, "Who was in charge of this woman?" Abbey spoke and explained that they picked her up and put her on the chair after she fell early morning. Later, checking in on her, they found her where she was left that morning after her fall, so they decided to leave her undisturbed to rest. It was right before my arrival to the home that they checked on her to find her not breathing, very blue in the face. So Lucas called 911 and immediately, within minutes, an ambulance came to the home. Thelma went alone. They left her to go alone without help or support. It is sad to be alone in your darkest time in your life, to suffer alone. How lonely and full of grief she must have been, confused, unable to find her light, with old age hammering her strength. She was unable to find even that glimpse or flicker to fight back or to even know how to.

Kate

My husband encouraged me to leave the hospital after the initial visit with my mother and meet my friend, Kate, as planned. Later we would get a bite to eat. Now Kate is not just some ordinary friend but is a very unique and different being in a human body. Immediately, after I left the hospital room, Marten dropped me off at her home. She took one look at me and knew something was horribly wrong. Fumbling with my words and attempting to explain what just happened, all I could do was stand there. It was obvious I was in shock, and a horrible dreamlike state came over me that stuck like glue. This feeling was persistent, difficult to shake and remained with me for a long time. Patiently, she listened as the muddled sentences came out of my mouth and that is when she suggested, "Get more comfortable, Ember. Come, take your shoes off and sit down on the couch!" She sat in lotus position propped with fluffy pillows, tapping to the couch. Coaxing me, she said, "Please come, sit, take a load off your body! You must be exhausted from such a grueling trip. Here Ember, have some hot tea I just brewed." Mechanically moving to the couch, the tears started flowing. The story began to unravel and calmly but firmly she said, "I want to meet you at the hospital after you and Marten go out to get something to eat."

So, immediately after eating at the quaint Pizza Shoppe in Lititz, we departed for the hospital. Receiving authorization to leave our car engine on by the garage attendant, because by now my device used the car for energy and was running, using subspace to connect with my mother, we entered the hospital lobby. Already waiting at the hospital, Kate had inquired at the front desk as to my mom's whereabouts and found that Thelma was moved to another floor. Entering the room where Thelma lay connected to life support, I immediately noticed my mom was more at peace, which gave me some relief. While massaging her feet, I shared with her one more time my love for her and a sudden knowing came to me—she was gone.

Grief

On a dreary cold winter evening, dewey green eyes filled with sadness as she grieves with her mother. It is now the second visit of the day by this woman. Lovingly massaging her mother's feet, she senses that her mother looks more at peace than on her first visit. She mentions this to her husband who is with her. Expressing her love, she tells an old story of all the things they had the opportunity to do with each other and suddenly a light knock on the door is heard. He asks permission to enter the room; she nods her head.

One of the first things he says is, "It definitely does not look like Lucas followed through with taking Thelma to her hair appointments." She thinks, "Can you see my heart would not lie, there is no reason to!" She just wanted her dear parents to be safe because of her love for them. She remains quiet and looks on and is hurt by all the players in this cruel turn of events. Loneliness, resentment, and despair overwhelm her. The world seems to be a cold place, particularly the church.

Present flash

Jeffrie, the man responsible for the estate, is finding drug needles hidden in the nooks and crannies of the mansion as it is being cleaned. The evidence is found indicating that money is being extracted out of this elderly couple's bank account which has been switched from the Fulton to the Sovereign Bank for some time. This is the bank where Abbey worked; later she is let go after some investigation on this matter.

Chapter Twelve
What do Churches Represent?

A little blonde girl with the cutest dimples and the brightest green eyes steps in front of the whole congregation to recite her Bible verse from memory. She has been waiting for this moment anxiously, feeling a bit awkward. Turning and standing in front of the congregation, she stands tall and looks out bravely at all the people. Taking a deep breath she begins to proudly recite her verse by heart. As she begins, she hears chuckles and laughter. Did she do something wrong? Not realizing they are smiling and laughing because she looks adorable, she thinks that they are laughing at her and her cheeks become a bright pink as she blushes.

Our parents donated their time and money to the church every year, not just little sums but huge amounts of money to help the church. They gave much of their time in helping with fundraisers and other activities which revolved around the church and its needs. Various construction projects for the expansion of the church were taken on by Lester. The church played the role of a surrogate family for Lester and Thelma, fulfilling their longing for a family life. When children, we accompanied them to most of these church functions and, as we grew into adulthood, became involved in the church in our own activities. Unfortunately, the church did not reciprocate the same devotion to our parents in their time of hardship. They did not have to believe us or take sides; all they had to do was pay social visits, take meals over to them. They were disillusioned into thinking that Lucas was well capable of taking care of his grandparents. Therefore, the world turned its back on us and all went sour. Taking this to court this young man would have fought us using his big bank account and Thelma would have supported him in doing so because by now she had allowed him to take total control of her. He used her fear to propel him forward, covertly.

Proving her mentally incompetent in order to lift the no trespassing would have been very difficult with Lucas in the situation, so we allowed the Office of the Aging to take that responsibility. Unfortunately, they went through the process unaware and blinded with their disillusioned minds as to the gravity or ramifications of the seriousness of this situation, which became very dark and desolate. They did not seem to want to do their homework on the case. They had not a clue what they were doing which was affecting the lives of the loved ones of Lester and Thelma. Therefore, they played a big part of one of the weeds in the garden. They first supported the no trespassing and then they unsupported it, which just took time and padded their pocket books with money for the time they put in on this case which they were not connected to emotionally.

During all this confusion, he was ransacking their home. My dad was so thin, very incoherent and frightened, when I came to visit them on that first day I was able to step onto the property. The trees bowed and drops of dew descended, as we entered the driveway, weary and exhausted from just getting off the plane from the long flight from Hawaii. We had stepped into the nightmare.

The Visit

Late evening, she sets up her computer at the home of her friend. Using quantum biofeedback through subspace, messages are sent giving her mother permission to make her next step. Later that evening, finally finishing, she lets out a long sigh. Everything corrects with ease and as an electrical current goes through and around her body, she does not give it much thought because it is not the only time this was experienced. But she does know that whatever the outcome, her mother was going to be okay and turns the device off.

That morning she experiences what most people do not have the opportunity to ever witness. The walls begin to rattle and creak, bringing forth an extraordinarily powerful energy from a higher energetic dimension in time and space. Once it arrives, her body, as well as her husband's, are being softly caressed from their heads to the bottoms of their feet. Music plays, not just music in their imaginations, but audible music coming from the front right-hand corner of the room.

Chapter Thirteen
Love is Invincible

That evening after the hospital visit, we drove back to the home of our good friend and I continued to work with Thelma. Receiving the message that she was happy, I told her, "Go to the brightest light but if you want and are able to, I am here for you. We can have fun together and I love you." Visions went through my head of times playing tennis together, purchasing her new bike, riding our bikes together, doing her nails and rubbing her feet. Love in such a deep way radiated from my whole being, a love for all her faults as well as for her beauty. Having helped many people using quantum biofeedback, I had never seen rectifications resembling what was being shown to me. Emotional components of joy, peace, love, happiness and ecstasy were rectifying one hundred percent. It appeared as if this is what bliss looks like and a knowing came to me that she was going to pass or had already made that step.

That morning around 3:00 a.m. my eyes opened wide. I was awakened by the sounds of intense crackling, it felt as if the bedroom came alive, harboring such an intense energy impossible to describe. It simply was amazing. Alone, I had this amazing encounter. I witnessed a true miracle, a breakthrough of energy from a higher parallel dimension. My first thought was this only happens in movies and my second thought was about being alone experiencing this enormous breakthrough of energy. No one else had the opportunity to witness its power. Wow, why me!? Paralyzed in the experience, I was in awe. After the enormous amount of energy entered the room and I was able to move again, I tapped my husband and said, "She's here!" Waking from a deep sleep, he said, "What is happening!" By now a soft but very distinct vibration was going up and down our bodies. I was already experiencing this vibration which was like soft waves of love caressing our bodies as we lay there on the bed. Then music commenced to play, which was coming from the right corner of our room, very audible almost childlike, playful and joyful. This seemed to go on for a long time. I don't know exactly when it stopped but at the time my body could not process all this energy. I knew a beautiful phenomenon just happened, what would be called a miracle. I now have a humble understanding as to why the Three Wise Men were sore afraid when the Glory of God came down upon them. This event did not happen only one night but for each night while staying at our friend's home in Pennsylvania that he so graciously offered.

The sound of the music appears as if it is coming from a xylophone, a very happy and joyful song, almost childlike, which happens every early morning around three o'clock while staying at her friend's home. Although this was a beautiful occurrence, on a physical level this unusual phenomenon totally freaks her body out. Every night, she commences to medicate herself with all kinds of natural herbal sleeping remedies and later decides that potato vodka is also a great bedtime tonic. It takes her nervous system a long time to calm down, giving her very little sleep. She's unable to close those anxious jade green eyes.

The vision of her perfection in love and the quantum entanglement created the collapse of what she knew to be true, her love for me. She had already made that decision to make her next step even on life support while her body still breathed and her heart pumped blood. My mom was experiencing ecstasy. Visiting me with maybe other angels in the wee hours of the morning she was finally set free from the pain which covered her beautiful spirit. When her body died, she wanted to come back and see me, having a heartfelt message to share and nothing was going to stop her.

The next day, each of our children shared their love to their grandma using my cell phone which was held up to Thelma's ear. When our youngest daughter talked to her grandma, her tears flowed tenderly down her cheeks and with the phone in her hand she walked to the kitchen. Every aroma imaginable was in the air of all different kinds of foods which were a component of the countless holidays spent together as a family. The many meals of Thanksgiving, Christmas, and Easter which were generously and lovingly prepared by her grandma were detected so strongly in the kitchen. When Roslyn came out to the kitchen, they turned and looked at each other in wonderment and awe, realizing that they both were having the same experience. Their grandma's love shines through the veil of darkness and is letting them know that truly all is well. Her love goes on eternally.

Life

Thelma is now being prepared for her next step and is going to be taken off the life support which is keeping her alive. As her body is prepared for this big moment, Ember rubs her back with baby cream. Later, Lester is pushed right next to Thelma, and his hand is put into Thelma's hand. Incoherent, his face is blank of emotion, but he knows the love of his life is gone forever.

It was difficult to let her go but she already was gone—lying there was a lifeless body. I could not help but notice her bruised and battered back—black and blue from her tailbone up to the back of her head. It made me question 'how did that all take place?' It appeared she did not have just one fall but fell countless times, plunging forcefully as she struck her back. Mairzy pushed Lester's wheelchair next to her bed and put his hand in hers, as Thelma was removed from the machine that was supposedly keeping her alive. This situation created so much distress in me and disbelief. It made me question my faith or value in mankind. I wasn't sure if Lester knew exactly what was going on, but I am sure his spirit knew and anger was my friend that fueled me forward through the grief and sadness. It was so impossible to process all that was going on. It took me years to fully come to terms with most of it.

My heart felt so heavy and I mourned, but then, remembering my experience in our bedroom gave me a whole different perspective. Such an intense energy of happiness and love from a higher dimension came through that morning. It totally amazed me, bringing me to my knees in awe with reverence for the divine. She is alive.

After she's been taken off life support, Lucas reaches for Thelma's hand. Covertly, he twists and turns her diamond ring on her finger, trying so hard to pull it off. Mairzy's hawk eyes are watching him while tears relentlessly flow, blinding her sister's eyes. Later, Ember is told the ring would not budge and she entertains the thought that another dimensional being of light held it tight saying, "Stop, you scoundrel! Enough is enough, don't you see, love wins always!"

Her mother succumbs on the dark and dreary day of Dec.15, 2011 at the age of 92.

Thelma's entire personal jewelry and belongings were all missing because of jealousy and hate which took hold. Entering Thelma's bedroom, I slowly opened her closets and found them barren, making it impossible to find an outfit for her funeral. All was amiss. Gloomily, I kept on searching each closet, hoping to find something for my mother to wear and this is when Lucas suddenly appeared holding an outfit. With the eeriest certainty in his high-pitched voice, he said, "This is what she would have wanted to wear. You need to have the funeral attendant put this on her, Aunt Ember." At the time I did not think or even stop to wonder, why did he have an outfit all ready for her?

My body was very distraught during this time, utterly in shock. The funeral was a very cold and dismal day as rain poured tears from the dark heavens and winds of chilly air blew, swirling the last few leaves that were left from autumn. My dad was transported by Lucas to the site where they laid the coffin. He was unable to leave the car. I am not sure if Lester knew exactly what was going on at the time although he might have been totally aware. However his body had let him down; he was frail and unable to walk or communicate. Feeling utterly out of control regarding his safety, the day of my mother's funeral was very dark, gloomy and cold, which went along with how I was feeling as the heavenly doors stood mourning with me.

'Proof of Heaven,' Eben Alexander, M.D. says *"There is a sense in which all the losses that we undergo here on earth are in truth variations of one absolutely central loss: the loss of Heaven. On the day that the doors of Heaven were closed to me, I felt a sense of sadness unlike any I'd ever known. Emotions are different up there. All the human emotions are present, but they're deeper, more spacious; they're not just inside but outside as well. Imagine that every time your mood changed here on earth, the weather changed instantly along with it. That your tears would bring on a torrential downpour and your joy would make the clouds instantly disappear. That gives a hint of how much more vast and consequential changes of mood feel like up there, how strange and powerfully what we think of as "inside" and "outside" don't really exist at all. The prayers of others gave me energy. That's probably why, profoundly sad as I was, something in me felt a strange confidence that everything would be all right. These beings knew I was undergoing a transition, and they were singing and praying to help me keep my spirits up. I was headed into the unknown, but by that point, I had complete faith and trust that I would be taken care of, ..."*

Potato Vodka and the Church

During Thelma's funeral and the planning stages, potato vodka became a good friend of mine. Interestingly, alcohol is not a drink I use frequently, but it helped tremendously to soften the blows of all the energy of the funeral and the quantum happening that came through to our bedroom at my friend's home every night and was experienced on several other occasions other than the wee hours of the morning. During the funeral which was held at the church, Kate accompanied me and my water bottle which had more than just water in it. Singing together the church hymns that were requested by the church, and at times laughing quietly, my magic beverage was sipped throughout the funeral and when it was time to go to the graveside, 'pain' was not even a word in my vocabulary. Roses were handed out freely to people I thought somehow were related to me, but was told later that they were acquaintances. It simply did not matter anymore. Kate's love and long hugs will always be remembered; her love carried me through this period of my life.

Chapter Fourteen
Devaluing of Human Life

The door creaks open and dry brown leaves enter, bringing in the cold frigid air. The leaves swirl around lining a path as a woman dressed in black slowly approaches. Her hunched over back heaves as giant tears fall to the floor creating a bottomless abyss of water. The door opens wider, allowing the winter air to chill the room, welcoming the gust of the wind which slowly swirls and travels around this elderly woman. Steadily, she approaches the young woman who by now is sitting and watching. Nearing the bed she sits down beside her. It seems like an eternity. She sits quietly and then slowly lifts the black veil that covers her face. Their eyes connect. Startled, her jade eyes open.

The last week my mom was alive she confided to a friend about the lack of food, and how they were faint with hunger. Thelma cried, sharing with her friend that Lucas was gone all day and never around to help with Lester or to transport her to the spa on Saturdays. Later with a little detective work, we found out that the money for the salon was being used by Abbey for her own needs. Lester always loved to take his wife to the hairdresser but life changed, and unexpected events occurred in his life, and the stroke which almost took his life made him become incapable of doing what he loved, to be with the one he loved. He had been the rock and the foundation of their marriage and Thelma liked that part of him and felt lost without him. Therefore, the court had given Lucas this responsibility of transporting Thelma to the facility to get her hair done, which he ignored.

The magnitude of Thelma's friend acting upon information shared with her was of paramount importance, but this information was never given to any authorities. She only shared this information with me at the funeral about Thelma's last week of life.

Why were my parents neglected, and why weren't Office of the Aging staff checking on them each day, making sure they were okay. Theri, representing the organization, had everything taken care of or at least that is what she said, but why when it was so obvious that my parents were becoming malnourished and not properly cared for, was nothing done about it? Why not pop in on them in the morning to get the real picture instead of relying on Lucas's "schedule"? Common sense was not a word in their vocabulary.

During my stay in Pennsylvania, bits, and pieces of information were unfolded and discovered by talking to a few people who were troubled by the abuse which was taking place in the home. They left Thelma and Lester feeling very uneasy. Why wasn't this behavior reported to the police? Thelma confided in one friend that they were not being helped to get to appointments. She complained about the lack of food and that their refrigerator was always barren. She said that Lucas was never around. This information should have been given to the Office of the Aging and the Lancaster police. Life is so valuable and cannot be taken for granted or ignored in its pain. We need to confront it and find out how we can do our part to help in a situation. Our pleas and cries for help were ignored and not taken seriously, as well as the requests for help from their grandchildren. It appeared as if the world turned its back and closed its eyes. They stuck their heads in the sand, hiding as an ostrich.

Ostriches really don't hide their heads in the sand. Contrary to popular belief, when an ostrich feels genuinely threatened; it will actually take off running. Considering it is the fastest animal on two legs, it can pretty much outrun most other animals. In fact, ostriches have been clocked as high as 45 miles per hour when being chased by a close predator. Just as impressive, ostriches have been shown to be capable of a sustained run of around 30 miles per hour for an extended period. So they can pretty much outrun the vast majority of predators out there, with a few exceptions. And in the few cases they can't manage to outrun those hunting them, ostriches can be absolutely deadly with their powerful kicks combined with a large claw on each hoof-like foot. Ostriches can easily kill humans with a kick and have been observed to even be able to kill full grown lions if the lion doesn't get them first. The ostrich also has extremely good eyesight and hearing. Because of this, they are generally able to perceive predators before the predator sees them. So what they will do when they observe a predator is lie down on the ground and put their body as close to the ground as possible and wait. Often, living in very hot savannas in Africa, the heat haze, combined with how low they are to the ground, will make them appear to be just a mound of dirt in the distance to predators. If this fails to work and the predator approaches, the ostrich will stand up and take off running. Ostriches are very interesting and somewhat amusing. It would have been nice if the people involved with this situation lived out their ostrich attributes! We are a lot stronger than we can even fathom.

The agency that we chose to trust by inviting them to become involved did not have the awareness or the energy to understand how grave the circumstances were. We felt betrayed by them. They had no idea just how dangerous and manipulative this young man was in this particular state of affairs, nor equipped regarding what signs to look for. During all this, Kate supported me. Kate showed me how it felt to have a true friend and that experience will never be forgotten. On another very gloomy cold damp day, before I left to fly home, she bought me gifts, sparking my faith in mankind. Truly, she was an angel during my time of need. I had lost many of my friends, but I gained a few diamonds in turn. Her love shone through all the dark energy of those twelve days, which carried me for a long time and eventually encouraged me to take another inch forward through the mucky quicksand.

Looking out at the bayfront into the darkness, deep eyes of green become lost in the rhythm of the rain which pelts hard against the picture window. The wind bellows and howls across the stormy ocean. Suddenly, a Lion appears, letting out a loud roar as he struts proudly, showing off his magnificence. This picture disappears as quickly as it appears and there is only pitch blackness and the sounds of the rain against the window pane. As she looks again into the darkness, a slender deer appears which is very frightened. It bleats as their eyes connect. Looking into them is like peering into an endless prism which pierces her heart as time stands still for what seems an eternity. Blackness comes again and next the Lion appears again, strutting proudly, now holding the neck of the deer. Shaking its lifeless body, he snarls as fresh blood streams down its chin. The Lion stares boastfully into her dimming green eyes.

Artwork

Mairzy was encouraged to take down her many paintings. "Take them home, Aunt Mairzy, they are yours!" He said in his high pitched voice.

Reminiscing, she had become totally engrossed in the story behind an oil pastel she was holding in her hands. This painting was one of her last masterpieces she painted of Lester and Thelma. They were standing in front of their home holding hands looking at the Koi pond. She remembers how happy they were when this photograph was taken so she had captured it on canvas.

A couple flashes of light catch her attention and quickly she glances over her shoulder. She is caught by surprise as she discovers Lucas taking pictures of her. Resting beside her are a few of her other masterpieces gathered together to be taken home with her. Caught off guard, she forgets that Lucas might just have different motives. Allowing herself to get caught up in the moment with Lucas's possible façade of sincerity, quickly she regains her wits. Realizing what really might be going on and not wanting to take a chance, with sheer expediency Mairzy puts every piece of art back on the walls. She thought just maybe she was being set up. Was she?

We were informed by the financial guardian that nothing was allowed to leave the home, all items were going to be sold at auction. This included Thelma's necklace the guardian gave to Lucas and Abbey in the hallway of the emergency room which was removed from Thelma's thin body by the nurses. Family pictures and any personal items were part of those items; absolutely nothing could leave the home.

Pitifully, wild-eyed Lucas hovered over and protected Thelma's jewelry which was laid out in front of him in our parents' bedroom after her death, that is the very little that was left. It was as if he was scared that we were going to take it from him. Looking through the house it was very obvious that so many of Thelma's lovely things were missing, many gifts given to her as well as many of their other valuables were gone. He charmed them, winning their hearts. Lester and Thelma wanted to believe in him in the worst way. I'd become increasingly disheartened to watch the foundation of our family start to crack and tumble down until it was almost totally destroyed, but I hoped to find that love will always shine brighter.

The twenty-four-hour care now designated to Lester after Thelma was found upstairs unconscious and blue in the face still did not give us comfort. We knew that if Lucas wanted Lester out of the picture he would be smart enough to accomplish it. So the Office of the Aging were informed that if anything happened to Lester, we would hold them accountable and if that involved us going to court, so be it. Therefore, they concurred to help him settle into Moravian. It took some time to convince the financial guardian that removing Lucas from the home was the right thing to do, while also changing the locks. At first, he thought Lucas could keep an eye on the property, which really meant: let's give him more time to sell stolen items from the home using the money for his addiction while living rent free.

Lucas was discovered taking jewelry to various shops to collect money. This fact was reported by a friend of ours who caught sight of him in Lancaster heading toward a pawn shop. So out of curiosity, he decided to follow him into the store. Our friend listened as Lucas told the store owner that the jewelry was a gift given to him from his grandma and his reason for the visit was to find out how much money he could acquire by selling it. Later, after the friend made a few phone calls, this jewelry was retrieved, but my only thought to his actions was just maybe Thelma did give him the jewelry before her death. Nobody would really know except Lucas. It is one of those pieces of the puzzle that really is immaterial to me.

In shock from the events of Thelma's death, we were now returning back to our home in Hawaii, flying over the magnificent ocean. Justin is sitting on his big fluffy couch and staring at the television in his apartment in California. Feeling quite restless, with his thoughts and mind only on his grandma, he decides to go to sleep to block out his grief, and the noise in his head which eats at his soul. The reality that he is not ever going to be able to see her again only magnifies his loneliness.

—*Just as the clock strikes three o'clock, he awakens to hear the sound of his bureau shaking. The whole room begins to come alive and emits explosions of sound resembling cracking. Next, a ball of golden bright energy lingers over him which is way too much for him to bear. Tucking his body up in a ball he rolls over to his side, tugging the sheets over his head. Light caressing commences which begins at the top of his head making his hairs stand up and travels down his whole body, going to the bottom of his feet. The energy gradually becomes stronger in intensity continuing for what seems like an eternity. He knows without a doubt it is his grandma because it is done in love but a love he never felt before. It is much more multidimensional with great depth and strong magnitude.*

MERGING OUR MULTIDIMENSIONAL SELF
By: Soluntra King

From the Source of all that is, Creator, One, creation expresses itself in prisms of Light in worlds within worlds, a multi-dimensional jewel that is all one. As we went out from the One and experienced creation we explored worlds and dimensions, until we eventually fragmented to third density and our experience of it on the earth plane. This is where if we fragmented any further we would destroy our planet and ourselves; we are now shifting from destruction to creation, on the return journey home, merging all our fragments and parts of ourselves, unification of our multidimensional selves. We brought into the illusion on the third and fourth dimensions that have been controlled by the Astral Lords. Feeling that we were separate we invited fear into our experience with all that meant, death and rebirth, decay, illness, the victim, victimizer, and the belief that we could not ascend in our body.

But as we own and love our fears, and embrace all fragments of ourselves that have been controlled by fear, we release the hooks of duality, and so are clear to see ourselves as we truly are. We shift dimensions and come from our divine presence, from all levels and dimensional aspects of self; we become our body of Light. We are not just the ground crew for the Light Ship; we are the crew, on the ship and here at once. We are the Council of Light, the Angel, the Light Being, the Dark Lord, and the many ET aspects of self, Pleiadian, Sirian, Andromedan, Orion, Lyra, and Arcturus. We no longer think of them as someone else, or outside of us--as we merge we are them. We come from the One, and as we gradually fragmented we became Founder Creators, Creator Gods, and members of the Council of Light, members of the Galactic Federation. We became different extraterrestrial beings, until we fragmented so much that we became 7 billion people on Earth at this time. As we love and accept others, and ourselves seeing the Source within us, all beings and creation, we unify our fragments. This does not mean we lose our identity, we are still us, and so have compassion and love for all creation without judgment. We become the unlimited being we truly are, and can utilize all the incredible Light codings of who we are, to be a Co-Creator right here on Earth. Heaven and Earth are one, as we complete this beautiful experience in the Creation Story.

We become conscious of our divinity, and that we are responsible for what we create, we work with the Councils of Light consciously, and our Oversoul in all its magnificent expressions. This becomes clear as we love and embrace all the renegade parts of ourselves that separated from the Source and decided to create on their own will, the negative ET in us, the Dark Lord, the Magician always trying to control and run the energies. Until we got burnt enough times, for what we put out comes back to us, so as we explored power and control we became trapped in fear. Now as we embrace and love all these maverick multi-dimensional selves and align back to the source, we realize that if we really want to enjoy our experience, being aligned in the divine will is a lot easier, effortless effort. We become the universal flow.

The paradigm of duality served a great purpose; Prime Creator explored all the limitations of its unlimited universes. Now as we leave our limitations behind and step through the doorway and into our unlimited self, we move into a whole new paradigm of love and creation, out of chaos and into harmony, and onto new stories. So what are all these multi-dimensional selves of us and how do we find them? They start right here in our lives as we are right now, in the relationships we experience, negative or positive experiences that affect us. Obviously if negative we need to love and accept the gift that is being shown to us by the person/s pressing our buttons. As well as loving our mother in us, our father in us, our partner in us, our children in us, other family members, as well as others who give us a gift that creates a negative response. We can also explore who these people really are, not just good old Dad who I've had to go through heaps with, to learn to accept myself. But who is he on the inner planes, and for what purpose are we really together here at this time? Once you start seeing the higher aspects of people, whoever they are, it helps you shift out of the earthbound dramas.

We also have ourselves in parallel worlds right now from the earth experience, some call these past lives. All of these so-called past lives may not necessarily be you, but part of your group soul experience. To understand and unify the human condition for compassion and empathy, we only get hooked up by them when we are still in ego identity, but as we clear and unify we are not attached to whether it was us in our own soul experience or part of the group. It is all us and part of our learning and integration process. Then we have other dimensions and worlds within the Earth.

The whole scenario freaked him out, but Justin knew without a doubt as the unusual phenomena happened, it was Grandma. Sharing this experience with me, Justin said his room had become alive, and vibrated in such an enormous amount of energy, it was almost to the point of being unbearable.

Also, our daughters in Hawaii during the mid-morning hours for a second time, savored different smells, not of Thanksgiving but this time the whole house smelled of pork and sauerkraut. Thelma invited us over for this dish which she prepared for New Year's Day. She enjoyed preparing this wonderful feast, showing her love for us. They knew it was Grandma without a doubt.

When describing my experience to people, they want to know if Thelma was still on life support or did this happen after she was taken off of the life support. When discovering she was still on life support for this quantum happening they said, "Oh, how could it be? Oh no, it could have never been your mother! It was an evil spirit!"

Now a human spirit is strong and her desire to see me was so powerful. I believe she wanted me to know that she was so happy in a place of total bliss and love. Why did this happen to me? I do not know, but I like to think that the grander scheme of life was looking down at me frantically living my human life with such a heart of love, that it knew I needed encouragement to go forward, as well as my family. My intentions were pure and it seemed like life was not giving that back to me. My mom could see me from a higher place and even after being hooked up to life support, she had left that broken body, which I believe was the evening when they moved her to the upper floor. She waited until I came to make that final step.

Dark Angels

Pictures were found down in the basement of the twin sisters, where Lucas held his strange gatherings.

Angels are found in the Bible, which speaks about a spiritual world that is parallel along the physical. I believe the Spiritual realm is more real than the physical. All through the Bible, Satan tries to thwart God. Some people believe the spiritual world consists of convicts some of whom are the leaders of the demonic world, the fallen spirits. There is much information on this subject related to Satan's goal to destroy God's people. He thought he had succeeded because of the crucifixion of Jesus but Jesus went and preached to the demonic world and then arose to sit on the right hand of God. Some of the ideas that the Bible conveys to the reader includes how some of these demons actually can enter into people's bodies. The fallen angels created offspring. Satan walks the Earth as a roaring lion to see who can be devoured, and we are to armor ourselves with Christ's word and do greater things than Jesus did in the World. Christ's Love is so much more powerful than Satan's hate and deceit, Station 91.7. The speaker on this station goes on to speak about the spiritual realm and how he had become involved with satanic cults. After witnessing the strength of these occults, he said without a doubt, he has chosen the side of the highest angel beings of light and the Lord Jesus Christ. There is a lot of material to read on this subject matter with one good resource being Liberty University. Many different beliefs do pertain to material in the Bible and a multitude of different religions exist today but regardless of all the facts, and views, my faith and experience support that the spiritual world is very real nevertheless.

While taking flight, traveling home to Hawaii after Thelma's demise, a malicious article was already written about the twin daughters of Lester and Thelma.

Accidentally coming across an email found with information about the auction of her parent's home, Mairzy begins to read it, finding the contents very disturbing. In this article, the twin daughters of Lester and Thelma are portrayed as being very greedy, spiteful people taking advantage of their weak and elderly parents. Money is behind their selfish decision to remove their father from his home against his will and place him in a retirement center.

The Estate's contents were being advertised for an auction. Researching the web, Mairzy found pictures of the home with information pertaining to the public auction. Out of curiosity, she begins to read the comments below. That is when Mairzy came across a very nasty article about us.

Just as my plane landed in Hawaii, I received her phone call informing me of the horrible article written about us, found with the advertisement for the auction of the items of The Roslyn Estate. After reading it, I called the newspaper office to immediately have it removed. This email was seen in an article about the Estate found on Lancaster Online. It was hoping to get the interest of potential buyers for the home and entice visiting auction attendees.

The Auction April 23, 2012

Hundreds of bargain hunters and curiosity seekers descended Saturday on Roslyn, the grand old mansion that was once the home of Watt & Shand co-founder Peter T. Watt.

It was the belongings that were auctioned Saturday. The home has 25 rooms, but only the first floor was open for Saturday's sale. Many of those who walked through the home and around the grounds seemed as interested in the architecture as the contents, many carried cameras and took photos.

The home's contents were auctioned off and the property itself, at the northeast corner of Marietta and President Avenues, is listed for sale at $1.25 million.

People were lined up from the driveway out to the sidewalk to be able to get into the home and then there was just the interested bystander. Mairzy did not personally attend the auction, but her three children were there. I felt as if our lives were invaded on another level, taken over by people who were mere scavengers, clueless of the pain we suffered. Anger surged through my veins having nowhere to go, which made me feel out of control. Every night I was awakened with different dreams which visited and tortured me about our home and the new owners, who did not welcome us.

McKenzie and Lindsay ran into their Aunt Kay who was very contemptuous and angry. She said that the items of the home were rightfully hers and were not to be sold. She was very resistant to the auction and the pain it created in her being. Jackson was also at the auction to see what was going on and reported back to Mairzy. He was our trustworthy detective.

Later, the home was sold at a very low price which was used for Lester's stay at the retirement center. At first, mulling over many other places for Lester to stay, we decided that it was the best safe place for him to be because he needed and still needs assistance in getting dressed, bathed, toileted and a couple good pair of hands to transfer him from his bed into his wheelchair. The stroke was harsh on his body.

The guardian requests that warm clothing is retrieved. Reluctantly, Lucas searches through Lester's drawers and throws the clothing into a garbage bag. Arriving at Moravian the bag of clothing is dropped off at the front desk and immediately a car is seen speeding away hastily as the brown leaves trail after it into the night's frosty air, never to return.

The lead-grey skies stared silently outside as the fire's flames licked the hearth in the care facility where Lester sat gazing into the flames.

After returning home to Hawaii, she rests, meditates and does her own hyperbaric oxygen therapy as well as many other therapies to work on healing the multitude of emotions that her body was holding onto, unprocessed. She visits several 10-day silent retreats to learn the technique of Vipassana Meditation. It is where she learns the basics of the method and practices sufficiently to experience its beneficial results.

But within a year, she is in flight to visit her dad. A special passcode is needed now in order to talk to Lester because of a nasty phone call which was overheard by one of the nurses. This call is malicious, berating Lester for not coming home, making demands for more money.

Returning each year, they are welcomed at their friend's home. This home has a well kept organic garden full of fresh vegetables for them to choose from for their meals. Their friend's office is next door to the home and he pops in to say hi once in awhile—such a likable guy and a top notch medical doctor highly respected in the community. His wife is a very gracious woman, a highly evolved soul beautiful inside as well as having a gorgeous presence.

Holding on to memories associated with her mother's passing, a feeling overtakes her that is impossible for her to shake. With the arrival of the night, her body becomes intolerably anxious and severe panic attacks overcome her. This is where she had experienced a paranormal happening. Her brain and body are still unable to release and are compressed with the shock of the whole experience of her mother's passing. Her death and the events stretch every nerve in her body, the quantum happening so fresh in her mind, the strangest and most bizarre incident in her life, only found in movies and never thought remotely possible in real life. As night arrives, she drinks vodka until 4:00 a.m. and then goes to bed. Returning to this home every year she has the same issue, but the year 2014 is the time when changes start occurring and occasional relief is welcomed as her body begins to relax. She makes the decision to let go, commencing to make a conscious resolution to trust that all was truly well or at least that is what she kept telling herself. Her weary deep green eyes begin to close.

The year 2014 was the turning point. Very excited about their new adventure, Kate and her husband invited us to see their new business, a pizzeria shop. At our first opportunity to see this place, it rocked with awesome food and many loyal customers. After arriving, proceeding back to a private room with a bar, we chatted and laughed into the wee hours of the morning. Mike, Kate's husband, listened patiently as I fumbled for the words about my quantum experience and he said, "Ember, just remember you were chosen to have such a wonderful experience; look at it as a privilege and choose not to be afraid." Simple as that, it became my turning point and I truly knew all was well. Love is a beautiful safe revitalizing energy.

"Love and compassion are necessities, not luxuries. Without them, humanity cannot survive." ~Dalai Lama

"To have a respect for ourselves, guides our morals; and to have deference for others, governs our manners." —Laurence Sterne (1713-1768). Respect emerges from within. The wanton disrespect we sometimes show toward things and others is really just a manifestation of our lack of self-respect.

Eventually, the truth is shared, catching me off guard, as Lester describes what happened to him, "All was stolen by this scoundrel who gets to go free with all my hard-earned belongings. Everything I worked so hard for is now all gone. What can be done about it? I guess he will just get to go free?"

Later, Lester conveys another strong message to Marten by telephone, recounting a struggle resulting from trying to acquire control of a shotgun that was being pointed at him and Thelma. Crying, he says, "The prick demanded control of all my assets. I lost the battle with the bastard because I was not strong enough to retrieve the shotgun." Lester fumbled through to form words and described as best he could what had happened during the latter years of his life, saying how both of them were so very frightened for their lives and he began to cry. This conversation was taped by my husband.

"Truth is incontrovertible. Malice may attack it and ignorance may deride it, but, in the end, there it is." —Winston Churchill (1874-1965)

Why did the Universe allow this? My parents were not bad people; neither were their twin daughters. Why? I would like to think and hope there was a bigger picture involved. Was it a battle between the Spiritual Worlds that parallel the physical world to break the bonds of evil? Could it be interrelated somehow to the pharmaceuticals ingested while giving birth which gave opportunist energies an opening to inhabit this young soul's being? Was the occult involved with this, opening the door for evil to enter? What about the large sized rectangular hole, looking very much like a grave, found hidden under bushes to the side of the home where the puppy was found in the fountain? How much of an effect did that energy have on the dynamics of our family? Was it responsible for what helped fuel the evil upon our family which ran rampant like a vampire, sucking out all the strength from its victim, leaving behind the deepest darkest depression? Did this evil work through the perpetrator, giving him a deep satisfaction through dispersing the family, separating any unity by ruining all with lies and deceit? Was he encouraged to scheme these plots and dramas to cause havoc? I do know love is stronger than any kind of demonic energy. This darkness followed me back to Hawaii for one last jolt to take me down. But love is so much more powerful and will always win.

Razzle

A year later after Thelma's death, we decided to go on a shopping spree to Macy's with Linnea—the first time going out since Thelma's death. Piling into the car and waving goodbye to Roslyn, we pulled out of the driveway. It was not unusual for Roslyn to stay home because shopping at that time with all of us would have been way too stressful on her nervous system. At the time she was holding my sweetest Razzle, not just some ordinary dog but unique because of her heart of gold, carefully chosen because of her quiet demeanor from a huge litter of cockapoos. The day she became a member of our family was a very special time in our lives. Going into the barn, we carefully looked at the many different types of dogs and came across the cockapoos, which were all squealing with delight and barking, "Take me, take me!" But this one little cockapoo just stood back quietly with her big brown eyes looking at me. Just to entertain myself, I walked around to look at all the other dogs but already knew there was no need to really search further. She already had cemented the deal and came home with us that day, going everywhere with me.

Razzle was found in my pocketbook at clothing stores and grocery stores, peeking out from my sweatshirt pocket when running the bike path and any other place imaginable. Receiving many baths in the kitchen sink with her special companion, they were scrubbed until they were squeaky clean and later laughter could be heard as they played together. Mischievously, Linnea gathered up bubbles in her cup and dumped them onto Razzle's head, in return, Razzle shook briskly making bubbles fly everywhere. Many became airborne, floating lazily above them like small rainbows as the sun shone through them from the kitchen window.

Razzle acquired a beautiful winter coat and boots for the frigid air of winter. Her teeth were scrubbed every day as well as her body pampered with massages. She was surprised with new toys purchased every month, and Razzle's teeth dazzled all her onlookers winning the hearts of many people as well as her dog friends. Gentle but curious, she went off to explore many times on her own, sometimes beyond the boundaries of our property but always came back.

When we prepared to move, Razzle appeared as if she had a stroke, so using an animal pad for her to lie upon, I worked throughout the night using quantum biofeedback. She knew she had to regain her health because big plans were being undertaken, and by morning, feeling better, her bags were packed for the sunny bright world of Hawaii, accompanied by Jasmine, a fluffy cat, and Lavender, a cute black and white parti poodle.

But this particular day, we decided to take our youngest daughter shopping at Macy's and resume a normal family life, at least for Linnea's sake. As we all piled into the car, a strong feeling came over me to put Razzle behind our gate around the home. This thought was not given the attention it should have been given. Instead, I rationalized over my strong feelings, thinking Razzle was being taken care of by my older daughter. By now we were heading to the trampoline on the right side of our property loaded with macadamia trees. It is important when you get a strong feeling, heed it.

A final attempt to bring a woman down to her knees by the cruel hearts of a nest of devils that preyed upon her and her family deviously finds and controls her weakened puppy, taking advantage of her ripe age of fourteen years. This evil force pushes her forward to the front of this five-acre property of macadamia trees where two happy Siberian huskies live on an acre of land.

When arriving home, there is no Razzle waiting to greet them. This is so unusual for her not to be on the front porch. Something must be horribly amiss with Razzle. Normally she would have been waiting patiently for their return, wagging her tail. Immediately, Marten and Linnea go searching with flashlights on a four wheeler, looking for Razzle.

Mournful cries can be heard filling the night air, the macadamia trees bow their weary heads in prayer as they come traveling up to the home after scoping the five acres of property. She knows and waits in her place of refuge and her green eyes begin to emit endless streams of tears. Closing her office windows, she falls face down on the office floor and with such angst, and hysteria encompassing her being, she screams. Her eyes turn gray. The macadamia trees grieve as Linnea and her father slowly ride to the home on their four wheelers carrying the furry lifeless body of Razzle.

The stars and moon mourn that night and thick clouds, like a stormy blanket for the inky black sky, begin to pour wetness upon the Earth. Streaks of lightning light up the darkness, shrouding hot grayish clouds with a blinding incandescence, emanating the might of an imminent tempest. Searching, finally finding her, he kneels down to pull her from the cold floor into his arms. Hysterical, she sobs relentlessly, so angry at God for allowing such a horrible act. She wants to just die and give up. Life really sucks and it is impossible to forgive. But as always, time passes before her and helps soften the blow of death and slowly she comes to terms with the loss of such a wonderful friend so abruptly following her mother's death. Razzle no longer exists in the physical sense and she would no longer be able to enjoy touching her soft white fur and look lovingly into that smiley glowing face.

How did I create this? Flashes of Razzle at her happiest times, rolling on her back, smiling as my youngest daughter tickled her. I am not my pictures and can get through this. These pictures do not define me because I am a special soul/body connection. The Earth School is difficult—In fact, the most difficult thing I ever did.

The Gift in it all is that your love climbs above to become stronger, which makes evil a laughingstock.

Chapter Fifteen
The Gift

Freshman Roslyn Singleton Named East Atlantic Gymnastics League Specialist of the Week

1/21/2003

Singleton is the first Pittsburgh gymnast to earn a weekly honor from the EAGL since 2000 and only the third in Panthers history. Pittsburgh—Freshman Roslyn Singleton was named the East Atlantic Gymnastics League (EAGL) Specialist of the Week for her performance in Saturday's record-setting meet by the Panthers in a 195.4-194.1 victory over No. 27 Missouri.

Singleton (Lancaster, Pa. /Manheim Township) was competing for only the second time in her collegiate career and finished in a tie for first place on the floor exercise with a score of 9.875. It was her first floor routine as she didn't compete in that event in the season opener on Jan. 11. Singleton also placed fifth on the balance beam with a score of 9.775 from the judges.

The award is given to a gymnast who competes and excels in fewer than three events in a meet. It is the first year for the award, which is given along with the EAGL Gymnast of the Week honor. It is the first EAGL weekly honor for a Pittsburgh gymnast since Danielle "Freddie" Alba was named Co-Gymnast of the Week on March 7, 2000. Singleton joins Alba and Brenda Stevens as the only Panthers gymnasts to be honored since the inception of the awards in 1996.

The Panthers' 195.4 points were the second most in team history and the total placed them at 18th in this week's national rankings by Gym Info. Pittsburgh is ranked second in the Northeast Region behind Michigan and first among the eight teams in the EAGL.

Excerpts from Thesis

Knowing that I was being guided, I refused to look back, only to look forward.

This paper will give a detailed account on the positive outcome of using quantum biofeedback with my daughter. No one in the medical field had a clue as to how to help her. The only suggestions were the use of pharmaceuticals, sedatives, and confining her to a mental ward. In fact, I was told later, I had harmed her by not going along with the psychiatric medications—and given reasons why, which did not make sense to me.

Searching for help for six years, I knew that something had gone terribly amiss with my daughter. She was a student at the University of Pittsburgh. Offered five scholarships for her gymnastics ability, she proudly chose the University of Pittsburgh, where she was given recognition for her high grades during her first year as well as for her exquisite talent in gymnastics, honored by an Eagles award.

Making simple decisions in school was becoming more difficult. The decision to let go of her dream, giving up the scholarship she acquired with the University of Pittsburg was decided under much duress.

Eventually, she deteriorated, and became uncommunicative, going through many different stages of behavior.

During this time Roslyn frequented the Amish fields, lying on her back in the tall grass surrounded by the curious cattle. The only sign of where Roslyn might be found was the clue of her red bicycle parked along the winding country road. Her motor and mental skills had declined, making it nearly impossible to follow along in a simple yoga class

Acceptance

Sometimes the Amish would take her in and feed her dinner at a long table. They knew that this young girl struggled and gave her space to just be.

After summer break and working in the Grand Tetons with her brother, she decides after much agonizing to give up her scholarship with the University of Pittsburgh. There is a period of time after working in the Grand Tetons that she enrolls and attends the University of Hawaii but studying becomes increasingly difficult and she never does finish her degree.

After being home for a while, Roslyn expresses interest in seeing her brother in New Mexico. Agreeing, we think it might be good for her to be around other people her age. She enrolls in the university and takes a few college courses in Albuquerque to occupy her time. She struggles with these classes and is unable to acquire a passing grade. Her health begins to take a spiral downhill but Roslyn is well enough to work in the school cafeteria. It is here where she slowly declines and ends up in a catatonic state. Her face becomes void of any expression and she spends time alone for days, not interacting at all, losing all sense of reality. During this period of time of her life, I visit her and stay for stretches of time to help support her, hoping her body will heal in time. I do not act on any input or help from doctors as to why she is having such difficulty; they only want to medicate and institutionalize her.

During the time Roslyn visits her brother in New Mexico, I spend much time alone in Hawaii. Encouraging Roslyn to come visit me from Albuquerque, I arrange appointments for her with different doctors. Sometimes Roslyn is dropped off and instructed to wait for me to pick her up later. Heavily involved with the clairvoyant classes, many times I pick her up after my class is finished which works out perfectly.

It was at this one particular doctor's office where very important information is going to be received which is going to change Roslyn's life. Later, visiting this particular doctor's office to receive feedback about Roslyn's condition, she immediately approaches me and smiles, inviting me to come into her office. Guiding me to sit down, she takes both my hands and softly looks into my worried eyes with deep concern, inquiring, "What happened to Roslyn?" I begin to weep. Bingo, finally a doctor is taking an interest in Roslyn's condition and has the time to listen to me. After patiently listening, she says it appears to her as if Roslyn had a total nervous breakdown. Disturbed at seeing such a beautiful young lady in such a horrible predicament, she begins to talk about a technology involving the quantum world. She has witnessed huge comebacks with situations appearing hopeless and, in confidence, guarantees me that Roslyn can be helped, "Well, maybe she will not be the same Roslyn, but she will be a coherent viable being. Please be patient, it will take some time because I have witnessed amazing results using this technology."

This doctor was pointing me in the correct direction and will never be forgotten because she is the key who opened the door for endless possibilities for this young girl's life. She went out on a limb in making such a strong statement because by now this device was getting some bad publicity. It had become the pharmaceutical companies and FDA's worst nightmare. People experienced amazing recoveries and made testimonials and claims but they should not have done so in such a brazen manner. This did not go over very well with the FDA, even if they were true. The pharmaceutical companies were not happy because quantum biofeedback alleviates the stressors that create the disease in the first place and therefore removes the need for their expensive drugs. The idea that Roslyn was going to be helped by using quantum biofeedback fueled my passion, prompting me to eventually pursue the science behind it in my studies with Quantum University of Integrative Medicine, particularly after seeing some movement with Roslyn, who by now had travelled back to be with her brother in Albuquerque, New Mexico. This is where she received her first entrainment using subspace and it opened my eyes, giving me hope for her recovery.

The first ten appointments were long distance, which might boggle some minds. Roslyn could not be calibrated (found energetically) on her first session.. There was NO calibration of her energy, but after a few tries, there was a BREATH of relief, a connection, bringing hope!

Finally, after my lengthy time alone in Hawaii, a plan fell into place and very shortly after meeting with this doctor, I returned to Pennsylvania and found a buyer for the building that Lanco Gymnastics Training Center and many other smaller businesses occupied. In turn, this money was used to buy a device. First, I took beginner classes, next, intermediate and last, advanced classes making me a specialist in biofeedback. All these three-day courses were held in different states.

Roslyn fueled my journey with focus and spurred my forward motion. The plan already was set in motion with patience as one of the key players. What is money without health?

It was during this time that our masonry business struggled and we were warned by the bank that if our business went over our line of credit that things could get very nasty. Unfortunately, our focus was on helping Roslyn. My full attention was on our daughter and not heeding the bank's warning. Marten was more concerned than I about the business's outcome but I did not help him at all in this matter because I absolutely did not want to put my energy into anything else other than helping our daughter who was fighting for her life. In fact, I hardly noticed what was going on about me other than my focus to help Roslyn. It was most imperative to find answers to help Roslyn pull the pieces of her life back together—the part of her that she lost, making it impossible to find her way back to her own essence. She needed help and we were not finding it in Pennsylvania. It was horrible watching her go through so many different stages of her sickness.

Roslyn's Journey

She left. It is hard to explain what that means but there was no longer a trace of her in that beautiful body. She had previously told me in Pennsylvania before she visited her brother in New Mexico that she had an urgent sense. She had to hold my hand because if she did not, she would be lost forever.

In Pennsylvania

The medical professionals and neurologist did not have answers regarding how to help her. In the beginning, before quantum biofeedback, it was difficult to listen to her mournful cries as she wailed throughout the night in her bedroom in Pennsylvania. During the time she talked about visiting her brother in New Mexico, most of her gymnast friends began to judge her as crazy. These were the girls she competed with at Berks and many had also received scholarships or were still doing gymnastics in various universities. Gymnastics was Roslyn's life. She'd practice twenty hours or more at a time while in high school with these girls and absolutely loved every minute of it. She went on to compete for the University of Pittsburgh. This was a huge commitment. Many phone calls were received, informing us that Roslyn needed to be institutionalized, which wracked our souls. Many of her gymnast friends judged her and I knew we were going to have to leave so she could heal. I explained to them that she was going through a transition but they argued their point as they read verbatim to me information about schizophrenia found on the internet, seemingly angry because we did not agree.

Only one friend from gymnastics stuck by her, a true friend to Roslyn. Visiting often, they went out for lunch together. Also, Roslyn was invited to go along to the many different youth meetings with Sally.

Another young woman stuck by Roslyn whom she met at yoga, overlooking the sometimes odd behavior.

Both of these young women understood Roslyn was struggling and created that safe nonjudgmental space to be in their company.

A good friend of mine said, "Wow, what happened to Roslyn? She's so different. Oh well, at least she had a good eighteen years of her life and during that time had so many accomplishments!"

Many times we had to deal with people's insensitivities, but this was among the worst. "Too bad," she said, "it looks as if she will never be the same." Clenching my teeth, I answered her, "She is working things out and will be just fine."

She was one of the friends that got the message on my recorder that huge changes were being made to better my life and if I did not return the phone call, please understand that this is one of my changes. I did not return her phone call.

Roslyn was still there. I knew that she just acted a bit odd. So expressing a desire to see her brother, we agreed, thinking it might do her some good to go somewhere where she'd be accepted and to get away from the judgments of her gymnast friends.

While Roslyn went to New Mexico to stay with her brother, I stayed in Hawaii for a rather long stretch of time, taking classes with the Clairvoyant Center. If I could let go, answers would come into consciousness, but first I had to let go of her and the outcome. It was imperative to change my energy so she could model me energetically on a higher dimension. This was the key to open up possibilities for her healing. Answers eventually did come for her healing after I was alone for six months in Hawaii, one being quantum biofeedback which led to taking classes at Iquim University of Integrative Medicine and the use of many other healing modalities. This journey is documented in my thesis, giving a full account of Roslyn's miraculous recovery, which was published because of Doctor Paul Drouin's encouragement. I felt as if there was not enough time in the day to learn and I worked diligently, staying calm. Panic had to be assuaged many times because I knew it would ruin my focus to stay on task.

More Excerpts

How can you explain or try to explain what fuels a mother when her child is involved? It is as if she develops a part of herself—or maybe I should say is able to let go of herself—and connects with the divine to be led in a steadfast way. It was all about that twinkling-eyed little girl who definitely had a mind of her own. Instead of crawling, she scooted on the floor, eventually pulling herself up to walk on those wobbly legs. She definitely had my heart from the beginning.

A Mother's Love

This paper will give a detailed account on the positive outcome of using quantum biofeedback with my daughter. No one in the medical field had a clue as to how to help her. The only suggestions were the use of pharmaceuticals, sedatives, and confining her to a mental ward. In fact, I was told later, I had harmed her by not going along with the psychiatric medications—and given reasons why which did not make sense to me.

Searching for help for six years, I knew....

As Roslyn started to awake from her catatonic state, she exhibited many odd behaviors and appeared as if she had a huge amount of neurological damage. At the onset of treatment, she was unable to stop her busy mind and talked nonsensically throughout the night. While visiting her in New Mexico, I was very disturbed to listen to her chatter. Incapable of joining in a conversation at this time of her life, she made her own conversation. Her hands shook uncontrollably as well as her head, which would at times jerk back unexpectedly. It appeared as if she was totally out of control of her body. She later told me that in New Mexico she had befriended a being who was the color of red, I listened.

Hawaii

Getting in touch with her through her world, creating humorous silly children's songs became our thread of connection. Now we engaged in conversation or listened to people that we could not see on this physical plane of life. Were these people nonexistent or were they in another dimension of time? How about her many visions? In order to get into her world, I encouraged her to talk about the people with whom she was now engaging in conversation. I asked questions as to where they came from and any other information that she knew about them. Usually, with crisp clear answers, she'd tell me a little bit about them and let me know when they came and left. She was able to talk freely about these people. But when you tried to have a conversation with her in real time, she was unresponsive.

Becoming delusional, she thought something very gruesome was happening within our family members and exhibited horrible panic attacks. She experienced uncontrollable bouts of rage, inappropriate language, crude and lucid remarks, hints about taking her life as well as mine, obnoxious behavior, staying alone, unable to join the family, deadpan staring at walls, visions of horrible events outside the family as well as inside the family with the members of our family doing atrocious horrible acts of violence and absolutely believing they were occurring at the present moment. These were only some of the behaviors which were part of her healing journey. Roslyn talked often about death and how easy it would be for anyone to die. This was very eerie as if something else was talking inside her.

Many times, choosing to get out of the car, they walk. Tonight using only the light of their cell phones in their hands, they travel slowly along the narrow country road listening to the wild boars squeal as they scatter to hide in the trees and bushes close by.

Marten drove Roslyn home because she was having out of control bouts of unrelenting rage and delusional thought patterns that could not be assuaged. If Marten was not with us, my car would be found parked along the side of the road, abandoned for a while. Linnea and I would start walking home, picking my car up later. Usually, Roslyn was waiting, sitting in it, but on this occasion, we were in luck. Marten had accompanied us.

Songs and stories are made up as they walk toward their destination. Sometimes this walk is a rather long journey. Tonight they travel slowly into the darkness, listening closely to the sounds of cars traveling in the night. As cars approach, they move over onto the grassy area away from the curb because of the heavy blanket of blackness which covers, now monochromatic, terrain. The moon and stars are hidden by the dark stormy clouds as the wind begins to blow. Curving, the sky storm clouds arch into the ocean. Darkening the countryside, the steel smoky clouds melt into the earth. Suddenly a brilliant flash flickers and dies, like an almighty camera flash that blankets everything at once. Moments later the rumbling thunder arrives and right on cue the rain begins to fall haphazardly from the sky and then all at once it falls in great sheets. There is nowhere to hide. Another flash of bright light follows its cracking boom but they're too far from home to run. They keep walking with the coqui frogs serenading them into the night at a steady pace toward home.

Getting out of the car with Linnea was imperative because it was not fair for her to witness the rage and the obscenities that were seething out of Roslyn's mouth. Many times the words were directed at Linnea, but it was not really Roslyn. Dramatic weird thought processes were caused by the inflammation of her brain, part of the reason for her out of control outbursts. She has no remembrance of most of them. These bouts of psychotic behavior evoking out of control rage began to occur a lot as her healing journey moved forward. Sometimes it was directed at Linnea and sometimes at me. Roslyn's strength was enhanced substantially with these outbreaks, which made her very capable of doing damage and harm to others, especially when her rage escalated. Many items were broken in the home. Doors, walls, and outside fences were broken by her increased strength and hurled objects. Very heavy, sharp objects whizzed past my head unexpectedly. Did some dark being occupy her body working through my daughter? It is as if she turned into some kind of psychotic monster full of venom and foul language, unlike the Roslyn I knew. Disconnected from her external world, she often did not respond or if she did it was in a very slow manner, having to be prompted. Sometimes her behavior resembled the negative symptoms of schizophrenia: inexpressiveness, blankness, lack of feeling, monotone and monosyllabic speech. There were times she just stared or had conversations with people we did not see but which she befriended. Having any kind of conversation with her was totally impossible because her nervous system was constantly misfiring. Her conversation did not make sense nor could it be quieted during the night.

In the beginning of her journey, we visited many different medical doctors and neurologists to find help but a plan to get her back to her feet seemed to be an impossible feat without drugs. Instead, we were told repeatedly how pharmaceutical drugs and enrolling her in a psychiatric unit was the only answer. One neurologist did agree with me from Hershey Medical Center. She understood what I believed to be true about Roslyn.

The Golden Globe of Light

Later in her journey of healing, excitedly she went looking for me because she had some exciting news. She recounted the visitation of a golden globe that hovered over her body which told her, "Please do not to be afraid; we have come to heal you." Her healing journey is amazing as recorded in the *Power of the Entangled Hierarchy*. During this time she was active in the mental health outpatient program as we were directed, so she could receive financial help. Roslyn was unable to communicate but her brain worked when she shared her experience of being in other dimensions and so when she began to share her vision with her doctor, he became very perturbed and agitated. Listening to his response, I suggested that many people do not understand and therefore will not appreciate her visions, so it probably is best not to share these experiences with them. When talking about these paranormal happenings, her doctor became more adamant about her taking the pharmaceuticals drugs that he prescribed, explaining that they would help to subdue these visions. In response to my advice, she was quiet, only sharing her many visions and dreams with me.

More excerpts from Thesis

See: http://www.neurofeedbacknj.com/neurofeedback/qeeg/

She was discovered by a doctor in the mental health unit at Kona Hospital who attributed her dysfunctional behavior to head trauma. The results of a neurofeedback test (called a QEEG) of Roslyn's brainwaves determined his suspicions to be correct. He told me that he was very surprised that she could have been overlooked and not recognized as having symptoms from a traumatic brain injury. He was very excited to talk about Roslyn. The test told it all.

Since working with so many cases related to sports accidents in his career, he had never seen a case so severe and was surprised by her progression in therapy. The severe disruption of brain waves was also attributed to the slight calcification in the upper brain stem and Roslyn's chiari (oversized brain). Her brain was in such a state of severe disruption, physically, it could not recover on its own. The encouraging result of neurofeedback done three times a week was enhanced by the use of quantum biofeedback. Also, hyperbaric oxygen therapy was prescribed four times a week with the neurofeedback to grow new brain waves. Vipassana was a type of breath work also explored in conjunction with the neurofeedback. More information can be found on the website: http://www.dhamma.org/en/vipassana.shtml.

Four months previous, Roslyn had a QEEG and we proceeded to make an appointment for neurofeedback. When this practitioner looked at the QEEG, he refused to work with Roslyn because her brain was so askew but suggested medicating her with drugs. I ignored this information and kept looking toward our goal of full recovery. Never Give Up, NEVER!

Later, Roslyn was seen by a doctor who'd just arrived at Kona Hospital, where she was enrolled as an outpatient in the psychiatric care unit. Disturbed after meeting with her, he had good reason to believe that her problem was not stemming from mental illness. The medical community was overlooking what he believed to be the true diagnosis. This doctor, by divine appointment, had replaced Roslyn's previous psychiatrist who was annoyed by my persistence in supporting Roslyn's decision to not take the drugs prescribed. It was strongly proposed by her caseworker that she claim mental issues, instead of a head injury. A diagnosis of psychosis would enable her to receive financial assistance. Therefore this is why she attended the mental outpatient unit, visiting once a week. This is where she was discovered by a medical doctor who came over from the mainland and landed in the mental health unit, working in the outpatient facility. Immediately upon seeing Roslyn, he knew without a doubt that her bizarre behavior was the result of a head injury or thought so and wanted to find out more information about Roslyn. Unable to communicate, Roslyn was incoherent at the time and appeared as if she had major neurological damage. He left a message on my cell phone during my stay in Mexico, while I took classes with the quantum masters, asking me to please call him. Listening to his message gave me hope and promptly a meeting was arranged with him, upon my return.

When meeting with Dr. Brite, the first question he asked was, "What do you think happened to Roslyn?" Bingo, the second time someone in the medical field sought after my opinion! After sharing with him about her history of head injuries, he proceeded to read a list of behavior abnormalities associated with a head injury. Although the behavior exhibited by Roslyn was much more extreme, this information supported me and fueled my focus, igniting the torch of hope. We made an appointment for her in his personal office and a second brain map (QEEG) was done which proved him correct in his assumption. But instead of feeling the case was hopeless and her brain waves too disrupted, he wanted to take the challenge to help her. By now, my suspicions were confirmed without a doubt that the behavior being exhibited resulted from a head injury which was exacerbating other complications, making her lose total control. The test results using a quantum biofeedback device pointed me in the direction of a head injury being the underlying cause of the total disruption of her brain and my findings were backed up by the QEEG brain map.

The QEEG enables the practitioner to see the unique pattern of mental strengths and weaknesses–areas of the brain where there is too little or too much activity and areas that are not coordinating their activity the best they could. Never seeing someone with such severe damage come back to be a healthy viable person, he asked me if I was prepared for the emotional outbursts and unconventional behavior she most likely would exhibit as she healed. We were definitely on the frontier of something that was never accomplished before in the history of science but he believed we were on to what was ultimately going to help Roslyn. Receiving neurofeedback for a year while she still continued receiving quantum biofeedback, her jerky head motions and her flailing hands started to become less severe. But she still had a long way to go before becoming a viable living human being. She appeared unconscious to the world around her and her awareness as to how to participate in a conversation was void. During this period of time, she worked through huge amounts of rage and had many flagrant emotional outbursts exhibiting foul language, destroying things with her insurmountable strength. We tried to stay neutral to these outbursts the best we could, but it was difficult.

Losing our family business made it impossible to pay this doctor, so we traded Marten's beautiful burnt orange jeep for services rendered. This jeep was not just an ordinary jeep but had all the chrome in just the right places. It had a special license plate and was garnished with interior lights which could be changed by a switch to set the mood; it was my husband's dream car. Wanting in the worse way to have this doctor work with Roslyn, I convinced him to give our jeep in exchange for this doctor's help. Marten reluctantly agreed.

Informed by this doctor that the neurological damage most likely would always be a part of her life, I secretly refused to accept this information but expanded my knowledge, awareness, and expertise, continuing to take classes with Quantum University and worked with Roslyn every day.

Unfortunately, he had some deep personal issues. He came to heal, but his demons followed him, growing in strength, torturing him unrelentingly. Later, he abruptly vacated his office without notice after a year of working with Roslyn. Inwardly, he was such a good-hearted, kind and an extremely intelligent man. Marten felt betrayed, because of giving his jeep for payment, but the doctor did play a significant part in Roslyn's life, giving us hope and supporting us in what we believed happened to Roslyn.

The Portal

Roslyn was found often staring at the TV looking at the pictures with no sound. On several occasions, she accompanied us to the movies but after the movie was finished, she did not have a clue as to what happened and made up her own storyline. Happy, she was well enough to travel to the movies because we were by now seeing a huge shift with Roslyn because of the entrainments using quantum biofeedback and neurofeedback, but we knew she still had a long way to go before becoming a coherent being.

Where was Roslyn? Much later, Roslyn inquires if she could join me on my afternoon walk taking me totally by surprise. This was definitely not the norm for Roslyn who by now tried to avoid me at all costs. It was the first time in years that Roslyn expressed interest in joining me. She was quiet at first but halfway through the walk she said, "Do you know where I was, Mom?" Stopping right in my tracks, I looked at her and in a calm and a deliberate voice asked her where. The doors were opened and she began a detailed account of entering a portal. She described her stay in this portal which she described as a gray fuzzy hole she entered while staying in Albuquerque. It was here people entered and stayed to receive healings for various ailments, a place she was not certain that she would ever be able to leave: "It seemed like forever and I questioned if I would be allowed to return, that is if I would be well enough to return. I thought that I would never be able to see you again."

While in the portal, she saw random people come and go that she did not know. They came to receive various healings for their different chakras. As we were finishing our walk, she said that she also saw people she knew enter the portal. She saw me in the portal having my throat chakra healed, as well as other people in our family come and leave. Acquaintances and friends came and received a healing specific for that person, making it a very busy place. "I was relieved when I finally was able to leave this place," she said.

Later that afternoon, she suggests she give our parti poodle Lavender a haircut. After spending a rather lengthy time with her, Lavender comes out of the bathroom looking beautiful and Roslyn comes out with no hair. She shaved her whole head with dog clippers!

More Excerpts from Thesis

When Roslyn first did yoga at the Big Island Yoga Center, she had to be led and helped with each pose. In 2010, loud outbursts were exhibited in yoga and there was always that possibility of having to exit the class early because of panic attacks that came at unexpected times. These panic attacks mimicked a heart attack and, therefore, were exacerbated by the thought that she was actually having a heart attack. In 2011, there were occasional bouts of anxiety and the feeling of being suffocated. As of 2013, the body is able to relax, the nervous system is able to unwind, and body awareness has increased.

A study investigation on the effects of an Iyengar yoga program on perceived stress, psychological and physical outcomes in distressed women showed that after three months, the women in the groups that did yoga showed significant improvements in stress, in reduced anxiety, depression and mood swings. They had a sense of well-being and calmness when Iyengar yoga was a part of their lives.

Yoga and Stress by Ellen Serber states as follows: "When someone is suffering from the kind of condition where the body is still in the response to a physical threat or psychological distress, which generates and produces many chemical and hormonal reactions in the body, this fight or flight response is great for a short time but if it cannot shut down it is harmful. Research has been made on the benefits of Yoga practice in alleviating stress and its effects."

A very good summary of the research on the stress response is contained in Robert Sapolsky's book, "Why Zebras Don't Get Ulcers."A review of the current thinking on stress reveals that the process is both biochemical and psychological. Sapolsky first outlines the physiological experience of stress, explaining that the sympathetic nervous system is responsible for reacting to emergencies, employing the fright and flight reflexes. "Originating in the brain, sympathetic projections exit your spine and branch out to nearly every organ, every blood vessel, and every sweat gland in your body," Sapolsky writes. "The sympathetic nervous system kicks into action during emergencies, or what you think are emergencies....The nerve endings of this system release adrenaline....Sympathetic nerve endings also release the closely related substance: noradrenaline." In the United States, adrenaline, which is secreted by the sympathetic nerve endings in the adrenal gland, is referred to as epinephrine; noradrenaline, which is secreted by all other sympathetic nerve endings throughout the body, is referred to as norepinephrine. These are the chemicals which, within seconds, signal the organs into action. This is called the "neural route," because the action of one cell, a neuron, travels to the next cell in line and through that cellular link mobilizes activity in response to a stressor. When the neuron secretes a messenger that "percolates into the bloodstream and affects events far and wide, that messenger is a hormone," Sapolsky continues. "All sorts of glands secrete hormones; the secretion of some of them is turned on during stress, and the secretion of others is turned off. The parasympathetic nervous system, which mediates calm, is inhibited by the sympathetic nervous system during a stressful emergency."

The brain is the master gland. "It is now recognized that the base of the brain, the hypothalamus, contains a huge array of these releasing and inhibiting hormones, which instruct the pituitary, which in turn regulates the secretions of the peripheral glands."

When the brain experiences or thinks of something stressful, these hormones will be released. Along with epinephrine and norepinephrine, another group of hormones is released during stress. These are called glucocorticoids. *Whereas epinephrine acts immediately, the glucocorticoids come into play within minutes or hours. According to Sapolsky, the hormonal path of the stress response moves like this: "When something stressful happens or you think a stressful thought, the hypothalamus secretes an array of releasing hormones into the hypothalamic-pituitary circulatory system. The principal such releaser is called CRF (corticotropin releasing factor), while a variety of minor players synergize with CRF. Within fifteen seconds or so, CRF triggers the pituitary to release hormone ACTH (also known as corticotropin). After ACTH is released into the bloodstream, it reaches the adrenal gland, and, within a few minutes, triggers glucocorticoid release. Together, glucocorticoids and the secretions of the sympathetic nervous system (epinephrine and norepinephrine) account for a large percentage of what happens in your body during stress. These are the workhorses of the stress response." One way researchers measure stress is by taking blood levels of glucocorticoids.*

There are other chemical changes in the body that facilitate the stress response and are crucial in an emergency. The pituitary and brain secrete substances to blunt pain; these are endorphins and enkephalin. The pancreas is stimulated to produce glucagon which helps raise levels of sugar glucose needed by the muscles to mobilize energy. The pituitary secretes prolactin, which suppresses reproduction. Other reproductive hormones—estrogen, progesterone, and testosterone—are inhibited. Emergencies are obviously no time to reproduce. Vasopressin, an antidiuretic, is secreted from the pituitary. Growth-related hormones and insulin are both inhibited as the body mobilizes its resources for immediate survival and future needs are disregarded. And therein is the catch.

All this arousal in an emergency becomes pathological if it is not turned off when the threat is over. But it is not just the threat of physical danger that must recede for the response to end. The brain must think and understand that it is over or the cycle continues, becoming a hindrance to health. It is not that stress itself makes us sick, but its continuation creates the conditions for other ailments to make us ill. In order to change the very complex stress response, it is very important to become familiar with relaxation and learn to let go. Shivasana is a very important part in yoga for letting go, lying on your back with arms at a 45-degree angle with legs stretched out to the edge of the mat and the head slightly elevated with a blanket and an eye pillow which helps relax the eyes. Training the body to respond to the request for relaxation on a muscular level and breathing deeply creates a habit of relaxation that can be very helpful in turning off the stress response.

Prayer is very powerful. Many people pray for their loved ones when they are seriously ill. They hope that a divine force will hear and respect their request and cure the patient. Others pray by using their inner powers and believe that they can heal at a distance using their sheer intention to help the patient. What do you believe about the Power of Prayer? Please read scientific studies done at http://www.plim.org/PrayerDeb.htm: These studies have shown conclusive evidence of the power of prayer. Time after time the outcomes of these tests have shown the reality of the force of higher spiritual beings and our ability to communicate with them.

We have also learned from viewing the results of these studies that the expectations we have while praying factor into the outcome of our prayers. Though the faithful will always believe that there need not be any physical evidence of the power and effects of prayer, science has come a long way toward showing just that: prayer is real, and it works

HUMOR

It is important to look past the behavior and see the person's spirit-- who she/he is, not becoming attached to the behavior. I detached myself from all offensive behavior, I learned to let go and found humor in the healing process, (2010, D.E.Singleton). In fact, the first time there was communication with Roslyn, humor, and silly children's songs were used to get into her world, the world that she resided. I was detached from the outcome, but knew that there would be one and was confident that I was being guided with answers for her complete healing. This healing was going to happen at its own pace. I am not aware of anyone that has displayed such severe symptoms as this young lady, who has eventually integrated into society.

As time went on, she used her hands to have her own conversation which only she understood.

Each one of us is an artist creating an authentic life and the real art of listening involves awareness and sensitivity to the feelings of the person speaking because it is at the feeling level that genuine connection, relationship, and healing occurs. By Sarah Ban Breathnach

A SAFE space is a crucial ingredient needed to make that leap.

2012. BioSuperfood, discovered at the World Congress of Integrative Medicine, is a whole food product formulated with nutritionally rich microalgae, four of the most nutrient and phytonutrient dense algae found on earth. At least 160,000 children suffered from Chernobyl radiation illnesses. BAC saved many thousands and miracles were numerous. Given the super nutrients in BAC, rapid progress in healing was observed and several of the victims treated that survived are still alive today. It restores the inner genius of the endocrine system which regulates all aspects of health. It also gives nutritional support for people in their everyday struggle with common or difficult health conditions, sparking the body's own revolution against aging and declining health. Organic, vegan, pure and one hundred percent natural, veggie capsules, a powerful antioxidant supporting the immune, and cardiovascular system, it is a complete protein including all essential amino acids, rich in all required vitamins A, B complex, C, D, E, K, and abundant in all known minerals and trace elements, complete with essential fatty acids. It is a great source of enzymes and most efficient source of chlorophyll, rich in nucleic acids containing a rare form of B12. We saw remarkable improvement using this product. Roslyn was able to speak sentences, her energy increased and her brain began to turn on, increasing her healing capabilities.

9/6/2013. The memory and appreciation of being part of the Pittsburgh gymnastics team are expressed. "As she becomes more conscious and her body regains strength, the reality of how her life has been affected as well as her brain is becoming clearer to her. She is vividly remembering her past accomplishments; she mourns and yearns to come back as strong as before. She has so much yet to process." Now the body is able to relax, the nervous system is beginning to unwind and body awareness has increased.

The angle taken with this particular case was not with a diagnosis because the medical community wanted to diagnose this client with a mental illness. The use of a diagnosis can help if it is done with awareness of the core factor that is creating the illness. This takes much training and education. Also, the use of medication is appropriate when used with awareness in certain situations particularly in short-term use and, of course, needs to be monitored very closely. Pharmaceuticals were not used because of the belief of the client as well as the practitioner that the body must be allowed to heal without masking the symptoms.

The book, Brain on Fire by Susannah Cahalan is a book about a disease (anti-NMDA-receptor encephalitis) that affected her brain and the many misdiagnoses' she had to endure until the correct diagnosis was found. In her book, she talks about how she believes children are misdiagnosed with autism as well as adults misdiagnosed with severe mental disorders such as schizophrenia. These never receive the proper help to enjoy a normal life. She states that there is research being done on the link between autoimmune diseases and mental illnesses. Based on this she believes that some forms of schizophrenia, bipolar disorders, obsessive-compulsive disorders, and depression are actually caused by inflammatory conditions in the brain. Just maybe there is a relationship to some of the bizarre behavior associated with traumatic brain injury and this type of inflammatory condition of the brain. Susannah goes on to say, unfortunately for most people suffering from severe psychiatric conditions, it is nearly impossible to give the proper testing to receive the proper help for them because of the exorbitant cost to diagnose and to treat properly.

Why is this so?

More excerpts from Thesis

The term catatonia represents a stage defined by absence, by inability, and by non-behaviors. It is a miswiring that creates this condition. Some of the behavior associated with catatonic is muscular rigidity and fixedness of posture, immobility or stupor, refusal to eat or drink, excitement, deadpan staring, mutism, impulsivity, negativism, rigidity, automatic repetition of words or statements said by another person, and direct observation. Catatonia comes from the misfiring of neurons. The "muscular" rigidity occurs when the chemical link is severed between the patient's awareness of her body and the feeling of comfort and appropriateness of movement. Roslyn developed autonomic symptoms, her blood pressure and heart rate vacillated between high and low. The catatonic stage marks the height of the disease and precedes breathing failure, coma, and sometimes death. Sometimes and most likely the stages of recovery often occur in reverse order. Before Roslyn got to catatonia she had passed through psychosis so she had to pass through it again on her road back to normality.

This compelled quite an array of emotions and it was a wild ride for her and for our family to observe, always knowing that she was getting a little closer to normalcy. Despite all the weird behavior we could see Roslyn's spirit shine through gradually, and hope held the space for her return.

Later, when Roslyn was brought out in social situations we did much of the talking for her and during social eating she usually soiled her shirt or outfit with whatever food she was eating. As she became more coherent, she realized people were embarrassed or uncomfortable being around her and became well aware of being treated as if she was retarded, at times with very little respect. She was very hyper-attuned, small things such as tapping of silverware were way too much for her to deal with and therefore, she held her ears shut to block out the noise.

The vagus nerve is the 10th of our 12 cranial nerves. What makes cranial nerves unique is their emergence in pairs from the brain, as opposed to the nerves that thread outward through the spinal cord. With the exception of the optic nerve, the cranial nerves are components of the peripheral nervous system, which serves as a communication relay between the brain and the extremities.

In Medieval Latin, "vagus" literally means "wandering." What a perfect fit, because the cord-thick vagus nerve originates in the brain stem, extends through the neck and chest, and terminates in the abdomen. It supplies parasympathetic fibers to our organs from the neck to the top of the colon, with the exception of the adrenal glands. The parasympathetic nervous system is responsible for stimulation of "rest-and-digest"/"feed and breed" activities that occur when we're at "rest." Its action is considered complementary to that of the sympathetic nervous system–responsible for stimulating fight/flight response activities. So that means the vagus nerve orchestrates dynamics such as lowering heart rate and blood pressure, downward movement through the gastrointestinal tract, a number of muscle movements in the mouth (including speech), and keeping the larynx open for breathing.

Excessive activation of the vagus nerve during emotional stress–a parasympathetic overcompensation of a strong stress/anxiety-induced response–is at play. It's all about a sudden drop in heart rate and blood pressure which can even result in loss of bladder control during moments of extreme fear.

The Vagus Nerve | (Self) Stimulation

Vagus nerve stimulation (VNS) has been used to control seizures since 1979. The procedure, which uses a pacemaker-like device implanted in the chest, has recently been approved for treating tough cases of depression.

But when it comes to depression and anxiety relief, you don't have to fool with invasive or non-invasive vagus nerve stimulation. You can learn and practice vagal maneuvers. Here are just a few...

Immersing your face in cold water called the (diving reflex).

Attempting to exhale against a closed airway is usually done by closing your mouth, and pinching your nose shut while pressing out as if blowing up a balloon.

A modified version, less impactful on the Eustachian tubes, can be performed by breathing with the glottis (the vocal folds and the opening between them) partially closed. Just do the exhale while making an "Hhhh" sound, like when you're cleaning your glasses

Tensing your stomach muscles as if to bear down to have a bowel movement, diaphragm breathing techniques and basic yoga routines can stimulate the vagus nerve as well as yoga-associated activities with chanting, listening and vocalizing.

The mystique of heaven meeting earth, water meeting land as snowflakes gently drop from heaven, blanketing earth in its white embrace, always puts her in awe of nature's rhythms. She feels gratitude in the witnessing of a kiss, the kiss of the Divine and the mundane.

Pictures of snow and the night sky illuminated by the full moon lull this mother's imagination as her eyes deepen into pools of green water, remembering a scene which takes her into a magical snowy scene. She remembers.

Snow is falling steadily and there is excitement in the air. It is a magical winter land scene being observed by an all loving God. Yelps of happiness can be heard under the star-laden sky. A young boy with a head of sandy blond hair is laughing as he mounts his red wooden sled with a little long-haired cockapoo, sporting nut-brown woolen booties which keep her paws warm. His sister, Roslyn, is following closely behind on her inner tube. You can hear her giggles as Wilbur, a Gordon setter, runs next to her in the cold frosty air. Wilbur gallops alongside the sled as it swiftly moves down the snowy hill, making a new path in the freshly falling snow.

Sharing a strong bond with her brother who is a few years older than she, Roslyn rolls off her sled at the bottom of the hill. Giggles can be heard as they lie making angels in the freshly fallen snow. The snow pours freely from the heavens as they gaze upward, catching snowflakes on their tongues.

Tenacity is important. Tenacious

Adjective \tə-'nā-shəs\

: Not easily stopped or pulled apart: firm or strong

: continuing for a long time

: Very determined to do something

According to the Merriam Dictionary

Dance

Dance is a beautiful way for expression of your deepest feelings, creating a feeling of wholeness just as swimming does in the ocean. Swimming alone grants a sense of peace and awe, liberating the body. Swim in the sparkling ocean, touching its softness and the energy it emits; and as you invite the salt water to caress your face it will elicit freedom to enter the body, generating a type of dance.

One gorgeous picture perfect afternoon while swimming far out into the ocean waters, I stopped to observe the sunlight's rays shimmering on the surface of the water. It created a kaleidoscope of beautiful lights penetrating deep into the blue ocean. Looking up to see how far I had wandered from the beach shoreline, I spotted a herd of fins coming toward me which startled me from my serene feeling. For a moment I wondered, "Are these fins of dolphins?" I sure hope so, because it was not looking like a very promising predicament if they were not. As the fins headed toward me I waited, knowing that swimming to shore was not much of an option at the moment, being that the shoreline was barely detectable. Deciding to see who the fins belonged to, I took a long look under the water and saw beautiful smiling dolphins and better yet, each one was showing me their baby. As they circled me, they somersaulted, danced and did all kinds of gymnastics honoring motherhood. They knew what it meant to be a mother fighting for her baby's life and stayed with me for a long time, coming close enough to touch me their voices were heard as they sang, encouraging me in my journey. Their babies jumped, performing all kinds of tricks while the smaller babies stayed very close by their mother's side. I will never forget the immersion of love felt all around and over me which went on for quite some time. I swam back to shore feeling supported, changed forever.

The Walmart Shed

Going through a stage of ingesting a lot of water at one time, Roslyn did not have the awareness nor the discipline to stop this heavy consumption of water which was consumed in such a short period of time and discovered by following the path of the stream of water, many times found lying on the cement floor of a bathroom in town. Because of God's grace, the water gushed from her, moving continuously through her stomach. If not in town, Roslyn was often found face down on the grass writhing in pain in front of her small hale (in Hawaii, a house). Sometimes catching the driver by surprise, the car had to be stopped inconveniently alongside the road because she'd just ingested a gallon of water before getting into the car.

Living in Hawaii, you can become very creative. Since we decided it best to have Roslyn close to us, we made a bedroom from a large shed bought at Wal-Mart, with a bed, shelves, couch and a television which fitted in very conveniently. Roslyn's hale had windows constructed that extended out with screens and a nice sized screened-in outside porch protected from any nasty mosquitoes, where she had the luxury to enjoy the sounds, smells, taste and sights of nature.

My focused intention was to see Roslyn's beautiful spirit shine through, knowing her obnoxious behavior was just part of her healing journey. The more movement displayed in her emotions usually meant she was going through a shift, finding a little bit more of Roslyn and letting go of that which was not her. Many of Roslyn's amazing visions and dreams during her healing journey were recorded in *The Power of the Entangled Hierarchy*.

After cutting up all of her belongings and placing them in bags to hang in the neighborhood coffee trees, eventually, she had nothing to wear and only a vague remembrance of most of these actions. Asking her why she had to cut her clothing to shreds and hide them, she paused and said, "I feel compelled to punish myself."

I felt like I had to buy her more clothing to wear, but they also found their way into the trash can or trash bin at some random apartment complex and many times cut to shreds. Jewelry was discarded at whim and items of value were tossed out. I became frustrated with her attitude but knew remaining neutral to this behavior was imperative because materialistic things were not important enough to cause a dissension between us, which would not help her heal.

On this unique healing journey, she repeatedly had vivid dreams about her gymnastics team. Many times they were cheering her on, wanting her to wake up in the worse way. They were patiently waiting for her return, so looking forward to celebrating her victory with her. There were numerous dreams about her team and coach desiring her back while she lay in a coffin. Every time a new dream came, it brought her one more inch forward to freedom.

Truly a walking miracle, her journey, dreams, and visions were documented as she reconnected to her spirit/soul body. All of the head and hand jerking gradually disappeared and Roslyn began to connect with her eyes. Honored to be a part of her healing journey, I learned much invaluable information to help others.

Tourette's has been linked to different parts of the brain, including an area called the basal ganglia, which helps control body movements. Differences there may affect nerve cells and the chemicals that carry messages between them. Researchers think the trouble in this brain network may play a role in Tourette's. Repeatedly we were told by the medical professionals that Roslyn had neurological damage which would never change but she proved them wrong. The involuntary movements and vocal outbursts which resembled Tourette's have disappeared though they were diagnosed as being irreversible. The human body has such amazing healing abilities; all you have to do is tap into them. College classes in Hawaii forced her to learn how to read, write and actually comprehend the material read. She became more aware of the people around her as well as her surroundings. At first, appearing as if she was severely retarded, slowly Roslyn re-integrated into the classroom. Grasping the importance of social skills and proper etiquette, she reinvented herself. This did not happen all at once but took years. In the beginning, her sister was a great support in helping her work through her college courses, assisting her in writing her papers and reading her college textbooks with her. Roslyn had no clue how to write paragraphs or how to begin a paper, let alone support what she wrote. Having no comprehension skills she made up her own story and her own rules in what she read. Everything had to be learned from scratch. Marten talked to each professor, sharing the background about Roslyn and her challenges as she healed and they patiently supported and guided her along the way.

A Miracle

"And he said unto her, Daughter, thy faith hath made thee whole; go in peace, and be whole of thy plague" (Mark 5:34, KJV) The Bible has many verses indicating the strength of our healing capabilities. It works, but it is easy to get sidetracked with negativity. Depression, grief and lower energies can come knocking at your door and will rob you of your faith if you allow them in, creating doubts of your own power within. Keep your eyes on the goal, be an observer and never look back! "And Jesus said unto them, 'Because of your unbelief: for verily I say unto you, If ye have faith as a grain of mustard seed, ye shall say unto this mountain, Remove hence to yonder place; and it shall remove; and nothing shall be impossible unto you'." (Matthew 17:20, KJV).

Now a graduate of the Hawaii Community College, she has aspirations of exploring her life journey and career. She attends yoga classes and is involved with a very upbeat church in Hawaii. Taking lessons for ballroom dancing she is now dancing to her own rhythm, coherent, viable—an energetic young woman back in the game of life.

Asking for honesty and true relationships filled with love and commitment, I found most people are not ready for that kind of relationship. Instead, forced to find my answers in a higher spiritual dimension and to trust and be led by it, I find compassion for the people in my life, expecting them not to be anybody but themselves and perfect exactly where they are on their path. It was lonely on my path but I was supported and nurtured by higher dimensional beings, and found my answers to the questions: Who am I, why am I here, and where am I going?

I found the template that was me and it fit perfectly. I had to embrace forgiveness for blaming myself for my mother's death. Before I made the move, my dad asked me, "Ember, do you really have to go?" I looked at him and said yes. In my mind's eye, I did all that was possible to help my parents. It was a very gloomy, depressing and very difficult time in my life because I knew without a doubt that a new life would have to be discovered, a place that welcomed me in love or I would choose to die.

You really can't keep on asking why but must learn to accept, not resist, and move forward in your life. One has to learn to let go and get in touch with your own body-spirit connection and know that you are not any of the pictures. Somehow you are interconnected, but you need to learn to become neutral to all your pictures so you are not holding onto a storyline that plays over and over again in your life, preventing all the magic and wonder from entering your life. That is exactly how it worked for me because life goes on and you are the captain of it. You can choose to go forward or you can stay stuck in the story. Knowing death was knocking at my door, I chose life and so gradually developed skills to let go and bring in my essence. This enabled me to see the beauty of my life and the energy to make that conscious decision to step off the hamster wheel into freedom. This, in turn, opened my eyes. Getting in touch with me, I found love for my own uniqueness by detachment, making that conscious decision to let go of the people that I loved. This brought confidence in my own self-value, and a deeper compassion for others—their faults as well as my faults.

Humor in life is another key which opened a door of reality. This brought a sense that worries in this realm are not important anymore.

We must really know it because this life is not what it appears to be. There is another dimension that can be reached where peace and joy can be found.

Finding the gift--literally forced to do so because of my thick bullheadedness--I kicked my arms and legs in resistance and exhibited tantrums of sheer frustration through a lot of it. "When is this ever going to stop? Why am I here on Earth? God, is this just a bad joke? Why me? What did I do to deserve these horrible events in my life?" After this resistance, which only caused pain and suffering, was released changes did occur. I became a person that had not existed before, but in order to discover peace and leave the pain-wracked writhing body, I had to let go. There was no other choice but to do so.

All the players, the people that helped bring this situation to a higher consciousness, especially all the support by angels and ascended masters—these are the true stars of this story. There is much we really do not know. Why do Angels come to visit us? Why are there miracles, messages we can hear? We are guided if we only choose to listen. This life on the planet Earth School can be fun. We can find that feeling again if we only take the time to know that it is there waiting for us if we choose. We struggle but are only fighting against our pictures. This makes it hard because we are afraid to face ourselves. Life is beautiful and its beauty is all around us, just waiting for us to notice. Our individual magic is waiting for each of us if you let go of your expectations and what you think they should be. We are perfect exactly the way we are and the star of our own movie, whether it's bad or good, perfect with all our faults. If you listen you will be led. There is no wrong or right but if you learn from your life experiences and grow that is the success.

As a little girl who played, ran free and wild, I had no idea that all these different events would eventually happen in my life. I had no real vision of the future. I didn't yearn to grow up. As a little girl, I did find that magic of life, and my work was to find that magic as an adult which took some time—in fact, a good part of my life. Definitely, this was a very laborious journey and many times was painful.

As I hand-mowed our yard there was plenty of time to reflect upon my life. Time and time again my thoughts came back to the fact that; my life on planet Earth was a test. From a very young age, somehow I knew that energy existed and some energy is not always so nice: it is dark, scary and lurking. Growing in stature and having visions of the old lady sobbing and the lion with the deer in its mouth, I saw the curtain unfurled to show what was to transpire in my life as well as to the people dear to my heart. Many other feelings and thoughts as a child rose within my being which were very hard to share but they were associated with a feeling of great foreboding, and a knowledge that something was amiss. Knowing every moment spent with my parents was precious, I was deeply saddened as I saw the road my parents decided to venture down, knowing there was no hope of a return.

My magic place, the world of Ember, is a place where I can visit often. At first, electrical currents were experienced which went from my left big toe and up the left side of my body, eventually coursing throughout my whole body. It is where I remained for hours soaking in all the energy and light, seeing colors. This is a beautiful place, not only for me. Everyone has that world where all really is well. Now on several occasions when sitting in a room full of people, a feeling comes over me of such happiness and love, lights of all colors can be seen bouncing off people and around the room. "Do these people feel as good as I?" Such a feeling of euphoria comes over me and all the cares of the world disappear into nothing. This must be the feeling of bliss.

Sitting side by side on the lava rock enjoying the quiet, as the ocean breeze softly caresses their bodies, they listen to the sounds of nature. Suddenly a breeze picks up at the shoreline, wrinkling the water as the waves slowly roll toward them in silver lines.

Gazing softly out toward the ocean with deep reflecting blue eyes, the young woman stands excitedly and points to something she detects way beyond. Now, the ocean looks calm with no activity but if you really look, the movement is seen far out on the horizon in the deeper ocean water. Watching patiently, she finally sights powerful creatures which appear as if they are traveling in toward shallower waters. At first, only their fins are seen emerging from the cool waters as they swim in unison. Coming closer and becoming more discernible, they begin to show off as they jump, tumble and perform all kinds of acrobatics for these two observers. Many dolphins perform with their children in close proximity, and later to the left a humpback whale is seen from afar joining them, creating a huge fountain, shooting water high up into the blue sky. What a celebration!

Such a heightened awareness is behind those electric bright blue eyes.

Roslyn made a beautiful bookmark with a poem about her grandma's death etched on it which she created in her Writing Intensive of Modern

Literature, written when she just commenced to understand how to write sentences again. It is as read:

Each day I wake up
Each night I go to sleep tight
Each sound captivates me here
Smells of old thanksgiving dinner
I can sense my grandma's spirit walking it has been two years
My grandpa is single now; He resides in the Moravian, a Buccaneer
He is so angry losing
Lucas got kicked out permanently
He no longer can hurt my grandma
She is in the ground
My mother left at home
She is so saddened by her death
We cry together for hours

Observing the dance at Lanco Gymnastic Center was such a wonderful feeling. I loved creating something so beautiful for children, knowing that they will remember the experience for the rest of their lives. It was where they can express their deepest part of themselves by movement of their bodies in the prayer of dance and gymnastics.

Waiting, she holds her tight and watches as her body takes its last breath. Emitting rays of green flickering light, her eyes close in prayer.

As we sat in a coffee shop in Lititz, we called the hospital very shortly after leaving Thelma, inquiring of the possibility of keeping her body for investigation. Already on it, they were doing their own investigation because of the nature of the death. A detective was appointed.

Death

Choosing to look beyond her idiosyncrasies I found compassion for a woman who struggled for a long time and hid in that struggle. Death frees a person to dance with life in a different way than we know in our bodies. I heard time and the trivialities of life are not important once you have made that step. People who have died and come back from the grip of death are forever changed. Roslyn, when she was able to express herself, told me of places that she visited and the description of the experiences on her journey was sharp, very clear and with color, which validates my thoughts and knowledge that there are other worlds that we do not see. Death to my mother was finding that world of freedom from her broken body to be able to experience the freedom to dance to her own special rhythm, losing her dance on earth. Very frightened, lying on that cold hospital bed, she was afraid to let go of a body that could not support her. Quantum biofeedback helped her energetic body to relax and let go, finding enough energy to pass on to the brightest light. This spoke to me in a very auditory way, making sure I knew without a doubt. Her quantum entrance made the walls; pipes and the ceiling vibrate and crackle, ushering in such a gush of energy. The amount of energy experienced which entered into my bedroom that cold December morning cannot be put into words! This energy was so powerful, intense and strong, and it demonstrates the power of the human spirit. She loved me and wanted to tell me that all was truly well, expressing her appreciation and joy to have known me.

My heart of love shone through and with love all is possible.

There is so much not understood about death but somehow it was perfect exactly the way it all played out, even though it appeared very tragic to an outsider. The realization of how people can be deceived and be controlled so easily by someone, just as my parents were controlled, became very apparent to me. It is some kind of energy that creates a type of mind control by the perpetrator and it makes you think if he can do what he did, what else is out there controlling the public's mind. Can minds be controlled or influenced by radio waves, energies put out by different agencies? What fuels this control?

When first taken to assisted living, Lester was initially very despondent and totally confused. Understandably this was so because of just recovering from a massive cerebral hemorrhage and being taken from the home he loved. His life had turned upside down. Removed from rehabilitation early, he was not given the proper attention that he so desperately needed. Now residing at Moravian, he receives care and is loved by the staff. Lester sings as his brain heals and he becomes more coherent. Just turning ninety-nine years old, he is now at peace with the knowledge of his safety.

Grief

Visiting Lester at Moravian, we found him sitting in a wheelchair and from his eyes poured pools of water which flowed freely down his cheeks. Mentioning this to a few people and nurses responsible for him, the reply was that his allergies were responsible for his tears. Not convinced with that explanation, we tried getting his attention and waiting for a response from him. He waved his hand and put his head into his hand. This did not only happen once but many times. I believe he was grieving. Honor each other's emotions and support each other. Don't ignore. Recognize these emotions with neutrality; by doing so our compassion holds the space to allow the healing process. Last year, Lester started to become very aloof and unresponsive, not wanting to eat. Marten called him and it was as if a light bulb clicked in his brain. Lester and my husband had a very good working relationship, which later developed into a close personal relationship.

Lester absolutely loves Mr. Marten and remembers Mr. Marten's Grill.

"They had so much fun and my goodness, laugh they did. They loved these undisturbed times; they were precious."

Charlie

Emotions tied up in my life resembled a ball of string which was slowly unraveling. Charlie was a very important part of this process and helped me tremendously in the role he played. Charlie is a Siberian husky with a beautiful soul. The five acres of land in Hawaii seemed like such a perfect setup for my son's two Siberian huskies brought over from New Mexico. Charlie gave Justin so many good memories in New Mexico, being such a devoted companion.

Hiking all afternoon, he is quite ready to go home because of the threat of a winter storm which is brewing on the horizon. Reaching into his pocket to retrieve his keys, to his dismay, he finds they are missing. Worriedly, he peers out to the horizon with concerned blue eyes, seeing that the sun is now just starting to set. He knows it is going to be a long cold night in the mountains.

During the night of sub-zero weather, as promised, a winter storm spews snow from the sky in full force, showing off its magnitude. Charlie's thick coat of hair serves as a blanket which keeps his master warm during this cold blizzard night in the mountains of New Mexico.

The next morning when the sun's rays just begin to peek through the mountain trees, Charlie nudges his master awake from a dream filled with bright colors. Looking into his master's deep blue eyes he whines, begging for him to please follow as he excitedly leads the way. Then Charlie stops abruptly and begins to dig vigorously, uncovering the keys.

Sandia Mountains

Sandia means "watermelon" in Spanish and when you see the setting sun splash pink light over the rocky 10,600-foot peaks of the Sandia Mountains, you'll know exactly how they earned the name. To get a closer view of these spectacular peaks, you can ride the Sandia Peak Aerial Tramway which is the world's longest tramway, to the crest, where you can look out over 11,000 square miles of magical New Mexico landscape. To the west, the majestic Rio Grande meanders through a cottonwood-lined valley and dormant volcanoes are silhouetted against the brilliant sunset. As darkness blankets the city, thousands of lights below twinkle like diamonds, matching the stars scattered across the enormous sky.

On the New Mexico hiking trails, you can find breathtaking views and fascinating geological formations. You may also discover fossils, petroglyphs, and petrified wood or ancient ruins. With abundant New Mexico wildlife in the area, it is not uncommon to see roadrunners, deer, hawks or other woodland critters.

Like his master, Charlie loves adventure and hikes often with him. But it is on this one morning while hiking, Charlie's excitement overrides any concern of his whereabouts or for his master. He becomes distracted with all the different woodland critters.

Distraught and exhausted from searching the mountain for Charlie, Justin comes down the hill alone and immediately begins to look for help, very concerned about the whereabouts of his dog. Later that day, as Justin patiently waits, sitting cross-legged at the bottom of the mountain with his nomad-blue eyes deep in thought he reminisces about his lost friend. Suddenly, he hears shouting in the far distance. Perking up from his dismal thoughts, he squints toward the very animated voice and sees far beyond a person, sitting in one

of the carts of the tram, furiously waving his arms, appearing as if he might be trying to get his attention. As the enlivened traveler progresses down the mountain, Justin squints, looking for any signs of Charlie. Coming closer and barely recognizable, a form begins to take shape, sitting in the cart in front of the excited traveler. Finally, with a sigh of relief, his heart sings at the sight of Charlie who by now can be seen wagging his tail fiercely. Charlie has never looked so good to Justin as he jumps off the tram and sprints toward him with his ears pointing straight up, gleefully barreling his way to Justin and knocking him over, licking his master's face with his big rough pink tongue. Wrapping his arms around his furry nape, he settles his nose into his thick soft fur as streams of tears pour down his cheeks. What a reconnection!

The day it was time for Charlie's next step, was the hardest decision for Justin. We had been working as a family unit feeding Charlie and showering him because he was unable to stand up on his back legs. Justin and Roslyn massaged his body and washed him using the shower and changed his position frequently because bedsores had begun to develop on his weakened body. I was not home when this decision was made because Justin thought it better for me not to see the process of Charlie's demise. Painstakingly he went to the front of the five-acre property and dug his friend's grave. Later, Marten joined Justin with a shovel, helping him finish digging the grave. He stayed with him throughout the whole process of Charlie's last breath and burial. Mourning together, they created support for each other in this very difficult time.

Charlie fell to sleep outside in the velvety soft grass as the morning sun's rays shone upon his head. He had a slight smile on his lips that fine spring day never to wake again.

Never wanting to talk about Razzle, I consciously avoided the front of the property where she was found torn apart that fateful night. But three years later, right after Charlie's passing; I walked down to the front of the property with my three companions to look for Charlie's grave and came across a flat stone with Razzle's name etched on it with a beautiful rose quartz crystal on top of it. Next to Razzle's grave was where Charlie was laid to rest. A large clear quartz crystal was found in Charlie's personal dish on a flat stone upon his fresh dug grave. This dish was special because Justin had made it in New Mexico just for Charlie, engraving Charlie's name on the side of it. Both graves were found along the front edge of our property where succulent passion fruit grows abundantly. There was a stew of smells radiating through the warm air and that particular bright sunny afternoon Charlie gave me permission to mourn my Razzle and forgive, unraveling just one more string in my tight ball of emotions. Not ever knowing exactly what happened to Razzle, I have closed that chapter. He has given my body permission and has aided me to release those uncomfortable stuck emotions, making it possible for them to be replaced, giving me the opportunity to build a new life in a new energy again. He is telling me not to look back, but keep my eyes on the new Ember. Please forgive.

Chapter Sixteen
Celebration of Life

The fireworks dazzle and wow the passengers on a boat that displays proudly the name Thelma Jane. The full moon lights up the sky, illuminating the name of this humble boat, bringing sparkles of magic, compassion, and love to the passengers on the vast radiant silvery bay waters. The sounds of celebration are heard throughout the night as they give hoots of glee and shouts of joy at the beautiful display of colors exploding in the night sky. Fourth of July is important to this motley group of people. Holding hands, stretching them high above their heads they celebrate in the darkness of the night with only the light of the moon and sparkles in the sky. Love rains down upon them.

Razzle accompanied us many times on our adventures out fishing. But on this one particular time the harsh waves pounded and poured over our boat while we headed through the rough channel leading to the deep ocean, and we almost capsized. Thinking that she would not be noticed because of all the commotion, she tried to steal the raw fish off of the fishing hook but instead had the misfortune of getting the hook caught into the side of her mouth. This act taught her a hard lesson because the hook was impossible to remove. So as a group, we came together in a circle and held her close to our bodies helping to calm her anxious shaking body. Slowly, she began to relax and released her hysteria, making it possible to remove the hook with ease. Her eyes looked at me with a knowing that something special just happened, comforted by the energy and unity of our love.

Heaven

Arising early to see the morning masterpiece, Lester has decided that it would be lots of fun to go walking on the boardwalk. As we made our way up the steps with him and onto the worn, splintering boards, looking down both lengths we saw that the numerous stores that line the expanse were closed. Their lights, once welcoming and bright, are off, and we proceeded to take our walk in the serene darkness of early morning. Later, after walking for awhile, we make our way across and finally off of the wooded walkway. The undeniable and easily recognized smell of the beach, a combination of salt and seaweed, engulfed us. Passing through the dunes covered with ocean grass we are greeted by the most beautifully natural sight—

"Tranquil," I think to myself. If any words could possibly be fitting enough to describe the beautiful sight of the ocean and moon before my very eyes, it was tranquil, serene and peaceful.

We spread our colorful towels and sit on the cool sand and wait. Then it commences to happen. This is something I have witnessed on countless occasions before, yet it still never ceases to amaze me and never will. The sun begins to make its appearance over the distant, ever-present yet mysterious horizon as splendorous rays of soft blues, radiant pinks, and delicate violets begin to peek beyond the horizon. The sun's likeness reflects off of the vast ocean waters in front of us. Despite its blinding qualities, it is captivating. I don't blink at all for fear that a single second of the most wonderful sight is missed, which is far too beautiful for words, beyond mere mortal understanding.

Later, heading back onto the wooden boardwalk the memories abound within me from childhood summers spent at the ocean: bike rides I've shared with my family, trips up to the shops in the evenings for French fries, ice cream, water taffy and Italian sausage sandwiches. I recall chasing seagulls and even learning how to fly a kite. This boardwalk defines my past, each individual board somehow tells a part of my life story. As we head back to the boardwalk, Lester makes the suggestion that we get some French fries. The French fry sellers on the boardwalk are renowned for their "vinegar fries"— fries with cider vinegar and salt on them served in paper cones. One such place we visit often is Thrasher's, established in 1929. Laughing and talking of old stories, we munch on French fries together until our stomachs are full and satisfied. After dining on this wonderful delectable food, Lester and Thelma take a stroll on the boardwalk, while Marten and I sit on the sand watching the ocean.

A great reverence has developed for the ocean, and the driving force of nature, and my communion with it. Sitting on the sand, still slightly cool from the previous night, I realized beyond a doubt that I am the luckiest person on the planet. The waves were breaking in perfect sets of four, some splashing into the jetties, while others made their way to greet us on the shore. Closing my eyes, I saw that everything was free and completely at rest.

Like the pieces of even the most intricate puzzle, everything just seemed to fit.

In the far distance, an elderly couple strolls happily, holding hands as they walk the wooden planks toward their meeting ground. White seagulls excitedly soar around them being part of their walk, swooping down, dancing as they twirl and tumble in the late morning sky etched in soft clouds with only hues of pink.

This memory is forever etched in my mind's eye. Though we were special, unique souls on a very different journey in life, Thelma won a special place in my heart, remembered as a woman who was generous and did so much for us girls, sending us to college—something she never got to experience. She also bought beautiful clothing for us and provided times that were unforgettable with the many different festivities of Easter, Christmas, Thanksgiving, New Year's day and the unique celebration of each and everyone's birthday. Looking at my parents' background has given me great respect and a feeling of gratefulness. They are my parents and so much appreciated for all that they have taught me. Life does go on; events do happen that can change our lives forever but the one thing I did learn is that love shines through it all and is more powerful than anything. Everything is possible with love. Love creates miracles in those lives that need a miracle. Light shines through the darkness to show the truth that cannot be hidden.

In his death experience, Eben Alexander, M.D. states in his book *Proof of Heaven* that he had the opportunity to tour many Worlds unseen by those living and that he could move from the lower realm and to the higher realm by mere intention. As he practiced this movement by mere thinking of the higher worlds he found it became easier to return to the higher worlds where a Spinning Melody was to be heard with notes, and gorgeous music, with a spinning ball of light emitting from it which blossomed into his awareness. He was asked what he learned there and he said if he had to boil it down to just one word, it would be, simply: *Love.* "Love is, without a doubt, the basis of everything. Not some abstract, hard-to-fathom kind of love but the day-today kind that everyone knows the kind of love we feel when we look at our spouse and our children, or even our animals. In its purest and most powerful form, this love is not jealous or selfish but unconditional. This is the reality of realities, the incomprehensibly glorious truth of truths that lives and breathes at the core of everything that exists or that ever will exist, and no remotely accurate understanding of who and what we are can be achieved by anyone who does not know it and embody it in all of their actions.

"Not much of a scientific insight? Well, I beg to differ. I'm back from that place, and nothing could convince me that this is not only the single most important *scientific* truth as well." He goes on to say, "In an almost eerie way, my discoveries beyond the body echoed the lessons I had learned just a year earlier through reconnecting with my birth family. Ultimately, none of us are orphans. We are all in the position I was, in that we have other family: beings that are watching and looking out for us—beings we have momentarily forgotten, but who, if we open ourselves to their presence, are waiting to help us navigate our time here on earth. None of us are ever unloved. Each and every one of us is deeply known and cared for by a Creator who cherishes us beyond any ability we have to comprehend. That knowledge must no longer remain a secret."

Chapter Seventeen
Love

On February 14, 2016, the subject and significance of Valentine's Day is the focus for today. Lester says, "Valentine's Day is a very important day, you do know that, Ember?" Before the conversation began, I had reminded him it was me and he exclaimed, "Oh my, I thought that you were Mairzy!" It was very amazing for him to be so cognizant.

When he reminds her of the importance of Valentine's Day, she replies, "Yes, I know it is a very special day." He professes his love for her from the bottom of his heart, saying she is his one and only Valentine. Of course, she is sure this message has been given to her twin sister, but it is the way he expresses himself, making her feel so very special. Reiterating his message, it links right to her heart as her eyes glow a soft hue of green.

He inquires if her studies are completed and if so, does she have any future plans? Becoming quiet, he begins to cough, "Can you help me?"

"Okay sir, I'll see what can be done!" She laughs.

I have found simplicity brings forth elegance and archery is like meditation. In archery you have to concentrate on one object and aim, whereas in meditation you gather all your consciousness to concentrate on your nose and breathing. Discovery of your body is finding your soul and being in grace and communion with your body. This creates peace, not pain. Knowing that I am on a pilgrimage just as everyone else is I have come to know that I will never know exactly who I am but do know death is inevitable. In this pilgrimage, parts of me will be discovered along the way. Life is almost like a scavenger hunt, full of fun and excitement in what will be discovered.

Vipassana, meditation, swimming in the ocean, ballroom dancing, fasting, and yoga helped me tremendously to break through the grief and trauma of losing my mother on a very physical level. Regular quantum biofeedback sessions, massage, light therapy and Dr. Patrick Porter Mind Fit glasses and his many programs also have been a tremendous help in my journey forward. See for more information: www.quantumhealthhawaii.

com. Barry Goldstein's music has helped me reconnect to my heart and brain. And yes, better yet, time to heal was my saving grace as nature supported me on my path in grace—in recreating hope.

Every day you live in hope to face the fact of death. People are scared when it is their time to graduate to their next step but even in death, do not give up your hope. Let go and know all is well. Your body dies but not you as a spirit, which creates continuous communication found in your heart. Hope takes to the heart and grace creates a fusion to the Spirit of God, a safe haven within you, creating a prayer of continuous communication with the living God who resides in you and around you. Do not let your heart be broken, energize it by hope, building your foundation of self-love which radiates out for others to see your light within.

Experiencing communication through an Orb, Om, Eben Alexander M.D. was told that there is not one universe but many—In fact, more than he could conceive, but that love lay at the center of them all. Evil was present in all the other universes as well, but only in the tiniest trace amounts. Evil was necessary because without it free will would be impossible, and without free will, there could be no growth—no forward movement, no chance for us to become what God longed for us to be. Horrible and all-powerful as evil sometimes seemed to be in a world like ours, in the larger picture love was overwhelmingly dominant, and it would ultimately be triumphant. "I saw the abundance of life throughout the countless universes, including some whose intelligence was advanced far beyond that of humanity. I saw that there are countless higher dimensions, but that the only way to know these dimensions is to enter and experience them directly. They cannot be known or understood from lower dimensional space. Cause and effect exist in these higher realms, but outside of our earthly conception of them. The world of time and space in which we move in this terrestrial realm is tightly and intricately meshed within these higher worlds. In other words, these worlds aren't totally apart from us, because all worlds are part of the same overarching divine Reality. From those higher worlds, one could access any time or place in our world.

He said his experience was in ways a perfect storm of near-death experiences. As a practicing neurosurgeon with decades of research and hands-on work in the operating room behind him, he was in a better-than-average position to judge not only the reality but also the implications of what happened to him. "Those implications are tremendous beyond description. My experience showed me that the death of the body and the brain are not the end of consciousness—that human experience continues beyond the grave. More important, it continues under the gaze of a God who loves and cares about each one of us and about where the universe itself and all the beings within it are ultimately going. The place I went was real. Real in a way that makes the life we are living here and now completely dreamlike by comparison. This doesn't mean I don't value the life I'm living now, however. In fact, I value it more than I ever did before. I do so because I now see it in its true context."

She knew that whatever curse was on her home and family was being broken. Love breaks the hold of evil and hate, and returns it to the pool of energy in neutrality. Love wins, always. Hearing the music was the melody of love, freedom, release and ecstasy to say that, "Ember, everything is ok, life is magical and the gift of love creates miracles. You are special and do not forget it!"

The day my mother passed was not just an ordinary day but was one of those extraordinary days which will never be forgotten. It was a day when God made sure that it was known without a doubt that I am not alone and that death is not the end. This was made known by a sensational encounter with angelic beings that celebrated and made music with my mom's passing. I believe she was there with them, not at all alone but do know it has changed my life.

Today, she visits a favorite spot where macadamia trees stand tall over a large trampoline. This place welcomes a lot of contemplation and meditation. Three companions accompany her on the huge trampoline: Lilo, a red miniature poodle, Lavender, a parti poodle and Gunther being the biggest, a mix between a Rottweiler and Shar-Pei are all so happy to be a part of the party. Exhausted, laughing and falling down onto her back, she looks up with her light green eyes, peering into the branches of the macadamia trees, as the sun rays shimmer through them. She giggles as each furry friend lays their chins on her belly. How much fun it is to be alive! This tree shares its fragrance with the white flowers that bloom so abundantly and later manifest macadamia nuts, which are harvested as they fall to the ground. This tree has shown her the way back home. Love symbolizes this area of the yard for her, as she feels the love that surrounds her and is in her, feeling supported by beings from another dimension which she always knew existed, making her heart sing again.

Tinker Bell a very tiny puppy, a miniature Chihuahua, runs circles around Ember as if she has known her for a lifetime. She squeals and is so excited to see Ember who is visiting her twin sister, Mairzy, in Pennsylvania. It is the first time she has seen Tinker Bell. Do dog spirits come back looking for their masters?

Lester continues to receive quantum biofeedback sessions every week from his daughter, Ember. He has become more aware and vibrant, appearing as if he does not belong in the mental dementia and Alzheimer's unit, but can hold a conversation, remembering back to when he was a boy. Diagnosed with heart failure and cancer, Lester was only given a few weeks to live but is still going strong. He is 99 years old.

The End

The time to claim your sovereignty is here now. Open your heart to the glory of it all.

Change has happened, shift has happened and the New Earth is now here. The true level of love is here and waiting for you all to perceive it and welcome yourselves home.

The love for you all is real, feel this love flow through your heart and through every cell in your body, and embrace the divinity that you are.

Wait no more for saviors, wait no more for an outside trigger but instead allow yourselves to be revealed as the true masters that you all are.

Make your wish, and accept it, love it, live it, be it and flow with happiness.

We are all connected by the thread of life that is our connection to the divine, to our true source, our loving home.

Soar like there is no limit because in the heart there are no such limitations, and only you can decide which direction to go.